Samuel Thurber

Select Essays of Addison

Together with Macaulay's Essay on Addison's Life and Writings

Samuel Thurber

Select Essays of Addison
Together with Macaulay's Essay on Addison's Life and Writings

ISBN/EAN: 9783337055714

Printed in Europe, USA, Canada, Australia, Japan

Cover: Foto ©Raphael Reischuk / pixelio.de

More available books at **www.hansebooks.com**

The Academy Classics

SELECT
ESSAYS OF ADDISO

TOGETHER WITH

MACAULAY'S ESSAY ON ADDISON'S LIFE AND WRITINGS

EDITED BY

SAMUEL THURBER

1942

ALLYN AND BACON

Boston   New York   Chicago

CONTENTS.

PAGE

EDITORIAL.

THE STAGE.

MANNERS.

POLITICS.

INTRODUCTION.

IT is coming to be understood that the object of education is rather the attainment of power than the acquisition of knowledge. To know either many things or very much about any one thing is less important than to know how to do things. The recognition of this principle is transforming methods of teaching in all departments. Research is the new watchword. Once regarded as the special function of the most advanced students, research is now seen to be the proper activity even of children in the lower grades. The elation of discovery is the best stimulus for minds of all classes and at all stages.

How to apply the principles of research to the teaching of literature is now the main problem to be solved in the department of English. Once it was the custom to give students of literature books to learn about authors. Then the manuals and histories of literature were displaced, and the masterpieces themselves were introduced into the schools, to be read and expounded in recitation. The ancient practice of annotating Latin and Greek texts for school use was allowed to set the example for books in the mother tongue, and these too appeared, and are still wont to appear, with explanations and definitions to facilitate the getting of lessons.

At the present moment the teaching of literature may be said to have developed to the point when question and answer, problem and solution, obscurity and elucidation, are simultaneously thrust upon the learner's attention, in order that he may for not one conscious moment entertain the feeling of curiosity and interest, that he may be saved all need of exploration, that he may be excused from independent thinking and have merely to bend over his book and learn his lesson. Such is the note stage thus far reached in the evolution of literature teaching.

In order that our condition may not become one of arrested development, teachers must accept cordially and without misgiving the idea that the making of notes is precisely the business of the student himself, and that he cannot be denied this exercise without suffering irreparable loss. Youthful curiosity at length becomes atrophied if left unemployed. The work of research that the maker of notes has to undertake is too pleasant and stimulating to be withheld from the learner. For the teacher to explain everything in advance, or to allow notes to explain it in advance, and then to expect of the class only to say back what has just been said to them, is to reduce teaching to the lowest depths of imbecility.

I have always found that pupils like to be given something to do. They like to be set at work to find out things not obvious at a glance. They like to conquer difficulties. They like the adventure of searching a library for a hidden reference. What a note gives them they accept without emotion, — almost without consciousness, — such long years have they spent already over the books and paper in their desks. For further

burrowing in that petty area it is no longer possible to
rouse their zeal.   They are old enough to go hunting in
larger fields.   High school youth are in the note-making
period of mental growth.   They should annotate their
own texts, and should be taught to scorn silly offerings
of help.   They too can handle dictionaries and encyclopædias, tease librarians, rummage in histories and biog-
raphies: and this is all that the note-maker can do for
them.

Having found the presence of a mass of explanatory
notes an obstacle to my endeavor to interest my pupils
in their English reading, I have essayed to suggest a
better method of procedure by preparing texts in such
a manner as rather to call for research than to make
research needless by giving its results.   A note that
tells at once what is wanted forestalls the teacher.   I
would co-operate with the teacher by aiding him to set
the pupils at work.   Accordingly I have offered no
notes whatever on passages easily explained by reference
to dictionaries and encyclopædias, except perchance to
give a warning that such research should not be omitted.
Only when I have found the way of research a little
dark or crooked have I hinted at the path to be pursued.
The "notes" in this volume, therefore, are distinctly
meant to send the learner away from the little books in
his little desk to the larger and more abundant books of
the school library, and to the public and other libraries
to which he may have access.   I have myself found it a
joy to conquer these small difficulties: this joy I would
share with my pupils.

For the general reader an English text may be furnished with any amount of labor-saving apparatus.   The

general reader wants to luxuriate in his reading and not be constantly sent to books of reference. To him it is intolerably tedious to be obliged to make work of his reading. But the pupil in school is the very antithesis of the general reader. The pupil will not read to while away his time, but to learn how to investigate; he is not to court his ease at his tasks, but to whet his curiosity and give it free range; he is not so enamoured of his school desk and his long hours at it but he will be at least willing to rise and try new postures and new muscles. Pedagogic annotation, therefore, should not be directed toward the saving of labor: much rather should it be full of exhortations and promptings to labor. This point, dear learner, you do not understand; but the way to attain an understanding of it is a pleasant one; here are a few directions to enable you to make a start. In this spirit, I conceive, should English texts for schools be annotated.

Intelligent reading implies the use of certain literary apparatus, access to which is possible to almost every member of an American community. The function of the school, with regard to this apparatus, is to show its value and to train in the methods of putting it to use. High schools should graduate their pupils expert in the handling of dictionaries and encyclopædias, quick to surmise which way to turn to find information about men and things. To make the little text-book self-sufficing is to make it false to the facts of real life, for the real books of the world are bound together by infinite links of mutual explanation, and every book of value must be read with reference to other books. Pupils are to be trained in the art of literary exploration. They are to be trained to the habit of satisfying their curios⸗ity. The youth who is capable of curiosity, and who knows how to proceed to find the thing he wants, has one of the best gifts that the school course in literature can bestow upon him. The youth who read his English in books where notes told him what he wanted before he knew that he wanted it, is left in the lurch when he comes to read the books that imply knowledge or skill in finding knowledge.

No self-respecting teacher will accept a text-book that presupposes his own ignorance or his utter lack of opportunity to communicate his knowledge. We are very much engrossed with our work, of course, and have not much time for extraneous matters: but explaining difficulties, so far from being a business extraneous to our ·duty, is its very heart and soul. First of all things, the teacher is presumed to know his subject. If he teaches literature, he claims to know how to teach literature, to be at home in the literary field. A generation of teachers bred on explanatory notes undergoes paralysis of the teaching faculty, and sinks into inane dependence on adventitious aids. For their own culture, as well as for their control of wise methods, teachers of English need to qualify themselves to be their own expositors of texts. The literature of the mother tongue herein differs from that in the ancient languages. We may grant that classic philology is too recondite for secondary teachers to master. Teachers of Latin and Greek may cleave to their notes. But English philology is near to our homes and lies patent to the seeker of average industry and acumen. To treat English literature as if it lay the other side of the middle ages is to commit the absurdest mistake of modern scholastic methods.

The notes appended to this selection from the writings of Addison and Macaulay are therefore not explanatory. They will be found to be rather queries than answers to queries. They have grown out of my own experience in reading this very matter with high school classes. My way of procedure is this.

As soon as a point appears that evidently needs elucidation, I assign it to a particular pupil for research. If this research threatens to lead the pupil into a maze so hopeless as to cause discouragement and waste of time, I give hints more or less broad as to the course to be pursued. Pupils will search long and eagerly for the .thing they want; but they have other studies, and their limitations must be respected. Hence they usually need help. But they take infinite pleasure in finding the object of their quest and in reporting their successes. At each recitation a few pupils are ready with their reports. Meanwhile they have been in the various libraries of the city, calling for books, searching indexes, taking notes. In short, they have been ardently at work studying literature. They have been in contact with books, and have learned to appreciate somewhat the interrelationship of the members of the great literary family. Often they make independent discoveries, and report the most interesting and amusing facts, more or less germane to the strict object of their commission.

Whatever historical knowledge pupils have acquired comes of course directly into play in this work of literary research. History and literature go hand in hand. Books of history and biography are oftenest the ones to which students of literature must resort. The past begins to open only to the student who explores many sources and sees things from many sides. The world being full of books, it is pedagogic high treason to act as if the text-book contained the whole canon of knowledge.

In culling the Addisonian specimens included in this volume I have had distinctly in view a juvenile public. To compile a good book for pupils to read either in public or in private, was the first consideration. Secondarily, I have endeavored to represent fairly the wonderful diversity of Addison's themes, illustrating with careful selection each of the more conspicuous classes into which the essays may be grouped.

The De Coverley papers I have placed together in the order of their appearance; and that this series may lack no important member, I have included in it the contributions of Steele and Budgell. The pupil will take pleasure in comparing these papers with Addison's to see if he can detect any difference in the styles of the three writers.

The remaining essays in this collection have been selected from Addison's work in the Spectator, the Tatler, the Guardian, and the Freeholder. Following the example of Arnold and other editors, I have given to these selections a slight grouping, though without making such grouping conspicuous to the eye. It appears sufficiently in the table of contents. Under the rubrics, Editorial, The Stage, Manners, Politics, Tales, Varia, Morals and Religion, Hymns, I have brought together forty-five of the more famous papers. The only distinct class of essays of which I have admitted no representative is that of formal criticism. Writing of this kind is but little apt to prove stimulating to youth.

An ideal selection from Addison's prose writings would of course be a perfect miniature, omitting no feature of the original. Some features of the original should, however, be omitted from an edition intended to be read and worked over in school. Generally, I may say, I have allowed my selection to give an impression of more gravity and seriousness than one brings from the reading of any undivided portion of Addison's papers. The whims, fashions, frivolities of the day, that were duly discussed in the Addisonian periodicals, remain to us still amusing and historically important. That which was light in its day is light still; but it inevitably comes to pass that whatever is undertaken in the class-room has to be dwelt upon more or less, and a clear congruity between the content of a passage and the labor given to the mastery of its meaning recommends the work to the juvenile sense of propriety and proportion.

It has not seemed to me important to give all the chosen papers absolutely entire. In no sense are these essays artistic wholes, possessing a structure that is ruined by the excision of the least portion. I wished to compress into a small compass a considerable variety of specimens. Lightness, readableness, cleanness, I deemed to be the true principles to govern my editing.

Macaulay's essay on the Life and Writings of Addison I have also shortened, without, however, mutilating it as a biography. For school use Macaulay's essay is rather long and rather overloaded with historical erudition. Young readers can work out most of it with the teacher's help, but parts of it require more collateral reading than such readers can profitably undertake. I have shortened this essay, therefore, by about a fifth. Only persons familiar with Macaulay will miss this fifth. To the pupil the essay will not be found to lack consecutiveness and clearness.

While working at this limited selection from Addison's writings, the class will have frequent occasion to consult the writer's complete works. A complete Addison and a complete Spectator and Tatler should lie on the table for easy reference during the time devoted to this period of literature. Two good editions of Addison's works are accessible, — the edition of Bishop Hurd, enlarged by Henry G. Bohn, published, in six volumes, in the Bohn Standard Library; and the edition, also in six volumes, of Professor George Washington Greene, published by J. B. Lippincott and Co.

The Spectator can be had in numerous shapes. Chiefly to be recommended is the edition of Professor Henry Morley, published, in three volumes, by George Routledge and Sons. This edition has notes and an index. The Spectator, Tatler, and Guardian are included in the series of British Essayists, edited by A. Chalmers.

Books and articles bearing directly on Addison and Steele and their writings will be found in endless profusion. Macaulay's essay is here presented. The Life of Addison by Miss Aikin, which Macaulay criticises, is republished in this country and may easily be looked up in the libraries. Still more accessible is Mr. Courthope's Addison, in the English Men of Letters series. In 1889 appeared the Life of Richard Steele by George A. Aitken. This handsome book, in two octavo volumes, will be found extremely valuable for frequent reference. It contains interesting portraits. Much smaller is Austin Dobson's Steele, in the English Worthies series. A book not yet quite superseded by all the literary researches of nearly three generations is Nathan Drake's Essays, biographical, critical, and historical, illustrative of the Tatler, Spectator, and Guardian, London, 1805. The book entitled Addisoniana, published in two small volumes in 1803, will be found worth looking up. It contains a curious portrait of "Mr. Addison at Button's." With a little enterprise pupils will hunt up many portraits of Addison.

On the manners and customs of the eighteenth century, the student will find useful and interesting, either for consultation or for continuous reading, England and the English in the Eighteenth Century, by William Connor Sydney, Macmillan and Co., 1891. Still more interesting, by reason of its numerous illustrations, is Social Life in the Reign of Queen Anne, by John Ashton, Chatto and Windus, 1882.

On the general history of Addison's times the reader will naturally refer to Macaulay, so far as Macaulay's History extends, and should learn to refer to the index to the Essays even for eighteenth century matters not reached by the History. Charles Knight's Popular History of England is a book that every high school should possess. Its pictures and its frequent reference to social and literary matters make it a work of supreme interest to youth. Works so large as Lecky's History of England in the Eighteenth Century, Burton's History of the Reign of Queen Anne, Wyon's History of Great

Britain during the Reign of Queen Anne, and Lord Mahon's three works on eighteenth century periods, while too formidable for high school pupils to think of reading as wholes, are not too large for consultation in the investigation of special subjects. The War of the Spanish Succession is treated on a scale suitable for high school digestion in G. W. Kitchin's History of France. A most excellent book, both for reading and for handy reference on all topics of English history, is Samuel Rawson Gardiner's Student's History of England. Every high school should have this work. The notes in this volume refer to it constantly.

Merely verbal difficulties in texts no older than Addison's writings are usually explained by the larger dictionaries. When all the common dictionaries fail, then •the Century should be tried. It is a great blessing to a school to possess the Century. The possibilities of profit from a course of English study are doubled when such a book lies accessible for easy reference.

S. T.

April 4, 1892.

DR. SAMUEL JOHNSON ON ADDISON.

As a describer of life and manners Addison must be allowed to stand perhaps the first of the first rank. His humor, which, as Steele observes, is peculiar to himself, is so happily diffused as to give the grace of novelty to domestic scenes and daily occurrences. He never "o'ersteps the modesty of nature," nor raises merriment or wonder by the violation of truth. His figures neither divert by distortion nor amaze by aggravation. He copies life with so much fidelity that he can be hardly said to invent; yet his exhibitions have an air so original that it is difficult to suppose them not merely the product of imagination.

As a teacher of wisdom he may be confidently followed. His religion has nothing in it enthusiastic or superstitious; he appears neither weakly credulous nor wantonly sceptical; his morality is neither dangerously lax nor impracticably rigid. All the enchantment of fancy and all the cogency of argument are employed to recommend to the reader his real interest, the care of pleasing the Author of his being. Truth is shown sometimes as the phantom of a vision; sometimes appears half-veiled in an allegory; sometimes attracts regard in the robes of fancy; and sometimes steps forth in the confidence of reason. She wears a thousand dresses, and in all is pleasing.

> " Mille habet ornatus, mille decenter habet."

His prose is tne model of the middle style; on grave subjects not formal, on light occasions not grovelling; pure without scrupulosity, and exact without apparent elaboration; always equable and always easy, without glowing words and pointed sentences. Addison never deviates from his track to snatch a grace; he seeks no ambitious ornaments and tries no hazardous innovations. His page is always luminous, but never blazes in unexpected splendor.

It was apparently his principal endeavor to avoid all harshness and severity of diction; he is therefore sometimes verbose in his transitions and connections, and sometimes descends too much to the language of conversation; yet if his language had been less idiomatical it might have lost somewhat of its genuine Anglicism. What he attempted he performed; he is not feeble, and he did not wish to be energetic; he is never rapid and he never stagnates. His sentences have neither studied amplitude nor affected brevity; his periods, though not diligently rounded, are voluble and easy. Whoever wishes to attain an English style, familiar but not coarse, and elegant but not ostentatious, must give his days and nights to the volumes of Addison.

FROM TAINE'S *HISTOIRE DE LA LITTÉRATURE ANGLAISE.*

QUE d'art il faut pour plaire! D'abord l'art de se faire entendre, du premier coup, toujours, jusqu'au fond, sans peine pour le lecteur, sans réflexion, sans attention! Figurez-vous des hommes du monde qui lisent une page entre deux bouchées de gâteaux, des dames qui interrompent une phrase pour demander l'heure du bal: trois mots spéciaux ou savants leur feraient jeter le journal. Ils ne veulent que des termes clairs, de l'usage commun, où l'esprit entre de primesaut comme dans les sentiers de la causerie ordinaire; en effet, pour eux, la lecture n'est qu'une causerie et meilleure que l'autre. Car le monde choisi raffine le langage. Il ne souffre point les hasards ni les à-peu-près de l'improvisation et de l'inexpérience. Il exige la science du style comme la science des façons. Il veut des mots exacts qui expriment les fines nuances de la pensée, et des mots mesurés qui écartent les impressions choquantes ou extrêmes. Il souhaite des phrases développées qui, lui présentant la même idée sous plusieurs faces, l'impriment aisément dans son esprit distrait. Il demande des alliances de mots qui, présentant une idée comme sous une forme piquante, l'enfoncent vivement dans son imagination distraite. Addison lui donne tout ce qu'il désire; ses écrits sont la pure source du style classique; jamais en Angleterre on n'a parlé de meilleur ton. Les ornements y abondent, et jamais la rhétorique n'y a part. Partout de justes oppositions qui ne servent qu'à la clarté et ne sont point trop prolongées; d'heureuses expressions aisément trouvées qui donnent aux choses un tour

ingénieux et nouveau ; des périodes harmonieuses où les sons
coulent les uns dans les autres avec la diversité et la douceur
d'un ruisseau calme ; une veine féconde d'inventions et d'images
où luit la plus aimable ironie.

FROM BELJAME'S *LE PUBLIC ET LES HOMMES DE LETTRES EN ANGLETERRE AU XVIIIme SIÈCLE.*

REPRÉSENTEZ-VOUS un homme du monde, poli sans recherche,
grave sans raideur, instruit sans pédantisme, aimant et goûtant les
plaisirs de l'esprit, avec cela chrétien, chrétien convaincu, mais ni
rigide, ni bigot, ni intolérant, et de sa religion pratiquant surtout
la charité ; figurez-vous cet homme causant dans une société de
gens distingués et cultivés, ét leur communiquant, selon les hasards
de la conversation, ses idées sur toutes les questions que peut agiter
une réunion pareille, sur la littérature, sur les amusements ou les
mœurs du jour, quelquefois sur des questions plus hautes touchant
aux grands intérêts de cette vie ou de l'autre ; dans ces causeries
variées de sujets et de ton, il est aimable, spirituel, intéressant
toujours, souvent élevé, mais jamais il ne prend le langage dog-
matique et sentencieux ; il se garde discrètement des longs dével-
oppements monotones sur le même thème, car il est à ses yeux de
mauvais goût et de mauvaise politique d'ennuyer ses auditeurs ;
ennemi de toute exagération, il n'emploie ni les grandes phrases,
ni les grands gestes ; il loue plus volontiers qu'il ne blâme, et s'il
est forcé de blâmer, il ne se laisse pas aller aux paroles blessantes,
auxquelles son savoir-vivre répugne autant que sa religion ; il
indique son blâme par un mot grave et calme, plus souvent par une
intonation ironique, par un clignement de l'œil, par un plissement
de la lèvre. Jamais sa conversation n'a le caractère apprêté et
raide d'un enseignement, et cependant elle instruit, et l'on n'aura
pas vécu dans le commerce de son esprit sans en retirer, en même
temps que le plaisir le plus délicat, le plus sérieux profit intellectuel
et moral. Tels sont les essais d'Addison : ce sont les causeries
attrayantes d'un homme du monde chez qui l'esprit est élevé par
le savoir et la raison, et tempéré par la bonté.

SELECT ESSAYS OF ADDISON.

Spectator No. 1.   *Thursday, March 1, 1711: — The Spectator introduces himself to the reader.*

I HAVE observed that a reader seldom peruses a book with pleasure, until he knows whether the writer of it be a black or a fair man, of a mild or choleric disposition, married or a bachelor, with other particulars of the like nature, that conduce very much to the right understanding of an author. To gratify this curiosity, which is so natural to a reader, I design this paper, and my next, as prefatory discourses to my following writings, and shall give some account in them of the several persons that are engaged in this work. As the chief trouble of compiling, digesting, and correcting, will fall to my share, I must do myself the justice to open the work with my own history.

I was born to a small hereditary estate, which, according to the tradition of the village where it lies, was bounded by the same hedges and ditches in William the Conqueror's time that it is at present, and has been delivered down from father to son whole and entire, without the loss or acquisition of a single field or meadow, during the space of six hundred years. There runs a story in the family, that my mother dreamed that her child was destined to be a judge : whether this might proceed from a law-suit which was then depending in the family, or my father's being a justice of the peace, I cannot determine; for I am not so vain as to think it presaged any dignity that I should arrive at in my future life, though that was the interpretation which the neighborhood put upon it. The gravity of my behavior at my very first appearance in the world seemed to favor my mother's dream: for as she has often told me, I threw away my rattle before I was two months old, and would not make use of my coral until they had taken away the bells from it.

As for the rest of my infancy, there being nothing in it remarkable, I shall pass it over in silence. I find, that, during my nonage, I had the reputation of a very sullen youth, but was always a favorite of my schoolmaster, who used to say, that my parts were solid, and would wear well. I had not been long at the university, before I distinguished myself by a most profound silence; for, during the space of eight years, excepting in the public exercises of the college, I scarce uttered the quantity of an hundred words; and indeed do not remember that I ever spoke three sentences together in my whole life. Whilst I was in this learned body, I applied myself with so much diligence to my studies, that there are very few celebrated books, either in the learned or the modern tongues, which I am not acquainted with.

Upon the death of my father, I was resolved to travel into foreign countries, and therefore left the university, with the character of an odd unaccountable fellow, that had a great deal of learning, if I would but show it. An insatiable thirst after knowledge carried me into all the countries of Europe, in which there was any thing new or strange to be seen; nay, to such a degree was my curiosity raised, that having read the controversies of some great men concerning the antiquities of Egypt, I made a voyage to Grand Cairo, on purpose to take the measure of a pyramid; and as soon as I had set myself right in that particular, returned to my native country with great satis faction.

I have passed my latter years in this city, where I am frequently seen in most public places, though there are not above half-a-dozen of my select friends that know me; of whom my next paper shall give a more particular account. There is no place of general resort, wherein I do not often make my appearance: sometimes I am seen thrusting my head into a round of politicians at Will's, and listening with great attention to the narratives that are made in those little circular audiences. Sometimes I smoke a pipe at Child's, and whilst I seem attentive to nothing but the postman, overhear the conversation of every table in the room. I appear on Sunday nights at St. James's coffee-house, and sometimes join the little committee of politics in the inner room, as one who comes there to hear and improve. My face is likewise very well known at the Grecian, the Cocoa-tree, and in the theatres both of Drury Lane and the Hay Market. I have been taken for a merchant upon the exchange for above these ten years, and sometimes pass for a Jew in the assembly of stock-jobbers at Jonathan's: in short, wherever I see a cluster of people, I always mix with them, though I never open my lips but in my own club.

Thus I live in the world rather as a spectator of mankind, than as one of the species, by which means I have made myself a speculative statesman, soldier, merchant, and artisan, without ever meddling with any practical part in life. I am very well versed in the theory of a husband or a father, and can discern the errors in the economy, business, and diversion of others, better than those who are engaged in them; as standers-by discover blots, which are apt to escape those who are in the game. I never espoused any party with violence, and am resolved to observe an exact neutrality between the Whigs and Tories, unless I shall be forced to

declare myself by the hostilities of either side. In short, I
have acted in all the parts of my life as a looker-on, which
is the character I intend to preserve in this paper.

I have given the reader just so much of my history and
character, as to let him see I am not altogether unqualified
for the business I have undertaken. As for other particulars
in my life and adventures, I shall insert them in following
papers, as I shall see occasion. In the mean time, when I
consider how much I have seen, read, and heard, I begin to
blame my own taciturnity; and since I have neither time
nor inclination to communicate the fulness of my heart in
speech, I am resolved to do it in writing, and to print myself out, if possible, before I die. I have been often told by
my friends, that it is a pity so many useful discoveries which
I have made should be in the possession of a silent man.
For this reason therefore, I shall publish a sheet-full of
thoughts every morning, for the benefit of my contemporaries: and if I can any way contribute to the diversion or
improvement of the country in which I live, I shall leave it,
when I am summoned out of it, with the secret satisfaction
of thinking that I have not lived in vain.

There are three very material points which I have not
spoken to in this paper; and which, for several important
reasons, I must keep to myself, at least for some time; I
mean, an account of my name, my age, and my lodgings. I
must confess, I would gratify my reader in any thing that
is reasonable; but as for these three particulars, though I
am sensible they might tend very much to the embellishment
of my paper, I cannot yet come to a resolution of communicating them to the public. They would indeed draw me
out of that obscurity which I have enjoyed for many years,
and expose me in public places to several salutes and civilities, which have been always very disagreeable to me; for
the greatest pain I can suffer is the being talked to and being
stared at. It is for this reason likewise that I keep my

complexion and dress as very great secrets; though it is not impossible but I may make discoveries of both in the progress of the work I have undertaken.

After having been thus particular upon myself, I shall in to-morrow's paper, give an account of those gentlemen who are concerned with me in this work; for, as I have before intimated, a plan of it is laid and concerted, as all other matters of importance are, in a club.

Spectator No. 2. *The Spectator Club: Sir Roger de Coverley, the Templar, Sir Andrew Freeport, Captain Sentry, Will Honeycomb, the Clergyman.*

The first of our society is a gentleman of Worcestershire, of ancient descent, a baronet, his name Sir Roger de Coverley. His great grandfather was inventor of that famous country-dance which is called after him. All who know that shire are very well acquainted with the parts and merits of Sir Roger. He is a gentleman that is very singular in his behavior, but his singularities proceed from his good sense, and are contradictions to the manners of the world, only as he thinks the world is in the wrong. However, this humor creates him no enemies, for he does nothing with sourness or obstinacy; and his being unconfined to modes and forms makes him but the readier and more capable to please and oblige all who know him. When he is in town, he lives in Soho Square. It is said he keeps himself a bachelor, by reason he was crossed in love by a perverse beautiful widow of the next county to him. Before this disappointment, Sir Roger was what you call a fine gentleman, had often supped with my Lord Rochester and Sir George Etherege, fought a duel upon his first coming to town, and kicked Bully Dawson in a public coffeehouse for calling him youngster. But, being ill used by the above mentioned widow, he was very serious for a year and a half; and though, his temper being naturally jovial, he at last got over it, he grew careless of himself, and never dressed afterwards. He continues to wear a coat and doublet of the same cut that were in fashion at the time of his repulse, which, in his merry humors, he tells us, has been in and out twelve times since he first wore it. He is now in his fifty-sixth year, cheerful, gay and hearty; keeps a good house both in town and country; a great lover of mankind; but there is such a mirthful cast in his behavior, that he is rather beloved than esteemed. His tenants grow rich, his servants look satisfied, all the young women profess love to him, and the young men are glad of his company; when he comes into a house, he calls the servants by their names, and talks all the way up stairs to a visit. I must not omit, that Sir Roger is a justice of the *quorum;* that he fills the chair at a quarter-session with great abilities, and three months ago gained universal applause by explaining a passage in the game-act.

The gentleman next in esteem and authority among us is another bachelor, who is a member of the Inner Temple; a man of great probity, wit and understanding; but he has chosen his place of residence rather to obey the direction of an old humorsome father, than in pursuit of his own inclinations. He was placed there to study the laws of the land, and is the most learned of any of the house in those of the stage. Aristotle and Longinus are much better understood by him than Littleton or Coke. The father sends up every post questions relating to marriage-articles, leases and tenures, in the neighborhood; all which questions he agrees with an attorney to answer and take care of in the lump. He is studying the passions themselves, when he should be inquiring into the debates among men which arise from them. He knows the argument of each of the orations of Demosthenes and Tully; but not one case in the reports of our own courts. No one ever took him for a fool, but

none, except his intimate friends, know he has a great deal
of wit. This turn makes him at once both disinterested and
agreeable; as few of his thoughts are drawn from business,
they are most of them fit for conversation. His taste of
books is a little too just for the age he lives in; he has read
all, but approves of very few. His familiarity with the
customs, manners, actions and writings of the ancients,
makes him a very delicate observer of what occurs to him
in the present world. He is an excellent critic, and the
time of the play is his hour of business; exactly at five he
passes through New Inn, crosses through Russell Court,
and takes a turn at Will's, till the play begins; he has his
shoes rubbed and his periwig powdered at the barber's as
you go into the Rose. It is for the good of the audience
when he is at a play; for the actors have an ambition to
please him.

The person of next consideration is Sir Andrew Freeport,
a merchant of great eminence in the city of London. A
person of indefatigable industry, strong reason, and great
experience. His notions of trade are noble and generous,
and (as every rich man has usually some sly way of jesting
which would make no great figure were he not a rich man)
he calls the sea the British Common. He is acquainted
with commerce in all its parts, and will tell you that it is a
stupid and barbarous way to extend dominion by arms, for
true power is to be got by arts and industry. He will often
argue, that if this part of our trade were well cultivated,
we should gain from one nation, — and if another, from another. I have heard him prove that diligence makes more
lasting acquisitions than valor, and that sloth has ruined
more nations than the sword. He abounds in several frugal
maxims, amongst which the greatest favorite is, "A penny
saved is a penny got." A general trader of good sense is
pleasanter company than a general scholar; and Sir Andrew
having a natural unaffected eloquence, the perspicuity of

his discourse gives the same pleasure that wit would in another man. He has made his fortunes himself; and says that England may be richer than other kingdoms, by as plain methods as he himself is richer than other men; though at the same time I can say this of him, that there is not a point in the compass but blows home a ship in which he is an owner.

Next to Sir Andrew in the club-room sits Captain Sentry, a gentleman of great courage, good understanding, but invincible modesty. He is one of those that deserve very well, but are very awkward at putting their talents within the observation of such as should take notice of them. He was some years a captain, and behaved himself with great gallantry in several engagements, and at several sieges; but having a small estate of his own, and being next heir to Sir Roger, he has quitted a way of life, in which no man can rise suitably to his merit, who is not something of a courtier as well as a soldier. I have heard him often lament that in a profession where merit is placed in so conspicuous a view, impudence should get the better of modesty. He says it is a civil cowardice to be backward in asserting what you ought to expect, as it is a military fear to be slow in attacking when it is your duty. With this candor does the gentleman speak of himself and others. The same frankness runs through all his conversation. The military part of his life has furnished him with many adventures, in the relation of which he is very agreeable to the company; for he is never over-bearing, though accustomed to command men in the utmost degree below him; nor ever too obsequious, from an habit of obeying men highly above him.

But, that our society may not appear a set of humorists, unacquainted with the gallantries and pleasures of the age, we have among us the gallant Will Honeycomb, a gentleman who, according to his years, should be in the decline of his life, but, having ever been very careful of his person, and always had a very easy fortune, time has made but a very little impression, either by wrinkles on his forehead, or traces in his brain. His person is well turned, of a good height. He is very ready at that sort of discourse with which men usually entertain women. He has all his life dressed very well, and remembers habits as others do men. He can smile when one speaks to him, and laughs easily. He knows the history of every mode, and can inform you from what Frenchwoman our wives and daughters had this manner of curling their hair, that way of placing their hoods; and whose vanity to show her foot made that part of the dress so short in such a year. In a word, all his conversation and knowledge have been in the female world; as other men of his age will take notice to you what such a minister said upon such and such an occasion, he will tell you when the Duke of Monmouth danced at court, such a woman was then smitten, another was taken with him at the head of his troop in the Park. For all these important relations, he has ever about the same time received a kind glance or a blow of a fan from some celebrated beauty, mother of the present Lord such-a-one.

I cannot tell whether I am to account him whom I am next to speak of, as one of our company; for he visits us but seldom, but when he does, it adds to every man else a new enjoyment of himself. He is a clergyman, a very philosophic man, of general learning, great sanctity of life, and the most exact good breeding. He has the misfortune to be of a very weak constitution; and consequently cannot accept of such cares and business as preferments in his function would oblige him to; he is therefore among divines what a chamber councillor is among lawyers. The probity of his mind, and the integrity of his life, create him followers, as being eloquent or loud advances others. He seldom introduces the subject he speaks upon; but we are so far gone in years that he observes, when he is among us, an earnestness to have him fall on some divine topic, which he always treats with much authority, as one who has no interests in this world, as one who is hastening to the object of all his wishes, and conceives hope from his decays and infirmities.   These are my ordinary companions. — *Steele.*

———

Spectator No. 34.   *Members of the Club discuss the Spectator's papers.*

The club of which I am a member is very luckily composed of such persons as are engaged in different ways of life, and deputed as it were out of the most conspicuous classes of mankind: by this means I am furnished with the greatest variety of hints and materials, and know everything that passes in the different quarters and divisions, not only of this great city, but of the whole kingdom.   My readers too have the satisfaction to find, that there is no rank or degree among them who have not their representative in this club, and that there is always somebody present who will take care of their respective interests, that nothing may be written or published to the prejudice or infringement of their just rights and privileges.

I last night sat very late in company with this select body of friends, who entertained me with several remarks which they and others had made upon these my speculations, as also with the various success which they had met with among their several ranks and degrees of readers. Will Honeycomb told me, in the softest manner he could, that there were some ladies (but for your comfort, says Will, they are not those of the most wit) that were offended at the liberties I had taken with the opera and the puppet show; that some of them were likewise very much surprised, that I should think such serious points as the dress and equipage of persons of quality, proper subjects for raillery.

He was going on, when Sir Andrew Freeport took him up short, and told him that the papers he hinted at had done great good in the city, and that all their wives and daughters were the better for them; and further added, that the whole city thought themselves very much obliged to me for declaring my generous intentions to scourge vice and folly as they appear in a multitude, without condescending to be a publisher of particular intrigues. "In short," says Sir Andrew, "if you avoid that foolish beaten road of falling upon aldermen and citizens, and employ your pen upon the vanity and luxury of courts, your paper must needs be of general use."

Upon this my friend the Templar told Sir Andrew, that he wondered to hear a man of his sense talk after that manner; that the city had always been the province for satire; and that the wits of King Charles's time jested upon nothing else during his whole reign. He then showed, by the examples of Horace, Juvenal, Boileau, and the best writers of every age, that the follies of the stage and court had never been accounted too sacred for ridicule, how great soever the persons might be that patronized them: "But after all," says he, "I think your raillery has made too great an excursion in attacking several persons of the Inns of Court; and I do not believe you can show me any precedent for your behavior in that particular."

My good friend Sir Roger de Coverley, who had said nothing all this while, began his speech with a pish! and told us, that he wondered to see so many men of sense so very serious upon fooleries. "Let our good friend," says he, "attack every one that deserves it: I would only advise you, Mr. Spectator," applying himself to me, "to take care how you meddle with country squires: they are the ornaments of the English nation; men of good heads and sound bodies; and let me tell you, some of them take it ill of you, that you mention fox hunters with so little respect."

Captain Sentry spoke very sparingly on this occasion. What he said was only to commend my prudence in not touching upon the army, and advised me to continue to act discreetly in that point.

By this time I found every subject of my speculations was taken away from me, by one or other of the club; and began to think myself in the condition of the good man that had one wife who took a dislike to his gray hairs, and another to his black, till by their picking out what each of them had an aversion to, they left his head altogether bald and naked.

While I was thus musing with myself, my worthy friend the clergyman, who, very luckily for me, was at the club that night, undertook my cause. He told us that he wondered any order of persons should think themselves too considerable to be advised: that it was not quality, but innocence, which exempted men from reproof: that vice and folly ought to be attacked wherever they could be met with, and especially when they were placed in high and conspicuous stations of life. He further added, that my paper would only serve to aggravate the pains of poverty, if it chiefly exposed those who were already depressed, and in some measure turned into ridicule, by the meanness of their conditions and circumstances. He afterwards proceeded to take notice of the great use this paper might be of to the public, by reprehending those vices which are too trivial for the chastisement of the law, and too fantastical for the cognizance of the pulpit. He then advised me to prosecute my undertaking with cheerfulness, and assured me, that whoever might be displeased with me, I should be approved by all those whose praises do honor to the persons on whom they are bestowed.

The whole club pays a particular deference to the discourse of this gentleman, and are drawn into what he says as much by the candid ingenuous manner with which he delivers himself, as by the strength of argument and force of reason which he makes use of. Will Honeycomb immediately agreed, that what he had said was right; and that, for his part, he would not insist upon the quarter which he had demanded for the ladies. Sir Andrew gave up the city with the same frankness. The Templar would not stand out; and was followed by Sir Roger and the Captain; who all agreed that I should be at liberty to carry the war into what quarter I pleased; provided I continued to combat with criminals in a body, and to assault the vice without hurting the person.

This debate, which was held for the good of mankind, put me in mind of that which the Roman triumvirate were formerly engaged in for their destruction. Every man at first stood hard for his friend, till they found that by this means they should spoil their proscription : and at last making a sacrifice of all their acquaintance and relations, furnished out a very decent execution.

Having thus taken my resolutions, to march on boldly in the cause of virtue and good sense, and to annoy their adversaries in whatever degree or rank of men they may be found, I shall be deaf for the future to all the remonstrances that shall be made to me on this account. If Punch grows extravagant, I shall reprimand him very freely : if the stage becomes a nursery of folly and impertinence, I shall not be afraid to animadvert upon it. In short, if I meet with anything in city, court, or country, that shocks modesty or good manners, I shall use my utmost endeavors to make an example of it. I must however entreat every particular person who does me the honor to be a reader of this paper, never to think himself, or any one of his friends or enemies, aimed at in what is said : for I promise him, never to draw a faulty character which does not fit at least a thousand people : or to publish a single paper, that is not written in the spirit of benevolence, and with a love to

Spectator No. 105.   *Will Honeycomb's dislike of pedantry leads the Spectator to moralize on this subject.*

My friend Will Honeycomb values himself very much upon what he calls the knowledge of mankind, which has cost him many disasters in his youth; for Will reckons every misfortune that he has met with among the women, and every rencounter among the men, as parts of his education, and fancies he should never have been the man he is, had not he broke windows, knocked down constables, and disturbed honest people with his midnight serenades, when he was a young fellow. The engaging in adventures of this nature Will calls the studying of mankind, and terms this knowledge of the town, the knowledge of the world. Will ingenuously confesses, that for half of his life his head ached every morning with reading of men over night; and at present comforts himself under sundry infirmities with the reflection, that without them he could not have been acquainted with the gallantries of the age. This Will looks upon as the learning of a gentleman, and regards all other kinds of science as the accomplishments of one whom he calls a scholar, a bookish man, or a philosopher.

For these reasons Will shines in a mixed company, where he has the discretion not to go out of his depth, and has often a certain way of making his real ignorance appear a seeming one. Our club however has frequently caught him tripping, at which times they never spare him. For as Will often insults us with the knowledge of the town, we sometimes take our revenge upon him by our knowledge of books.

He was last week producing two or three letters which he writ in his youth to a coquette lady. The raillery of them was natural, and well enough for a mere man of the town; but, very unluckily, several of the words were wrong spelt. Will laughed this off at first as well as he could, but finding himself pushed on all sides, and especially by the Templar, he told us, with a little passion, that he never liked pedantry in spelling, and that he spelt like a gentleman, and not like a scholar : upon this Will had recourse to his old topic of showing the narrow-spiritedness, the pride and ignorance of pedants ; which he carried so far, that upon my retiring to my lodgings, I could not forbear throwing together such reflections as occurred to me upon that subject.

A man who has been brought up among books, and is able to talk of nothing else, is a very indifferent companion, and what we call a pedant. But, methinks, we should enlarge the title, and give it every one that does not know how to think out of his profession and particular way of life.

What is a greater pedant than a mere man of the town? Bar him the play-houses, a catalogue of the reigning beauties, and an account of a few fashionable distempers that have befallen him, and you strike him dumb. How many a pretty gentleman's knowledge lies all within the verge of the court? He will tell you the names of the principal favorites, repeat the shrewd sayings of a man of quality, whisper an intrigue that is not yet blown upon by common fame : or, if the sphere of his observation is a little larger than ordinary, will perhaps enter into all the incidents, turns, and revolutions in a game of ombre. When he has gone thus far, he has shown you the whole circle of his accomplishments, his parts are drained, and he is disabled from any farther conversation. What are these but rank pedants ? And yet these are the men who value themselves most on their exemption from the pedantry of colleges.

I might here mention the military pedant, who always talks in a camp, and is storming towns, making lodgments, and fighting battles from one end of the year to the other. Everything he speaks smells of gunpowder; if you take away

his artillery from him, he has not a word to say for himself
I might likewise mention the law pedant, that is perpetually
putting cases, repeating the transactions of Westminster
Hall, wrangling with you upon the most indifferent circumstances of life, and not to be convinced of the distance of a
place, or of the most trivial point in conversation, but by
dint of argument. The state pedant is wrapped up in news,
and lost in politics. If you mention either of the kings of
Spain or Poland, he talks very notably; but if you go out
of the gazette, you drop him. In short, a mere courtier, a
mere soldier, a mere scholar, a mere anything, is an insipid
pedantic character, and equally ridiculous.

Of all the species of pedants, which I have mentioned,
the book pedant is much the most supportable; he has at
least an exercised understanding, and a head which is full
though confused, so that a man who converses with him may
often receive from him hints of things that are worth knowing, and what he may possibly turn to his own advantage,
though they are of little use to the owner. The worst kind
of pedants among learned men, are such as are naturally
endowed with a very small share of common sense, and have
read a great number of books without taste or distinction.

The truth of it is, learning, like travelling, and all other
methods of improvement, as it finishes good sense, so it
makes a silly man ten thousand times more insufferable, by
supplying variety of matter to his impertinence, and giving
him an opportunity of abounding in absurdities.

Shallow pedants cry up one another much more than men
of solid and useful learning. To read the titles they give
an editor, or collator of a manuscript, you would take him
for the glory of the commonwealth of letters, and the wonder of his age, when perhaps upon examination you find that
he has only rectified a Greek particle, or laid out a whole
sentence in proper commas.

They are obliged indeed to be thus lavish of their praises,

that they may keep one another in countenance, and it is no wonder if a great deal of knowledge, which is not capable of making a man wise, has a natural tendency to make him vain and arrogant.

Spectator No. 106. *The Spectator's observations at Sir Roger's country-house.*

Having often received an invitation from my friend Sir Roger de Coverley to pass away a month with him in the country, I last week accompanied him thither, and am settled with him for some time at his country-house, where I intend to form several of my ensuing speculations. Sir Roger, who is very well acquainted with my humor, lets me rise and go to bed when I please; dine at his own table or in my chamber as I think fit, sit still and say nothing without bidding me be merry. When the gentlemen of the country come to see him, he only shows me at a distance: as I have been walking in his fields I have observed them stealing a sight of me over an hedge, and have heard the knight desiring them not to let me see them, for that I hated to be stared at.

I am the more at ease in Sir Roger's family, because it consists of sober and staid persons: for as the knight is the best master in the world, he seldom changes his servants; and as he is beloved by all about him, his servants never care for leaving him; by this means his domestics are all in years, and grown old with their master. You would take his Valet-de-chambre for his brother, his butler is grey-headed, his groom is one of the gravest men that I have ever seen, and his coachman has the looks of a privy-counsellor. You see the goodness of the master even in the old house-dog, and in a grey pad that is kept in the stable with great care and tenderness out of regard to his past services, though he has been useless for several years.

I could not but observe with a great deal of pleasure the joy that appeared in the countenance of these ancient domestics upon my friend's arrival at his country-seat. Some of them could not refrain from tears at the sight of their old master; every one of them pressed forward to do something for him, and seemed discouraged if they were not employed. At the same time the good old knight, with a mixture of the father and the master of the family, tempered the inquiries after his own affairs with several kind questions relating to themselves. This humanity and good nature engages everybody to him, so that when he is pleasant upon any of them, all his family are in good humor, and none so much as the person whom he diverts himself with: on the contrary, if he coughs, or betrays any infirmity of old age, it is easy for a stander by to observe a secret concern in the looks of all his servants.

My worthy friend has put me under the particular care of his butler, who is a very prudent man, and, as well as the rest of his fellow-servants, wonderfully desirous of pleasing me, because they have often heard their master talk of me as of his particular friend.

My chief companion, when Sir Roger is diverting himself in the woods or the fields, is a very venerable man who is ever with Sir Roger, and has lived at his house in the nature of a chaplain above thirty years. This gentleman is a person of good sense and some learning, of a very regular life and obliging conversation: he heartily loves Sir Roger, and knows that he is very much in the old knight's esteem, so that he lives in the family rather as a relation than a dependent.

I have observed in several of my papers, that my friend Sir Roger, amidst all his good qualities, is something of an humorist; and that his virtues, as well as imperfections, are, as it were, tinged by a certain extravagance, which makes them particularly his, and distinguishes them from those of other men. This cast of mind, as it is generally very innocent in itself, so it renders his conversation highly agreeable, and more delightful than the same degree of sense and virtue would appear in their common or ordinary colors. As I was walking with him last night, he asked me how I liked the good man whom I have just now mentioned; and, without staying for my answer, told me that he was afraid of being insulted with Latin and Greek at his own table; for which reason he desired a particular friend of his at the university to find him out a clergyman rather of plain sense than much learning, of a good aspect, a clear voice, a sociable temper: and, if possible, a man that understood a little of back-gammon. "My friend," says Sir Roger, "found me out this gentleman, who, besides the endowments required of him, is, they tell me, a good scholar, though he does not show it: I have given him the parsonage of the parish; and because I know his value, have settled upon him a good annuity for life. If he outlives me, he shall find that he was higher in my esteem than perhaps he thinks he is. He has now been with me thirty years; and though he does not know I have taken notice of it, has never in all that time asked anything of me for himself, though he is every day soliciting me for something in behalf of one or other of my tenants, his parishioners. There has not been a law-suit in the parish since he has lived among them; if any dispute arises they apply themselves to him for the decision; if they do not acquiesce in his judgment, which I think never happened above once or twice at most, they appeal to me. At his first settling with me, I made him a present of all the good sermons which have been printed in English, and only begged of him that every Sunday he would pronounce one of them in the pulpit. Accordingly, he has digested them into such a series, that they follow one another naturally, and make a continued system of practical divinity."

As Sir Roger was going on in his story, the gentle-man we were talking of came up to us; and upon the knight's asking him who preached to-morrow (for it was Saturday night) told us, the Bishop of St. Asaph in the morning, and Dr. South in the afternoon. He then showed us his list of preachers for the whole year, where I saw with a great deal of pleasure archbishop Tillotson, bishop Saunderson, Dr. Barrow, Dr. Calamy, with several living authors who have published discourses of practical divinity. I no sooner saw this venerable man in the pulpit, but I very much approved of my friend's insisting upon the qualifications of a good aspect and a clear voice; for I was so charmed with the gracefulness of his figure and delivery, as well as with the discourses he pronounced, that I think I never passed any time more to my satisfaction. A sermon repeated after this manner is like the composition of a poet in the mouth of a graceful actor.

I could heartily wish that more of our country clergy would follow this example; and instead of wasting their spirits in laborious compositions of their own, would endeavor after a handsome elocution, and all those other talents that are proper to enforce what has been penned by greater masters. This would not only be more easy to themselves, but more edifying to the people.

Spectator No. 107.　*The Coverley household: Sir Roger's treatment of his servants.*

The reception, manner of attendance, undisturbed freedom, and quiet, which I meet with here in the country, has confirmed me in the opinion I always had, that the general corruption of manners in servants is owing to the conduct of masters. The aspect of every one in the family carries so much satisfaction that it appears he knows the happy lot which has befallen him in being a member of it. There is one particular which I have seldom seen but at Sir Roger's; it is usual in all other places, that servants fly from the parts of the house through which their master is passing: on the contrary, here they industriously place themselves in his way; and it is on both sides, as it were, understood as a visit, when the servants appear without calling. This proceeds from the humane and equal temper of the man of the house, who also perfectly well knows how to enjoy a great estate with such economy as ever to be much beforehand. This makes his own mind untroubled, and consequently unapt to vent peevish expressions, or give passionate or inconsistent orders to those about him. Thus respect and love go together, and a certain cheerfulness in performance of their duty is the particular distinction of the lower part of this family. When a servant is called before his master, he does not come with an expectation to hear himself rated for some trivial fault, threatened to be stripped, or used with any other unbecoming language, which mean masters often give to worthy servants; but it is often to know what road he took that he came so readily back according to order; whether he passed by such a ground; if the old man who rents it is in good health; or whether he gave Sir Roger's love to him, or the like.

One might, on this occasion, recount the sense that great persons in all ages have had of the merit of their dependents, and the heroic services which men have done their masters in the extremity of their fortunes; and shown to their undone patrons that fortune was all the difference between them; but as I design this my speculation only as a gentle admonition to thankless masters, I shall not go out of the occurrences of common life, but assert it as a general observation, that I never saw, but in Sir Roger's family, and one or two more, good servants treated as they ought to be.

Sir Roger's kindness extends to their children's children, and this very morning he sent his coachman's grandson to prentice. I shall conclude this paper with an account of a picture in his gallery, where there are many which will deserve my future observation.

At the very upper end of this handsome structure I saw the portraiture of two young men standing in a river, the one naked, the other in a livery. The person supported seemed half dead, but still so much alive as to show in his face exquisite joy and love towards the other. I thought the fainting figure resembled my friend Sir Roger; and looking at the butler, who stood by me, for an account of it, he informed me that the person in the livery was a servant of Sir Roger's, who stood on the shore while his master was swimming, and observing him taken with some sudden illness, and sink under water, jumped in and saved him. He told me Sir Roger took off the dress he was in as soon as he came home, and by a great bounty at that time, followed by his favor ever since, had made him master of that pretty seat which we saw at a distance as we came to this house. I remembered indeed Sir Roger said there lived a very worthy gentleman, to whom he was highly obliged, without mentioning anything further. Upon my looking a little dissatisfied at some part of the picture, my attendant informed me that it was against Sir Roger's will, and at the earnest request of the gentleman himself, that he was drawn in the habit in which he had saved his master. — *Steele.*

Spectator No. 108.   *The Spectator describes Will Wimble, whom he meets at Sir Roger's.*

As I was yesterday morning walking with Sir Roger before his house, a country fellow brought him a huge fish, which, he told him, Mr. William Wimble had caught that

very morning; and that he presented it, with his service to
him, and intended to come and dine with him. At the same
time he delivered a letter, which my friend read to me as
soon as the messenger left him.

SIR ROGER,—I desire you to accept of a jack, which is the best
I have caught this season. I intend to come and stay with you a
week, and see how the perch bite in the Black River. I observed with
some concern, the last time I saw you upon the bowling-green, that
your whip wanted a lash to it; I will bring half a dozen with me
that I twisted last week, which I hope will serve you all the time you
are in the country. I have not been out of the saddle for six days
last past, having been at Eton with Sir John's eldest son. He takes
to his learning hugely.

I am, sir, your humble servant,

WILL WIMBLE.

This extraordinary letter, and message that accompanied
it, made me very curious to know the character and quality
of the gentleman who sent them; which I found to be as
follows. Will Wimble is younger brother to a baronet, and
descended of the ancient family of the Wimbles. He is now
between forty and fifty; but being bred to no business and
born to no estate, he generally lives with his elder brother
as superintendent of his game. He hunts a pack of dogs
better than any man in the country, and is very famous for
finding out a hare. He is extremely well versed in all the
little handicrafts of an idle man: he makes a may-fly to a
miracle, and furnishes the whole country with angle-rods.
As he is a good-natured officious fellow, and very much esteemed upon account of his family, he is a welcome guest
at every house, and keeps up a good correspondence among
all the gentlemen about him. He carries a tulip-root in his
pocket from one to another, or exchanges a puppy between
a couple of friends that live perhaps in the opposite sides
of the county. Will is a particular favorite of all the young
heirs, whom he frequently obliges with a net that he has

weaved, or a setting-dog that he has made himself. He now and then presents a pair of garters of his own knitting to their mothers or sisters; and raises a great deal of mirth among them, by inquiring as often as he meets them how they wear. These gentleman-like manufactures and obliging little humors make Will the darling of the country.

Sir Roger was proceeding in the character of him, when we saw him make up to us with two or three hazel-twigs in his hand that he had cut in Sir Roger's woods, as he came through them, in his way to the house. I was very much pleased to observe on one side the hearty and sincere welcome with which Sir Roger received him, and on the other, the secret joy which his guest discovered at sight of the good old Knight. After the first salutes were over, Will desired Sir Roger to lend him one of his servants to carry a set of shuttlecocks he had with him in a little box to a lady that lived about a mile off, to whom it seems he had promised such a present for above this half year. Sir Roger's back was no sooner turned but honest Will began to tell me of a large cock-pheasant that he had sprung in one of the neighboring woods, with two or three other adventures of the same nature. Odd and uncommon characters are the game that I look for and most delight in; for which reason I was as much pleased with the novelty of the person that talked to me, as he could be for his life with the springing of a pheasant, and therefore listened to him with more than ordinary attention.

In the midst of his discourse the bell rung to dinner, where the gentleman I have been speaking of had the pleasure of seeing the huge jack he had caught served up for the first dish in a most sumptuous manner. Upon our sitting down to it he gave us a long account how he had hooked it, played with it, foiled it, and at length drew it out upon the bank, with several other particulars that lasted all the first course. A dish of wild fowl that came afterwards furnished conversation for the rest of the dinner, which concluded with a late invention of Will's for improving the quail-pipe.

Upon withdrawing into my room after dinner, I was secretly touched with compassion towards the honest gentleman that had dined with us, and could not but consider, with a great deal of concern, how so good an heart and such busy hands were wholly employed in trifles; that so much humanity should be so little beneficial to others, and so much industry so little advantageous to himself. The same temper of mind and application to affairs might have recommended him to the public esteem, and have raised his fortune in another station of life. What good to his country or himself might not a trader or a merchant have done with such useful though ordinary qualifications?

Will Wimble's is the case of many a younger brother of a great family, who had rather see their children starve like gentlemen than thrive in a trade or profession that is beneath their quality. This humor fills several parts of Europe with pride and beggary. It is the happiness of a trading nation, like ours, that the younger sons, though uncapable of any liberal art or profession, may be placed in such a way of life as may perhaps enable them to vie with the best of their family. Accordingly, we find several citizens that were launched into the world with narrow fortunes, rising by an honest industry to greater estates than those of their elder brothers. It is not improbable but Will was formerly tried at divinity, law, or physic; and that finding his genius did not lie that way, his parents gave him up at length to his own inventions. But certainly, however improper he might have been for studies of a higher nature, he was perfectly well turned for the occupations of trade and commerce. As I think this is a point which cannot be too much inculcated, I shall desire my reader to compare what I have here written with what I have said in my twenty-first speculation.

Spectator No. 109. *Sir Roger's account of his ancestors.*

I was this morning walking in the gallery, when Sir Roger entered at the end opposite to me, and, advancing towards me, said he was glad to meet me among his relations the De Coverleys, and hoped I liked the conversation of so much good company, who were as silent as myself. I knew he alluded to the pictures; and, as he is a gentleman who does not a little value himself upon his ancient descent, I expected he would give me some account of them. We were now arrived at the upper end of the gallery, when the Knight faced towards one of the pictures, and, as we stood before it, he entered into the matter, after his blunt way of saying things as they occur to his imagination without regular introduction or care to preserve the appearance of chain of thought.

"It is," said he, "worth while to consider the force of dress, and how the persons of one age differ from those of another merely by that only. One may observe, also, that the general fashion of one age has been followed by one particular set of people in another, and by them preserved from one generation to another. Thus the vast jetting coat and small bonnet, which was the habit in Harry the Seventh's time, is kept on in the yeoman of the guard; not without a good and politic view, because they look a foot taller, and a foot and a half broader: besides that the cap leaves the face expanded, and consequently more terrible, and fitter to stand at the entrances of palaces.

"This predecessor of ours, you see, is dressed after this manner, and his cheeks would be no larger than mine were he in a hat as I am. He was the last man that won a prize in the Tilt Yard (which is now a common street before Whitehall). You see the broken lance that lies there by his right foot: he shivered that lance of his adversary all to pieces; and, bearing himself, look you, sir, in this manner, at the same time he came within the target of the gentleman who rode against him, and taking him with incredible force before him on the pommel of his saddle, he in that manner rid the tournament over, with an air that showed he did it rather to perform the rule of the lists than expose his enemy : however, it appeared he knew how to make use of a victory, and, with a gentle trot, he marched up to a gallery where their mistress sat (for they were rivals) and let him down with laudable courtesy and pardonable insolence. I don't know but it might be exactly where the coffee-house is now.

"You are to know this my ancestor was not only of a military genius, but fit also for the arts of peace, for he played on the bass-viol as well as any gentleman at court : you see where his viol hangs by his basket-hilt sword. The action at the Tilt Yard you may be sure won the fair lady, who was a maid of honor, and the greatest beauty of her time; here she stands, the next picture. You see, sir, my great-great-great-grandmother has on the new-fashioned petticoat, except that the modern is gathered at the waist : my grandmother appears as if she stood in a large drum, whereas the ladies now walk as if they were in a go-cart. For all this lady was bred at court, she became an excellent country wife, she brought ten children, and, when I show you the library, you shall see, in her own hand (allowing for the difference of the language), the best receipt now in England both for a hasty-pudding and a white-pot.

"If you please to fall back a little, because 'tis necessary to look at the three next pictures at one view; these are three sisters. She on the right hand, who is so very beautiful, died a maid; the next to her, still handsomer, had the same fate, against her will; this homely thing in the middle had both their portions added to her own, and was stolen by a neighboring gentleman, a man of stratagem and resolution, for he poisoned three mastiffs to come at her,

and knocked down two deer-stealers in carrying her off.
Misfortunes happen in all families. The theft of this
romp and so much money, was no great matter to our estate. But the next heir that possessed it was this soft
gentleman, whom you see there : observe the small buttons,
the little boots, the laces, the slashes about his clothes,
and, above all, the posture he is drawn in (which to be sure
was his own choosing); you see he sits with one hand on
a desk writing and looking as it were another way, like an
easy writer, or a sonneteer. He was one of those that had
too much wit to know how to live in the world : he was a
man of no justice, but great good manners; he ruined everybody that had anything to do with him, but never said a
rude thing in his life; the most indolent person in the
world, he would sign a deed that passed away half his estate with his gloves on, but would not put on his hat before
a lady if it were to save his country. He is said to be the
first that made love by squeezing the hand. He left the
estate with ten thousand pounds debt upon it : but, however, by all hands I have been informed that he was every
way the finest gentleman in the world."

Sir Roger went on with his account of the gallery in the
following manner. "This man" (pointing to him I looked
at) "I take to be the honor of our house, Sir Humphrey de
Coverley; he was in his dealings as punctual as a tradesman, and as generous as a gentleman. He would have
thought himself as much undone by breaking his word, as
if it were to be followed by bankruptcy. He served his
country as knight of this shire to his dying day. He found
it no easy matter to maintain an integrity in his words and
actions, even in things that regarded the offices which were
incumbent upon him, in the care of his own affairs and relations of life, and therefore dreaded (though he had great
talents) to go into employments of state, where he must be
exposed to the snares of ambition. Innocence of life and

great ability were the distinguishing parts of his character; the latter, he had often observed, had led to the destruction of the former, and used frequently to lament that great and good had not the same signification. He was an excellent husbandman, but had resolved not to exceed such a degree of wealth: all above it he bestowed in secret bounties many years after the sum he aimed at for his own use was attained. Yet he did not slacken his industry, but to a decent old age spent the life and fortune which was superfluous to himself in the service of his friends and neighbors."

Here we were called to dinner, and Sir Roger ended the discourse of this gentleman by telling me, as we followed the servant, that this his ancestor was a brave man, and narrowly escaped being killed in the Civil Wars; "For," said he, "he was sent out of the field upon a private message the day before the battle of Worcester."

The whim of narrowly escaping by having been within a day of danger, with other matters above mentioned, mixed with good sense, left me at a loss whether I was more delighted with my friend's wisdom or simplicity.— *Steele.*

Spectator No. 110. *Ghosts and haunted houses.*

At a little distance from Sir Roger's house, among the ruins of an old abbey, there is a long walk of aged elms; which are shot up so very high, that when one passes under them, the rooks and crows that rest upon the tops of them, seem to be cawing in another region. I am very much delighted with this sort of noise, which I consider as a kind of natural prayer to that Being who supplies the wants of his whole creation, and who, in the beautiful language of the Psalms, feedeth the young ravens that call upon him.

I like this retirement the better, because of an ill report it lies under of being haunted; for which reason, as I have been told in the family, no living creature ever walks in it besides the chaplain. My good friend the butler desired me, with a very grave face, not to venture myself in it after sunset, for that one of the footmen had been almost frighted out of his wits by a spirit that appeared to him in the shape of a black horse without an head; to which he added, that about a month ago, one of the maids coming home late that way, with a pail of milk upon her head, heard such a rustling among the bushes, that she let it fall.

I was taking a walk in this place last night between the hours of nine and ten, and could not but fancy it one of the most proper scenes in the world for a ghost to appear in. The ruins of the abbey are scattered up and down on every side, and half covered with ivy and elder bushes, the harbors of several solitary birds, which seldom make their appearance till the dusk of the evening. The place was formerly a churchyard, and has still several marks in it of graves and burying-places. There is such an echo among the old ruins and vaults, that if you stamp but a little louder than ordinary, you hear the sound repeated. At the same time the walk of elms, with the croaking of the ravens, which from time to time are heard from the tops of them, looks exceeding solemn and venerable. These objects naturally raise seriousness and attention; and when night heightens the awfulness of the place, and pours out her supernumerary horrors upon everything in it, I do not at all wonder that weak minds fill it with spectres and apparitions.

Mr. Locke, in his chapter of the association of ideas, has very curious remarks, to show how, by the prejudice of education, one idea often introduces into the mind a whole set that bear no resemblance to one another in the nature of things. Among several examples of this kind, he produces the following instance: —

The ideas of goblins and sprights have really no more to do with darkness than light; yet let but a foolish maid inculcate these often on the mind of a child, and raise them there together, possibly he shall never be able to separate them again so long as he lives; but darkness shall ever afterwards bring with it those frightful ideas, and they shall be so joined, that he can no more bear the one than the other.

As I was walking in this solitude, where the dusk of the evening conspired with so many other occasions of terror, I observed a cow grazing not far from me, which an imagination that was apt to startle might easily have construed into a black horse without an head; and I daresay the poor footman lost his wits upon some such trivial occasion.

My friend Sir Roger has often told me, with a good deal of mirth, that at his first coming to his estate, he found three parts of his house altogether useless; that the best room in it had the reputation of being haunted, and by that means was locked up; that noises had been heard in his long gallery, so that he could not get a servant to enter it after eight o'clock at night; that the door of one of his chambers was nailed up, because there went a story in the family that a butler had formerly hanged himself in it; and that his mother, who lived to a great age, had shut up half the rooms in the house, in which either her husband, a son, or a daughter had died. The knight seeing his habitation reduced to so small a compass, and himself in a manner shut out of his own house, upon the death of his mother, ordered all the apartments to be flung open, and exorcised by his chaplain, who lay in every room one after another, and by that means dissipated the fears which had ·so long reigned in the family.

Spectator No. 112. *Sunday in the country : Sir Roger at church.*

I am always very well pleased with a country Sunday, and think, if keeping holy the seventh day were only a human institution, it would be the best method that could have been thought of for the polishing and civilizing of mankind. It is certain the country people would soon degenerate into a kind of savages and barbarians, were there not such frequent returns of a stated time in which the whole village meet together with their best faces, and in their cleanliest habits, to converse with one another upon indifferent subjects, hear their duties explained to them, and join together in adoration of the Supreme Being. Sunday clears away the rust of the whole week, not only as it refreshes in their minds the notions of religion, but as it puts both the sexes upon appearing in their most agreeable forms, and exerting all such qualities as are apt to give them a figure in the eye of the village. A country fellow distinguishes himself as much in the churchyard, as a citizen does upon the Change, the whole parish politics being generally discussed in that place either after sermon or before the bell rings.

My friend Sir Roger, being a good churchman, has beautified the inside of his church with several texts of his own choosing; he has likewise given a handsome pulpit-cloth, and railed in the communion table at his own expense. He has often told me, that at his coming to his estate he found his parishioners very irregular; and that in order to make them kneel and join in the responses, he gave every one of them a hassock and a common-prayer book: and at the same time employed an itinerant singing master, who goes about the country for that purpose, to instruct them rightly in the tunes of the psalms; upon which they now very much value themselves, and indeed outdo most of the country churches that I have ever heard.

As Sir Roger is landlord to the whole congregation, he keeps them in very good order, and will suffer nobody to sleep in it besides himself; for if by chance he has been surprised into a short nap at sermon, upon recovering out of it he stands up and looks about him, and if he sees anybody else nodding, either wakes them himself, or sends his servants to them. Several other of the old knight's particularities break out upon these occasions : sometimes he will be lengthening out a verse in the singing-psalms, half a minute after the rest of the congregation have done with it; sometimes, when he is pleased with the matter of his devotion, he pronounces *Amen* three or four times to the same prayer; and sometimes stands up when everybody else is upon their knees, to count the congregation, or see if any of his tenants are missing.

I was yesterday very much surprised to hear my old friend, in the midst of the service, calling out to one John Matthews to mind what he was about, and not disturb the congregation. This John Matthews it seems is remarkable for being an idle fellow, and at that time was kicking his heels for his diversion. This authority of the knight, though exerted in that odd manner which accompanies him in all circumstances of life, has a very good effect upon the parish, who are not polite enough to see anything ridiculous in his behavior; besides that the general good sense and worthiness of his character makes his friends observe these little singularities as foils that rather set off than blemish his good qualities.

As soon as the sermon is finished, nobody presumes to stir till Sir Roger is gone out of the church. The knight walks down from his seat in the chancel between a double row of his tenants, that stand bowing to him on each side; and every now and then inquires how such an one's wife, or mother, or son, or father do, whom he does not see at church; which is understood as a secret reprimand to the person that is absent.

The chaplain has often told me, that upon a catechising day, when Sir Roger has been pleased with a boy that answers well, he has ordered a bible to be given him next day for his encouragement; and sometimes accompanies it with a flitch of bacon for his mother. Sir Roger has likewise added five pounds a year to the clerk's place; and that he may encourage the young fellows to make themselves perfect in the church service, has promised, upon the death of the present incumbent, who is very old, to bestow it according to merit.

The fair understanding between Sir Roger and his chaplain, and their mutual concurrence in doing good, is the more remarkable, because the very next village is famous for the differences and contentions that rise between the parson and the 'squire, who live in a perpetual state of war. The parson is always preaching at the 'squire, and the 'squire to be revenged on the parson never comes to church. The 'squire has made all his tenants atheists and tithe-stealers; while the parson instructs them every Sunday in the dignity of his order, and insinuates to them in almost every sermon that he is a better man than his patron. In short matters are come to such an extremity, that the 'squire has not said his prayers either in public or private this half year; and that the parson threatens him, if he does not mend his manners, to pray for him in the face of the whole congregation.

Feuds of this nature, though too frequent in the country, are very fatal to the ordinary people; who are so used to be dazzled with riches, that they pay as much deference to the understanding of a man of an estate, as of a man of learning: and are very hardly brought to regard any truth, how important soever it may be, that is preached to them, when they know there are several men of five hundred a year who do not believe it.

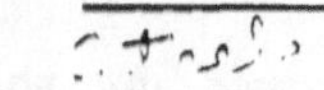

Spectator No. 113.   *Sir Roger in love.*

In my first description of the company in which I pass most of my time it may be remembered that I mentioned a great affliction which my friend Sir Roger had met with in his youth: which was no less than a disappointment in love. It happened this evening that we fell into a very pleasing walk at a distance from his house: as soon as we came into it, "It is," quoth the good old man, looking round him with a smile, "very hard, that any part of my land should be settled upon one who has used me so ill as the perverse Widow did; and yet I am sure I could not see a sprig of any bough of this whole walk of trees, but I should reflect upon her and her severity. She has certainly the finest hand of any woman in the world. You are to know this was the place wherein I used to muse upon her; and by that custom I can never come into it, but the same tender sentiments revive in my mind as if I had actually walked with that beautiful creature under these shades. I have been fool enough to carve her name on the bark of several of these trees; so unhappy is the condition of men in love to attempt the removing of their passion by the methods which serve only to imprint it deeper. She has certainly the finest hand of any woman in the world."

Here followed a profound silence; and I was not dis-pleased to observe my friend falling so naturally into a discourse which I had ever before taken notice he industri-ously avoided. After a very long pause he entered upon an account of this great circumstance in his life, with an air which I thought raised my idea of him above what I had ever had before; and gave me the picture of that cheerful mind of his, before it received that stroke which has ever since affected his words and actions. But he went on as follows:—

"I came to my estate in my twenty-second year, and re-solved to follow the steps of the most worthy of my ances-tors who have inhabited this spot of earth before me, in all the methods of hospitality and good neighborhood, for the sake of my fame, and in country sports and recreations, for the sake of my health. In my twenty-third year I was obliged to serve as sheriff of the county; and in my servants, officers, and whole equipage, indulged the pleasure of a young man (who did not think ill of his own person) in taking that public occasion of showing my figure and behavior to advantage. You may easily imagine to yourself what appearance I made, who am pretty tall, rid well, and was very well dressed, at the head of a whole county, with music before me, a feather in my hat, and my horse well bitted. I can assure you I was not a little pleased with the kind looks and glances I had from all the balconies and windows as I rode to the hall where the assizes were held. But when I came there, a beautiful creature in a widow's habit sat in court, to hear the event of a cause concerning her dower. This commanding creature (who was born for the destruction of all who behold her) put on such a resignation in her countenance, and bore the whispers of all around the court, with such a pretty uneasiness, I warrant you, and then recovered herself from one eye to another, till she was perfectly confused by meeting something so wistful in all she encountered, that at last, with a murrain to her, she cast her bewitching eye upon me. I no sooner met it but I bowed like a great surprised booby; and knowing her cause to be the first which came on, I cried, like a captivated calf as I was, 'Make way for the defendant's witnesses.' This sudden partiality made all the county immediately see the sheriff also was become a slave to the fine widow. During the time her cause was upon trial, she behaved herself, I warrant you, with such a deep attention to her business, took opportunities to have little billets handed to her counsel, then would be in such a pretty confusion, occasioned, you must know, by acting before so much company, that not only I but the whole court was prejudiced in her favor; and all that the next heir to her husband had to urge was thought so groundless and frivolous, that when it came to her counsel to reply, there was not half so much

said as every one besides in the court thought he could
have urged to her advantage. You must understand, sir,
this perverse woman is one of those unaccountable creatures,
that secretly rejoice in the admiration of men, but indulge
themselves in no further consequences. Hence it is that
she has ever had a train of admirers, and she removes from
her slaves in town to those in the country, according to the
seasons of the year. She is a reading lady, and far gone
in the pleasures of friendship: she is always accompanied
by a confidante, who is witness to her daily protestations
against our sex, and consequently a bar to her first steps
towards love, upon the strength of her own maxims and
declarations.

"She is such a desperate scholar, that no country gentleman can approach her without being a jest. As I was going
to tell you, when I came to her house I was admitted to
her presence with great civility; at the same time she
placed herself to be first seen by me in such an attitude,
as I think you call the posture of a picture, that she discovered new charms, and I at last came towards her with such
an awe as made me speechless. This she no sooner observed
but she made her advantage of it, and began a discourse to
me concerning love and honor, as they both are followed by
pretenders, and the real votaries to them. When she discussed these points in a discourse, which I verily believe
was as learned as the best philosopher in Europe could
possibly make, she asked me whether she was so happy
as to fall in with my sentiments on these important particulars. Her confidante sat by her, and upon my being in
the last confusion and silence, this malicious aid of hers
turning to her says, 'I am very glad to observe Sir Roger
pauses upon this subject, and seems resolved to deliver all
his sentiments upon the matter when he pleases to speak.'
They both kept their countenances, and after I had sat half
an hour meditating how to behave before such profound

casuists, I rose up and took my leave. Chance has since that time thrown me very often in her way, and she as often has directed a discourse to me which I do not understand. This barbarity has kept me ever at a distance from the most beautiful object my eyes ever beheld. It is thus also she deals with all mankind, and you must make love to her, as you would conquer the sphinx, by posing her. But were she like other women, and that there were any talking to her, how constant must the pleasure of that man be, who could converse with a creature—— But, after all, you may be sure her heart is fixed on some one or other; and yet I have been credibly informed—but who can believe half that is said ?"

I found my friend begin to rave, and insensibly led him towards the house, that we might be joined by some other company ; and am convinced that the Widow is the secret cause of all that inconsistency which appears in some parts of my friend's discourse ; though he has so much command of himself as not directly to mention her, yet according to that passage of Martial, which one knows not how to render into English, *Dum tacet hanc loquitur.—Steele.*

Spectator No. 115. *Exercise the best means of preserving health :*
Sir Roger as a hunter.

Bodily labor is of two kinds, either that which a man submits to for his livelihood, or that which he undergoes for his pleasure. The latter of them generally changes the name of labor for that of exercise, but differs only from ordinary labor as it rises from another motive.

That we might not want inducements to engage us in such an exercise of the body as is proper for its welfare, it is so ordered, that nothing valuable can be procured without it. Not to mention riches and honor, even food and raiment are not to be come at without the toil of the hands and sweat of the brows. Providence furnishes materials, but expects that we should work them up ourselves. The earth must be labored before it gives its increase, and when it is forced into its several products, how many hands must they pass through before they are fit for use? Manufactures, trade and agriculture, naturally employ more than nineteen parts of the species in twenty; and as for those who are not obliged to labor, by the condition in which they are born, they are more miserable than the rest of mankind, unless they indulge themselves in that voluntary labor which goes by the name of exercise.

My friend Sir Roger has been an indefatigable man in business of this kind, and has hung several parts of his house with the trophies of his former labors. The walls of his great hall are covered with the horns of several kinds of deer that he has killed in the chase, which he thinks the most valuable furniture of his house, as they afford him frequent topics of discourse, and show that he has not been idle. At the lower end of the hall is a large otter's skin stuffed with hay, which his mother ordered to be hung up in that manner, and the knight looks upon it with great satisfaction, because it seems he was but nine years old when his dog killed him. A little room adjoining to the hall is a kind of arsenal filled with guns of several sizes and inventions, with which the knight has made great havoc in the woods, and destroyed many thousands of pheasants, partridges, and woodcocks. His stable doors are patched with noses that belonged to foxes of the knight's own hunting down. Sir Roger showed me one of them, that for distinction's sake has a brass nail struck through it, which cost him about fifteen hours' riding, carried him through half a dozen counties, killed him a brace of horses, and lost above half his dogs. This the knight looks upon as one of the greatest exploits of his life. The perverse widow, whom I have given some account of, was the death of several foxes; for Sir Roger has told me, that in the course of his amours he patched the western door of his stable. Whenever the widow was cruel, the foxes were sure to pay for it. In proportion as his passion for the widow abated, and old age came on, he left off fox-hunting; but a hare is not yet safe that sits within ten miles of his house.

There is no kind of exercise which I would so recommend to my readers of both sexes as this of riding, as there is none which so much conduces to health, and is every way accommodated to the body, according to the idea which I have given of it. For my own part, when I am in town, for want of these opportunities, I exercise myself an hour every morning upon a dumb bell that is placed in a corner of my room, and pleases me the more, because it does everything I require of it in the most profound silence. My landlady and her daughters are so well acquainted with my hours of exercise, that they never come into my room to disturb me whilst I am ringing.

When I was some years younger than I am at present, I used to employ myself in a more laborious diversion, which I learned from a Latin treatise of exercises, that is written with great erudition: it is there called the σκιομαχία, or the fighting with a man's own shadow, and consists in the brandishing of two short sticks grasped in each hand, and loaden with plugs of lead at either end. This opens the chest, exercises the limbs, and gives a man all the pleasure of boxing without the blows. I could wish that several learned men would lay out that time which they employ in controversies and disputes about nothing, in this method of fighting with their own shadows. It might conduce very much to evaporate the spleen, which makes them uneasy to the public as well as to themselves.

To conclude, as I am a compound of soul and body, I consider myself as obliged to a double scheme of duties; and think I have not fulfilled the business of the day, when I do not thus employ the one in labor and exercise, as well as the other in study and contemplation.

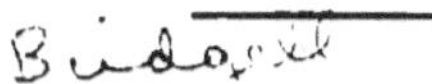

Spectator No. 116. *The Spectator accompanies Sir Roger to the hunting-field.*

Those who have searched into human nature observe that nothing so much shows the nobleness of the soul, as that its felicity consists in action. Every man has such an active principle in him, that he will find out something to employ himself upon, in whatever place or state of life he is posted. I have heard of a gentleman who was under close confinement in the Bastile seven years; during which time he amused himself in scattering a few small pins about his chamber, gathering them up again, and placing them in different figures on the arm of a great chair. He often told his friends afterwards, that unless he had found out this piece of exercise, he verily believed he should have lost his senses.

After what has been said, I need not inform my readers, that Sir Roger, with whose character I hope they are at present pretty well acquainted, has in his youth gone through the whole course of those rural diversions which the country abounds in; and which seem to be extremely well suited to that laborious industry a man may observe here in a far greater degree than in towns and cities. I have before hinted at some of my friend's exploits: he has in his youthful days taken forty coveys of partridges in a season; and tired many a salmon with a line consisting but of a single hair. The constant thanks and good wishes of the neighborhood always attended him on account of his remarkable enmity towards foxes; having destroyed more of these vermin in one year than it was thought the whole country could have produced. Indeed, the knight does not scruple to own among his most intimate friends, that in order to establish his reputation this way, he has secretly sent for great numbers of them out of other counties, which he used to turn loose about the country by night, that he might the better signalize himself in their destruction the next day. His hunting horses were the finest and best managed in all these parts : his tenants are still full of the praises of a gray stone horse that unhappily staked himself several years since, and was buried with great solemnity in the orchard.

Sir Roger, being at present too old for fox-hunting, to keep himself in action, has disposed of his beagles and got a pack of stop-hounds. What these want in speed he endeavors to make amends for by the deepness of their mouths and the variety of their notes, which are suited in such manner to each other that the whole cry makes up a complete concert. He is so nice in this particular, that a gentleman having made him a present of a very fine hound the other day, the knight returned it by the servant with a great many expressions of civility; but desired him to tell his master that the dog he had sent was indeed a most excellent bass, but that at present he only wanted a counter-tenor. Could I believe my friend had ever read Shakespeare I should certainly conclude he had taken the hint from Theseus in the Midsummer Night's Dream.

> My hounds are bred out of the Spartan kind,
> So flu'd, so sanded ; and their heads are hung
> With ears that sweep away the morning dew ;
> Crook-kneed and dew-lap'd like Thessalian bulls ;
> Slow in pursuit, but match'd in mouths like bells,
> Each under each : a cry more tunable
> Was never holla'd to, nor cheer'd with horn.

Sir Roger is so keen at this sport that he has been out almost every day since I came down; and upon the chaplain's offering to lend me his easy pad, I was prevailed on yesterday morning to make one of the company. I was extremely pleased, as we rid along, to observe the general benevolence of all the neighborhood towards my friend. The farmer's sons thought themselves happy if they could open a gate for the good old Knight as he passed by; which he generally requited with a nod or a smile, and a kind inquiry after their fathers and uncles.

After we had rid about a mile from home, we came upon a large heath, and the sportsmen began to beat. They had done so for some time, when, as I was at a little distance from the rest of the company, I saw a hare pop out from a small furze-brake almost under my horse's feet. I marked the way she took, which I endeavored to make the company sensible of by extending my arm; but to no purpose, till Sir Roger, who knows that none of my extraordinary motions are insignificant, rode up to me, and asked me if puss was gone that way. Upon my answering "Yes," he immediately called in the dogs and put them upon the scent. As they were going off, I heard one of the country-fellows muttering to his companion that 'twas a wonder they had not lost all their sport, for want of the silent gentleman's crying "Stole away!"

This, with my aversion to leaping hedges, made me withdraw to a rising ground, from whence I could have the picture of the whole chase, without the fatigue of keeping in with the hounds. The hare immediately threw them above a mile behind her: but I was pleased to find that instead of running straight forward, or in hunter's language, "flying the country," as I was afraid she might have done, she wheeled about, and described a sort of circle round the hill where I had taken my station, in such a manner as gave me a very distinct view of the sport. I could see her first pass by, and the dogs some time afterwards unravelling the whole track she had made, and following her through all her doubles.   I was at the same time delighted in observing that deference which the rest of the pack paid to each particular hound, according to the character he had acquired amongst them : if they were at fault, and an old hound of reputation opened but once, he was immediately followed by the whole cry; while a raw dog, or one who was a noted liar, might have yelped his heart out, without being taken notice of.

The hare now, after having squatted two or three times, and been put up again as often, came still nearer to the place where she was at first started. The dogs pursued her, and these were followed by the jolly Knight, who rode upon a white horse, encompassed by his tenants and servants, and cheering his hounds with all the gaiety of five-and-twenty. One of the sportsmen rode up to me, and told me that he was sure the chase was almost at an end, because the old dogs, which had hitherto lain behind, now headed the pack. The fellow was in the right. Our hare took a large field just under us, followed by the full cry "In view." I must confess the brightness of the weather, the cheerfulness of every thing around me, the chiding of the hounds, which was returned upon us in a double echo from two neighboring hills, with the hollowing of the sportsmen, and the sounding of the horn, lifted my spirits into a most lively pleasure, which I freely indulged because I was sure it was innocent. If I was under any concern, it was on the account of the poor hare, that was now quite spent, and almost within the reach of her enemies ; when the huntsman, getting forward, threw down his pole before the dogs. They were now within eight yards of that game which they had been pursuing for almost as many hours; yet on the signal before-mentioned they all made a sudden stand, and though they continued opening as much as before, durst not once attempt to pass beyond the pole. At the same time Sir Roger rode forward, and alighting, took up the hare in his arms; which he soon delivered up to one of his servants with an order, if she could be kept alive, to let her go in his great orchard: where it seems he has several of these prisoners of war, who live together in a very comfortable captivity. I was highly pleased to see the discipline of the pack, and the good-nature of the Knight, who could not find in his heart to murder a creature that had given him so much diversion.

For my own part I intend to hunt twice a week during my stay with Sir Roger; and shall prescribe the moderate use of this exercise to all my country friends, as the best kind of physic for mending a bad constitution, and preserving a good one.

I cannot do this better than in the following lines out of Mr. Dryden: —

> The first physicians by debauch were made;
> Excess began, and sloth sustains the trade.
> By chase our long-lived fathers earned their food;
> Toil strung the nerves, and purified the blood;
> But we their sons, a pamper'd race of men,
> Are dwindled down to threescore years and ten.
> Better to hunt in fields for health unbought
> Than fee the doctor for a nauseous draught.
> The wise for cure on exercise depend:
> God never made His work for man to mend. — *Budgell.*

Spectator No. 117. *The Spectator discusses witchcraft: with Sir Roger he visits Moll White.*

There are some opinions in which a man should stand neuter, without engaging his assent to one side or the other. Such a hovering faith as this, which refuses to settle upon any determination, is absolutely necessary to a mind that is careful to avoid errors and prepossessions. When the arguments press equally on both sides in matters that are indifferent to us, the safest method is to give up ourselves to neither.

It is with this temper of mind that I consider the subject of witchcraft. When I hear the relations that are made from all parts of the world, not only from Norway and Lapland, from the East and West Indies, but from every particular nation in Europe, I cannot forbear thinking that there is such an intercourse and commerce with evil spirits, as that which we express by the name of witchcraft. But when I consider that the ignorant and credulous parts of the world abound most in these relations, and that the persons among us who are supposed to engage in such an infernal commerce are people of a weak understanding and a crazed imagination, and at the same time reflect upon the many impostures and delusions of this nature that have been detected in all ages, I endeavor to suspend my belief till I hear more certain accounts than any which have yet come to my knowledge. In short, when I consider the question, whether there are such persons in the world as those we call witches, my mind is divided between the two opposite opinions: or rather (to speak my thoughts freely) I believe in general that there is, and has been such a thing as witchcraft; but at the same time can give no credit to any particular instance of it.

I am engaged in this speculation by some occurrences that I met with yesterday, which I shall give my reader an account of at large. As I was walking with my friend Sir Roger by the side of one of his woods, an old woman applied herself to me for charity. The Knight told me that this old woman had the reputation of a witch all over the country, that her lips were observed to be always in motion, and that there was not a switch about her house which her neighbor did not believe had carried her several hundreds of miles. If she chanced to stumble, they always found sticks or straws that lay in the figure of a cross before her.

If she made any mistake at church, and cried *Amen* in a wrong place, they never failed to conclude that she was saying her prayers backwards. There was not a maid in the parish that would take a pin of her, though she would offer a bag of money with it. She goes by the name of Moll White, and has made the country ring with several imaginary exploits which are palmed upon her. If the dairy maid does not make her butter come as soon as she should have it, Moll White is at the bottom of the churn. If a horse sweats in the stable, Moll White has been upon his back. If a hare makes an unexpected escape from the hounds, the huntsman curses Moll White. "Nay" (says Sir Roger), "I have known the master of the pack upon such an occasion, send one of his servants to see if Moll White had been out that morning."

This account raised my curiosity so far, that I begged my friend Sir Roger to go with me into her hovel, which stood in a solitary corner under the side of the wood. Upon our first entering Sir Roger winked to me, and pointed at something that stood behind the door, which, upon looking that way, I found to be an old broomstaff. At the same time he whispered me in the ear to take notice of a tabby cat that sat in the chimney corner, which, as the old Knight told me, lay under as bad a report as Moll White herself; for besides that Moll is said often to accompany her in the same shape, the cat is reported to have spoken twice or thrice in her life, and to have played several pranks above the capacity of an ordinary cat.

I was secretly concerned to see human nature in so much wretchedness and disgrace, but at the same time could not forbear smiling to hear Sir Roger, who is a little puzzled about the old woman, advising her as a justice of peace to avoid all communication with the devil, and never to hurt any of her neighbors' cattle. We concluded our visit with a bounty, which was very acceptable.

In our return home, Sir Roger told me that old Moll had been often brought before him for making children spit pins, and giving maids the night-mare; and that the country people would be tossing her into a pond and trying experiments with her every day, if it was not for him and his chaplain.

I have since found upon inquiry that Sir Roger was several times staggered with the reports that had been brought him concerning this old woman, and would frequently have bound her over to the county sessions had not his chaplain with much ado persuaded him to the contrary.

I have been the more particular in this account, because I hear there is scarce a village in England that has not a Moll White in it. When an old woman begins to dote, and grow chargeable to a parish, she is generally turned into a witch, and fills the whole country with extravagant fancies, imaginary distempers and terrifying dreams. In the mean time, the poor wretch that is the innocent occasion of so many evils begins to be frightened at herself, and sometimes confesses secret commerce and familiarities that her imagination forms in a delirious old age. This frequently cuts off charity from the greatest objects of compassion, and inspires people with a malevolence towards those poor decrepit parts of our species, in whom human nature is defaced by infirmity and dotage.

Spectator No. 122. *Sir Roger at the assizes.*

A man's first care should be to avoid the reproaches of his own heart; the next to escape the censures of the world. If the last interferes with the former, it ought to be entirely neglected; but otherwise there cannot be a greater satisfaction to an honest mind than to see those approbations which it gives itself seconded by the applauses of the public. A man is more sure of his conduct when the verdict which he passes upon his own behavior is thus warranted and confirmed by the opinion of all that know him.

My worthy friend Sir Roger is one of those who is not only at peace within himself but beloved and esteemed by all about him. He receives a suitable tribute for his universal benevolence to mankind in the returns of affection and goodwill which are paid him by every one that lives within his neighborhood. I lately met with two or three odd instances of that general respect which is shown to the good old Knight. He would needs carry Will Wimble and myself with him to the county assizes. As we were upon the road, Will Wimble joined a couple of plain men who rid before us, and conversed with them for some time; during which my friend Sir Roger acquainted me with their characters.

"The first of them," says he, "that has a spaniel by his side, is a yeoman of about an hundred pounds a year, an honest man. He is just within the Game Act, and qualified to kill a hare or a pheasant. He knocks down a dinner with his gun twice or thrice a week; and by that means lives much cheaper than those who have not so good an estate as himself. He would be a good neighbor if he did not destroy so many partridges; in short, he is a very sensible man, shoots flying, and has been several times foreman of the petty jury.

"The other that rides along with him is Tom Touchy, a fellow famous for taking the law of every body. There is not one in the town where he lives that he has not sued at a quarter sessions. The rogue had once the impudence to go to law with the Widow. His head is full of costs, damages, and ejectments; he plagued a couple of honest gentlemen so long for a trespass in breaking one of his hedges, till he was forced to sell the ground it enclosed to defray the charges of the prosecution. His father left him four-score pounds a year, but he has cast, and been cast so often, that he is not now worth thirty. I suppose he is going upon the old business of the willow tree."

As Sir Roger was giving me this account of Tom Touchy, Will Wimble and his two companions stopped short till we came up to them. After having paid their respects to Sir Roger, Will told them that Mr. Touchy and he must appeal to him upon a dispute that arose between them. Will, it seems, had been giving his fellow travellers an account of his angling one day in such a hole; when Tom Touchy, instead of hearing out his story, told him that Mr. Such-an-one, if he pleased, might take the law of him for fishing in that part of the river. My friend Sir Roger heard them both, upon a round trot; and, after having paused some time, told them, with the air of a man who would not give his judgment rashly, that much might be said on both sides. They were neither of them dissatisfied with the Knight's determination, because neither of them found himself in the wrong by it. Upon which we made the best of our way to the assizes.

The court was sat before Sir Roger came; but notwithstanding all the justices had taken their places upon the bench, they made room for the old Knight at the head of them; who, for his reputation in the country, took occasion to whisper in the judge's ear, that he was glad his lordship had met with so much good weather in his circuit. I was listening to the proceeding of the court with much attention, and infinitely pleased with that great appearance and solemnity which so properly accompanies such a public administration of our laws; when, after about an hour's sitting, I observed, to my great surprise, in the midst of a trial, that my friend Sir Roger was getting up to speak. I was in some pain for him, till I found he had acquitted himself of two or three sentences, with a look of much business and great intrepidity.

Upon his first rising the court was hushed, and a general

whisper ran among the country people that Sir Roger was up. The speech he made was so little to the purpose, that I shall not trouble my readers with an account of it; and I believe was not so much designed by the Knight himself to inform the court, as to give him a figure in my eye, and keep up his credit in the country.

I was highly delighted, when the court rose, to see the gentlemen of the country gathering about my old friend, and striving who should compliment him most; at the same time that the ordinary people gazed upon him at a distance, not a little admiring his courage, that was not afraid to speak to the judge.

In our return home we met with a very odd accident, which I cannot forbear relating, because it shows how desirous all who know Sir Roger are of giving him marks of their esteem. When we were arrived upon the verge of his estate, we stopped at a little inn to rest ourselves and our horses. The man of the house had, it seems, been formerly a servant in the Knight's family; and, to do honor to his old master, had some time since, unknown to Sir Roger, put him up in a sign-post before the door; so that the Knight's head had hung out upon the road about a week before he himself knew anything of the matter. As soon as Sir Roger was acquainted with it, finding that his servant's indiscretion proceeded wholly from affection and goodwill, he only told him that he had made him too high a compliment; and when the fellow seemed to think that could hardly be, added, with a more decisive look, that it was too great an honor for any man under a duke; but told him at the same time that it might be altered with a very few touches, and that he himself would be at the charge of it. Accordingly they got a painter, by the Knight's directions, to add a pair of whiskers to the face, and by a little aggravation of the features to change it into the Saracen's Head. I should not have known this story had not the inn-keeper, upon Sir

Roger's alighting, told him in my hearing, that his honor's
head was brought back last night with the alterations that
he had ordered to be made in it. Upon this, my friend,
with his usual cheerfulness, related the particulars above
mentioned, and ordered the head to be brought into the
room. I could not forbear discovering greater expressions
of mirth than ordinary upon the appearance of this monstrous face, under which, notwithstanding it was made
to frown and stare in a most extraordinary manner, I could
still discover a distant resemblance of my old friend. Sir
Roger, upon seeing me laugh, desired me to tell him truly
if I thought it possible for people to know him in that
disguise. I at first kept my usual silence; but upon the
Knight's conjuring me to tell him whether it was not still
more like himself than a Saracen, I composed my countenance in the best manner I could, and replied that much
might be said on both sides.

These several adventures, with the Knight's behavior in
them, gave me as pleasant a day as ever I met with in any
of my travels.

Spectator No. 125. *Sir Roger tells a story of his boyhood, which
leads the Spectator to discuss the evils of party-spirit.*

My worthy friend Sir Roger, when we are talking of the
malice of parties, very frequently tells us an accident that
happened to him when he was a school-boy, which was at a
time when the feuds ran high between the round-heads and
cavaliers. This worthy knight, being then but a stripling,
had occasion to inquire which was the way to St. Anne's
lane; upon which the person whom he spoke to, instead of
answering his question, called him a young Popish cur, and
asked him who had made Anne a saint! The boy, being in
some confusion, inquired of the next he met, which was the
way to Anne's lane; but was called a prick-eared cur for

his pains, and instead of being shown the way, was told, that she had been a saint before he was born, and would be one after he was hanged. Upon this, says Sir Roger, I did not think fit to repeat the former question, but going into every lane of the neighborhood, asked what they called the name of that lane. By which ingenious artifice he found out the place he inquired after, without giving offence to any party. Sir Roger generally closes this narrative with reflections on the mischief that parties do in the country; how they spoil good neighborhood, and make honest gentlemen hate one another; besides that they manifestly tend to the prejudice of the land-tax, and the destruction of the game.

There cannot a greater judgment befall a country than such a dreadful spirit of division as rends a government into two distinct people, and makes them greater strangers and more averse to one another, than if they were actually two different nations. The effects of such a division are pernicious to the last degree, not only with regard to those advantages which they give the common enemy, but to those private evils which they produce in the heart of almost every particular person. This influence is very fatal both to men's morals and their understandings; it sinks the virtue of a nation, and not only so, but destroys even common sense.

A furious party-spirit, when it rages in its full violence, exerts itself in civil war and bloodshed; and, when it is under its greatest restraints, naturally breaks out in falsehood, detraction, calumny, and a partial administration of justice. In a word, it fills a nation with spleen and rancor, and extinguishes all the seeds of good-nature, compassion, and humanity.

Plutarch says very finely, that a man should not allow himself to hate even his enemies, because, says he, "if you indulge this passion on some occasions, it will rise of itself in others; if you hate your enemies, you will contract such a vicious habit of mind, as by degrees will break out upon those who are your friends, or those who are indifferent to you." I might here observe how admirably this precept of morality (which derives the malignity of hatred from the passion itself, and not from its object) answers to that great rule which was dictated to the world about an hundred years before this philosopher wrote; but instead of that, I shall only take notice, with a real grief of heart, that the minds of many good men among us appear soured with party-principles, and alienated from one another in such a manner, as seems to me altogether inconsistent with the dictates either of reason or religion. Zeal for a public cause is apt to breed passions in the hearts of virtuous persons, to which the regard of their own private interest would never have betrayed them.

If this party-spirit has so ill an effect on our morals, it has likewise a very great one upon our judgments. We often hear a poor insipid paper or pamphlet cried up, and sometimes a noble piece depreciated, by those who are of a different principle from the author. One who is actuated by this spirit is almost under an incapacity of discerning either real blemishes or beauties. A man of merit in a different principle, is like an object seen in two different mediums, that appears crooked or broken, however straight and entire it may be in itself. For this reason there is scarce a person of any figure in England who does not go by two contrary characters, as opposite to one another as light and darkness. Knowledge and learning suffer in a particular manner from this strange prejudice, which at present prevails amongst all ranks and degrees in the British nation. As men formerly became eminent in learned societies by their parts and acquisitions, they now distinguish themselves by the warmth and violence with which they espouse their respective parties. Books are valued upon the like considerations: an abusive scurrilous style passes for satire, and a dull scheme of party notions is called fine writing.

There is one piece of sophistry practised by both sides, and that is the taking any scandalous story, that has been ever whispered or invented of a private man, for a known undoubted truth, and raising suitable speculations upon it. Calumnies that have been never proved, or have been often refuted, are the ordinary postulatums of these infamous scribblers, upon which they proceed as upon first principles granted by all men, though in their hearts they know they are false, or at best very doubtful. When they have laid these foundations of scurrility, it is no wonder that their superstructure is every way answerable to them. If this shameless practice of the present age endures much longer, praise and reproach will cease to be motives of .action in good men.

For my own part, I could heartily wish that all honest men would enter into an association, for the support of one another against the endeavors of those whom they ought to look upon as their common enemies, whatsoever side they may belong to. Were there such an honest body of neutral forces, we should never see the worst of men in great figures of life, because they are useful to a party; nor the best unregarded, because they are above practising those methods which would be grateful to their faction. We should then single every criminal out of the herd, and hunt him down, however formidable and overgrown he might appear: on the contrary, we should shelter distressed innocence, and defend virtue, however beset with contempt or ridicule, envy or defamation. In short, we should not any longer regard our fellow-subjects as Whigs or Tories, but should make the man of merit our friend, and the villain, our enemy.

Spectator No. 126. *Strictures on party-spirit continued.*

In my yesterday's paper I proposed, that the honest men of all parties should enter into a kind of association for the defence of one another, and the confusion of their common enemies. As it is designed this neutral body should act with a regard to nothing but truth and equity, and divest themselves of the little heats and prepossessions that cleave to parties of all kinds, I have prepared for them the following form of an association, which may express their intentions in the most plain and simple manner.

We whose names are hereunto subscribed, do solemnly declare, that we do in our consciences believe two and two make four; and that we shall adjudge any man whatsoever to be our enemy who endeavors to persuade us to the contrary. We are likewise ready to maintain with the hazard of all that is near and dear to us, that six is less than seven in all times and all places; and that ten will not be more three years hence than it is at present. We do also firmly declare, that it is our resolution as long as we live to call black black, and white white. And we shall upon all occasions oppose such persons that upon any day of the year shall call black white, or white black, with the utmost peril of our lives and fortunes.

Were there such a combination of honest men, who without any regard to places would endeavor to extirpate all such furious zealots as would sacrifice one-half of their country to the passion and interest of the other; as also such infamous hypocrites, that are for promoting their own advantage under color of the public good; with all the profligate immoral retainers to each side, that have nothing to recommend them but an implicit submission to their leaders; we should soon see that furious party-spirit extinguished, which may in time expose us to the derision and contempt of all the nations about us.

A member of this society, that would thus carefully employ himself in making room for merit, by throwing down the worthless and depraved part of mankind from those conspicuous stations of life to which they have been sometimes advanced, and all this without any regard to his private interest, would be no small benefactor to his country.

I remember to have read in Diodorus Siculus an account of a very active little animal, which I think he calls ichneumon, that makes it the whole business of his life to break the eggs of the crocodile, which he is always in search after. This instinct is the more remarkable, because the ichneumon never feeds upon the eggs he has broken, nor any other way finds his account in them. Were it not for the incessant labors of this industrious animal, Egypt, says the historian, would be over-run with crocodiles; for the Egyptians are so far from destroying those pernicious creatures, that they worship them as gods.

If we look into the behavior of ordinary partisans, we shall find them far from resembling this disinterested animal; and rather acting after the example of the wild Tartars, who are ambitious of destroying a man of the most extraordinary parts and accomplishments, as thinking that upon his decease, the same talents, whatever posts they qualified him for, enter of course into his destroyer.

I do not know whether I have observed in any of my former papers, that my friends Sir Roger de Coverley and Sir Andrew Freeport are of different principles, the first of them inclined to the *landed* and the other to the *monied* interest. This humor is so moderate in each of them, that it proceeds no farther than to an agreeable raillery, which very often diverts the rest of the club. I find, however, that the Knight is a much stronger Tory in the country than in the town, which, as he has told me in my ear, is absolutely necessary for the keeping up his interest. In all our journey from London to his house we did not so much as bait at a Whig inn: or if by chance the coach-man stopped at a wrong place, one of Sir Roger's servants would ride up to

his master full speed, and whisper to him that the master
of the house was against such a one in the last election.
This often betrayed us into hard beds and bad cheer; for
we were not so inquisitive about the inn as the inn-keeper;
and provided our landlord's principles were sound, did not
take any notice of the staleness of his provisions. This I
found still the more inconvenient, because the better the
host was, the worse generally were his accommodations; the
fellow knowing very well that those who were his friends
would take up with coarse diet and hard lodging. For these
reasons, all the while I was upon the road I dreaded entering into an house of any one that Sir Roger had applauded
for an honest man.

Since my stay at Sir Roger's in the country, I daily find
more instances of this narrow party-humor. Being upon a
bowling-green at a neighboring market-town the other day
(for that is the place where the gentlemen of one side meet
once a week), I observed a stranger among them of a better
presence and genteeler behavior than ordinary; but was
much surprised, that notwithstanding he was a very fair
better, nobody would take him up. But upon inquiry I
found, that he was one who had given a disagreeable vote
in a former parliament, for which reason there was not a
man upon that bowling-green who would have so much correspondence with him as to win his money of him.

Among other instances of this nature, I must not omit
one which concerns myself. Will Wimble was the other
day relating several strange stories that he had picked up,
nobody knows where, of a certain great man; and upon my
staring at him, as one that was surprised to hear such
things in the country, which had never been so much as
whispered in the town, Will stopped short in the thread of
his discourse, and after dinner asked my friend Sir Roger
in his ear, if he were sure that I was not a fanatic.

It gives me a serious concern to see such a spirit of dissension in the country; not only as it destroys virtue and common sense, and renders us in a manner barbarians towards one another, but as it perpetuates our animosities, widens our breaches, and transmits our present passions and prejudices to our posterity. For my own part, I am sometimes afraid that I discover the seeds of a civil war in these our divisions; and therefore cannot but bewail, as in their first principles, the miseries and calamities of our children.

Spectator No. 130. *Sir Roger and the gypsies.*

As I was yesterday riding out in the fields with my friend Sir Roger, we saw at a little distance from us a troop of gypsies. Upon the first discovering of them, my friend was in some doubt whether he should not exert the *Justice of the peace* upon such a band of lawless vagrants; but not having his clerk with him, who is a necessary counsellor on those occasions, and fearing that his poultry might fare the worse for it, he let the thought drop: but at the same time gave me a particular account of the mischiefs they do in the country, in stealing people's goods and spoiling their servants. "If a stray piece of linen hangs upon an hedge," says Sir Roger, "they are sure to have it; if a hog loses his way in the fields, it is ten to one but he becomes their prey; our geese cannot live in peace for them: if a man prosecutes them with severity, his henroost is sure to pay for it. They generally straggle into these parts about this time of the year; and set the heads of our servant-maids so agog for husbands, that we do not expect to have any business done as it should be whilst they are in the country. I have an honest dairy-maid who crosses their hands with a piece of silver every summer, and never fails being promised the handsomest young fellow in the parish for her pains. Your friend the butler has been fool enough to be seduced by them; and, though he is sure to lose a knife, a fork, or a spoon every time his fortune is told him, generally shuts himself up in the pantry with an old gypsy for above half an hour once in a twelvemonth. Sweet-hearts are the things they live upon, which they bestow very plentifully upon all those that apply themselves to them. You see now and then some handsome young jades among them: the girls have very often white teeth and black eyes."

Sir Roger observing that I listened with great attention to his account of a people who were so entirely new to me, told me, that if I would they should tell us our fortunes.

As I was very well pleased with the Knight's proposal, we rid up and communicated our hands to them. A Cassandra of the crew, after having examined my lines very diligently, told me, that I was a good woman's man, with some other particulars which I do not think proper to relate. My friend Sir Roger alighted from his horse, and exposing his palm to two or three of them that stood by him, they crumpled it into all shapes, and diligently scanned every wrinkle that could be made in it; when one of them who was elder and more sun-burnt than the rest, told him, that he had a widow in his line of life; upon which the Knight cried, " Go, go, you are an idle baggage "; and at the same time smiled upon me. The gypsy finding he was not displeased in his heart, told him after a farther inquiry into his hand, that his true love was constant, and that she should dream of him to-night: my old friend cried, " Pish," and bid her go on. The gypsy told him that he was a bachelor, but would not be so long; and that he was dearer to somebody than he thought; the Knight still repeated that she was an idle baggage, and bid her go on. " Ah master," says the gypsy, "that roguish leer of yours makes a pretty woman's heart ache; you han't that simper about the mouth for nothing." The uncouth gibberish with which all this was uttered, like the darkness of an oracle, made us the more attentive to it. To be short, the Knight left the money with her that he had crossed her hand with, and got up again on his horse.

As we were riding away, Sir Roger told me, that he knew several sensible people who believed these gypsies now and then foretold very strange things; and for half an hour together appeared more jocund than ordinary. In the height of his good humor, meeting a common beggar upon the road who was no conjuror, as he went to relieve him, he found his pocket was picked; that being a kind of palmistry at which this race of vermin are very dexterous.

Spectator No. 131. *The Spectator sees reasons why he had better return to town.*

It is usual for a man who loves country sports to preserve the game in his own grounds, and divert himself upon those that belong to his neighbor. My friend Sir Roger generally goes two or three miles from his house, and gets into the frontiers of his estate, before he beats about in search of a hare or partridge, on purpose to spare his own fields, where he is always sure of finding diversion when the worst comes to the worst. By this means the breed about his house has time to increase and multiply; besides that the sport is the more agreeable where the game is the harder to come at, and where it does not lie so thick as to produce any perplexity or confusion in the pursuit. For these reasons the country gentleman, like the fox, seldom preys near his own home.

In the same manner I have made a month's excursion out of the town, which is the great field of game for sportsmen of my species, to try my fortune in the country, where I have started several subjects, and hunted them down, with some pleasure to myself, and I hope to others. I am here forced to use a great deal of diligence before I can spring anything to my mind; whereas in town, whilst I am following one character, it is ten to one but I am crossed in my way by another, and put up such a variety of odd creatures in both sexes, that they foil the scent of one another, and puzzle the chase. My greatest difficulty in the country is to find sport, and, in town, to choose it. In the meantime, as I have given a whole month's rest to the cities of London and Westminster, I promise myself abundance of new game upon my return thither.

It is indeed high time for me to leave the country, since I find the whole neighborhood begin to grow very inquisitive after my name and character; my love of solitude, taciturnity, and particular way of life having raised a great curiosity in all these parts.

The notions which have been framed of me are various: some look upon me as very proud, some as very modest, and some as very melancholy. Will Wimble, as my friend the butler tells me, observing me very much alone, and extremely silent when I am in company, is afraid I have killed a man. The country people seem to suspect me for a conjuror; and, some of them hearing of the visit which I made to Moll White, will needs have it that Sir Roger has brought down a cunning man with him, to cure the old woman, and free the country from her charms. So that the character which I go under in part of the neighborhood, is what they here call a " white witch."

A justice of peace, who lives about five miles off, and is not of Sir Roger's party, has, it seems, said twice or thrice at his table, that he wishes Sir Roger does not harbor a Jesuit in his house, and that he thinks the gentlemen of the country would do very well to make me give some account of myself.

On the other side, some of Sir Roger's friends are afraid the old Knight is imposed upon by a designing fellow, and

as they have heard that he converses very promiscuously,
when he is in town, do not know but he has brought down
with him some discarded Whig, that is sullen and says
nothing because he is out of place.

Such is the variety of opinions which are here entertained of me, so that I pass among some for a disaffected
person, among some for a wizard, and among others for
a murderer; and all this for no other reason, that I can
imagine, but because I do not hoot and holloa and make a
noise. It is true, my friend Sir Roger tells them, *that it is
my way*, and that I am only a philosopher; but this will
not satisfy them. They think there is more in me than he
discovers, and that I do not hold my tongue for nothing.

For these and other reasons I shall set out for London
to-morrow, having found by experience that the country
is not a place for a person of my temper, who does not
love jollity, and what they call good neighborhood. A man
that is out of humor when an unexpected guest breaks in
upon him, and does not care for sacrificing an afternoon to
every chance-comer, that will be the master of his own
time, and the pursuer of his own inclinations, makes but a
very unsociable figure in this kind of life. I shall therefore
retire into the town, if I may make use of that phrase, and
get into the crowd again as fast as I can, in order to be
alone. I can there raise what speculations I please upon
others, without being observed myself, and at the same
time enjoy all the advantages of company with all the
privileges of solitude.

Spectator No. 269. *Sir Roger in town.*

I was this morning surprised with a great knocking at the
door, when my landlady's daughter came up to me, and
told me that there was a man below desired to speak with

me. Upon my asking her who it was, she told me it was a very grave elderly person, but that she did not know his name. I immediately went down to him, and found him to be the coachman of my worthy friend Sir Roger de Coverley. He told me that his master came to town last night, and would be glad to take a turn with me in Gray's Inn Walks. As I was wondering in myself what had brought Sir Roger to town, not having lately received any letter from him, he told me that his master was come up to get a sight of Prince Eugene, and that he desired I would immediately meet him.

I was not a little pleased with the curiosity of the old Knight, though I did not much wonder at it, having heard him say more than once in private discourse, that he looked upon Prince Eugenio (for so the Knight always calls him) to be a greater man than Scanderbeg.

I was no sooner come into Gray's Inn Walks, but I heard my friend upon the terrace hemming twice or thrice to himself with great vigor, for he loves to clear his pipes in good air (to make use of his own phrase), and is not a little pleased with any one who takes notice of the strength which he still exerts in his morning hems.

I was touched with a secret joy at the sight of the good old man, who before he saw me was engaged in conversation with a beggar-man that had asked an alms of him. I could hear my friend chide him for not finding out some work; but at the same time saw him put his hand in his pocket and give him six-pence.

Our salutations were very hearty on both sides, consisting of many kind shakes of the hand, and several affectionate looks which we cast upon one another. After which the Knight told me my good friend his chaplain was very well, and much at my service, and that the Sunday before he had made a most incomparable sermon out of Doctor Barrow. "I have left," says he, "all my affairs in his hands, and being willing to lay an obligation upon him, have deposited with him thirty marks, to be distributed among his poor parishioners."

He then proceeded to acquaint me with the welfare of Will Wimble. Upon which he put his hand into his fob and presented me in his name with a tobacco-stopper, telling me that Will had been busy all the beginning of the winter, in turning great quantities of them; and that he made a present of one to every gentleman in the country who has good principles, and smokes. He added, that poor Will was at present under great tribulation, for that Tom Touchy had taken the law of him for cutting some hazel sticks out of one of his hedges.

Among other pieces of news which the Knight brought from his country seat, he informed me that Moll White was dead; and that about a month after her death the wind was so very high, that it blew down the end of one of his barns. "But for my own part," says Sir Roger, "I do not think that the old woman had any hand in it."

He afterwards fell into an account of the diversions which had passed in his house during the holidays; for Sir Roger, after the laudable custom of his ancestors, always keeps open house at Christmas. I learned from him that he had killed eight fat hogs for this season, that he had dealt about his chines very liberally amongst his neighbors, and that in particular he had sent a string of hogs-puddings with a pack of cards to every poor family in the parish. "I have often thought," says Sir Roger, "it happens very well that Christmas should fall out in the middle of winter. It is the most dead uncomfortable time of the year, when the poor people would suffer very much from their poverty and cold, if they had not good cheer, warm fires, and Christmas gambols to support them. I love to rejoice their poor hearts at this season, and to see the whole village merry in my great hall. I allow a double quantity of malt to my small beer, and set it a running for twelve days to every one that calls for it. I have always a piece of cold beef and a mince-pie upon the table, and am wonderfully pleased to see my tenants pass away a whole evening in playing their innocent tricks, and smutting one another. Our friend Will Wimble is as merry as any of them, and shows a thousand roguish tricks upon these occasions."

I was very much delighted with the reflection of my old friend, which carried so much goodness in it. He then launched out into the praise of the late Act of Parliament for securing the Church of England, and told me, with great satisfaction, that he believed it already began to take effect, for that a rigid Dissenter, who chanced to dine at his house on Christmas day, had been observed to eat very plentifully of his plum-porridge.

After having dispatched all our country matters, Sir Roger made several inquiries concerning the club, and particularly of his old antagonist, Sir Andrew Freeport. He asked me with a kind of a smile whether Sir Andrew had not taken the advantage of his absence to vent among them some of his republican doctrines; but soon after, gathering up his countenance into a more than ordinary seriousness, "Tell me truly," says he, "don't you think Sir Andrew had a hand in the Pope's Procession?" — but without giving me time to answer him, "Well, well," says he, "I know you are a wary man, and do not care to talk of public matters."

The Knight then asked me if I had seen Prince Eugenio, and made me promise to get him a stand in some convenient place where he might have a full sight of that extraordinary man, whose presence does so much honor to the British nation. He dwelt very long on the praises of this great general, and I found that, since I was with him in the country, he had drawn many observations together out of his reading in Baker's Chronicle, and other authors, who always lie in his hall window, which very much redound to the honor of this prince.

Having passed away the greatest part of the morning in hearing the Knight's reflections, which were partly private, and partly political, he asked me if I would smoke a pipe with him over a dish of coffee at Squire's. As I love the old man, I take delight in complying with every thing that is agreeable to him, and accordingly waited on him to the coffee-house, where his venerable figure drew upon us the eyes of the whole room. He had no sooner seated himself at the upper end of the high table, but he called for a clean pipe, a paper of tobacco, a dish of coffee, a wax-candle, and the Supplement, with such an air of cheerfulness and good-humor, that all the boys in the coffee-room (who seemed to take pleasure in serving him) were at once employed on his several errands, insomuch that nobody else could come at a dish of tea, till the Knight had got all his conveniences about him.

Spectator No. 329. *Sir Roger visits Westminster Abbey.*

My friend Sir Roger de Coverley told me t'other night that he had been reading my paper upon Westminster Abbey, in which, says he, there are a great many ingenious fancies. He told me, at the same time, that he observed I had promised another paper upon the tombs, and that he should be glad to go and see them with me, not having visited them since he had read history. I could not at first imagine how this came into the Knight's head, till I recollected that he had been very busy all last summer upon Baker's Chronicle, which he has quoted several times in his disputes with Sir Andrew Freeport since his last coming to town. Accordingly, I promised to call upon him the next morning, that we might go together to the Abbey.

I found the Knight under his butler's hands, who always

shaves him. He was no sooner dressed than he called for a glass of the Widow Trueby's water, which he told me he always drank before he went abroad. He recommended to me a dram of it at the same time with so much heartiness, that I could not forbear drinking it. As soon as I had got it down, I found it very unpalatable; upon which the Knight, observing that I had made several wry faces, told me that he knew I should not like it at first, but that it was the best thing in the world against the stone or gravel.

I could have wished, indeed, that he had acquainted me with the virtues of it sooner; but it was too late to complain, and I knew what he had done was out of good will. Sir Roger told me, further, that he looked upon it to be very good for a man whilst he stayed in town, to keep off infection; and that he got together a quantity of it upon the first news of the sickness being at Dantzic. When of a sudden turning short to one of his servants, who stood behind him, he bade him call a hackney-coach, and take care it was an elderly man that drove it.

He then resumed his discourse upon Mrs. Trueby's water, telling me that the Widow Trueby was one who did more good than all the doctors and apothecaries in the country; that she distilled every poppy that grew within five miles of her; that she distributed her water gratis among all sorts of people: to which the Knight added, that she had a very great jointure, and that the whole country would fain have it a match between him and her; "And truly," said Sir Roger, "if I had not been engaged, perhaps I could not have done better."

His discourse was broken off by his man telling him he had called a coach. Upon our going to it, after having cast his eye upon the wheels, he asked the coachman if his axle-tree was good; upon the fellow telling him he would warrant it, the Knight turned to me, told me he looked like an honest man, and went in without further ceremony.

We had not gone far, when Sir Roger, popping out his head, called the coachman down from his box, and upon his presenting himself at the window, asked him if he smoked: as I was considering what this would end in, he bade him stop by the way at any good tobacconist's, and take in a roll of their best Virginia. Nothing material happened in the remaining part of our journey till we were set down at the west end of the Abbey.

As we went up the body of the church, the Knight pointed at the trophies upon one of the new monuments, and cried out, "A brave man, I warrant him!" Passing afterwards by Sir Cloudesley Shovel, he flung his hand that way, and cried, "Sir Cloudesley Shovel, a very gallant man!" As we stood before Busby's tomb, the Knight uttered himself again after the same manner, — "Dr. Busby — a great man! he whipped my grandfather — a very great man! I should have gone to him myself if I had not been a blockhead — a very great man!"

We were immediately conducted into the little chapel on the right hand. Sir Roger, planting himself at our historian's elbow, was very attentive to every thing he said, particularly to the account he gave us of the lord who had cut off the King of Morocco's head. Among several other figures, he was very well pleased to see the statesman Cecil upon his knees; and, concluding them all to be great men, was conducted to the figure which represents that martyr to good housewifery, who died by the prick of a needle. Upon our interpreter telling us that she was a maid of honor to Queen Elizabeth, the Knight was very inquisitive into her name and family; and, after having regarded her finger for some time, "I wonder," says he, "that Sir Richard Baker has said nothing of her in his Chronicle."

We were then conveyed to the two coronation chairs, where my old friend, after having heard that the stone from Scotland, was called Jacob's Pillar, sat himself down in the chair; and, looking like the figure of an old Gothic king, asked our interpreter what authority they had to say that Jacob had ever been in Scotland. The fellow, instead of returning him an answer, told him that he hoped his honor would pay his forfeit. I could observe Sir Roger a little ruffled upon being thus trepanned; but, our guide not insisting upon his demand, the Knight soon recovered his good humor, and whispered in my ear that if Will Wimble were with us, and saw those two chairs, it would go hard but he would get a tobacco-stopper out of one or t'other of them.

Sir Roger, in the next place, laid his hand upon Edward the Third's sword, and, leaning upon the pommel of it, gave us the whole history of the Black Prince; concluding that, in Sir Richard Baker's opinion, Edward the Third was one of the greatest princes that ever sat upon the English throne.

We were then shown Edward the Confessor's tomb, upon which Sir Roger acquainted us that he was the first who touched for the evil, and afterwards Henry the Fourth's, upon which he shook his head, and told us that there was fine reading in the casualties of that reign.

Our conductor then pointed to that monument where there is the figure of one of our English kings without a head; and upon giving us to know that the head, which was of beaten silver, had been stolen away several years since, "Some Whig, I'll warrant you," says Sir Roger: "you ought to lock up your kings better; they will carry off the body too if you don't take care."

The glorious names of Henry the Fifth and Queen Elizabeth gave the Knight great opportunities of shining and of doing justice to Sir Richard Baker, who, as our Knight observed with some surprise, had a great many kings in him whose monuments he had not seen in the Abbey.

For my own part, I could not but be pleased to see the Knight show such an honest passion for the glory of his country, and such a respectful gratitude to the memory of its princes.

I must not omit that the benevolence of my good old friend, which flows out towards every one he converses with, made him very kind to our interpreter, whom he looked upon as an extraordinary man; for which reason he shook him by the hand at parting, telling him that he should be very glad to see him at his lodgings in Norfolk Buildings, and talk over these matters with him more at leisure.

Spectator No. 335.   *Sir Roger goes to the play.*

My friend Sir Roger de Coverley, when we last met together at the club, told me that he had a great mind to see the new tragedy with me, assuring me, at the same time, that he had not been at a play these twenty years. "The last I saw," said Sir Roger, "was the 'Committee,' which I should not have gone to neither, had not I been told beforehand that it was a good Church of England comedy." He then proceeded to inquire of me who this distressed mother was, and, upon hearing that she was Hector's widow, he told me that her husband was a brave man, and that when he was a school-boy, he had read his life at the end of the dictionary. My friend asked me, in the next place, if there would not be some danger in coming home late, in case the Mohocks should be abroad. "I assure you," says he, "I thought I had fallen into their hands last night, for I observed two or three lusty black men that followed me half way up Fleet Street, and mended their pace behind me in proportion as I put on to get away from them. You must know," continued the Knight with a smile, "I fancied they had a mind to *hunt* me, for I remember an honest gentleman in my neighborhood who was served such a trick in King Charles the Second's time; for which reason he has not ventured himself in town ever since. I might have shown them very good sport had this been their design; for, as I am an old fox-hunter, I should have turned and dodged, and have played them a thousand tricks they had never seen in their lives before." Sir Roger added that if these gentlemen had any such intention they did not succeed very well in it; "for I threw them out," says he, "at the end of Norfolk Street, where I doubled the corner and got shelter in my lodgings before they could imagine what was become of me. However," says the Knight, "if Captain Sentry will make one with us to-morrow night, and if you will both of you call upon me about four o'clock, that we may be at the house before it is full, I will have my own coach in readiness to attend you, for John tells me he has got the fore wheels mended."

The captain, who did not fail to meet me there at the appointed hour, bid Sir Roger fear nothing, for that he had put on the same sword which he made use of at the battle of Steenkirk. Sir Roger's servants, and among the rest my old friend the butler, had, I found, provided themselves with good oaken plants to attend their master upon this occasion. When we had placed him in his coach, with myself at his left hand, the captain before him, and his butler at the head of his footmen in the rear, we convoyed him in safety to the playhouse, where, after having marched up the entry in good order, the captain and I went in with him, and seated him betwixt us in the pit. As soon as the house was full, and the candles lighted, my old friend stood up and looked about him with that pleasure which a mind seasoned with humanity naturally feels at the sight of a multitude of people who seem pleased with one another, and partake of the same common entertainment. I could not but fancy to myself, as the old man stood up in the middle of the pit, that he made a very proper centre to a tragic audience. Upon the entering of Pyrrhus, the Knight told me that he did not believe the King of France himself had a better strut. I was, indeed, very attentive to my old friend's remarks, because I looked upon them as a piece of natural criticism; and was well pleased to hear him, at the conclusion of almost every scene, telling me that he could not imagine how the play would end. One while he appeared much concerned for Andromache; and a little while after as much for Hermione; and was extremely puzzled to think what would become of Pyrrhus.

When Sir Roger saw Andromache's obstinate refusal to her lover's importunities, he whispered me in the ear, that he was sure she would never have him; to which he added, with a more than ordinary vehemence, "You can't imagine, Sir, what 'tis to have to do with a widow." Upon Pyrrhus's threatening afterwards to leave her, the Knight shook his head, and muttered to himself, "Ay, do if you can." This part dwelt so much upon my friend's imagination, that at the close of the third act, as I was thinking of something else, he whispered me in my ear, "These widows, Sir, are the most perverse creatures in the world. But pray," says he, "you that are a critic, is the play according to your dramatic rules, as you call them? Should your people in tragedy always talk to be understood? Why, there is not a single sentence in this play that I do not know the meaning of."

The fourth act very luckily began before I had time to give the old gentleman an answer: "Well," says the Knight, sitting down with great satisfaction, "I suppose we are now to see Hector's ghost." He then renewed his attention, and, from time to time, fell a praising the widow. He made, indeed, a little mistake as to one of her pages, whom at his first entering he took for Astyanax; but quickly set himself right in that particular, though, at the same time, he owned he should have been very glad to have seen the little boy, "who," says he, "must needs be a very fine child by the account that is given of him." Upon Hermione's going off with a menace to Pyrrhus, the audience gave a loud clap, to which Sir Roger added, "On my word, a notable young baggage!"

As there was a very remarkable silence and stiffness in the audience during the whole action, it was natural for them to take the opportunity of these intervals between the acts to express their opinion of the players and of their respective parts. Sir Roger hearing a cluster of them praise Orestes, struck in with them, and told them that he thought his friend Pylades was a very sensible man; as they were afterwards applauding Pyrrhus, Sir Roger put in a second time: "And let me tell you," says he, "though he speaks but little, I like the old fellow in whiskers as well as any of them." Captain Sentry seeing two or three wags, who sat near us, lean with an attentive ear towards Sir Roger, and fearing lest they should smoke the Knight, plucked him by the elbow, and whispered something in his ear, that lasted till the opening of the fifth act. The Knight was wonderfully attentive to the account which Orestes gives of Pyrrhus's death, and at the conclusion of it, told me it was such a bloody piece of work that he was glad it was not done upon the stage. Seeing afterwards Orestes in his raving fit, he grew more than ordinary serious, and took occasion to moralize (in his way) upon an evil conscience, adding, that Orestes, in his madness, looked as if he saw something.

As we were the first that came into the house, so we were the last that went out of it; being resolved to have a clear passage for our old friend, whom we did not care to venture among the jostling of the crowd. Sir Roger went out fully satisfied with his entertainment, and we guarded him to his lodging in the same manner that we brought him to the playhouse; being highly pleased, for my own part, not only with the performance of the excellent piece which had been presented, but with the satisfaction which it had given to the old man.

Spectator No. 383. *Sir Roger and the Spectator go by water to Vauxhall Gardens.*

As I was sitting in my chamber and thinking on a subject for my next *Spectator*, I heard two or three irregular bounces at my landlady's door, and upon the opening of it, a loud cheerful voice inquiring whether the philosopher was at home. The child who went to the door answered very innocently, that he did not lodge there. I immediately recollected that it was my good friend Sir Roger's voice; and that I had promised to go with him on the water to Spring Gardens, in case it proved a good evening. The Knight put me in mind of my promise from the bottom of the stair-case, but told me that if I was speculating he would stay below till I had done. Upon my coming down, I found all the children of the family got about my old friend, and my landlady herself, who is a notable prating gossip, engaged in a conference with him, being mightily pleased with his stroking her little boy upon the head, and bidding him be a good child, and mind his book.

We were no sooner come to the Temple Stairs, but we were surrounded with a crowd of watermen, offering us their respective services. Sir Roger, after having looked about him very attentively, spied one with a wooden leg, and immediately gave him orders to get his boat ready. As we were walking towards it, "You must know," says Sir Roger, "I never make use of any body to row me, that has not either lost a leg or an arm. I would rather bate him a few strokes of his oar than not employ an honest man that has been wounded in the Queen's service. If I was a lord or a bishop, and kept a barge, I would not put a fellow in my livery that had not a wooden leg."

My old friend, after having seated himself, and trimmed the boat with his coachman, who being a very sober man, always serves for ballast on these occasions, we made the best of our way for Vauxhall. Sir Roger obliged the waterman to give us the history of his right leg, and hearing that he had left it at La Hogue, with many particulars which passed in that glorious action, the Knight, in the triumph of his heart, made several reflections on the greatness of the British nation; as, that one Englishman could beat three Frenchmen; that the Thames was the noblest river in Europe; that London Bridge was a greater piece of work than any of the seven wonders of the world; with many other honest prejudices which naturally cleave to the heart of a true Englishman.

After some short pause, the old Knight turning about his head twice or thrice, to take a survey of this great Metropolis, bid me observe how thick the city was set with churches, and that there was scarce a single steeple on this side Temple Bar. "A most heathenish sight!" says Sir Roger; "there is no religion at this end of the town. The fifty new churches will very much mend the prospect; but church work is slow, church work is slow!"

I do not remember I have any where mentioned, in Sir Roger's character, his custom of saluting every body that passes by him with a good-morrow or a good-night. This the old man does out of the overflowings of his humanity, though at the same time it renders him so popular among all his country neighbors, that it is thought to have gone a good way in making him once or twice knight of the shire. He cannot forbear this exercise of benevolence even in town, when he meets with any one in his morning or evening walk. It broke from him to several boats that passed by us upon the water; but to the Knight's great surprise, as he gave the good-night to two or three young fellows a little before our landing, one of them, instead of returning the civility, asked us, what queer old put we had in the boat, with a great deal of the like Thames ribaldry. Sir Roger seemed a little shocked at first, but at length, assuming a face of magistracy, told us that if he were a Middlesex justice, he would make such vagrants know that Her Majesty's subjects were no more to be abused by water than by land.

We were now arrived at Spring Gardens, which is exquisitely pleasant at this time of the year. When I considered the fragrancy of the walks and bowers, with the choirs of birds that sang upon the trees, and the loose tribe of people that walked under their shades, I could not but look upon the place as a kind of Mahometan paradise. Sir Roger told me it put him in mind of a little coppice by his house in the country, which his chaplain used to call an aviary of nightingales. "You must understand," says the Knight, "there is nothing in the world that pleases a man in love so much as your nightingale. Ah, Mr. Spectator! the many moonlight nights that I have walked by myself, and thought on the Widow by the music of the nightingale!" He here fetched a deep sigh, and was falling into a fit of musing, when a mask, who came behind him, gave him a gentle tap upon the shoulder, and asked him if he would drink a bottle of mead with her. But the Knight being startled at so unexpected a familiarity, and displeased to be interrupted in his thoughts of the Widow, told her she was a wanton baggage, and bid her go about her business.

We concluded our walk with a glass of Burton ale, and a slice of hung beef. When we had done eating ourselves, the Knight called a waiter to him, and bid him carry the remainder to the waterman that had but one leg. I perceived the fellow stared upon him at the oddness of the message, and was going to be saucy; upon which I ratified the Knight's commands with a peremptory look.

Spectator No. 517.   *The death of Sir Roger.*

We last night received a piece of ill news at our club, which very sensibly afflicted every one of us. I question not but my readers themselves will be troubled at the hearing of it. To keep them no longer in suspense, Sir Roger de Coverley *is dead.* He departed this life at his house in the country, after a few weeks' sickness. Sir Andrew Freeport has a letter from one of his correspondents in those parts, that informs him the old man caught a cold at the county-sessions, as he was very warmly promoting an address of his own penning, in which he succeeded according to his wishes. But this particular comes from a Whig justice of peace, who was always Sir Roger's enemy and antagonist. I have letters both from the chaplain and Captain Sentry which mention nothing of it, but are filled with many particulars to the honor of the good old man. I have likewise a letter from the butler, who took so much care of me last summer when I was at the Knight's house. As my friend the butler mentions, in the simplicity of his heart, several circumstances the others have passed over in silence, I shall give my reader a copy of his letter, without any alteration or diminution.

Honored Sir,

Knowing that you was my old master's good friend, I could not forbear sending you the melancholy news of his death, which has afflicted the whole country, as well as his poor servants, who loved him, I may say, better than we did our lives. I am afraid he caught his death the last county-sessions, where he would go to see justice done to a poor widow woman and her fatherless children, that had been wronged by a neighboring gentleman; for you know, Sir, my good master was always the poor man's friend. Upon his coming home, the first complaint he made was, that he had lost his roast-beef stomach, not being able to touch a sirloin, which was served up according to custom; and you know he used to take great delight in it. From that time forward he grew worse and worse, but still kept a good heart to the last. Indeed we were once in great hope of his recovery, upon a kind message that was sent him from the widow lady whom he had made love to the forty last years of his life; but this only proved a lightning before death. He has bequeathed to this lady, as a token of his love, a great pearl necklace, and a couple of silver bracelets set with jewels, which belonged to my good old lady his mother: he has bequeathed the fine white gelding, that he used to ride a hunting upon, to his chaplain, because he thought he would be kind to him, and has left you all his books. He has, moreover, bequeathed to the chaplain a very pretty tenement with good lands about it. It being a very cold day when he made his will, he left for mourning, to every man in the parish, a great frieze coat, and to every woman a black riding-hood. It was a most moving sight to see him take leave of his poor servants, commending us all for our fidelity, whilst we were not able to speak a word for weeping. As we most of us are grown gray-headed in our dear master's service, he has left us pensions and legacies, which we may live very comfortably upon, the remaining part of our days. He has bequeathed a great deal more in charity, which is not yet come to my knowledge, and it is peremptorily said in the parish that he has left money to build a steeple to the church; for he was heard to say some time ago, that if he lived two years longer, Coverley Church should have a steeple to it. The chaplain tells everybody that he made a very good end, and never speaks of him without tears. He was buried, according to his own directions, among the family of the Coverleys, on the left hand of his father, Sir Arthur. The coffin was carried by six of his tenants, and the pall held up by six of the quorum: the whole parish followed the corpse with heavy hearts, and in their mourning suits, the men in frieze, and the women in riding-hoods. Captain Sentry, my master's nephew, has taken possession of the hall-house and the whole estate. When my old master saw him a little before his death he shook him by the hand, and wished him joy of the estate which was falling to him, desiring him only to make a good use of it, and to pay the several legacies, and the gifts of charity which he told him he had left as quit-rents upon the estate. The captain truly seems a courteous man, though he says but little. He makes much of those whom my master loved, and shows great kindnesses to the old house-dog, that you know my poor master was so fond of. It would have gone to your heart to have heard the moans the dumb creature made on the day of my master's death. He has never joyed himself since; no more has any of us. 'Twas the melancholiest day for the poor people that ever happened in Worcestershire. This is all from,

Honored Sir, your most sorrowful Servant,

EDWARD BISCUIT.

P.S. My master desired, some weeks before he died, that a book which comes up to you by the carrier should be given to Sir Andrew Freeport, in his name.

This letter, notwithstanding the poor butler's manner of writing it, gave us such an idea of our good old friend, that upon the reading of it there was not a dry eye in the club. Sir Andrew opening the book, found it to be a collection of Acts of Parliament. There was in particular the Act of Uniformity, with some passages in it marked by Sir Roger's own hand. Sir Andrew found that they related to two or three points, which he had disputed with Sir Roger the last time he appeared at the club. Sir Andrew, who would have been merry at such an incident on another occasion, at the sight of the old man's handwriting burst into tears and put the book into his pocket. Captain Sentry informs us, that the Knight has left rings and mourning for every one in the club.

Spectator No. 10. *The Spectator commends his papers to sundry classes of men, and especially to women.*

It is with much satisfaction that I hear this great city inquiring, day by day, after these my papers, and receiving my morning lectures with a becoming seriousness and attention. My publisher tells me that there are already three thousand of them distributed every day, so that if I allow twenty readers to every paper, which I look upon as a modest computation, I may reckon about threescore thousand disciples in London and Westminster, who I hope will take care to distinguish themselves from the thoughtless herd of their ignorant and unattentive brethren. Since I have raised to myself so great an audience, I shall spare no pains to make their instruction agreeable, and their diversion useful. For which reasons I shall endeavor to enliven morality with wit, and to temper wit with morality, that my readers may, if possible, both ways find their account in the speculation of the day. And to the end that their virtue and discretion may not be short, transient, intermitting starts of thought, I have resolved to refresh their memories from day to day, till I have recovered them out of that desperate state of vice and folly into which the age is fallen. The mind that lies fallow but a single day, sprouts up in follies that are only to be killed by a constant and assiduous culture. It was said of Socrates that he brought philosophy down from heaven, to inhabit among men; and I shall be ambitious to have it said of me, that I have brought philosophy out of closets and libraries, schools and colleges, to dwell in clubs and assemblies, at tea-tables and in coffee-houses.

I would, therefore, in a very particular manner, recommend these my speculations to all well-regulated families, that set apart an hour in every morning for tea and bread and butter; and would earnestly advise them for their good, to order this paper to be punctually served up, and to be looked upon as a part of the tea-equipage.

Sir Francis Bacon observes, that a well written book, compared with its rivals and antagonists, is like Moses's serpent, that immediately swallowed up and devoured those of the Egyptians. I shall not be so vain as to think, that where the *Spectator* appears, the other public prints will vanish; but shall leave it to my reader's consideration, whether it is not much better to be let into the knowledge of one's self, than to hear what passes in Muscovy or Poland; and to amuse ourselves with such writings as tend to the wearing out of ignorance, passion, and prejudice, than such as naturally conduce to inflame hatreds, and make enmities irreconcilable.

In the next place, I would recommend this paper to the daily perusal of those gentlemen whom I cannot but consider as my good brothers and allies, I mean the fraternity of spectators, who live in the world without having anything to do in it; and either by the affluence of their fortunes, or laziness of their dispositions, have no other business with the rest of mankind but to look upon them. Under this class of men are comprehended all contemplative tradesmen, titular physicians, fellows of the Royal Society, Templars that are not given to be contentious, and statesmen that are out of business; in short, every one that considers the world as a theatre, and desires to form a right judgment of those who are actors on it.

There is another set of men that I must likewise lay a claim to, whom I have lately called the blanks of society, as being altogether unfurnished with ideas, till the business and conversation of the day has supplied them. I have often considered these poor souls with an eye of great commiseration, when I have heard them asking the first man they have met with, whether there was any news stirring, and, by that means, gathering together materials for thinking. These needy persons do not know what to talk of till about twelve o'clock in the morning; for, by that time, they are pretty good judges of the weather, know which way the wind sits, and whether the Dutch mail be come in. As they lie at the mercy of the first man they meet, and are grave or impertinent all the day long, according to the notions which they have imbibed in the morning, I would earnestly entreat them not to stir out of their chambers till they have read this paper, and do promise them that I will daily instill into them such sound and wholesome sentiments, as shall have a good effect on their conversation for the ensuing twelve hours.

But there are none to whom this paper will be more useful than to the female world. I have often thought there has not been sufficient pains taken in finding out proper employments and diversions for the fair ones. Their amusements seem contrived for them, rather as they are women, than as they are reasonable creatures, and are more adapted to the sex than to the species. The toilet is their great scene of business, and the right adjusting of their hair the principal employment of their lives. The sorting of a suit of ribbons is reckoned a very good morning's work; and if they make an excursion to a mercer's or a toy-shop, so great a fatigue makes them unfit for anything else all the day after. Their more serious occupations are sewing and embroidery, and their greatest drudgery the preparation of jellies and sweet-meats. This, I say, is the state of ordinary women; though I know there are multitudes of those of a more elevated life and conversation, that move in an exalted sphere of knowledge and virtue, that join all the beauties of the mind to the ornaments of dress, and inspire a kind of awe and respect, as well as love, into their male beholders. I hope to increase the number of these by publishing this daily paper, which I shall always endeavor to make an innocent, if not an improving entertainment, and by that means at least divert the minds of my female readers from greater trifles. At the same time, as I would fain give some finishing touches to those which are already the most beautiful pieces of human nature, I shall endeavor to point out all those imperfections that are the blemishes, as well as those virtues which are the embellishments of the sex. In the meanwhile I hope these my gentle readers, who have so much time on their hands, will not grudge throwing away a quarter of an hour in a day on this paper, since they may do it without any hindrance to business.

I know several of my friends and well-wishers are in great pain for me, lest I should not be able to keep up the spirit of a paper which I oblige myself to furnish every day : but to make them easy in this particular, I will prom-

ise them faithfullly to give it over as soon as I grow dull.
This I know will be matter of great raillery to the small
wits; who will frequently put me in mind of my promise,
desire me to keep my word, assure me that it is high time
to give over, with many other little pleasantries of the like
nature, which men of a little smart genius cannot forbear
throwing out against their best friends, when they have
such a handle given them of being witty. But let them
remember that I do hereby enter my caveat against this
piece of raillery.

Spectator No. 101. *The Spectator imagines himself described by
an antiquarian of a future age.*

I cannot forbear entertaining myself very often with
the idea of an imaginary historian describing the reign of
Anne the First and introducing it with a preface to his
reader, that he is now entering upon the most shining part
of English story. The great rivals in fame will be then
distinguished according to their respective merits, and shine
in their proper points of light. "Such an one," says the
historian, "though variously represented by the writers of
his own age, appears to have been a man of more than
ordinary abilities, great application, and uncommon integrity: nor was such a one, though of an opposite party and
interest, inferior to him in any of these respects." The
several antagonists who now endeavor to depreciate one
another, and are celebrated or traduced by different parties,
will then have the same body of admirers, and appear
illustrious in the opinion of the whole British nation. The
deserving man, who can now recommend himself to the
esteem of but half his countrymen, will then receive
the approbations and applauses of a whole age.

Among the several persons who flourish in this glorious
reign, there is no question but such a future historian, as

the person of whom I am speaking, will make mention of the men of genius and learning who have now any figure in the British nation. For my own part, I often flatter myself with the honorable mention which will then be made of me; and have drawn up a paragraph in my own imagination, that I fancy will not be altogether unlike what will be found in some page or other of this imaginary historian.

"It was under this reign," says he, "that the Spectator published those little diurnal essays which are still extant. We know very little of the name or person of this author, except only that he was a man of a very short face, extremely addicted to silence, and so great a lover of knowledge, that he made a voyage to Grand Cairo for no other reason but to take the measure of a pyramid. His chief friend was one Sir Roger de Coverley, a whimsical country knight, and a Templar, whose name he has not transmitted to us. He lived as a lodger at the house of a widow-woman, and was a great humorist in all parts of his life. This is all we can affirm with any certainty of his person and character. As for his speculations, notwithstanding the several obsolete words and obscure phrases of the age in which he lived, we still understand enough of them to see the diversions and characters of the English nation in his time: not but that we are to make allowance for the mirth and humor of the author, who has doubtless strained many representations of things beyond the truth. For if we interpret his words in their literal meaning, we must suppose that women of the first quality used to pass away whole mornings at a puppet-show: that they attested their principles by their *patches :* that an audience would sit out an evening to hear a dramatical performance written in a language which they did not understand : that chairs and flower-pots were introduced as actors upon the British stage: that a promiscuous assembly of men and women were allowed to meet at midnight in masques within the verge of the court; with many improbabilities of the like nature. We must therefore, in these and the like cases, suppose that these remote hints and allusions aimed at some certain follies which were then in vogue, and which at present we have not any notion of. We may guess by several passages in the speculations, that there were writers who endeavored to detract from the works of this author, but as nothing of this nature has come down to us, we cannot guess at any objections that could be

made to his paper.   If we consider his style with that indulgence which
we must show to old English writers, or if we look into the variety of his
subjects, with those several dissertations, moral reflections. . . ."

* * * * *

The following part of the paragraph is so much to my
advantage, and beyond anything I can pretend to, that I
hope my reader will excuse me for not inserting it.

Spectator No. 124.   *Large books versus pamphlets and newspapers.*

A man who publishes his works in a volume, has an infinite advantage over one who communicates his writings to
the world in loose tracts and single pieces.   We do not
expect to meet with anything in a bulky volume, till after
some heavy preamble, and several words of course, to prepare the reader for what follows : nay, authors have established it as a kind of rule, that a man ought to be dull
sometimes, as the most severe reader makes allowances for
many rests and nodding places in a voluminous writer.
This gave occasion to the famous Greek proverb "That a
great book is a great evil."

On the contrary, those who publish their thoughts in distinct sheets, and as it were by piece-meal, have none of these
advantages.   We must immediately fall into our subject,
and treat every part of it in a lively manner, or our papers
are thrown by as dull and insipid : our matter must lie
close together, and either be wholly new in itself, or in the
turn it receives from our expressions.   Were the books of
our best authors thus to be retailed to the public, and every
page submitted to the taste of forty or fifty thousand
readers, I am afraid we should complain of many flat
expressions, trivial observations, beaten topics, and common
thoughts, which go off very well in the lump.   At the same
time, notwithstanding some papers may be made up of

broken hints and irregular sketches, it is often expected that every sheet should be a kind of treatise, and make out in thought what it wants in bulk: that a point of humor should be worked up in all its parts; and a subject touched upon in its most essential articles, without the repetitions, tautologies, and enlargements, that are indulged to longer labors. The ordinary writers of morality prescribe to their readers after the Galenic way; their medicines are made up in large quantities. An essay writer must practise in the chymical method, and give the virtue of a full draught in a few drops. Were all books reduced thus to their quintessence, many a bulky author would make his appearance in a penny-paper: there would be scarce such a thing in nature as a folio: the works of an age would be contained on a few shelves; not to mention millions of volumes that would be utterly annihilated.

I cannot think that the difficulty of furnishing out separate papers of this nature, has hindered authors from communicating their thoughts to the world after such a manner: though I must confess I am amazed that the press should be only made use of in this way by news-writers, and the zealots of parties; as if it were not more advantageous to mankind, to be instructed in wisdom and virtue, than in politics; and to be made good fathers, husbands, and sons, than counsellors and statesmen. Had the philosophers and great men of antiquity, who took so much pains in order to instruct mankind, and leave the world wiser and better than they found it, — had they, I say, been possessed of the art of printing, there is no question but they would have made such an advantage of it, in dealing out their lectures to the public. Our common prints would be of great use were they thus calculated to diffuse good sense through the bulk of a people, to clear up their understandings, animate their minds with virtue, dissipate the sorrows of a heavy heart, or unbend the mind from its more severe employments, with innocent amusements. When knowledge, instead of being bound up in books, and kept in libraries and retirements, is thus obtruded upon the public; when it is canvassed in every assembly, and exposed upon every table; I cannot forbear reflecting upon that passage in the Proverbs, "Wisdom crieth without, she uttereth her voice in the streets; she crieth in the chief place of concourse, in the openings of the gates. In the city she uttereth her words, saying, 'How long, ye simple ones, will ye love simplicity, and the scorners delight in their scorning, and fools hate knowledge?'"

I am not at all mortified, when sometimes I see my works thrown aside by men of no taste nor learning. There is a kind of heaviness and ignorance that hangs upon the minds of ordinary men, which is too thick for knowledge to break through. Their souls are not to be enlightened.

To these I must apply the fable of the mole, that after having consulted many oculists for the bettering of his sight, was at last provided with a good pair of spectacles; but upon his endeavoring to make use of them, his mother told him very prudently, "that spectacles, though they might help the eye of a man, could be of no use to a mole." It is not therefore for the benefit of moles that I publish these my daily essays.

But besides such as are moles through ignorance, there are others who are moles through envy. As it is said in the Latin proverb, "that one man is a wolf to another;" so, generally speaking, one author is a mole to another author. It is impossible for them to discover beauties in one another's works, they have eyes only for spots and blemishes: they can indeed see the light, as it is said of the animals which are their name-sakes, but the idea of it is painful to them; they immediately shut their eyes upon it, and withdraw themselves into a wilful obscurity. I have already caught two or three of these dark undermining vermin, and intend to make a string of them, in order to hang them up in one of my papers, as an example to such voluntary moles.

Spectator No. 445. *Effect of the newly imposed stamp duty on periodical publications. The Spectator defends his non-partisan course.*

This is the day on which many eminent authors will probably publish their last words. I am afraid that few of our weekly historians, who are men that above all others delight in war, will be able to subsist under the weight of a stamp, and an approaching peace. A sheet of blank paper that must have this new *imprimatur* clapped upon it, before it is qualified to communicate anything to the public, will make its way in the world very heavily. In short, the necessity of carrying a stamp, and the improbability of notifying a bloody battle, will, I am afraid, both concur to the sinking of those thin folios, which have every other day retailed to us the history of Europe for several years last past. A facetious friend of mine, who loves a pun, calls this present mortality among authors "the fall of the leaf."

I remember, upon Mr. Baxter's death, there was published a sheet of very good sayings, inscribed, "The last words of Mr. Baxter." The title sold so great a number of these papers, that about a week after there came out a second sheet, inscribed, "More last words of Mr. Baxter." In the same manner, I have reason to think, that several ingenious writers, who have taken their leave of the public, in farewell papers, will not give over so, but intend to appear again, though perhaps under another form, and with a different title. Be that as it will, it is my business in this place to give an account of my own intentions, and to acquaint my reader with the motives by which I act in this great crisis of the republic of letters.

I have been long debating in my own heart, whether I should throw up my pen, as an author that is cashiered by the act of parliament, which is to operate within these four and twenty hours, or whether I should still persist in laying my speculations from day to day before the public. The argument which prevails with me most on the first side of the question is, that I am informed by my bookseller he must raise the price of every single paper to twopence, or that he shall not be able to pay the duty of it. Now, as I am very desirous my readers should have their learning as cheap as possible, it is with great difficulty that I comply with him in this particular.

However, upon laying my reasons together in the balance, I find that those which plead for the continuance of this work have much the greater weight. For, in the first place, in recompense for the expense to which this will put my readers, it is to be hoped they may receive from every paper so much instruction as will be a very good equivalent. And, in order to this, I would not advise any one to take it in, who, after the perusal of it, does not find himself twopence the wiser or the better man for it; or who, upon examination, does not believe that he has had two penny worth of mirth or instruction for his money.

But I must confess there is another motive which prevails with me more than the former. I consider that the tax on paper was given for the support of the government; and as I have enemies, who are apt to pervert every thing I do or say, I fear they would ascribe the laying down my paper, on such an occasion, to a spirit of malcontentedness, which I am resolved none shall ever justly upbraid me with. No! I shall glory in contributing my utmost to the weal public; and if my country receives five or six pounds a day by my labors, I shall be very well pleased to find myself so useful a member. It is a received maxim, that no honest man should enrich himself by methods that are prejudicial to the community in which he lives: and by the same rule I think we may pronounce the person to deserve very well of his countrymen, whose labors bring more into the public coffers than into his own pocket.

Since I have mentioned the word enemies, I must explain myself so far as to acquaint my reader, that I mean only the insignificant party-zealots on both sides; men of such poor narrow souls, that they are not capable of thinking on any thing but with an eye to Whig or Tory. During the course of this paper, I have been accused by these despicable wretches of trimming, time serving, personal reflection, secret satire, and the like. Now though, in these my compositions, it is visible to any reader of common sense that I consider nothing but my subject, which is always of an indifferent nature; how is it possible for me to write so clear of party, as not to lie open to the censure of those who will be applying every sentence, and finding out persons and things in it, which it has no regard to?

Several <u>paltry scribblers</u> and declaimers have done me the honor to be dull upon me in reflections of this nature; but notwithstanding my name has been sometimes traduced by this contemptible tribe of men, I have hitherto avoided all animadversions upon 'em. The truth of it is, I am afraid of making them appear considerable by taking notice of them, for they are like those imperceptible insects which are discovered by the microscope, and cannot be made the subject of observation without being magnified.

Having mentioned those few who have shown themselves the enemies of this paper, I should be very ungrateful to the public, did not I at the same time testify my gratitude to those who are its friends, in which number I may reckon many of the most distinguished persons of all conditions, parties, and professions in the isle of Great Britain. I am not so vain as to think this approbation is so much due to the performance as to the design. There is, and ever will be, justice enough in the world, to afford patronage and protection for those who endeavor to advance truth and virtue, without regard to the passions and prejudices of any particular cause or faction. If I have any other merit in me, it is that I have new-pointed all the batteries of ridicule. They have been generally planted against persons, who have appeared serious rather than absurd, or at best have aimed rather at what is unfashionable than what is vicious. For my own part, I have endeavored to make nothing ridiculous that is not in some measure criminal. I have set up the immoral man as the object of derision: in short, if I have not formed a new weapon against vice and irreligion, I have at least shown how that weapon may be put to a right use, which has so often fought the battles of impiety and profaneness.

Spectator No. 488.　*The Spectator defends the raised price.*

I find, by several letters which I receive daily, that many of my readers would be better pleased to pay three halfpence for my paper, than twopence. The ingenious T. W. tells me, that I have deprived him of the best part of his breakfast, for that since the rise of my paper, he is forced every morning to drink his dish of coffee by itself, without the addition of the *Spectator*, that used to be better than lace to it. Eugenius informs me very obligingly that he never thought he should have disliked any passage in my paper, but that of late there have been two words in every one of them, which he could heartily wish left out, viz. "Price Twopence." I have a letter from a soap-boiler, who condoles with me very affectionately upon the necessity we both lie under of setting an higher price on our commodities, since the late tax has been laid upon them, and desiring me, when I write next on that subject, to speak a word or two upon the duties upon Castile soap. But there is none of these my correspondents, who writes with a greater turn of good sense and elegance of expression, than the generous Philomedes, who advises me to value every *Spectator* at sixpence, and promises that he himself will engage for above a hundred of his acquaintance, who shall take it at that price.

Letters from the female world are likewise come to me, in great quantities, upon the same occasion; and as I naturally bear a great deference to this part of our species, I am very glad to find that those who approve my conduct in this particular, are much more numerous than those who condemn it. A large family of daughters have drawn me up a very handsome remonstrance, in which they set forth that their father having refused to take in the *Spectator*, since the additional price was set upon it, they offered him unanimously to bate him the article of bread and butter in the tea-table account, provided the *Spectator* might be served up to them every morning as usual. Upon this the old gentleman, being pleased it seems with their desire of improving themselves, has granted them the continuance both of the *Spectator* and their bread and butter, having given particular orders that the tea-table shall be set forth every morning with its customary bill of fare, and without any manner of defalcation. I thought myself obliged to mention this particular, as it does honor to this worthy gentleman; and if the young lady Letitia, who sent me this account, will acquaint me with his name, I will insert it at length in one of my papers, if he desires it.

I should be very glad to find out any expedient that might alleviate the expense which this my paper brings to any of my readers; and, in order to it, must propose two points to their consideration. First, that if they retrench any the smallest particular in their ordinary expense, it will easily make up the halfpenny a day, which we have now under consideration. Let a lady sacrifice but a single ribbon to her morning studies, and it will be sufficient: let a family burn but a candle a-night less than their usual number, and they may take in the *Spectator* without detriment to their private affairs.

In the next place, if my readers will not go to the price of buying my papers by retail, let them have patience, and they may buy them in the lump, without the burden of a tax upon them. My speculations, when they are sold single like cherries upon the stick, are delights for the rich and wealthy; after some time they come to market in greater quantities, and are every ordinary man's money. The truth of it is, they have a certain flavor at their first appearance, from several accidental circumstances of time, place, and person, which they may lose if they are not taken early; but in this case every reader is to consider, whether it is not better for him to be a half a year behind-hand with the fashionable and polite part of the world, than to strain himself beyond his circumstances. My bookseller has now about ten thousand of the third and fourth volumes, which he has ready to publish, having already disposed of as large an edition both of the first and second volumes. As he is a person whose head is very well turned for his business, he thinks they would be a very proper present to be made to persons at christenings, marriages, visiting-days, and the like joyful solemnities, as several other books are frequently given at funerals. He has printed them in such a little portable volume, that many of them may be ranged together upon a single plate; and is of opinion that a salver of *Spectators* would be as acceptable an entertainment to the ladies, as a salver of sweetmeats.

I shall conclude this paper with an epigram lately sent to the writer of the *Spectator*, after having returned my thanks to the ingenious author of it.

Sir,.

Having heard the following epigram very much commended, I wonder that it has not yet had a place in any of your papers. I think the suffrage of our poet laureat should not be overlooked, which shows the opinion he entertains of your paper, whether the notion he proceeds upon be true or false. I make bold to convey it to you, not knowing if it has yet come to your hands.

ON THE SPECTATOR.

BY MR. TATE.

When first the *Tatler* to a mute was turn'd
Great Britain for her censor's silence mourn'd;
Robb'd of his sprightly beams, she wept the night,
'Till the *Spectator* rose, and blaz'd as bright.
So the first man the sun's first setting view'd,
And sigh'd, till circling day his joys renew'd;
Yet doubtful how that second sun to name,
Whether a bright successor, or the same.
So we: but now from this suspense are freed,
Since all agree, who both with judgment read,
'Tis the same sun, and doth himself succeed.

Spectator No. 529.   *Precedence in literature.*

Upon the hearing of several late disputes concerning rank and precedence, I could not forbear amusing myself with some observations, which I have made upon the learned world, as to this great particular. By the learned world I here mean at large all those who are in any way concerned in works of literature, whether in the writing, printing, or repeating part. To begin with the writers: I have observed that the author of a folio, in all companies and conversations, sets himself above the author of a quarto; the author of a quarto above the author of an octavo; and so on, by a gradual descent and subordination, to an author in twenty-fours. This distinction is so well observed, that in an assembly of the learned, I have seen a folio writer place himself in an elbow-chair, when the author of a duo-decimo has, out of a just deference to his superior quality, seated himself upon a squab. In a word, authors are usually ranged in company after the same manner as their works are upon a shelf.

The most minute pocket author has beneath him the writers of all pamphlets, or works that are only stitched. As for the pamphleteer, he takes place of none but of the authors of single sheets, and of that fraternity who publish their labors on certain days, or on every day of the week. I do not find that the precedency among the individuals in this latter class of writers is yet settled.

For my own part, I have had so strict a regard to the ceremonial which prevails in the learned world, that I never presumed to take place of a pamphleteer till my daily papers were gathered into those two first volumes which have already appeared. After which, I naturally jumped over the heads, not only of all pamphleteers, but of every octavo writer in Great Britain that had written but one book. I am also informed by my bookseller that six octavos have at all times been looked upon as an equivalent to a folio; which I take notice of the rather, because I would not have the learned world surprised if, after the publication of half a dozen volumes, I take my place accordingly. When my scattered forces are thus rallied, and reduced into regular bodies, I shall flatter myself that I shall make no despicable figure at the head of them.

Whether these rules, which have been received time out of mind in the commonwealth of letters, were not originally established with an eye to our paper-manufacture, I shall leave to the discussion of others; and shall only remark further in this place, that all printers and booksellers take the wall of one another according to the above-mentioned merits of the authors to whom they respectively belong.

I come now to that point of precedency which is settled

among the three learned professions by the wisdom of our laws. I need not here take notice of the rank which is allotted to every doctor in each of these professions, who are all of them, though not so high as knights, yet a degree above 'squires; this last order of men, being the illiterate body of the nation, are consequently thrown together into a class below the three learned professions.

There is another tribe of persons who are retainers to the learned world, and who regulate themselves upon all occasions by several laws peculiar to their body; I mean the players, or actors, of both sexes. Among these it is a standing and uncontroverted principle, that a tragedian always takes place of a comedian; and it is very well known that the merry drolls who make us laugh are always placed at the lower end of the table, and in every entertainment give way to the dignity of the buskin. It is a stage maxim, " Once a king, and always a king."

I shall only add that, by parity of reason, all writers of tragedy look upon it as their due to be seated, served, or saluted, before comic writers; those who deal in tragicomedy usually taking their place between the authors of either side. There has been a long dispute for precedency between the tragic and heroic poets. Aristotle would have the latter yield the *pas* to the former; but Mr. Dryden, and many others, would never submit to this decision. Burlesque writers pay the same deference to the heroic, as comic writers to their serious brothers in the drama.

By this short table of laws order is kept up, and distinction preserved, in the whole republic of letters.

Spectator No. 13. *Signor Nicolini and his lions.*

There is nothing that of late years has afforded matter of greater amusement to the town than Signor Nicolini's combat with a lion in the Haymarket, which has been very often exhibited to the general satisfaction of most of the nobility and gentry in the kingdom of Great Britain. Upon the first rumor of this intended combat it was confidently affirmed and is still believed by many in both galleries, that there would be a tame lion sent from the Tower every opera night, in order to be killed by Hydaspes; this report, though altogether groundless, so universally prevailed in the upper regions of the play-house, that some of the most refined politicians in those parts of the audience gave it out in a whisper, that the lion was a cousin-german of the tiger who made his appearance in King William's days, and that the stage would be supplied with lions at the public expense, during the whole session.   Many likewise were the conjectures of the treatment which this lion was to meet with from the hands of Signor Nicolini; some supposed that he was to subdue him in recitativo, as Orpheus used to serve the wild beasts in his time, and afterwards to knock him on the head; several, who pretended to have seen the opera in Italy, had informed their friends, that the lion was to act a part in High-Dutch, and roar twice or thrice to a thorough-base, before he fell at the feet of Hydaspes.   To clear up a matter that was so variously reported, I have made it my business to examine whether this pretended lion is really the savage he appears to be, or only a counterfeit.

But before I communicate my discoveries I must acquaint the reader, that upon my walking behind the scenes last winter, as I was thinking on something else, I accidentally justled against a monstrous animal that extremely startled me, and upon my nearer survey of it, appeared to be a lion rampant. The lion, seeing me very much surprised, told me, in a gentle voice, that I might come by him if I pleased: "for," says he, "I do not intend to hurt anybody." I thanked him very kindly and passed by him: and, in a little time after, saw him leap upon the stage, and act his part with very great applause. It has been observed by several, that the lion has changed his manner of acting twice or thrice since his first appearance; which will not seem strange, when I acquaint my reader that the lion has been changed upon the audience three several times. The first lion was a candlesnuffer, who, being a fellow of a testy, choleric temper, overdid his part, and would not suffer himself to be killed so easily as he ought to have done; besides, it was observed of him, that he grew more surly every time he came out of the lion; and having dropt some words in ordinary conversation, as if he had not fought his best, and that he suffered himself to be thrown on his back in the scuffle, and that he would wrestle with Mr. Nicolini for what he pleased, out of his lion's skin, it was thought proper to discard him : and it is verily believed to this day, that had he been brought upon the stage another time, he would certainly have done mischief. Besides, it was objected against the first lion, that he reared himself so high upon his hinder paws, and walked in so erect a posture, that he looked more like an old man than a lion.

The second lion was a tailor by trade, who belonged to the play-house, and had the character of a mild and peaceable man in his profession. If the former was too furious, this was too sheepish, for his part; insomuch that after a short modest walk upon the stage, he would fall at the first touch of Hydaspes, without grappling with him, and giving him an opportunity of showing his variety of Italian trips : it is said indeed, that he once gave him a rip in his flesh-color doublet; but this was only to make work for himself, in his private character of a tailor. I must not omit that it was this second lion who treated me with so much humanity behind the scenes.

The acting lion at present is, as I am informed, a country gentleman who does it for his diversion, but desires his name may be concealed. He says very handsomely, in his own excuse, that he does not act for gain, that he indulges an innocent pleasure in it; and that it is better to pass away an evening in this manner, than in gaming and drinking; but at the same time says, with a very agreeable raillery upon himself, that if his name should be known, the ill-natured world might call him, "The ass in the lion's skin." This gentleman's temper is made out of such a happy mixture of the mild and the choleric, that he outdoes both his predecessors, and has drawn together greater audiences than have been known in the memory of man.

I must not conclude my narrative without taking notice of a groundless report that has been raised, to a gentleman's disadvantage of whom I must declare myself an admirer; namely, that Signor Nicolini and the lion have been seen sitting peaceably by one another and smoking a pipe together behind the scenes; by which their common enemies would insinuate, that it is but a sham combat which they represent upon the stage; but, upon inquiry I find, that if any such correspondence has passed between them, it was not till the combat was over, when the lion was to be looked upon as dead, according to the received rules of the drama. Besides, this is what is practised every day in Westminster-hall, where nothing is more usual than to see a couple of lawyers, who have been tearing each other to pieces in the court, embracing one another as soon as they are out of it.

I would not be thought, in any part of this relation, to reflect upon Signor Nicolini, who in acting this part only complies with the wretched taste of his audience; he knows very well that the lion has many more admirers than himself; as they say of the famous equestrian statue on the Pont-Neuf at Paris, that more people go to see the horse than the king who sits upon it. On the contrary, it gives me a just indignation to see a person whose action gives new majesty to kings, resolution to heroes, and softness to lovers, thus sinking from the greatness of his behavior, and degraded into the character of the London Prentice. I have often wished that our tragedians would copy after this great master in action. Could they make the same use of their arms and legs, and inform their faces with as significant looks and passions, how glorious would an English tragedy appear with that action, which is capable of giving a dignity to the forced thoughts, cold conceits, and unnatural expressions of an Italian opera! In the meantime, I have related this combat of the lion, to show what are at present the reigning entertainments of the politer part of Great Britain.

Audiences have often been reproached by writers for the coarseness of their taste: but our present grievance does not seem to be the want of a good taste, but of common sense.

Spectator No. 44. *Artifices of the dramatic poets.*

Among the several artifices which are put in practice by the poets to fill the minds of an audience with terror, the first place is due to thunder and lightning, which are often made use of at the descending of a god, or the rising of a ghost, at the vanishing of a devil, or at the death of a tyrant. I have known a bell introduced into several tragedies with good effect; and have seen the whole assembly in a very great alarm all the while it has been ringing. But there is nothing which delights and terrifies our English theatre so much as a ghost, especially when he appears in a bloody shirt. A spectre has very often saved a play, though he has done nothing but stalked across the stage, or rose through a cleft of it, and sunk again without speaking one word. There may be a proper season for these several terrors; and when they only come in as aids and assistances to the poet, they are not only to be excused, but to be applauded. Thus the sounding of the clock, in "Venice Pre-

served," makes the hearts of the whole audience quake, and
conveys a stronger terror to the mind than it is possible for
words to do. The appearance of the ghost in Hamlet is a
masterpiece in its kind, and wrought up with all the circumstances that can create either attention or horror. The
mind of the reader is wonderfully prepared for his reception
by the discourses that precede it; his dumb behavior at his
first entrance strikes the imagination very strongly; but
every time he enters, he is still more terrifying. Who can
read the speech with which young Hamlet accosts him
without trembling ?

> *Hor.* Look, my Lord, it comes !
> *Ham.* Angels and ministers of grace defend us !
> Be thou a spirit of health, or goblin damn'd ;
> Bring with thee airs from heav'n, or blasts from hell ;
> Be thy intents wicked or charitable ;
> Thou com'st in such a questionable shape,
> That I will speak to thee.   I'll call thee Hamlet,
> King, Father, Royal Dane : Oh ! answer me,
> Let me not burst in ignorance ; but tell
> Why thy canonized bones, hearsed in death,
> Have burst their cerements ?   Why the sepulchre,
> Wherein we saw thee quietly inurn'd,
> Hath op'd his ponderous and marble jaws,
> To cast thee up again ?   What may this mean ?
> That thou, dead corse, again in complete steel
> Revisit'st thus the glimpses of the moon,
> Making night hideous ?

I do not therefore find fault with the artifices above mentioned, when they are introduced with skill, and accompanied by proportionable sentiments and expressions in
the writing.

For the moving of pity our principal machine is the hand-
kerchief; and indeed, in our common tragedies, we should
not know very often that the persons are in distress by anything they say, if they did not from time to time apply

their handkerchiefs to their eyes. Far be it from me to think of banishing this instrument of sorrow from the stage; I know a tragedy could not subsist without it; all that I would contend for is, to keep it from being misapplied. In a word, I would have the actor's tongue sympathize with his eyes.

A disconsolate mother, with a child in her hand, has frequently drawn compassion from the audience, and has therefore gained a place in several tragedies. A modern writer, that observed how this had took in other plays, being resolved to double the distress, and melt his audience twice as much as those before him had done, brought a princess upon the stage with a little boy in one hand, and a girl in the other. This too had a very good effect. A third poet, being resolved to outwrite all his predecessors, a few years ago introduced three children with great success: and, as I am informed, a young gentleman, who is fully determined to break the most obdurate hearts, has a tragedy by him, where the first person that appears upon the stage is an afflicted widow in her mourning weeds, with half a dozen fatherless children attending her, like those that usually hang about the figure of charity. Thus several incidents, that are beautiful in a good writer, become ridiculous by falling into the hands of a bad one.

But among all our methods of moving pity or terror, there is none so absurd and barbarous, and what more exposes us to the contempt and ridicule of our neighbors, than that dreadful butchering of one another, which is so very frequent upon the English stage. To delight in seeing men stabbed, poisoned, racked, or impaled, is certainly the sign of a cruel temper; and as this is often practised before the British audience, several French critics, who think these are grateful spectacles to us, take occasion from them to represent us as a people that delight in blood. It is indeed very odd to see our stage strewed with carcasses in the last scene of a tragedy; and to observe in the wardrobe of the playhouse several daggers, poniards, wheels, bowls for poison, and many other instruments of death. Murders and executions are always transacted behind the scenes in the French theatre; which in general is very agreeable to the manners of a polite and civilized people: but as there are no exceptions to this rule on the French stage, it leads them into absurdities almost as ridiculous as that which falls under our present censure. I remember in the famous play of Corneille, written upon the subject of the Horatii and Curiatii, the fierce young hero who had overcome the Curiatii one after another, (instead of being congratulated by his sister for his victory, being upbraided by her for having slain her lover), in the height of his passion and resentment kills her. If any thing could extenuate so brutal an action, it would be the doing of it on a sudden, before the sentiments of nature, reason, or manhood, could take place in him. However, to avoid *public bloodshed*, as soon as his passion is wrought to its height, he follows his sister the whole length of the stage, and forbears killing her till they are both withdrawn behind the scenes. I must confess, had he murdered her before the audience, the indecency might have been greater; but as it is, it appears very unnatural, and looks like killing in cold blood. To give my opinion upon this case, the fact ought not to have been represented, but to have been told, if there was any occasion for it.

Spectator No. 235.   *The trunk-maker at the theatre.*

There is nothing which lies more within the province of a Spectator than public shows and diversions: and as, among these, there are none which can pretend to vie with those elegant entertainments that are exhibited in our theatres, I think it particularly incumbent on me to take notice of everything that is remarkable in such numerous and refined assemblies.

It is observed, that of late years there has been a certain person in the upper gallery of the playhouse, who, when he is pleased with any thing that is acted upon the stage, expresses his approbation by a loud knock upon the benches or the wainscot, which may be heard over the whole theatre. This person is commonly known by the name of the trunk-maker in the upper gallery. Whether it be that the blow he gives on these occasions resembles that which is often heard in the shops of such artisans, or that he was supposed to have been a real trunk-maker, who, after the finishing of his day's work, used to unbend his mind at these public diversions with his hammer in his hand, I cannot certainly tell. There are some, I know, who have been foolish enough to imagine it is a spirit which haunts the upper gallery, and from time to time makes those strange noises; and the rather because he is observed to be louder than ordinary every time the ghost of Hamlet appears. Others have reported that it is a dumb man, who has chosen this way of uttering himself when he is transported with any thing he sees or hears. Others will have it to be the playhouse thunderer, that exerts himself after this manner in the upper gallery, when he has nothing to do upon the roof.

But having made it my business to get the best information I could in a matter of this moment, I find that the trunk-maker, as he is commonly called, is a large black man, whom nobody knows. He generally leans forward on a huge oaken plant, with great attention to everything that passes upon the stage. He is never seen to smile; but upon hearing anything that pleases him, he takes up his staff with both hands and lays it upon the next piece of timber that stands in his way with exceeding vehemence; after which he composes himself in his former posture, till such time as something new sets him again at work.

It has been observed, his blow is so well timed, that the most judicious critic could never except against it. As soon as any shining thought is expressed in the poet, or any uncommon grace appears in the actor, he smites the bench or wainscot. If the audience does not concur with him, he smites a second time, and if the audience is not yet awaked, looks around him with great wrath, and repeats the blow a third time, which never fails to produce the clap. He sometimes lets the audience begin the clap of themselves, and at the conclusion of their applause ratifies it with a single thwack.

He is of so great use to the playhouse, that it is said a former director of it, upon his not being able to pay his attendance by reason of sickness, kept one in pay to officiate for him till such time as he recovered; but the person so employed, though he laid about him with incredible violence, did it in such wrong places, that the audience soon found out that it was not their old friend the trunk-maker.

It has been remarked that he has not yet exerted himself with vigor this season. He sometimes plies at the opera; and upon Nicolini's first appearance, was said to have demolished three benches in the fury of his applause. He has broken half a dozen oaken plants upon Dogget, and seldom goes away from a tragedy of Shakespeare without leaving the wainscot extremely shattered.

The players do not only connive at his obstreperous approbation, but very cheerfully repair at their own cost whatever damages he makes. They had once a thought of erecting a kind of wooden anvil for his use, that should be made of a very sounding plank, in order to render his strokes more deep and mellow; but as this might not have been distinguished from the music of a kettle-drum, the project was laid aside.

In the meanwhile, I cannot but take notice of the great use it is to an audience, that a person should thus preside over their heads like the director of a concert, in order to awaken their attention, and beat time to their applauses; or, to raise my simile, I have sometimes fancied the trunk-maker in the upper gallery to be like Virgil's ruler of the wind, seated upon the top of a mountain, who, when he struck his sceptre upon the side of it roused an hurricane, and set the whole cavern in an uproar.

It is certain the trunk-maker has saved many a good play, and brought many a graceful actor into reputation, who would not otherwise have been taken notice of. It is very visible, — as the audience is not a little abashed, if they find themselves betrayed into a clap, when their friend in the upper gallery does not come into it, so the actors do not value themselves upon the clap, but regard it as a mere *brutum fulmen,* or empty noise, when it has not the sound of the oaken plant in it. I know it has been given out by those who are enemies to the trunk-maker, that he has sometimes been bribed to be in the interest of a bad poet or a vicious player; but this is a surmise which has no foundation; his strokes are always just, and his admonitions seasonable; he does not deal about his blows at random, but always hits the right nail upon the head. The inexpressible force wherewith he lays them on sufficiently shows the evidence and strength of his conviction. His zeal for a good author is indeed outrageous, and breaks down every fence and partition, every board and plank, that stands within the expression of his applause.

As I do not care for terminating my thoughts in barren speculations, or in reports of pure matter of fact, without drawing something from them for the advantage of my countrymen, I shall take the liberty to make an humble proposal, that whenever the trunk-maker shall depart this life, or whenever he shall have lost the spring of his arm by sickness, old age, infirmity, or the like, some able-bodied critic should be advanced to this post, and have a competent

salary settled on him for life, to be furnished with bamboos
for operas, crab-tree cudgels for comedies, and oaken plants
for tragedy, at the public expense. And to the end that
this place should be always disposed of according to merit,
I would have none preferred to it who has not given con-
vincing proofs both of a sound judgment and a strong arm,
and who could not, upon occasion, either knock down an ox,
or write a comment upon Horace's Art of Poetry. In short,
I would have him a due composition of Hercules and Apollo,
and so rightly qualified for this important office, that the
trunk-maker may not be missed by our posterity.

Spectator No. 592.   *Stage properties: dramatic critics.*

I look upon the playhouse as a world within itself. They
have lately furnished the middle region of it with a new set
of meteors, in order to give the sublime to many modern
tragedies. I was there last winter at the first rehearsal of
the new thunder, which is much more deep and sonorous
than any hitherto made use of. They have a Salmoneus
behind the scenes who plays it off with great success. Their
lightnings are made to flash more briskly than heretofore:
their clouds are also better furbelowed, and more voluminous: not to mention a violent storm locked up in a great
chest, that is designed for the Tempest. They are also
provided with above a dozen showers of snow, which, as I
am informed, are the plays of many unsuccessful poets arti-
ficially cut and shredded for that use. Mr. Rymer's Edgar
is to fall in snow at the next acting of King Lear, in order
to heighten, or rather to alleviate, the distress of that unfortunate prince; and to serve by way of decoration to a piece
which that great critic has written against.

I do not indeed wonder that the actors should be such
professed enemies to those among our nation who are com-

monly known by the name of critics, since it is a rule among these gentlemen to fall upon a play, not because it is ill written, but because it takes. Several of them lay it down as a maxim, that whatever dramatic performance has a long run must of necessity be good for nothing; as though the first precept in poetry were, *not to please.* Whether this rule holds good or not, I shall leave to the determination of those who are better judges than myself; if it does, I am sure it tends very much to the honor of those gentlemen, who have established it; few of their pieces having been disgraced by a run of three days, and most of them being so exquisitely written that the town would never give them more than one night's hearing.

I have a great esteem for a true critic, such as Aristotle and Longinus among the Greeks, Horace and Quintilian among the Romans, Boileau and Dacier among the French. But it is our misfortune, that some who set up for professed critics among us are so stupid, that they do not know how to put ten words together with elegance or common propriety, and withal so illiterate, that they have no taste of the learned languages, and therefore criticise upon old authors only at second hand. They judge of them by what others have written, and not by any notions they have of the authors themselves. The words unity, action, sentiment, and diction, pronounced with an air of authority, give them a figure among unlearned readers, who are apt to believe they are very deep, because they are unintelligible. The ancient critics are full of the praises of their contemporaries; they discover beauties which escaped the observation of the vulgar, and very often find out reasons for palliating and excusing such little slips and oversights as were committed in the writings of eminent authors. On the contrary, most of the smatterers in criticism who appear among us make it their business to vilify and depreciate every new production that gains applause, to descry imaginary blemishes, and to prove by far-fetched arguments, that what pass for beauties in any celebrated piece are faults and errors. In short, the writings of these critics, compared with those of the ancients, are like the works of the sophists compared with those of the old philosophers.

Envy and cavil are the natural fruits of laziness and ignorance; which was probably the reason that in the Heathen mythology Momus is said to be the son of Nox and Somnus, of darkness and sleep. Idle men, who have not been at the pains to accomplish or distinguish themselves, are very apt to detract from others; as ignorant men are very subject to decry those beauties in a celebrated work which they have not eyes to discover. Many of our sons of Momus, who dignify themselves by the name of critics, are the genuine descendants of those two illustrious ancestors. They are often led into those numerous absurdities in which they daily instruct the people, by not considering that, first, There is sometimes a greater judgment shown in deviating from the rules of art, than in adhering to them; and, secondly, That there is more beauty in the works of a great genius who is ignorant of all the rules of art, than in the works of a little genius, who not only knows but scrupulously observes them.

First, We may often take notice of men who are perfectly acquainted with all the rules of good writing, and notwithstanding choose to depart from them on extraordinary occasions. I could give instances out of all the tragic writers of antiquity who have shown their judgment in this particular, and purposely receded from an established rule of the drama, when it has made way for a much higher beauty than the observation of such a rule would have been. Those who have surveyed the noblest pieces of architecture and statuary, both ancient and modern, know very well that there are frequent deviations from art in the works of the greatest masters, which have produced a much nobler effect than a more accurate and exact way of proceeding could have done. This often arises from what the Italians call the *gusto grande* in these arts, which is what we call the sublime in writing.

In the next place, our critics do not seem sensible that there is more beauty in the works of a great genius who is ignorant of the rules of art, than in those of a little genius who knows and observes them.

A critic may have the same consolation in the ill success of his play, as Dr. South tells us a physician has at the death of a patient, that he was killed *secundum artem.* Our inimitable Shakespeare is a stumbling-block to the whole tribe of these rigid critics. Who would not rather read one of his plays, where there is not a single rule of the stage observed, than any production of a modern critic, where there is not one of them violated? Shakespeare was indeed born with all the seeds of poetry, and may be compared to the stone in Pyrrhus's ring, which, as Pliny tells us, had the figure of Apollo and the nine muses in the veins of it, produced by the spontaneous hand of nature, without any help from art.

Tatler No. 158. *Tom Folio.*

Tom Folio is a broker in learning, employed to get together good editions, and stock the libraries of great men. There is not a sale of books begins till Tom Folio is seen at the door. There is not an auction where his name is not heard, and that too in the very nick of time, in the critical moment, before the last decisive stroke of the hammer. There is not a subscription goes forward, in which Tom is not privy to the first rough draught of the proposals; nor a catalogue printed, that doth not come to him wet from the press. He is an universal scholar, so far as the title-page of all authors, knows the manuscripts in which they were discovered, the editions through which they have passed, with the praises or censures which they have received from the several members of the learned world.   He has a greater esteem for Aldus and Elzevir, than for Virgil and Horace. If you talk of Herodotus, he breaks out into a panegyric upon Harry Stephens.   He thinks he gives you an account of an author, when he tells the subject he treats of, the name of the editor, and the year in which it was printed. Or if you draw him into further particulars, he cries up the goodness of the paper, extols the diligence of the corrector, and is transported with the beauty of the letter.   This he looks upon to be sound learning and substantial criticism. As for those who talk of the fineness of style, and the justness of thought, or describe the brightness of any particular passages; nay, though they write themselves in the genius and spirit of the author they admire, Tom looks upon them as men of superficial learning and flashy parts.

I had yesterday morning a visit from this learned idiot, (for that is the light in which I consider every pedant), when I discovered in him some little touches of the coxcomb, which I had not before observed.   Being very full of the figure which he makes in the republic of letters, and wonderfully satisfied with his great stock of knowledge, he gave me broad intimations, that he did not "believe" in all points as his forefathers had done.   He then communicated to me a thought of a certain author upon a passage of Virgil's account of the dead, which I made the subject of a late paper.   This thought hath taken very much among men of Tom's pitch and understanding, though universally exploded by all that know how to construe Virgil, or have any relish of antiquity.   Not to trouble my reader with it, I found, upon the whole, that Tom did not believe a future state of rewards and punishments, because Æneas, at his leaving the empire of the dead, passed through the gate of ivory, and not through that of horn. Knowing that Tom had not sense enough to give up an opinion which he had once received, that I might avoid wrangling, I told him, that Virgil possibly had his oversights as well as another author. "Ah! Mr. Bickerstaff," says he, "you would have another opinion of him, if you would read him in Daniel Heinsius's edition. I have perused him myself several times in that edition," continued he; "and after the strictest and most malicious examination, could find but two faults in him: one of them is in the Æneid, where there are two commas instead of a parenthesis; and another in the third Georgic, where you may find a semicolon turned upside down." "Perhaps," said I, "these were not Virgil's thoughts, but those of the transcriber." "I do not design it," says Tom, "as a reflection on Virgil: on the contrary, I know that all the manuscripts 'reclaim' against such a punctuation. Oh, Mr. Bickerstaff," says he, "what would a man give to see one simile of Virgil writ in his own hand?" I asked him which was the simile he meant; but was answered, "Any simile in Virgil." He then told me all the secret history in the commonwealth of learning; of modern pieces that had the names of ancient authors annexed to them; of all the books that were now writing or printing in the several parts of Europe; of many amendments which are made, and not yet published; and a thousand other particulars, which I would not have my memory burdened with for a Vatican.

At length, being fully persuaded that I thoroughly admired him, and looked upon him as a prodigy of learning, he took his leave. I know several of Tom's class who are professed admirers of Tasso without understanding a word of Italian; and one in particular, that carries a *Pastor Fido* in his pocket, in which I am sure he is acquainted with no other beauty but the clearness of the character.

There is another kind of pedant, who, with all Tom Folio's

impertinencies, hath greater superstructures and embellishments of Greek and Latin, and is still more insupportable than the other, in the same degree as he is more learned. Of this kind very often are editors, commentators, interpreters, scholiasts, and critics; and in short, all men of deep learning without common sense. These persons set a greater value on themselves for having found out the meaning of a passage in Greek, than upon the author for having written it; nay, will allow the passage itself not to have any beauty in it, at the same time that they would be considered as the greatest men in the age for having interpreted it. They will look with contempt upon the most beautiful poems that have been composed by any of their contemporaries; but will lock themselves up in their studies for a twelvemonth together, to correct, publish, and expound, such trifles of antiquity as a modern author would be contemned for. Men of the strictest morals, severest lives, and the gravest professions, will write volumes upon an idle sonnet that is originally in Greek or Latin; give editions of the most immoral authors, and spin out whole pages upon the various readings of a lewd expression. All that can be said in excuse for them is, that their works sufficiently show they have no taste of their authors; and that what they do in this kind, is out of their great learning, and not out of any levity or lasciviousness of temper.

Tatler No. 163.   *Ned Softly.*

I yesterday came hither[1] about two hours before the company generally make their appearance, with a design to read over all the newspapers; but, upon my sitting down, I was accosted by Ned Softly, who saw me from a corner in

---

[1] Will's coffee-house.

the other end of the room, where I found he had been writing something. "Mr. Bickerstaff," says he, "I observe by a late Paper of yours, that you and I are just of a humor; for you must know, of all impertinences, there is nothing which I so much hate as news. I never read a Gazette in my life; and never trouble my head about our armies, whether they win or lose, or in what part of the world they lie encamped." Without giving me time to reply, he drew a paper of verses out of his pocket, telling me, "that he had something which would entertain me more agreeably; and that he would desire my judgment upon every line, for that we had time enough before us until the company came in."

Ned Softly is a very pretty poet, and a great admirer of easy lines. Waller is his favorite: and as that admirable writer has the best and worst verses of any among our great English poets, Ned Softly has got all the bad ones without book; which he repeats upon occasion, to show his reading, and garnish his conversation. Ned is indeed a true English reader, incapable of relishing the great and masterly strokes of this art; but wonderfully pleased with the little Gothic ornaments of epigrammatical conceits, turns, points, and quibbles, which are so frequent in the most admired of our English poets, and practised by those who want genius and strength to represent, after the manner of the ancients, simplicity in its natural beauty and perfection.

Finding myself unavoidably engaged in such a conversation, I was resolved to turn my pain into a pleasure, and to divert myself as well as I could with so very odd a fellow. "You must understand," says Ned, "that the sonnet I am going to read to you was written upon a lady, who showed me some verses of her own making, and is, perhaps, the best poet of our age. But you shall hear it."

Upon which he began to read as follows:

TO MIRA ON HER INCOMPARABLE POEMS.

I.

When dress'd in laurel wreaths you shine,
    And tune your soft melodious notes,
You seem a sister of the Nine,
    Or Phœbus' self in petticoats.

II.

I fancy, when your song you sing,
    (Your song you sing with so much art)
Your pen was plucked from Cupid's wing;
    For, ah! it wounds me like his dart.

"Why," says I, "this is a little nosegay of conceits, a very lump of salt: every verse has something in it that piques; and then the *dart* in the last line is certainly as pretty a sting in the tail of an epigram, for so I think you critics call it, as ever entered into the thought of a poet." "Dear Mr. Bickerstaff," says he, shaking me by the hand, "everybody knows you to be a judge of these things; and to tell you truly, I read over Roscommon's translation of 'Horace's Art of Poetry' three several times, before I sat down to write the sonnet which I have shown you. But you shall hear it again, and pray observe every line of it; for not one of them shall pass without your approbation.

> When dress'd in laurel wreaths you shine,

"That is," says he, "when you have your garland on; when you are writing verses." To which I replied, "I know your meaning: a metaphor!" "The same," said he, and went on.

> "And tune your soft melodious notes.

Pray observe the gliding of that verse; there is scarce a consonant in it: I took care to make it run upon liquids. Give me your opinion of it." "Truly," said I, "I think it as good as the former." "I am very glad to hear you say so," says he; "but mind the next.

You seem a sister of the Nine.

"That is," says he, "you seem a sister of the Muses; for, if you look into ancient authors, you will find it was their opinion that there were nine of them." "I remember it very well," said I; "but pray proceed."

"Or Phœbus' self in petticoats.

"Phœbus," says he, "was the god of poetry. These little instances, Mr. Bickerstaff, show a gentleman's reading. Then, to take off from the air of learning, which Phœbus and the Muses had given to this first stanza, you may observe, how it falls all of a sudden into the familiar; 'in Petticoats'!

Or Phœbus' self in petticoats."

"Let us now," says I, "enter upon the second stanza; I find the first line is still a continuation of the metaphor,

I fancy, when your song you sing."

"It is very right," says he, "but pray observe the turn of words in those two lines. I was a whole hour in adjusting of them, and have still a doubt upon me, whether in the second line it should be 'Your song you sing'; or, 'You sing your song.' You shall hear them both:

I fancy, when your song you sing,
(Your song you sing with so much art)
OR
I fancy, when your song you sing,
(You sing your song with so much art)."

"Truly," said I, "the turn is so natural either way, that you have made me almost giddy with it." "Dear sir," said he, grasping me by the hand, "you have a great deal of patience; but pray what do you think of the next verse?

Your pen was pluck'd from Cupid's wing."

"Think!" says I; "I think you have made Cupid look like a little goose."   "That was my meaning," says he: "I think the ridicule is well enough hit off.   But we come now to the last, which sums up the whole matter.

For, ah! it wounds me like his dart.

"Pray how do you like that *Ah!* doth it not make a pretty figure in that place?   *Ah!*——it looks.as if I felt the dart, and cried out as being pricked with it.

For, ah! it wounds me like his dart.

"My friend Dick Easy," continued he, "assured me, he would rather have written that *Ah!* than have been the author of the Æneid.   He indeed objected, that I made Mira's pen like a quill in one of the lines, and like a dart in the other.   But as to that——"   "Oh! as to that," says I, "it is but supposing Cupid to be like a porcupine, and his quills and darts will be the same thing."   He was going to embrace me for the hint; but half a dozen critics coming into the room, whose faces he did not like, he conveyed the sonnet into his pocket, and whispered me in the ear, "he would show it me again as soon as his man had written it over fair."

Spectator No. 21.   *Over-crowding of the learned professions.*

I am sometimes very much troubled when I reflect upon the three great professions of divinity, law, and physic: how they are each of them overburdened with practitioners, and filled with multitudes of ingenious gentlemen that starve one another.

We may divide the clergy into generals, field-officers, and subalterns. Among the first we may reckon bishops, deans, and archdeacons. Among the second are doctors of divinity, prebendaries, and all that wear scarves. The rest are comprehended under the subalterns. As for the first class, our constitution preserves it from any redundancy of incumbents, notwithstànding competitors are numberless. Upon a strict calculation, it is found that there has been a great exceeding of late years in the second division, several brevets having been granted for the converting of subalterns into scarf-officers; insomuch that within my memory the price of lutestring is raised above twopence in a yard. As for the subalterns, they are not to be numbered. . Should our clergy once enter into the corrupt practice of the laity, by the splitting of their freeholds, they would be able to carry most of the elections in England.

The body of the law is no less incumbered with superfluous members, that are like Virgil's army, which he tells us was so crowded, many of them had not room to use their weapons. This prodigious society of men may be divided into the litigious and peaceable. Under the first are comprehended all those who are carried down in coach-fuls to Westminster Hall, every morning in term-time. Martial's description of this species of lawyers is full of humor:

Iras et verba locant.

Men that hire out their words and anger; that are more or less passionate according as they are paid for it, and allow their client a quantity of wrath proportionable to the fee which they receive from him. I must however observe to the reader, that above three parts of those whom I reckon among the litigious, are such as are only quarrelsome in their hearts, and have no opportunity of showing their passion at the bar. Nevertheless, as they do not know what strifes may arise, they appear at the hall every day, that they may show themselves in a readiness to enter the lists, whenever there shall be occasion for them.

The peaceable lawyers are, in the first place, many of the benchers of the several Inns of Court, who seem to be the dignitaries of the law, and are endowed with those qualifications of mind that accomplish a man rather for a ruler than a pleader. These men live peaceably in their habitations, eating once a day, and dancing once a year, for the honor of their respective societies.

Another numberless branch of peaceable lawyers are those young men, who, being placed at the Inns of Court in order to study the laws of their country, frequent the playhouse more than Westminster Hall, and are seen in all public assemblies, except in a court of justice. I shall say nothing of those silent and busy multitudes that are employed within doors, in the drawing up of writings and conveyances; nor of those greater numbers that palliate their want of business with a pretence to such chamber-practice.

If, in the third place, we look into the profession of physic, we shall find a most formidable body of men; the sight of them is enough to make a man serious, for we may lay it down as a maxim, that when a nation abounds in physicians, it grows thin of people. Sir William Temple is very much puzzled to find out a reason why the northern hive, as he calls it, does not send out such prodigious swarms, and overrun the world with Goths and Vandals, as it did formerly; but had that excellent author observed that there were no students in physic among the subjects of Thor and Woden, and that this science very much flourishes in the north at present, he might have found a better solution for this difficulty than any of those he has made use of. This body of men, in our own country, may be described like the British army in Cæsar's time: some of them slay in chariots, and some on foot. If the infantry do less execution than the charioteers, it is because they cannot be carried so soon into all quarters of the town, and dispatch so much business in so short a time. Besides this body of regular troops, there are stragglers, who, without being duly listed and enrolled, do infinite mischief to those who are so unlucky as to fall into their hands.

There are, besides the above-mentioned, innumerable retainers to physic, who for want of other patients amuse themselves with the stifling of cats in an air-pump, cutting up dogs alive, or impaling of insects upon the point of a needle for microscopical observations; besides those that are employed in the gathering of weeds, and the chase of butterflies: not to mention the cockle-shell-merchants and spider-catchers.

When I consider how each of these professions are crowded with multitudes that seek their livelihood in them, and how many men of merit there are in each of them, who may be rather said to be of the science than the profession, I very much wonder at the humor of parents, who will not rather choose to place their sons in a way of life where an honest industry cannot but thrive, than in stations where the greatest probity, learning, and good sense may miscarry. How many men are country curates that might have made themselves aldermen of London, by a right improvement of a smaller sum of money than what is usually laid out upon a learned education! A sober frugal person, of slender parts and slow apprehension, might have thrived in trade, though he starves upon physic; as a man would be well enough pleased to buy silks of one whom he would not venture to feel his pulse. Vagellius is careful, studious, and obliging, but withal a little thick-skulled; he has not a single client, but might have had abundance of customers. The misfortune is, that parents take a liking to a particular profession, and therefore desire their sons may be of it. Whereas, in so great an affair of life, they should consider the genius and abilities of their children more than their own inclinations.

It is the great advantage of a trading nation, that there are very few in it so dull and heavy who may not be placed in stations of life, which may give them an opportunity of making their fortunes. A well-regulated commerce is not, like law, physic, or divinity, to be overstocked with hands; but, on the contrary, flourishes by multitudes, and gives employment to all its professors. Fleets of merchantmen are so many squadrons of floating shops, that vend our wares and manufactures in all the markets of the world, and find out chapmen under both the tropics.

Spectator No. 81. *On party patches.*

About the middle of last winter I went to see an opera at the theatre in the Hay Market, where I could not but take notice of two parties of very fine women, that had placed themselves in the opposite side boxes, and seemed drawn up in a kind of battle array one against another. After a short survey of them, I found they were patched differently; the faces on one hand being spotted on the right side of the forehead, and those upon the other on the left. I quickly perceived that they cast hostile glances upon one another; and that their patches were placed in those different situations, as party signals to distinguish friends from foes. In the middle boxes, between these two opposite bodies, were several ladies who patched indifferently on both sides of their faces, and seemed to sit there with no other intention but to see the opera. Upon inquiry I found, that the body of Amazons on my right hand were Whigs, and those on my left Tories : and that those who had placed themselves in the middle boxes were a neutral party, whose faces had not yet declared themselves. These last however, as I afterwards found, diminished daily, and took their party with one side or the other; insomuch that I observed in several of them, the patches, which were before dispersed equally, are now all gone over to the Whig or Tory side of the face. The censorious say that the men, whose hearts are aimed at, are very often the occasions that one part of the face is thus dishonored, and lies under a kind of disgrace, while the other is so much set off and adorned by the owners; and that the patches turn to the right or to the left, according to the principles of the man who is most in favor. But whatever may be the motives of a few fantastical coquettes, who do not patch for the public good so much as for their own private advantage, it is certain, that there are several women of honor, who patch out of principle, and with an eye to the interest of their country. Nay, I am informed that some of them adhere so steadfastly to their party, and are so far from sacrificing their zeal for the public to their passion for any particular person, that in a late draught of marriage articles a lady has stipulated with her husband, that whatever his opinions are, she shall be at liberty to patch on which side she pleases.

I must here take notice, that Rosalinda, a famous Whig partisan, has most unfortunately a very beautiful mole on the Tory part of her forehead; which, being very conspicuous, has occasioned many mistakes, and given an handle to her enemies to misrepresent her face, as though it had revolted from the Whig interest. But whatever this natural patch may seem to intimate, it is well known that her notions of government are still the same. This unlucky mole, however, has misled several coxcombs: and like the hanging out of false colors, made some of them converse with Rosalinda in what they thought the spirit of her party, when on a sudden she has given them an unexpected fire, that has sunk them all at once. If Rosalinda is unfortunate in her mole, Nigranilla is as unhappy in a pimple, which forces her, against her inclinations, to patch on the Whig side.

I am told that many virtuous matrons, who formerly have been taught to believe that this artificial spotting of the face was unlawful, are now reconciled, by a zeal for their cause, to what they could not be prompted by a concern for their beauty. This way of declaring war upon one another, puts me in mind of what is reported of the tigress, that several spots rise in her skin when she is angry, or, as Mr. Cowley says : —

> She swells with angry pride,
> And calls forth all her spots on ev'ry side.

When I was in the theatre the time above mentioned, I had the curiosity to count the patches on both sides, and found the Tory patches to be about twenty stronger than the Whig ; but to make amends for this small inequality, I the next morning found the whole puppet-show filled with faces spotted after the Whiggish manner. Whether or no the ladies had retreated hither in order to rally their forces I cannot tell ; but the next night they came in so great a body to the opera, that they out-numbered the enemy.

This account of party patches will, I am afraid, appear improbable to those who live at a distance from the fashionable world ; but as it is a distinction of a very singular nature, and what perhaps may never meet with a parallel, I think I should not have discharged the office of a faithful Spectator, had not I recorded it.

I have, in former papers, endeavored to expose this party rage in women, as it only serves to aggravate the hatred and animosities that reign among men, and in a great measure deprives the fair sex of those peculiar charms with which nature has endued them.

When the Romans and Sabines were at war, and just upon the point of giving battle, the women who were allied to both of them interposed with so many tears and entreaties, that they prevented the mutual slaughter which threatened both parties, and united them together in a firm and lasting peace.

I would recommend this noble example to our British ladies at a time when their country is torn with so many unnatural divisions, that, if they continue, it will be a misfortune to be born in it. The Greeks thought it so improper for women to interest themselves in competitions and contentions, that for this reason, among others, they forbade them under pain of death to be present at the Olympic games, notwithstanding these were the public diversions of all Greece.

As our English women excel those of all nations in beauty, they should endeavor to out-shine them in all other accomplishments proper to the sex, and to distinguish themselves as tender mothers and faithful wives, rather than as furious partisans. Female virtues are of a domestic turn. The family is the proper province for private women to shine in. If they must be showing their zeal for the public, let it not be against those who are perhaps of the same family, or at least of the same religion or nation, but against those who are the open, professed, undoubted enemies of their faith, liberty, and country. When the Romans were pressed with a foreign enemy, the ladies voluntarily contributed all their rings and jewels to assist the government under a public exigence; which appeared so laudable an action in the eyes of their countrymen, that from thenceforth it was permitted by a law to pronounce public orations at the funeral of a woman in the praise of the deceased person, which till that time was peculiar to men. Would our English ladies, instead of sticking on a patch against those of their own country, show themselves so truly public-spirited as to sacrifice every one her necklace against the common enemy, what decrees ought not to be made in favor of them!

Spectator No. 119.   *On country manners.*

The first and most obvious reflections which arise in a
man who changes the city for the country, are upon the
different manners of the people whom he meets with in
those two different scenes of life. By manners I do not
mean morals, but behavior and good breeding, as they show
themselves in the town and in the country.

And here, in the first place, I must observe a very great
revolution that has happened in this article of good breeding. Several obliging deferences, condescensions, and sub-
missions, with many outward forms and ceremonies that
accompany them, were first of all brought up among the
politer part of mankind, who lived in courts and cities, and
distinguished themselves from the rustic part of the species
(who on all occasions acted bluntly and naturally) by such
a mutual complaisance and intercourse of civilities. These
forms of conversation by degrees multiplied and grew
troublesome; the modish world found too great a constraint
in them, and have therefore thrown most of them aside.
Conversation was so encumbered with show and ceremony,
that it stood in need of a reformation to retrench its superfluities, and restore it to its natural good sense and beauty.
At present therefore an unconstrained carriage, and a certain openness of behavior, are the height of good breeding.
The fashionable world is grown free and easy; our manners
sit more loose upon us: nothing is so modish as an agreeable negligence. In a word, good breeding shows itself most
where to an ordinary eye it appears the least.

If after this we look on the people of mode in the country,
we find in them the manners of the last age. They have
no sooner fetched themselves up to the fashion of the polite
world, but the town has dropped them, and are nearer to
the first state of nature than to those refinements which formerly reigned in the court, and still prevail in the country.

One may now know a man that never conversed in the world, by his excess of good breeding. A polite country squire shall make you as many bows in half an hour, as would serve a courtier for a week. There is infinitely more to do about place and precedency in a meeting of justices' wives, than in an assembly of duchesses.

This rural politeness is very troublesome to a man of my temper, who generally take the chair that is next me, and walk first or last, in the front or in the rear, as chance directs. I have known my friend Sir Roger's dinner almost cold before the company could adjust the ceremonial, and be prevailed upon to sit down; and have heartily pitied my old friend, when I have seen him forced to pick and cull his guests, as they sat at the several parts of his table, that he might drink their healths according to their respective ranks and qualities. Honest Will Wimble, who I should have thought had been altogether uninfected with ceremony, gives me abundance of trouble in this particular. Though he has been fishing all the morning, he will not help himself at dinner, till I am served. When we are going out of the hall he runs behind me; and last night, as we were walking in the fields, stopped short at a stile till I came up to it, and upon my making signs to him to get over, told me, with a serious smile, that sure I believed they had no manners in the country.

There has happened another revolution in the point of good breeding, which relates to the conversation among men of mode, and which I cannot but look upon as very extraordinary. It was certainly one of the first distinctions of a well-bred man, to express every thing that had the most remote appearance of being obscene in modest terms and distant phrases; whilst the clown, who had no such delicacy of conception and expression, clothed his ideas in those plain, homely terms that are the most obvious and natural. This kind of good manners was perhaps carried to an excess, so as to make conversation too stiff, formal, and precise; for which reason (as hypocrisy in one age is generally succeeded by atheism in another) conversation is in a great measure relapsed into the first extreme; so that at present several of our men of the town, and particularly those who have been polished in France, make use of the most coarse, uncivilized words in our language, and utter themselves often in such a manner as a clown would blush to hear.

This infamous piece of good breeding, which reigns among the coxcombs of the town, has not yet made its way into the country; and as it is impossible for such an irrational way of conversation to last long among a people that make any profession of religion, or show of modesty, if the country gentlemen get into it, they will certainly be left in the lurch. Their good breeding will come too late to them, and they will be thought a parcel of lewd clowns, while they fancy themselves talking together like men of wit and pleasure.

Spectator No. 129. *The same subject.*

Great masters in painting never care for drawing people in the fashion; as very well knowing that the head-dress or periwig that now prevails, and gives a grace to their portraitures at present, will make a very odd figure, and perhaps look monstrous in the eyes of posterity. For this reason they often represent an illustrious poet in a Roman habit, or in some other dress that never varies. I could wish, for the sake of my country friends, that there was such a kind of everlasting drapery to be made use of by all who live at a certain distance from the town, and that they would agree upon such fashions as should never be liable to changes and innovations. For want of this standing dress, a man who takes a journey into the country is as much surprised as one who walks in a gallery of old family pictures; and finds as great a variety of garbs and habits in the persons he converses with. Did they keep to one constant dress they would sometimes be in the fashion, which they never are as matters are managed at present. If instead of running after the mode, they would continue fixed in one certain habit, the mode would sometime or other overtake them, as a clock that stands still is sure to point right once in twelve hours: in this case therefore I would advise them, as a gentleman did his friend who was hunting about the whole town after a rambling fellow, "If you follow him you will never find him, but if you plant yourself at the corner of any one street, I'll engage it will not be long before you see him."

I have already touched upon this subject, in a speculation which shows how cruelly the country are led astray in following the town, and equipped in a ridiculous habit, when they fancy themselves in the height of the mode. Since that speculation I have received a letter (which I there hinted at) from a gentleman who is now in the western circuit.

Mr. Spectator,

Being a lawyer of the Middle Temple, a Cornishman by birth, I generally ride the western circuit for my health, and as I am not interrupted with clients, have leisure to make many observations that escape the notice of my fellow-travellers.

One of the most fashionable women I met with in all the circuit was my landlady at Staines, where I chanced to be on a holiday. Her commode was not half a foot high, and her petticoat within some yards of a modish circumference. In the same place I observed a young fellow with a tolerable periwig, had it not been covered with a hat that was shaped in the Ramillie cock. As I proceeded in my journey I observed the petticoat grew scantier and scantier, and about threescore miles from London was so very unfashionable, that a woman might walk in it without any manner of inconvenience.

Not far from Salisbury I took notice of a justice of peace's lady, who was at least ten years behind-hand in her dress, but at the same time as fine as hands could make her. She was flounced and furbelowed from head to foot; every ribbon was wrinkled, and every part of her garments in curl, so that she looked like one of those animals which in the country we call a Friezeland hen.

Not many miles beyond this place I was informed, that one of the last year's little muffs had by some means or other straggled into those parts, and that all the women of fashion were cutting their old muffs in two, or retrenching them according to the little model which was got among them. I cannot believe the report they have there, that it was sent down franked by a parliament-man in a little packet; but probably by next winter this fashion will be at the height in the country, when it is quite out at London.

The greatest beau at our next county-sessions was dressed in a most monstrous flaxen periwig, that was made in king William's reign. The wearer of it goes, it seems, in his own hair, when he is at home, and lets his wig lie in buckle for a whole half-year, that he may put it on upon occasion to meet the judges in it.

I must not here omit an adventure which happened to us in a country church upon the frontiers of Cornwall. As we were in the midst of the service, a lady who is the chief woman of the place, and had passed the winter at London with her husband, entered the congregation in a little head-dress, and a hooped petticoat. The people, who were wonderfully startled at such a sight, all of them rose up. Some stared at the prodigious bottom, and some at the little top of this strange dress. In the mean time the lady of the manor filled the area of the church, and walked up to her pew with an unspeakable satisfaction, amidst the whispers, conjectures, and astonishments of the whole congregation.

Upon my way from hence we saw a young fellow riding towards us full gallop, with a bob-wig and a black silken bag tied to it. He stopt short at the coach, to ask us how far the judges were behind us. His stay was so very short, that we had only time to observe his new silk waistcoat, which was unbuttoned in several places to let us see that he had a clean shirt on, which was ruffled down to his middle.

From this place, during our progress through the most western parts of the kingdom, we fancied ourselves in king Charles the second's reign, the people having made very little variations in their dress since that time. The smartest of the country squires appear still in the Monmouth cock, and when they go a wooing (whether they have any post in the militia or not) they generally put on a red coat. We were, indeed, very much surprised at the place we lay at last night, to meet with a gentleman that had accoutered himself in a night-cap wig, a coat with long pockets and slit sleeves, and a pair of shoes with high scollop tops; but we soon found by his conversation that he was a person who laughed at the ignorance and rusticity of the country people, and was resolved to live and die in the mode.

Sir, if you think this account of my travels may be of any advantage to the public, I will next year trouble you with such occurrences as I shall meet with in other parts of England. For I am informed there are greater curiosities in the northern circuit than in the western; and that a fashion makes its progress much slower into Cumberland than into Cornwall. I have heard in particular, that the Steenkirk arrived but two months ago at Newcastle, and that there are several commodes in those parts which are worth taking a journey thither to see.

Spectator No. 295. *On pin money.*

Mr. Spectator,

I am turned of my great climacteric, and am naturally a man of a meek temper. About a dozen years ago I was married, for my sins, to a young woman of a good family, and of an high spirit; but could not bring her to close with me, before I had entered into a treaty with her longer than that of the Grand Alliance. Among other articles, it was therein stipulated that she should have 400*l.* a year for pin money, which I obliged myself to pay quarterly into the hands of one who acted as her plenipotentiary in that affair. I have ever since religiously observed my part in this solemn agreement. Now, Sir, so it is, that the lady has had several children since I married her. The education of these my children, who are born to me every year, straitens me so much that I have begged their mother to free me from the obligation of the above-mentioned pin money, that it may go towards making a provision for her family. This proposal makes her noble blood swell in her veins, insomuch that finding me a little tardy in her last quarter's payment, she threatens me every day to arrest me; and proceeds so far as to tell me, that if I do not do her justice, I shall die in a jail. To this she adds, when her passion would let her argue calmly, that she has several play-debts on her hand, which must be discharged very suddenly, and that she cannot lose her money as becomes a woman of her fashion, if she makes me any abatement in this article. I hope, Sir, you will take an occasion from hence to give your opinion upon a subject which you have not yet touched, and inform us if there are any precedents for this usage among our ancestors; or whether you find any mention of pin money in Grotius, Puffendorf, or any other of the civilians.

I am ever the humblest of your admirers,

JOSIAH FRIBBLE, Esq.

As there is no man living who is a more professed advocate for the fair sex than myself, so there is none that would be more unwilling to invade any of their ancient rights and privileges; but as the doctrine of pin money is of a very late date, unknown to our great grandmothers, and not yet received by many of our modern ladies, I think it is for the interest of both sexes to keep it from spreading.

We may indeed generally observe, that in proportion as a woman is more or less beautiful, and her husband advanced in years, she stands in need of a greater or less number of pins, and, upon a treaty of marriage, rises or falls in her demands accordingly. It must likewise be owned, that high quality in a mistress does very much inflame this article in the marriage reckoning.

But where the age and circumstances of both parties are pretty much upon a level, I cannot but think the insisting upon pin money is very extraordinary; and yet we find several matches broken off upon this very head. What would a foreigner, or one who is a stranger to this practice, think of a lover that forsakes his mistress because he is not willing to keep her in pins? But what would he think of the mistress, should he be informed that she asks five or six hundred pounds a year for this use? Should a man unacquainted with our customs be told the sums which are allowed in Great Britain under the title of pin money, what a prodigious consumption of pins would he think there was in this island! "A pin a day," says our frugal proverb, "is a groat a year"; so that according to this calculation, my friend Fribble's wife must every year make use of eight millions six hundred and forty thousand new pins!

I am not ignorant that our British ladies allege they comprehend under this general term several other conveniences of life; I could therefore wish, for the honor of my country women, that they had rather called it *Needle money*, which might have implied something of good housewifery, and not have given the malicious world occasion to think that dress and trifles have always the uppermost place in a woman's thoughts.

I know several of my fair readers urge, in defence of this practice, that it is but a necessary provision they make for themselves, in case their husband proves a churl or a miser; so that they consider this allowance as a kind of alimony, which they may lay their claim to without actually separating from their husbands. But with submission I think a woman who will give up herself to a man in marriage, where there is the least room for such an apprehension, and trust her person to one whom she will not rely on for the common necessaries of life, may very properly be accused (in the phrase of a homely proverb) of being "penny wise and pound foolish."

It is observed of over-cautious generals, that they never engage in a battle without securing a retreat, in case the event should not answer their expectations; on the other hand, the greatest conquerors have burnt their ships, or broke down the bridges behind them, as being determined either to succeed or die in the engagement. In the same manner, I should very much suspect a woman who takes such precautions for her retreat, and contrives methods how she may live happily, without the affection of one to whom she joins herself for life. Separate purses between man and wife are in my opinion unnatural. A marriage cannot be happy where the pleasures, inclinations, and interest of both parties are not the same. There is no greater enticement to love in the mind of man, than the sense of a person's depending upon him for her ease and happiness; as a woman uses all her endeavors to please the person whom she looks upon as her honor, her comfort, and her support.

For this reason I am not very much surprised at the behavior of a rough country squire, who, being not a little shocked at the proceeding of a young widow that would not recede from her demands of pin money, was so enraged at her mercenary temper, that he told her in great wrath, "As much as she thought him her slave, he would show all the world he did not care a pin for her." Upon which he flew out of the room, and never saw her more.

Socrates, in Plato's Alcibiades, says, he was informed by one who had travelled through Persia, that as he passed over a great tract of land, and inquired what the name of the place was, they told him it was the Queen's girdle; to which he adds, that another wide field which lay by it, was called the Queen's veil; and that in the same manner there was a large portion of ground set aside for every part of her majesty's dress. These lands might not be improperly called the Queen of Persia's pin money.

Spectator No. 403.　*The false rumor.*

When I consider this great city in its several quarters and divisions, I look upon it as an aggregate of various nations distinguished from each other by their respective customs, manners, and interests. The courts of two countries do not so much differ from one another, as the court and city in their peculiar ways of life and conversation. In short, the inhabitants of St. James's, notwithstanding they live under the same laws, and speak the same language, are a distinct people from those of Cheapside, who are likewise removed from those of the Temple on the one side, and those of Smithfield on the other, by several climates and degrees in their way of thinking and conversing together.

For this reason, when any public affair is upon the anvil, I love to hear the reflections that arise upon it in the several districts and parishes of London and Westminster, and to ramble up and down a whole day together, in order to make myself acquainted with the opinions of my ingenious countrymen. By this means I know the faces of all the principal politicians within the bills of mortality; and as every coffee-house has some particular statesman belonging to it, who is the mouth of the street where he lives, I always take care to place myself near him, in order to know his judgment on the present posture of affairs. The last progress that I made with this intention was about three months ago, when we had a current report of the king of France's death. As I foresaw this would produce a new face of things in Europe, and many curious speculations in our British coffee-houses, I was very desirous to learn the thoughts of our most eminent politicians on that occasion.

That I might begin as near the fountain-head as possible, I first of all called in at St. James's, where I found the whole outward room in a buzz of politics. The speculations were but very indifferent towards the door, but grew finer as you advanced to the upper end of the room, and were so very much improved by a knot of theorists who sat in the inner room, within the steams of the coffee-pot, that I there heard the whole Spanish monarchy disposed of, and all the line of Bourbon provided for, in less than a quarter of an hour.

I afterwards called in at Giles's, where I saw a board of French gentlemen sitting upon the life and death of their Grand Monarque. Those among them who had espoused the Whig interest very positively affirmed that he departed this life about a week since; and therefore proceeded without any further delay to the release of their friends in the galleys, and to their own re-establishment: but, finding they could not agree among themselves, I proceeded on my intended progress.

Upon my arrival at Jenny Man's, I saw an alert young fellow that cocked his hat upon a friend of his who entered just at the same time with myself, and accosted him after the following manner: "Well, Jack, the old prig is dead at last. Sharp's the word. Now or nevei, boy. Up to the walls of Paris directly." With several other deep reflections of the same nature.

I met with very little variation in the politics between Charing Cross and Covent Garden. And, upon my going into Will's, I found their discourse was gone off from the death of the French king to that of Monsieur Boileau, Racine, Corneille, and several other poets, whom they regretted upon this occasion, as persons who would have obliged the world with very noble elegies on the death of so great a prince, and so eminent a patron of learning.

At a coffee-house near the Temple, I found a couple of young gentlemen engaged very smartly in a dispute on the succession to the Spanish monarchy. One of them seemed to have been retained as advocate for the Duke of Anjou, the other for his Imperial Majesty. They were both for regulating the title to that kingdom by the statute-laws of England; but, finding them going out of my depth, I passed forward to Paul's church-yard, where I listened with great attention to a learned man, who gave the company an account of the deplorable state of France during the minority of the deceased king.

I then turned on my right hand into Fish-street; where the chief politician of that quarter, upon hearing the news, (after having taken a pipe of tobacco, and ruminated for some time), "If," says he, "the king of France is certainly dead, we shall have plenty of mackerel this season; our fishery will not be disturbed by privateers, as it has been for these ten years past." He afterwards considered how the death of this great man would affect our pilchards, and, by several other remarks, infused a general joy into his

I afterwards entered a by coffee-house that stood at the upper end of a narrow lane, where I met with a non-juror, engaged very warmly with a lace-man who was the great support of a neighboring conventicle. The matter in debate was whether the late French king was most like Augustus Cæsar or Nero. The controversy was carried on with great heat on both sides, and, as each of them looked upon me very frequently during the course of their debate, I was under some apprehension that they would appeal to me; and therefore laid down my penny at the bar, and made the best of my way to Cheapside.

I here gazed upon the signs for some time before I found one to my purpose. The first object I met in the coffee-room was a person who expressed a great grief for the death of the French king; but, upon his explaining himself, I found his sorrow did not arise from the loss of the monarch, but for his having sold out of the bank about three days before he heard the news of it: upon which a haberdasher, who was the oracle of the coffee-house, and had his circle of admirers about him, called several to witness that he had declared his opinion above a week before, that the French king was certainly dead; to which he added, that, considering the late advices we had received from France, it was impossible that it could be otherwise. As he was laying these together, and dictating to his hearers with great authority, there came in a gentleman from Garraway's, who told us that there were several letters from France just come in, with advice that the king was in good health, and was gone out a-hunting the very morning the post came away; upon which the haberdasher stole off his hat that hung upon a wooden peg by him, and retired to his shop with great confusion. This intelligence put a stop to my travels, which I had prosecuted with so much satisfaction; being not a little pleased to hear so many different opinions upon so great an event, and to observe how naturally upon such a piece of news every one is apt to consider it with a regard to his particular interest and advantage.

Guardian No. 166.   *A friend of mankind brought to grief by an alchemist.*

Charity is a virtue of the heart, and not of the hands, says an old writer. Gifts and alms are the expressions, not the essence, of this virtue. A man may bestow great sums on the poor and indigent, without being charitable, and may be charitable when he is not able to bestow anything. Charity is therefore a habit of good will, or benevolence, in the soul, which disposes us to the love, assistance, and relief of mankind, especially of those who stand in need of it. The poor man who has this excellent frame of mind. is no less entitled to the reward of this virtue, than the man who founds a college. For my own part, I am charitable to an extravagance this way. I never saw an indigent person in my life without reaching out to him some of this imaginary relief. I cannot but sympathize with every one I meet that is in affliction; and if my abilities were equal to my wishes, there should be neither pain nor poverty in the world.

To give my reader a right notion of myself in this particular, I shall present him with the secret history of one of the most remarkable parts of my life.

I was once engaged in search of the philosopher's stone. It is frequently observed of men who have been busied in this pursuit, that though they have failed in their principal design, they have, however, made such discoveries in their way to it, as have sufficiently recompensed their inquiries. In the same manner, though I cannot boast of my success in that affair, I do not repent of my engaging in it, because it produced in my mind such an habitual exercise of charity, as made it much better than perhaps it would have been, had I never been lost in so pleasing a delusion.

As I did not question but I should soon have a new Indies in my possession, I was perpetually taken up in considering how to turn it to the benefit of mankind. In order to it I employed a whole day in walking about this great city, to find out proper places for the erection of hospitals. I had likewise entertained that project, which has since succeeded in another place, of building churches at the court end of the town, with this only difference, that instead of fifty, I intended to have built a hundred, and to have seen them all finished in less than one year.

I had with great pains and application got together a list of all the French Protestants; and by the best accounts I could come at, had calculated the value of all those estates and effects which every one of them had left in his own country for the sake of his religion, being fully determined to make it up to him, and return some of them the double of what they had lost.

As I was one day in my laboratory, my operator, who was to fill my coffers for me, and used to foot it from the other end of the town every morning, complained of a sprain in his leg, that he had met with over against St. Clément's church. This so affected me, that, as a standing mark of my gratitude to him, and out of compassion to the rest of my fellow-citizens, I resolved to new pave every street within the liberties, and entered a memorandum in my pocket-book accordingly. About the same time I entertained some thoughts of mending all the highways on this side the Tweed, and of making all the rivers in England navigable.

But the project I had most at heart, was the settling upon every man in Great Britain three pounds a year, (in which sum may be comprised, according to Sir William Pettit's observations, all the necessities of life,) leaving to them whatever else they could get by their own industry, to lay out on superfluities.

I was above a week debating in myself what I should do in the matter of Impropriations; but at length came to a resolution to buy them all up, and restore them to the church.

As I was one day walking near St. Paul's, I took some time to survey that structure, and not being entirely satisfied with it, though I could not tell why, I had some thoughts of pulling it down, and building it up anew at my own expense.

For my own part, as I have no pride in me, I intended to take up with a coach and six, half a dozen footmen, and live like a private gentleman.

It happened about this time that public matters looked very gloomy, taxes came hard, the war went on heavily, people complained of the great burdens that were laid upon them; this made me resolve to set aside one morning, to consider seriously the state of the nation. I was the more ready to enter on it, because I was obliged, whether I would or no, to sit at home in my morning gown, having, after a most incredible expense, pawned a new suit of clothes, and a full-bottomed wig, for a sum of money which my operator assured me was the last he should want to bring all matters to bear.

After having considered many projects, I at length resolved to beat the common enemy at his own weapons, and laid a scheme which would have blown him up in a quarter of a year, had things succeeded to my wishes. As I was in this golden dream, somebody knocked at my door. I opened it, and found it was a messenger that brought me a letter from the laboratory. The fellow looked so miserably poor, that I was resolved to make his fortune before he delivered his message; but seeing he brought a letter from my operator, I concluded I was bound to it in honor, as much as a prince is to give a reward to one that brings him the first news of a victory. I knew this was the long-expected hour of projection, which I had waited for, with great impatience, above half a year. In short, I broke open my letter in a transport of joy, and found it as follows.

Sir,

After having got out of you everything you can conveniently spare, I scorn to trespass upon your generous nature, and, therefore, must ingenuously confess to you, that I know no more of the philosopher's stone than you do. I shall only tell you for your comfort, that I never yet could bubble a blockhead out of his money. They must be men of wit and parts who are for my purpose. This made me apply myself to a person of your wealth and ingenuity. How I have succeeded, you yourself can best tell.

Your humble servant to command,

Thomas White.

I have locked up the laboratory, and laid the key under the door.

I was very much shocked at the unworthy treatment of this man, and not a little mortified at my disappointment, though not so much for what I myself, as what the public, suffered by it. I think, however, I ought to let the world know what I designed for them, and hope that such of my readers who find they had a share in my good intentions, will accept the will for the deed.

Spectator No. 3. *The vision of public credit.*

In one of my late rambles, or rather speculations, I looked into the great hall where the Bank is kept, and was not a little pleased to see the directors, secretaries, and clerks, with all the other members of that wealthy corporation, ranged in their several stations, according to the parts they act in that just and regular economy. This revived in my

memory the many discourses which I had both read and
heard concerning the decay of public credit, with the
methods of restoring it, and which, in my opinion, have
always been defective, because they have been made with
an eye to separate interests and party principles.

The thoughts of the day gave my mind employment for
the whole night, so that I fell insensibly into a kind of
methodical dream, which disposed all my contemplations
into a vision or allegory, or what else the reader shall please
to call it.

Methought I returned to the great hall, where I had been
the morning before, but, to my surprise, instead of the company that I left there, I saw towards the upper end of the
hall a beautiful virgin, seated on a throne of gold. Her name
(as they told me) was Public Credit. The walls, instead of
being adorned with pictures and maps, were hung with many
Acts of Parliament written in golden letters. At the upper
end of the hall was the Magna Charta, with the Act of Uniformity on the right hand, and the Act of Toleration on the
left. At the lower end of the hall was the Act of Settlement, which was placed full in the eye of the virgin that sat
upon the throne. Both the sides of the hall were covered
with such Acts of Parliament as had been made for the
establishment of public funds. The lady seemed to set an
unspeakable value upon these several pieces of furniture,
insomuch that she often refreshed her eye with them, and
often smiled with a secret pleasure as she looked upon them;
but, at the same time, showed a very particular uneasiness,
if she saw anything approaching that might hurt them.
She appeared, indeed, infinitely timorous in all her behavior;
and, whether it was from the delicacy of her constitution,
or that she was troubled with vapors, as I was afterwards
told by one who I found was none of her well-wishers, she
changed color and startled at everything she heard. She
was likewise (as I afterwards found) a greater valetudina-

rian than any I had ever met with, even in her own sex, and subject to such momentary consumptions, that, in the twinkling of an eye, she would fall awáy from the most florid complexion, and the most healthful state of body, and wither into a skeleton. Her recoveries were often as sudden as her decays, insomuch that she would revive in a moment out of a wasting distemper, into a habit of the highest health and vigor.

I had very soon an opportunity of observing these quick turns and changes in her constitution. There sat at her feet a couple of secretaries, who received every hour letters from all parts of the world, which the one or the other of them was perpetually reading to her; and, according to the news she heard, to which she was exceedingly attentive, she changed color, and discovered many symptoms of health or sickness.

Behind the throne was a prodigious heap of bags of money, which were piled upon one another so high, that they touched the ceiling. The floor, on her right hand and on her left, was covered with vast sums of gold that rose up in pyramids on either side of her; but this I did not so much wonder at, when I heard, upon inquiry, that she had the same virtue in her touch, which the poets tell us a Lydian king was formerly possessed of; and that she could convert whatever she pleased into that precious metal.

After a little dizziness, and confused hurry of thought, which a man often meets with in a dream, methought the hall was alarmed, the doors flew open, and there entered half a dozen of the most hideous phantoms that I had ever seen (even in a dream) before that time. They came in two by two, though matched in the most dissociable manner, and mingled together in a kind of dance. It would be tedious to describe their habits and persons, for which reason I shall only inform my reader, that the first couple were Tyranny and Anarchy; the second were Bigotry and Atheism; the third, the genius of a commonwealth and a young man of about twenty-two. years of age, whose name I could not learn. He had a sword in his right hand, which in the dance he often brandished at the Act of Settlement; and a citizen, who stood by me, whispered in my ear, that he saw a sponge in his left hand. The dance of so many jarring natures put me in mind of the sun, moon, and earth, in the Rehearsal, that danced together for no other end but to eclipse one another.

The reader will easily suppose, by what has been before said, that the lady on the throne would have been almost frightened to distraction, had she seen but any one of these spectres: what then must have been her condition when she saw them all in a body? She fainted and died away at the sight.

There was a great change in the hill of money bags and the heaps of money; the former shrinking, and falling into so many empty bags, that I now found not above a tenth part of them had been filled with money. The rest that took up the same space, and made the same figure as the bags that were really filled with money, had been blown up with air, and called into my memory the bags full of wind, which Homer tells us his hero received as a present from Æolus. The great heaps of gold, on either side the throne, now appeared to be only heaps of paper, or little piles of notched sticks, bound up together in bundles, like Bath fagots.

Whilst I was lamenting this sudden desolation that had been made before me, the whole scene vanished: in the room of the frightful spectres, there now entered a second dance of apparitions very agreeably matched together, and made up of very amiable phantoms. The first pair was Liberty with Monarchy at her right hand; the second was Moderation leading in Religion; and the third a person, whom I had never seen, with the genius of Great Britain.

At the first entrance the lady revived; the bags swelled to their former bulk; the piles of fagots, and heaps of paper, changed into pyramids of guineas: and, for my own part, I was so transported with joy, that I awaked; though, I must confess, I would fain have fallen asleep again to have closed my vision, if I could have done it.

Spectator No. 69. *The Royal Exchange.*

There is no place in the town which I so much love to frequent as the Royal Exchange. It gives me a secret satisfaction, and, in some measure, gratifies my vanity, as I am an Englishman, to see so rich an assembly of country-men and foreigners consulting together upon the private business of mankind, and making this metropolis a kind of emporium for the whole earth. I must confess I look upon high-change to be a great council, in which all considerable nations have their representatives. Factors in the trading world are what ambassadors are in the politic world; they negotiate affairs, conclude treaties, and maintain a good correspondence between those wealthy societies of men that are divided from one another by seas and oceans, or live on the different extremities of a continent. I have often been pleased to hear disputes adjusted between an inhabitant of Japan and an alderman of London, or to see a subject of the Great Mogul entering into a league with one of the Czar of Muscovy. I am infinitely delighted in mixing with these several ministers of commerce, as they are distin-guished by their different walks and different languages: sometimes I am jostled among a body of Armenians; some-times I am lost in a crowd of Jews; and sometimes make one in a group of Dutchmen. I am a Dane, Swede, or Frenchman at different times: or rather fancy myself like the old philosopher, who upon being asked what country-man he was, replied, that he was a citizen of the world.

Though I very frequently visit this busy multitude of people, I am known to nobody there but my friend Sir Andrew, who often smiles upon me as he sees me bustling in the crowd, but at the same time connives at my presence without taking any further notice of me. There is indeed a merchant of Egypt, who just knows me by sight, having formerly remitted me some money to Grand Cairo; but as I am not versed in the modern Coptic, our conferences go no further than a bow and a grimace.

This grand scene of business gives me an infinite variety of solid and substantial entertainments. As I am a great lover of mankind, my heart naturally overflows with pleasure at the sight of a prosperous and happy multitude, insomuch, that at many public solemnities I cannot forbear expressing my joy with tears that have stolen down my cheeks. For this reason I am wonderfully delighted to see such a body of men thriving in their own private fortunes, and at the same time promoting the public stock; or, in other words, raising estates for their own families, by bringing into their country whatever is wanting, and carrying out of it whatever is superfluous.

Nature seems to have taken a peculiar care to disseminate the blessings among the different regions of the world, with an eye to this mutual intercourse and traffic among mankind, that the natives of the several parts of the globe might have a kind of dependence upon one another, and be united together by their common interest. Almost every degree produces something peculiar to it. The food often grows in one country, and the sauce in another. The fruits of Portugal are corrected by the products of Barbadoes; the infusion of a China plant sweetened with the pith of an Indian cane. The Philippine Islands give a flavor to our European bowls. The single dress of a woman of quality is often the product of a hundred climates. The muff and the fan come together from the different ends of the earth. The scarf is sent from the torrid zone, and the tippet from beneath the pole. The brocade petticoat rises out of the mines of Peru, and the diamond necklace out of the bowels of Indostan.

If we consider our own country in its natural prospect, without any of the benefits and advantages of commerce, what a barren, uncomfortable spot of earth falls to our share! Natural historians tell us, that no fruit grows originally among us besides hips and haws, acorns and pig-nuts, with other delicacies of the like nature; that our climate of itself, and without the assistance of art, can make no further advances towards a plum than to a sloe, and carries an apple to no greater perfection than a crab: that our melons, our peaches, our figs, our apricots, and cherries, are strangers among us, imported in different ages, and naturalized in our English gardens; and that they would all degenerate and fall away into the trash of our own country, if they were wholly neglected by the planter, and left to the mercy of our sun and soil. Nor has traffic more enriched our vegetable world, than it has improved the whole face of nature among us. Our ships are laden with the harvest of every climate: our tables are stored with spices, and oils, and wines; our rooms are filled with pyramids of China, and adorned with the workmanship of Japan: our morning's draught comes to us from the remot-est corners of the earth; we repair our bodies by the drugs of America, and repose ourselves under Indian canopies. My friend Sir Andrew calls the vineyards of France our gardens; the spice-islands our hot-beds; the Persians our silk-weavers, and the Chinese our potters. Nature indeed furnishes us with the bare necessities of life, but traffic gives us a great variety of what is useful, and at the same time supplies us with everything that is convenient and ornamental. Nor is it the least part of this our happiness, that while we enjoy the remotest products of the north and south, we are free from those extremities of weather which give them birth; that our eyes are refreshed with the green fields of Britain, at the same time that our palates are feasted with fruits that rise between the tropics.

For these reasons there are not more useful members in a commonwealth than merchants. They knit mankind together in a mutual intercourse of good offices, distribute the gifts of nature, find work for the poor, add wealth to the rich, and magnificence to the great. Our English merchant converts the tin of his own country into gold, and exchanges his wool for rubies. The Mahometans are clothed in our British manufacture, and the inhabitants of the frozen zone warmed with the fleeces of our sheep.

When I have been upon the Change, I have often fancied one of our old kings standing in person, where he is represented in effigy, and looking down upon the wealthy concourse of people with which that place is every day filled. In this case, how would he be surprised to hear all the languages of Europe spoken in this little spot of his former dominions, and to see so many private men, who in his time would have been the vassals of some powerful baron, negotiating like princes for greater sums of money than were formerly to be met with in the royal treasury! Trade, without enlarging the British territories, has given us a kind of additional empire: it has multiplied the number of the rich, made our landed estates infinitely more valuable than they were formerly, and added to them the accession of other estates as valuable as the lands themselves.

Freeholder No. 22.   *The Tory fox-hunter.*

For the honor of his Majesty, and the safety of his government, we cannot but observe, that those who have appeared the greatest enemies to both, are of that rank of men, who are commonly distinguished by the title of Fox-hunters. As several of these have had no part of their education in cities, camps, or courts, it is doubtful whether they are of greater ornament or use to the nation in which they live. It would be an everlasting reproach to politics, should such men be able to overturn an establishment which has been formed by the wisest laws, and is supported by the ablest heads. The wrong notions and prejudices which cleave to many of these country gentlemen, who have always lived out of the way of being better informed, are not easy to be conceived by a person who has never conversed with them.

That I may give my readers an image of these rural states-men, I shall, without further preface, set down an account of a discourse I chanced to have with one of them some time ago. I was travelling towards one of the remote parts of England, when about three o'clock in the afternoon, see-ing a country gentleman trotting before me with a spaniel by his horse's side, I made up to him. Our conversation opened, as usual, upon the weather; in which we were very unanimous; having both agreed that it was too dry for the season of the year. My fellow-traveller, upon this, observed to me, that there had been no good weather since the Revolution. I was a little startled at so extraordinary a remark, but would not interrupt him till he proceeded to tell me of the fine weather they used to have in King Charles the Second's reign. I only answered that I did not see how the badness of the weather could be the king's fault; and, without waiting for his reply, asked him whose house it was we saw upon the rising ground at a little distance from us.

He told me it belonged to an old fanatical cur, Mr. Such-a-one. "You must have heard of him," says he, "he's one of the Rump." I knew the gentleman's character upon hearing his name, but assured him, that to my knowledge he was a good churchman: "Ay!" says he, with a kind of surprise, "We were told in the country, that he spoke twice, in the queen's time, against taking off the duties upon French claret." This naturally led us to the proceedings of late parliaments, upon which occasion he affirmed roundly, that there had not been one good law passed since King William's accession to the throne, except the act for preserving the game. I had a mind to see him out, and therefore did not care for contradicting him. "Is it not hard," says he, "that honest gentlemen should be taken into custody of messengers to prevent them from acting according to their consciences? But," says he, "what can we expect when a parcel of factious——" He was going on in great passion, but chanced to miss his dog, who was amusing himself some distance behind us. We stood still till he had whistled him up; when he fell into a long panegyric upon his spaniel, who seemed, indeed, excellent in his kind: but I found the most remarkable adventure of his life was, that he had once like to have worried a dissenting teacher. The master could hardly sit on his horse for laughing all the while he was giving me the particulars of his story, which I found had mightily endeared his dog to him, and as he himself told me, had made him a great favorite among all the honest gentlemen of the country. We were at length diverted from this piece of mirth by a post-boy, who winding his horn at us, my companion gave him two or three curses, and left the way clear for him. "I fancy," said I, "that post brings news from Scotland. I shall long to see the next Gazette." "Sir," says he, "I make it a rule never to believe any of your printed news. We never see, sir, how things go, except now and then in Dyer's Letter, and

I read that more for the style than the news. The man has a clever pen, it must be owned. But is it not strange that we should be making war upon Church of England men with Dutch and Swiss soldiers, men of antimonarchical principles? These foreigners will never be loved in England, sir; they have not that wit and good-breeding that we have." I must confess I did not expect to hear my new acquaintance value himself upon these qualifications, but finding him such a critic upon foreigners, I asked him if he had ever travelled; he told me, he did not know what travelling was good for, but to teach a man to ride the great horse, to jabber French, and to talk against passive obedience: to which he added, that he scarce ever knew a traveller in his life who had not forsook his principles, and lost his hunting-seat. "For my part," says he, "I and my father before me have always been for passive obedience, and shall be always for opposing a prince who makes use of ministers that are of another opinion. But where do you intend to inn to-night? (for we were now come in sight of the next town;) I can help you to a very good landlord if you will go along with me. He is a lusty, jolly fellow, that lives well, at least three yards in the girt, and the best Church of England man upon the road." I had a curiosity to see this high-church inn-keeper, as well as to enjoy more of the conversation of my fellow-traveller, and therefore readily consented to set our horses together for that night. As we rode side by side through the town, I was let into the characters of all the principal inhabitants whom we met in our way. One was a dog, another a whelp, another a cur, under which several denominations were comprehended all that voted on the Whig side, in the last election of burgesses. As for those of his own party, he distinguished them by a nod of his head, and asking them how they did by their Christian names. Upon our arrival at the inn, my companion fetched out the jolly landlord, who knew him by his whistle. Many endearments and private whispers passed between them; though it was easy to see by the landlord's scratching his head that things did not go to their wishes. The landlord had sweiled his body to a prodigious size, and worked up his complexion to a standing crimson by his zeal for the prosperity of the church, which he expressed every hour of the day, as his customers dropt in, by repeated bumpers. He had not time to go to church himself, but, as my friend told me in my ear, had headed a mob at the pulling down of two or three meeting-houses. While supper was preparing, he enlarged upon the happiness of the neighboring shire; "For," says he, "there is scarce a Presbyterian in the whole county, except the bishop." In short, I found by his discourse that he had learned a great deal of politics, but not one word of religion, from the parson of his parish; and, indeed, that he had scarce any other notion of religion, but that it consisted in hating Presbyterians. I had a remarkable instance of his notions in this particular. Upon seeing a poor decrepit old woman pass under the window where we sat, he desired me to take notice of her; and afterwards informed me, that she was generally reputed a witch by the country people, but that, for his part, he was apt to believe she was a Presbyterian.

Supper was no sooner served in, than he took occasion from a shoulder of mutton that lay before us, to cry up the plenty of England, which would be the happiest country in the world, provided we would live within ourselves. Upon which, he expatiated on the inconveniences of trade, that carried from us the commodities of our country, and made a parcel of upstarts as rich as men of the most ancient families of England. He then declared frankly, that he had always been against all treaties and alliances with foreigners: "Our wooden walls," says he, "are our security, and we may bid defiance to the whole world, especially if they should attack us when the militia is out." I ventured

to reply, that I had as great an opinion of the English fleet
as he had; but I could not see how they could be paid, and
manned, and fitted out, unless we encouraged trade and
navigation. He replied, with some vehemence, that he
would undertake to prove trade would be the ruin of the
English nation. I would fain have put him upon it; but
he contented himself with affirming it more eagerly, to
which he added two or three curses upon the London merchants, not forgetting the directors of the bank. After
supper he asked me if I was an admirer of punch; and
immediately called for a sneaker. I took this occasion to
insinuate the advantages of trade, by observing to him that
water was the only native of England that could be made
use of on this occasion: but that the lemons, the brandy,
the sugar, and the nutmeg, were all foreigners. This put
him into some confusion; but the landlord, who overheard
'me, brought him off, by affirming, that for constant use,
there was no liquor like a cup of English water, provided
it had malt enough in it. My squire laughed heartily at
the conceit, and made the landlord sit down with us. We
sat pretty late over our punch; and, amidst a great deal of
improving discourse, drank the healths of several persons
in the country, whom I had never heard of, that, they both
assured me, were the ablest statesmen in the nation; and
of some Londoners, whom they extolled to the skies for
their wit, and who, I knew, passed in town for silly fellows.
It being now midnight, and my friend perceiving by his
almanac that the moon was up, he called for his horses, and
took a sudden resolution to go to his house, which was at
three miles' distance from the town, after having bethought
himself that he never slept well out of his own bed. He
shook me very heartily by the hand at parting, and discovered a great air of satisfaction in his looks, that he had met
with an opportunity of showing his parts, and left me a
much wiser man than he found me.

Spectator No. 56.	*Marraton and Yaratilda.*

The Americans believe that all creatures have souls, not only men and women, but brutes, vegetables, nay, even the most inanimate things, as stocks and stones. They believe the same of all the works of art, as of knives, boats, looking-glasses: and that as any of these things perish, their souls go into another world, which is habited by the ghosts of men and women. For this reason they always place by the corpse of their dead friend a bow and arrows, that he may make use of the souls of them in the other world, as he did of their wooden bodies in this. How absurd soever such an opinion as this may appear, our European philosophers have maintained several notions altogether as improbable. Some of Plato's followers in particular, when they talk of the world of ideas, entertain us with substances and beings no less extravagant and chimerical. Many Aristotelians have likewise spoken as unintelligibly of their substantial forms. I shall only instance Albertus Magnus, who in his dissertation upon the loadstone, observing that fire will destroy its magnetic virtues, tells us that he took particular notice of one as it lay glowing amidst an heap of burning coals, and that he perceived a certain blue vapor to arise from it, which he believed might be the substantial form, that is, in our West Indian phrase, the soul of the loadstone.

There is a tradition among the Americans, that one of their countrymen descended in a vision to the great repository of souls, or, as we call it here, to the other world; and that upon his return he gave his friends a distinct account of everything he saw among those regions of the dead. A friend of mine, whom I have formerly mentioned, prevailed upon one of the interpreters of the Indian kings, to inquire of them if possible, what tradition they have among them of this matter; which, as well as he could learn by those many questions which he asked them at several times, was in substance as follows.

The visionary, whose name was Marraton, after having travelled for a long space under an hollow mountain, arrived at length on the confines of this world of spirits; but could not enter it by reason of a thick forest made up of bushes, brambles, and pointed thorns, so perplexed and interwoven with one another, that it was impossible to find a passage through it. Whilst he was looking about for some track or pathway that might be worn in any part of it, he saw an huge lion couched under the side of it, who kept his eye upon him in the same posture as he watches for his prey. The Indian immediately started back, whilst the lion rose with a spring, and leaped towards him. Being wholly destitute of all other weapons, he stooped down to take up an huge stone in his hand: but to his infinite surprise grasped nothing, and found the supposed stone to be only the apparition of one. If he was disappointed on this side, he was as much pleased on the other, when he found the lion, which had seized on his left shoulder, had no power to hurt him, and was only the ghost of that ravenous creature which it appeared to be. He no sooner got rid of his impotent enemy, but he marched up to the wood, and after having surveyed it for some time, endeavored to press into one part of it that was a little thinner than the rest; when again, to his great surprise, he found the bushes made no resistance, but that he walked through briers and brambles with the same ease as through the open air; and, in short, that the whole wood was nothing else but a wood of shades. He immediately concluded, that this huge thicket of thorns and brakes was designed as a kind of fence or quick-set hedge to the ghosts it enclosed; and that probably their soft substances might be torn by these subtle points and prickles, which were too weak to make any impressions in flesh and blood. With this thought he resolved to travel through this intricate wood; when by degrees he felt a gale of perfumes breathing upon him, that grew stronger and sweeter in proportion as he advanced. He had not proceeded much farther when he observed the thorns and briers to end, and give place to a thousand beautiful green trees covered with blossoms of the finest scents and colors, that formed a wilderness of sweets, and were a kind of lining to those ragged scenes which he had before passed through. As he was coming out of this delightful part of the wood, and entering upon the plains it enclosed, he saw several horsemen rushing by him, and a little while after heard the cry of a pack of dogs. He had not listened long before he saw the apparition of a milk-white steed, with a young man on the back of it, advancing upon full stretch after the souls of about an hundred beagles that were hunting down the ghost of an hare, which ran away before them with an unspeakable swiftness. As the man on the milk-white steed came by him, he looked upon him very attentively, and found him to be the young prince Nicaragua, who died about half a year before, and by reason of his great virtues was at that time lamented over all the western parts of America.

He had no sooner got out of the wood, but he was entertained with such a landscape of flowery plains, green meadows, running streams, sunny hills, and shady vales, as were not to be represented by his own expressions, nor, as he said, by the conceptions of others. This happy region was peopled with innumerable swarms of spirits, who applied themselves to exercises and diversions according as their fancies led them. Some of them were tossing the figure of a quoit; others were pitching the shadow of a bar; others were breaking the apparition of a horse; and multitudes employing themselves upon ingenious handicrafts with the souls of departed utensils; for that is the name which in the Indian language they give their tools when they are burnt or broken. As he travelled through this delightful scene, he was very often tempted to pluck the flowers that rose everywhere about him in the greatest variety and pro- fusion, having never seen several of them in his own country; but he quickly found, that though they were objects of his sight, they were not liable to his touch. He at length came to the side of a great river, and being a good fisherman himself, stood upon the banks of it some time to look upon an angler that had taken a great many shapes of fishes, which lay flouncing up and down by him.

I should have told my reader, that this Indian had been formerly married to one of the greatest beauties of his country, by whom he had several children. This couple were so famous for their love and constancy to one another, that the Indians to this day, when they give a married man joy of his wife, wish that they may live together like Mar- raton and Yaratilda. Marraton had not stood long by the fisherman when he saw the shadow of his beloved Yaratilda, who had for some time fixed her eye upon him, before he discovered her. Her arms were stretched out towards him, floods of tears ran down her eyes; her looks, her hands, her voice called him over to her; and at the same time seemed to tell him that the river was unpassable. Who can describe the passion made up of joy, sorrow, love, desire, astonish- ment, that rose in the Indian upon the sight of his dear Yaratilda? He could express it by nothing but his tears, which ran like a river down his cheeks as he looked upon her. He had not stood in this posture long, before he plunged into the stream that lay before him; and finding it to be nothing but the phantom of a river, stalked on the bottom of it till he arose on the other side. At his approach Yaratilda flew into his arms, whilst Marraton wished him- self disencumbered of that body which kept her from his embraces. After many questions and endearments on both sides, she conducted him to a bower which she had dressed with her own hands with all the ornaments that could be met with in those blooming regions. She had made it gay beyond imagination, and was every day adding something new to it. As Marratou stood astonished at the unspeakable beauty of her habitation, and ravished with the fragrancy that came from every part of it, Yaratilda told him that she was preparing this bower for his reception, as well knowing that his piety to his God, and his faithful dealing towards men, would certainly bring him to that happy place, whenever his life should be at an end. She then brought two of her children to him, who died some years before, and resided with her in the same delightful bower; advising him to breed up those others which were still with him in such a manner, that they might hereafter all of them meet together in this happy place.

The tradition tells us further, that he had afterwards a sight of those dismal habitations which are the portion of ill men after death; and mentions several molten seas of gold, in which were plunged the souls of barbarous Europeans, who put to the sword so many thousands of poor Indians for the sake of that precious metal: but having already touched upon the chief points of this tradition, and exceeded the measure of my paper, I shall not give any further account of it.

Spectator No. 159. *The vision of Mirzah.*

When I was at Grand Cairo I picked up several oriental manuscripts, which I have still by me. Among others I met with one entitled, the Visions of Mirzah, which I have read over with great pleasure. I intend to give it to the public when I have no other entertainment for them; and shall begin with the first vision, which I have translated word for word as follows:

"On the fifth day of the moon, which according to the

custom of my forefathers I always kept holy, after having washed myself, and offered up my morning devotions, I ascended the high hills of Bagdat, in order to pass the rest of the day in meditation and prayer. As I was here airing myself on the tops of the mountains, I fell into a profound contemplation on the vanity of human life; and passing from one thought to another, 'surely,' said I, 'man is but a shadow and life a dream.' Whilst I was thus musing, I cast my eyes towards the summit of a rock that was not far from me, where I discovered one in the habit of a shepherd, with a musical instrument in his hand. As I looked upon him he applied it to his lips, and began to play upon it. The sound of it was exceeding sweet, and wrought into a variety of tunes that were inexpressibly melodious, and altogether different from anything I had ever heard. They put me in mind of those heavenly airs that are played to the departed souls of good men upon their first arrival in paradise, to wear out the impressions of their last agonies, and qualify them for the pleasures of that happy place. My heart melted away in secret raptures.

"I had been often told that the rock before me was the haunt of a genius; and that several had been entertained with music who had passed by it, but never heard that the musician had before made himself visible. When he had raised my thoughts, by those transporting airs which he played, to taste the pleasures of his conversation, as I looked upon him like one astonished, he beckoned to me, and by the waving of his hand directed me to approach the place where he sat. I drew near with that reverence which is due to a superior nature; and as my heart was entirely subdued by the captivating strains I had heard, I fell down at his feet and wept. The genius smiled upon me with a look of compassion and affability that familiarized him to my imagination, and at once dispelled all the fears and apprehensions with which I approached him. He lifted me from the ground, and taking me by the hand, 'Mirzah,' said he, 'I have heard thee in thy soliloquies, follow me.'

"He then led me to the highest pinnacle of the rock, and placed me on the top of it. 'Cast thy eyes eastward,' said he, 'and tell me what thou seest.' 'I see,' said I, 'a huge valley and a prodigious tide of water rolling through it.' 'The valley that thou seest,' said he, 'is the vale of misery, and the tide of water that thou seest is part of the great tide of eternity.' 'What is the reason,' said I, 'that the tide I see rises out of a thick mist at one end, and again loses itself in a thick mist at the other?' 'What thou seest,' said he, 'is that portion of eternity which is called time, measured out by the sun, and reaching from the beginning of the world to its consummation. Examine now,' said he, 'this sea that is thus bounded with darkness at both ends, and tell me what thou discoverest in it.' 'I see a bridge,' said I, 'standing in the midst of the tide.' 'The bridge thou seest,' said he, 'is human life; consider it attentively.' Upon a more leisurely survey of it, I found that it consisted of threescore and ten entire arches, with several broken arches, which added to those that were entire, made up the number about an hundred. As I was counting the arches the genius told me that this bridge consisted at first of a thousand arches; but that a great flood swept away the rest, and left the bridge in the ruinous condition I now beheld it. 'But tell me, further,' said he, 'what thou discoverest on it.' 'I see multitudes of people passing over it,' said I, 'and a black cloud hanging on each end of it.' As I looked more attentively, I saw several of the passengers dropping through the bridge, into the great tide that flowed underneath it; and upon further examination, perceived there were innumerable trap-doors that lay concealed in the bridge, which the passengers no sooner trod upon, but they fell through them into the tide and immediately disappeared. These hidden pitfalls were set very thick at the entrance of the bridge, so that throngs of people no sooner broke through the cloud, but many of them fell into them. They grew thinner towards the middle, but multiplied and lay closer together towards the end of the arches that were entire.

"There were indeed some persons, but their number was very small, that continued a kind of hobbling march on the broken arches, but fell through one after another, being quite tired and spent with so long a walk.

"I passed some time in the contemplation of this wonderful structure, and the great variety of objects which it presented. My heart was filled with a deep melancholy to see several dropping unexpectedly in the midst of mirth and jollity, and catching at everything that stood by them to save themselves. Some were looking up towards the heavens in a thoughtful posture, and in the midst of a speculation stumbled and fell out of sight. Multitudes were very busy in the pursuit of baubles that glittered in their eyes and danced before them, but often when they thought themselves within the reach of them, their footing failed and down they sunk. In this confusion of objects, I observed some with scimitars in their hands, and others with lancets, who ran to and fro upon the bridge, thrusting several persons upon trap-doors which did not seem to lie in their way, and which they might have escaped, had they not been thus forced upon them.

"The genius seeing me indulge myself in this melancholy prospect, told me I had dwelt long enough upon it: 'take thine eyes off the bridge,' said he, 'and tell me if thou yet seest anything thou dost not comprehend.' Upon looking up, 'what mean,' said I, 'those great flights of birds that are perpetually hovering about the bridge, and settling upon it from time to time? I see vultures, harpies, ravens, cormorants, and among many other feathered creatures, several little winged boys, that perch in great numbers upon the middle arches.' 'These,' said the genius, 'are envy, avarice, superstition, despair, love, with the like cares and passions, that infest human life.'

"I here fetched a deep sigh; 'alas,' said I, 'man was made in vain! How is he given away to misery and mortality! tortured in life, and swallowed up in death!' The genius, being moved with compassion towards me, bid me quit so uncomfortable a prospect. 'Look no more,' said he, 'on man in the first stage of his existence, in his setting out for eternity; but cast thine eye on that thick mist into which the tide bears the several generations of mortals that fall into it.' I directed my sight as I was ordered, and (whether or no the good genius strengthened it with any supernatural force, or dissipated part of the mist that was before too thick for the eye to penetrate) I saw the valley opening at the farther end, and spreading forth into an immense ocean, that had a huge rock of adamant running through the midst of it, and dividing it into two equal parts. The clouds still rested on one half of it, insomuch that I could discover nothing in it: but the other appeared to me a vast ocean planted with innumerable islands, that were covered with fruits and flowers, and interwoven with a thousand little shining seas that ran among them. I could see persons dressed in glorious habits with garlands upon their heads, passing among the trees, lying down by the sides of the fountains, or resting on beds of flowers; and could hear a confused harmony of singing birds, falling waters, human voices, and musical instruments. Gladness grew in me upon the discovery of so delightful a scene. I wished for the wings of an eagle, that I might fly away to those happy seats; but the genius told me there was no passage to them, except through the gates of death that I saw opening every moment upon the bridge. 'The islands,' said he, 'that lie so fresh and green before thee, and with which the whole face of the ocean appears spotted as far as thou canst see, are more in number than the sands on the sea-shore; there are myriads of islands behind those which thou here discoverest, reaching farther than thine eye, or even thine imagination, can extend itself. These are the mansions of good men after death, who, according to the degree and kinds of virtue in which they excelled, are distributed among these several islands, which abound with pleasures of different kinds and degrees, suitable to the relishes and perfections of those who are settled in them: every island is a paradise, accommodated to its respective inhabitants. Are not these, O Mirzah, habitations worth contending for? Does life appear miserable, that gives thee opportunities of earning such a reward? Is death to be feared, that will convey thee to so happy an existence? Think not man was made in vain, who has such an eternity reserved for him.' I gazed with inexpressible pleasure on these happy islands. At length, said I, ' show me now, I beseech thee, the secrets that lie hid under those dark clouds which cover the ocean on the other side of the rock of adamant.' The genius making me no answer, I turned about to address myself to him a second time, but I found that he had left me. I then turned again to the vision which I had been so long contemplating, but, instead of the rolling tide, the arched bridge, and the happy islands, I saw nothing but the long hollow valley of Bagdat, with oxen, sheep, and camels grazing upon the sides of it."

Spectator No. 463. *The golden scales.*

I was lately entertaining myself with comparing Homer's balance, in which Jupiter is represented as weighing the fates of Hector and Achilles, with a passage of Virgil, wherein that deity is introduced as weighing the fates of Turnus and Æneas. I then considered how the same way of thinking prevailed in the eastern parts of the world, as in those noble passages of Scripture, where we are told, that the great king of Babylon, the day before his death, had been weighed in the balance, and been found wanting. In other places of the holy writings, the Almighty is described as weighing the mountains in scales, making the weight for the winds, knowing the balancings of the clouds; and, in others, as weighing the actions of men, and laying their calamities together in a balance. Milton, as I have observed in a former paper, had an eye to several of these foregoing instances, in that beautiful description wherein he represents the archangel and the evil spirit as addressing themselves for the combat, but parted by the balance which appeared in the heavens and weighed the consequences of such a battle.

These several amusing thoughts having taken possession of my mind some time before I went to sleep, and mingling themselves with my ordinary ideas, raised in my imagination a very odd kind of vision. I was, methought, replaced in my study, and seated in my elbow-chair, where I had indulged the foregoing speculations, with my lamp burning by me, as usual. Whilst I was here meditating on several subjects of morality, and considering the nature of many virtues and vices, as materials for those discourses with which I daily entertain the public; I saw, methought, a pair of golden scales hanging by a chain of the same metal over the table that stood before me; when, on a sudden, there were great heaps of weights thrown down on each side of them. I found upon examining these weights, they showed the value of everything that is in esteem among men. I made an essay of them by putting the weight of wisdom in one scale, and that of riches in another, upon which the latter, to show its comparative lightness, immediately "flew up and kick'd the beam."

But, before I proceed, I must inform my reader, that these weights did not exert their natural gravity, till they were laid in the golden balance, insomuch that I could not guess which was light or heavy, whilst I held them in my hand. This I found by several instances, for upon my laying a weight in one of the scales, which was inscribed by the word Eternity; though I threw in that of time, prosperity, affliction, wealth, poverty, interest, success, with many other weights, which in my hand seemed very ponderous, they were not able to stir the opposite balance, nor could they have prevailed, though assisted with the weight of the sun, the stars, and the earth.

Upon emptying the scales, I laid several titles and honors, with pomps, triumphs, and many weights of the like nature, in one of them, and seeing a little glittering weight lie by me, I threw it accidentally into the other scale, when, to my great surprise, it proved so exact a counterpoise, that it kept the balance in an equilibrium. This little glittering weight was inscribed upon the edges of it with the word Vanity. I found there were several other weights which were equally heavy, and exact counterpoises to one another; a few of them I tried, as avarice and poverty, riches and content, with some others.

There were likewise several weights that were of the same figure, and seemed to correspond with each other, but were entirely different when thrown into the scales, as religion and hypocrisy, pedantry and learning, wit and vivacity, superstition and devotion, gravity and wisdom, with many others.

I observed one particular weight lettered on both sides, and upon applying myself to the reading of it, I found on one side written, "In the dialect of men," and underneath it, "CALAMITIES"; on the other side was written, "In the language of the gods," and underneath, "BLESSINGS." I found the intrinsic value of this weight to be much greater than I imagined, for it overpowered health, wealth, goodfortune, and many other weights, which were much more ponderous in my hand than the other.

There is a saying among the Scotch, that "an ounce of mother wit is worth a pound of clergy"; I was sensible of the truth of this saying, when I saw the difference between the weight of natural parts and that of learning. The observation which I made upon these two weights opened to me a new field of discoveries, for notwithstanding the weight of natural parts was much heavier than that of learning, I observed that it weighed an hundred times heavier than it did before, when I put learning into the same scale with it. I made the same observation upon faith and morality; for notwithstanding the latter outweighed the former separately, it received a thousand times more additional weight from its conjunction with the former, than what it had by itself. This odd phenomenon showed itself in other particulars, as in wit and judgment, philosophy and religion, justice and humanity, zeal and charity, depth of sense and perspicuity of style, with innumerable other particulars, too long to be mentioned in this paper.

As a dream seldom fails of dashing seriousness with impertinence, mirth with gravity, methought I made several other experiments of a more ludicrous nature, by one of which I found that an English octavo was very often heavier than a French folio; and by another, that an old Greek or Latin author weighed down a whole library of moderns. Seeing one of my Spectators lying by me, I laid it into one of the scales, and flung a twopenny piece in the other. The reader will not inquire into the event, if he remembers the first trial which I have recorded in this paper. I afterwards threw both the sexes into the balance; but as it is not for my interest to disoblige either of them, I shall desire to be excused from telling the result of this experiment. Having an opportunity of this nature in my hands, I could not forbear throwing into one scale the principles of a Tory, and in the other those of a Whig; but as I have all along declared this to be a neutral paper, I shall likewise desire to be silent under this head also, though upon examining one of the weights, I saw the word TEKEL engraven on it in capital letters.

I made many other experiments, and though I have not room for them all in this day's speculation, I may perhaps reserve them for another. I shall only add, that upon my awaking I was sorry to find my golden scales vanished, but resolved for the future to learn this lesson from them, not to despise or value any things for their appearances, but to regulate my esteem and passions towards them according to their real and intrinsic value.

Tatler No. 254. *Frozen words.*

There are no books which I more delight in than in travels, especially those that describe remote countries, and give the writer an opportunity of showing his parts without incurring any danger of being examined or contradicted. Among all the authors of this kind, our renowned country-man, Sir John Mandeville, has distinguished himself by the copiousness of his invention and the greatness of his genius. The second to Sir John I take to have been Ferdinand Mendez Pinto, a person of infinite adventure and unbounded imagination. One reads the voyages of these two great wits with as much astonishment as the travels of Ulysses in Homer, or of the Red-Cross Knight in Spenser. All is enchanted ground, and fairy-land.

I have got into my hands, by great chance, several *manuscripts* of these two eminent authors, which are filled with greater wonders than any of those they have communicated to the public; and indeed, were they not so well attested, they would appear altogether improbable. I am apt to think the ingenious authors did not publish them with the rest of their works, lest they should pass for fictions and fables : a caution not unnecessary, when the reputation ol their veracity was not yet established in the world. But as this reason has now no farther weight, I shall make the public a present of these curious pieces, at such times as I shall find myself unprovided with other subjects.

The present paper I intend to fill with an extract from Sir John's Journal, in which that learned and worthy knight gives an account of the freezing and thawing of several short speeches, which he made in the territories of Nova Zembla. I need not inform my reader, that the author of Hudibras alludes to this strange quality in that cold climate, when, speaking of abstracted notions clothed in a visible shape, he adds that apt simile,

Like words congeal'd in northern air.

Not to keep my reader any longer in suspense, the rela- tion put into modern language, is as follows :

"We were separated by a storm in the latitude of *seventy- three*, insomuch, that only the ship which I was in, with a Dutch and French vessel, got safe into a creek of Nova Zembla. We landed in order to refit our vessels and store ourselves with provisions. The crew of each vessel made themselves a cabin of turf and wood, at some distance from each other, to fence themselves against the inclemencies of the weather, which was severe beyond imagination. We soon observed, that in talking to one another we lost sev- eral of our words, and could not hear one another at above two yards distance, and that too when we sat very near the fire. After much perplexity, I found that our words froze in the air, before they could reach the ears of the persons to whom they were spoken. I was soon confirmed in this conjecture, when, upon the increase of the cold, the whole company grew dumb, or rather deaf; for every man was sensible, as we afterwards found, that he spoke as well as ever; but the sounds no sooner took air than they were condensed and lost. It was now a miserable spectacle to see us nodding and gaping at one another, every man talking, and no man heard. One might observe a seaman that could hail a ship at a league's distance, beckoning with his hand, straining his lungs, and tearing his throat; but all in vain.

" We continued here three weeks in this dismal plight. At length, upon a turn of wind, the air about us began to thaw. Our cabin was immediately filled with a dry clattering sound, which I afterwards found to be the crackling of consonants that broke above our heads, and were often mixed with a gentle hissing, which I imputed to the letter *s*, that occurs so frequently in the English tongue. I soon after felt a breeze of whispers rushing by my ear; for those, being of a soft and gentle substance, immediately liquefied in the warm wind that blew across our cabin. These were soon followed by syllables and short words, and at length by entire sentences, that melted sooner or later, as they were more or less congealed; so that we now heard every thing that had been *spoken* during the whole three weeks that we had been *silent*, if I may use that expression. It was now very early in the morning, and yet, to my surprise, I heard somebody say, 'Sir John, it is midnight, and time for the ship's crew to go to-bed.' This I knew to be the pilot's voice; and, upon recollecting myself, I concluded that he had spoken these words to me some days before, though I could not hear them until the present thaw. My reader will easily imagine how the whole crew was amazed to hear every man talking, and see no man opening his mouth. In the midst of this great surprise we were all in, we heard a volley of oaths and curses, lasting for a long while, and uttered in a very hoarse voice, which I knew belonged to the boatswain, who was a very choleric fellow, and had taken his opportunity of cursing and swearing at me, when he thought I could not hear him; for I had several times given him the strappado on that account, as I did not fail to repeat it for these his pious soliloquies, when I got him on ship-board.

"I must not omit the names of several beauties in Wapping, which were heard every now and then, in the midst of a long sigh that accompanied them; as, 'Dear Kate!' 'Pretty Mrs. Peggy!' 'When shall I see my Sue again!' This betrayed several amours which had been concealed until that time, and furnished us with a great deal of mirth in our return to England.

"When this confusion of voices was pretty well over, though I was afraid to offer at speaking, as fearing I should not be heard, I proposed a visit to the Dutch cabin, which lay about a mile farther up in the country. My crew were extremely rejoiced to find they had again recovered their hearing; though every man uttered his voice with the same apprehensions that I had done.

"At about half-a-mile's distance from our cabin we heard the groanings of a bear, which at first startled us; but, upon inquiry, we were informed by some of our company, that he was dead, and now lay in salt, having been killed upon that very spot about a fortnight before, in the time of the frost. Not far from the same place, we were likewise entertained with some posthumous snarls and barkings of a fox.

"We at length arrived at the little Dutch settlement; and, upon entering the room, found it filled with sighs that smelt of brandy, and several other unsavory sounds, that were altogether inarticulate. My valet, who was an Irishman, fell into so great a rage at what he heard, that he drew his sword; but not knowing where to lay the blame, he put it up again. We were stunned with these confused noises, but did not hear a single word until about half-an-hour after; which I ascribed to the harsh and obdurate sounds of that language, which wanted more time than ours to melt and become audible.

"After having here met with a very hearty welcome, we

went to the cabin of the French, who, to make amends for
their three weeks' silence, were talking and disputing with
greater rapidity and confusion than I ever heard in an
assembly, even of that nation. Their language, as I found,
upon the first giving of the weather, fell asunder and dissolved. I was here convinced of an error, into which I had
before fallen; for I fancied, that for the freezing of the
sound, it was necessary for it to be wrapped up, and, as it
were, preserved in breath: but I found my mistake when I
heard the sound of a kit playing a minuet over our heads.
I asked the occasion of it; upon which one of the company
told me that it would play there above a week longer; 'for,'
says he, 'finding ourselves bereft of speech, we prevailed
upon one of the company, who had his musical instrument
about him, to play to us from morning to night; all which
time was employed in dancing in order to dissipate our
chagrin, *et tuer le temps.*"

Here Sir John gives very good philosophical reasons
why the kit could not be heard during the frost; but, as
they are something prolix, I pass them over in silence, and
shall only observe, that the honorable author seems, by his
quotations, to have been well versed in the ancient poets,
which perhaps raised his fancy above the ordinary pitch of
historians, and very much contributed to the embellishments of his writings.

Spectator No. 584. *Hilpa and Shalum.*

Hilpa was one of the 150 daughters of Zilpah, of the
race of Cohu, by whom some of the learned think is meant
Cain. She was exceedingly beautiful, and when she was
but a girl of three score and ten years of age, received the
addresses of several who made love to her. Among these
were two brothers, Harpath and Shalum. Harpath, being

the first-born, was master of that fruitful region which lies
at the foot of mount Tirzah, in the southern parts of China.
Shalum (which is to say, the planter, in the Chinese language) possessed all the neighboring hills, and that great
range of mountains which goes under the name of Tirzah.
Harpath was of a haughty contemptuous spirit; Shalum
was of a gentle disposition, beloved both by God and man.

It is said that, among the antediluvian women, the
daughters of Cohu had their minds wholly set upon riches;
for which reason the beautiful Hilpa preferred Harpath to
Shalum, because of his numerous flocks and herds that
covered all the low country which runs along the foot of
mount Tirzah, and is watered by several fountains and
streams breaking out of the sides of that mountain.

Harpath made so quick a dispatch of his courtship, that
he married Hilpa in the hundredth year of her age; and
being of an insolent temper, laughed to scorn his brother
Shalum for having pretended to the beautiful Hilpa, when
he was master of nothing but a long chain of rocks and
mountains. This so much provoked Shalum, that he is
said to have cursed his brother in the bitterness of his
heart, and to have prayed that one of his mountains might
fall upon his head if ever he came within the shadow of it.

From this time forward Harpath would never venture
out of the valleys, but came to an untimely end in the 250th
year of his age, being drowned in a river as he attempted
to cross it. This river is called to this very day, from his
name who perished in it, the river Harpath, and what is
very remarkable, issues out of one of those mountains which
Shalum wished might fall upon his brother, when he cursed
him in the bitterness of his heart.

Hilpa was in the 160th year of her age at the death of
her husband, having brought him but 50 children before he
was snatched away, as has been already related. Many of
the antediluvians made love to the young widow, though

no one was thought so likely to succeed in her affections as her first lover Shalum, who renewed his court to her about ten years after the death of Harpath; for it was not thought decent in those days that a widow should be seen by a man within ten years after the decease of her husband.

Shalum falling into a deep melancholy, and resolving to take away that objection which had been raised against him when he made his first addresses to Hilpa, began, immediately after her marriage with Harpath, to plant all that mountainous region which fell to his lot in the division of this country. He knew how to adapt every plant to its proper soil, and is thought to have inherited many traditional secrets of that art from the first man. This employment turned at length to his profit as well as his amusement; his mountains were in a few years shaded with young trees, that gradually shot up into groves, woods, forests, intermixed with walks and lawns and gardens; insomuch that the whole region, from a naked and desolate prospect, began now to look like a second paradise. The pleasantness of the place, and the agreeable disposition of Shalum, who was reckoned one of the mildest and wisest of all who lived before the flood, drew into it multitudes of people, who were perpetually employed in the sinking of wells, the digging of trenches, and the hollowing of trees, for the better distribution of water through every part of this spacious plantation.

The habitations of Shalum looked every year more beautiful in the eyes of Hilpa, who, after the space of 70 autumns, was wonderfully pleased with the distant prospect of Shalum's hills, which were then covered with innumerable tufts of trees, and gloomy scenes that gave a magnificence to the place, and converted it into one of the finest landscapes the eye of man could behold.

The Chinese record a letter which Shalum is said to have written to Hilpa in the eleventh year of her widowhood. I shall here translate it, without departing from that noble simplicity of sentiments and plainness of manners which appears in the original.

Shalum was at this time 180 years old, and Hilpa 170.

Shalum, master of mount Tirzah, to Hilpa, mistress of the valleys.
                    In the 788th year of the creation.

What have I not suffered, O thou daughter of Zilpah, since thou gavest thyself away in marriage to my rival? I grew weary of the light of the sun, and have been ever since covering myself with woods and forests. These threescore and ten years have I bewailed the loss of thee on the top of mount Tirzah, and soothed my melancholy among a thousand gloomy shades of my own raising. My dwellings are at present as the garden of God; every part of them is filled with fruits and flowers and fountains. The whole mountain is perfumed for thy reception. Come up into it, O my beloved. Remember, O thou daughter of Zilpah, that the age of man is but a thousand years; that beauty is but the admiration of a few centuries. It flourishes as a mountain oak, or as a cedar on the top of Tirzah, which in three or four hundred years will fade away, and never be thought of by posterity, unless a young wood springs from its roots. Think well on this, and remember thy neighbor in the mountains.

Having here inserted this letter, which I look upon as the only antediluvian *billet doux* now extant, I shall in my next paper give the answer to it, and the sequel of this story.

Spectator No. 585.   *The sequel of the story of Hilpa and Shalum.*

The letter inserted in my last had so good an effect upon Hilpa, that she answered it in less than a twelvemonth, after the following manner.

Hilpa, mistress of the valleys, to Shalum, master of mount Tirzah.
                    In the year 789 of the creation.

What have I to do with thee, O Shalum? Thou praisest Hilpa's beauty, but art thou not secretly enamored with the verdure of her meadows? Art thou not more affected with the prospect of her green

valleys, than thou wouldst be with the sight of her person ? The low
ings of my herds, and the bleatings of my flocks, make a pleasant echo
in thy mountains, and sound sweetly in thy ears. What though I am
delighted with the wavings of thy forests, and those breezes of perfumes which flow from the top of Tirzah : are these like the riches of
the valley ?

I know thee, O Shalum ; thou art more wise and happy than
any of the sons of men. Thy dwellings are among the cedars ; thou
searchest out the diversity of soils, thou understandest the influences
of the stars, and markest the change of seasons. Can a woman appear lovely in the eyes of such a one ? Disquiet me not, O Shalum ;
let me alone that I may enjoy those goodly possessions which are
fallen to my lot. Win me not by thy enticing words. May thy trees
increase and multiply ; mayest thou add wood to wood, and shade to
shade ; but tempt not Hilpa to destroy thy solitude, and make thy
retirement populous.

The Chinese say, that a little time afterwards she accepted
of a treat in one of the neighboring hills to which Shalum
had invited her. This treat lasted for two years, and is
said to have cost Shalum five hundred antelopes, two thousand ostriches, and a thousand tun of milk; but what most
of all recommended it was that variety of delicious fruits
and pot-herbs, in which no person then living could any way
equal Shalum.

He treated her in the bower which he had planted amidst
the wood of nightingales. This wood was made up of such
fruit trees and plants as are most agreeable to the several
kinds of singing birds; so that it had drawn into it all the
music of the country, and was filled from one end of the
year to the other with the most agreeable concert in season.

He showed her every day some beautiful and surprising
scene in this new region of wood-lands; and as by this
means he had all the opportunities he could wish for of
opening his mind to her, he succeeded so well, that upon
her departure she made him a kind of promise, and gave
him her word to return him a positive answer in less than
fifty years.

She had not been long among her own people in the valleys, when she received new overtures, and at the same time a most splendid visit from Mishpach, who was a mighty man of old, and had built a great city, which he called after his own name. Every house was made for at least a thousand years, nay, there were some that were leased out for three lives; so that the quantity of stone and timber consumed in this building is scarce to be imagined by those who live in the present age of the world. This great man entertained her with the voice of musical instruments which had been lately invented, and danced before her to the sound of the timbrel. He also presented her with several domestic utensils wrought in brass and iron, which had been newly found out for the conveniency of life. In the mean time Shalum grew very uneasy with himself, and was sorely displeased at Hilpa for the reception which she had given to Mishpach, insomuch that he never wrote to her or spoke of her during a whole revolution of Saturn; but finding that this intercourse went no further than a visit, he again renewed his addresses to her, who, during his long silence, is said very often to have cast a wishing eye upon mount Tirzah.

Her mind continued wavering about twenty years longer between Shalum and Mishpach; for though her inclinations favored the former, her interest pleaded very powerfully for the other. While her heart was in this unsettled condition, the following accident happened, which determined her choice. A high tower of wood that stood in the city of Mishpach, having caught fire by a flash of lightning, in a few days reduced the whole town to ashes. Mishpach resolved to rebuild the place whatever it should cost him: and having already destroyed all the timber of the country, he was forced to have recourse to Shalum, whose forests were now two hundred years old. He purchased these woods with so many herds of cattle and flocks of sheep, and with such a vast extent of fields and pastures, that Shalum was now grown more wealthy than Mishpach; and therefore appeared so charming in the eyes of Zilpah's daughter, that she no longer refused him in marriage. On the day in which he brought her up into the mountains he raised a most prodigious pile of cedar, and of every sweet-smelling wood, which reached above three hundred cubits in height: he also cast into the pile bundles of myrrh and sheaves of spikenard, enriching it with every spicy shrub, and making it fat with the gums of his plantations. This was the burnt-offering which Shalum offered in the day of his espousals: the smoke of it ascended up to heaven, and filled the whole country with incense and perfume.

Spectator No. 26. *Thoughts in Westminster Abbey.*

When I am in a serious humor, I very often walk by myself in Westminster Abbey; where the gloominess of the place, and the use to which it is applied, with the solemnity of the building, and the condition of the people who lie in it, are apt to fill the mind with a kind of melancholy, or rather thoughtfulness, that is not disagreeable. I yesterday passed a whole afternoon in the churchyard, the cloisters, and the church, amusing myself with the tombstones and inscriptions which I met with in those several regions of the dead. Most of them recorded nothing else of the buried person, but that he was born upon one day, and died upon another: the whole history of his life being comprehended in those two circumstances, that are common to all mankind. I could not but look upon these registers of existence, whether of brass or marble, as a kind of satire upon the departed persons; who had left no other memorial of them but that they were born and that they died. They put me in mind of several persons mentioned in the battles of heroic poems, who have sounding names given them, for no other reason but that they may be killed, and are celebrated for nothing but being knocked on the head. The life of these men is finely described in holy writ by "the path of an arrow," which is immediately closed up and lost.

Upon my going into the church, I entertained myself with the digging of a grave; and saw in every shovelful of it that was thrown up, the fragment of a bone or skull intermixed with a kind of fresh mouldering earth, that some time or other had a place in the composition of a human body. Upon this I began to consider with myself what innumerable multitudes of people lay confused together under the pavement of that ancient cathedral; how men and women, friends and énemies, priests and soldiers, monks and prebendaries, were crumbled amongst one another, and blended together in the same common mass; how beauty, strength, and youth, with old age, weakness, and deformity, lay undistinguished in the same promiscuous heap of matter.

After having thus surveyed this great magazine of mortality, as it were, in the lump, I examined it more particularly by the accounts which I found on several of the monuments which are raised in every quarter of that ancient fabric. Some of them were covered with such extravagant epitaphs, that, if it were possible for the dead person to be acquainted with them, he would blush at the praises which his friends have bestowed upon him. There are others so excessively modest, that they deliver the character of the person departed in Greek or Hebrew, and by that means are not understood once in a twelvemonth. In the poetical quarter, I found there were poets who had no monuments, and monuments which had no poets. I observed, indeed, that the present war had filled the church with many of these uninhabited monuments, which had been erected to the memory of persons whose bodies were perhaps buried in the plains of Blenheim, or in the bosom of the ocean.

I could not but be very much delighted with several

modern epitaphs, which are written with great elegance of expression and justness of thought, and therefore do honor to the living as well as to the dead. As a foreigner is very apt to conceive an idea of the ignorance or politeness of a nation, from the turn of their public monuments and inscriptions, they should be submitted to the perusal of men of learning and genius, before they are put in execution. Sir Cloudesly Shovel's monument has very often given me great offence: instead of the brave rough English Admiral, which was the distinguishing character of that plain gallant man, he is represented on his tomb by the figure of a beau, dressed in a long periwig, and reposing himself upon velvet cushions under a canopy of state. The inscription is answerable to the monument; for instead of celebrating the many remarkable actions he had performed in the service of his country, it acquaints us only with the manner of his death, in which it was impossible for him to reap any honor. The Dutch, whom we are apt to despise for want of genius, show an infinitely greater taste of antiquity and politeness in their buildings and works of this nature, than what we meet with in those of our own country. The monuments of their admirals, which have been erected at the public expense, represent them like themselves; and are adorned with rostral crowns and naval ornaments, with beautiful festoons of seaweed, shells, and coral.

But to return to our subject. I have left the repository of our English kings for the contemplation of another day, when I shall find my mind disposed for so serious an amusement. I know that entertainments of this nature are apt to raise dark and dismal thoughts in timorous minds and gloomy imaginations; but for my own part, though I am always serious, I do not know what it is to be melancholy; and can therefore take a view of nature in her deep and solemn scenes, with the same pleasure as in her most gay and delightful ones. By this means I can improve myself

with those objects which others consider with terror. When
I look upon the tombs of the great, every emotion of envy
dies in me ; when I read the epitaphs of the beautiful, every
inordinate desire goes out; when I meet with the grief of
parents upon a tomb-stone, my heart melts with compassion;
when I see the tomb of the parents themselves, I consider
the vanity of grieving for those whom we must quickly
follow ; when I see kings lying by those who deposed them,
when I consider rival wits placed side by side, or the holy
men that divided the world with their contests and disputes,
I reflect with sorrow and astonishment on the little competitions, factions, and debates of mankind. When I read
the several dates of the tombs, of some that died yesterday,
and some six hundred years ago, I consider that great day
when we shall all of us be contemporaries, and make our
appearance together.

Spectator No. 343.   *Transmigrations of Pugg the monkey.*

Will Honeycomb, who loves to show upon occasion all
the little learning he has picked up, told us yesterday at
the club, that he thought there might be a great deal said
for the transmigration of souls, and that the eastern parts
of the world believed in that doctrine to this day. "Sir
Paul Rycaut," says he, "gives us an account of several well-
disposed Mahometans that purchase the freedom of any little bird they see confined to a cage, and think they merit as
much by it, as we should do here by ransoming any of our
countrymen from their captivity at Algiers. You must
know," says Will, "the reason is, because they consider
every animal as a brother or sister in disguise, and think
themselves obliged to extend their charity to them, though
under such mean circumstances. They'll tell you," says
Will, "that the soul of a man, when he dies, immediately

passes into the body of another man, or of some brute, which he resembled in his humor, or his fortune, when he was one of us."

As I was wondering what this profusion of learning would end in, Will told us that Jack Freelove, who was a fellow of whim, made love to one of those ladies who throw away all their fondness on parrots, monkeys, and lap-dogs. Upon going to pay her a visit one morning, he wrote a pretty epistle upon this hint. "Jack," says he, "was conducted into the parlor, where he diverted himself for some time with her favorite monkey, which was chained in one of the windows; till at length, observing a pen and ink lie by him, he writ the following letter to his mistress, in the person of the monkey; and upon her not coming down so soon as he expected, left it in the window, and went about his business.

"The lady soon after coming into the parlor, and seeing her monkey look upon a paper with great earnestness, took it up, and to this day is in some doubt," says Will, "whether it was writ by Jack or the monkey."

MADAM,

Not having the gift of speech, I have a long time waited in vain for an opportunity of making myself known to you; and having at present the conveniences of pen, ink, and paper by me, I gladly take the occasion of giving you my history in writing, which I could not do by word of mouth. You must know, Madam, that about a thousand years ago I was an Indian Brachman, and versed in all those mysterious secrets which your European philosopher, called Pythagoras, is said to have learned from our fraternity. I had so ingratiated myself by my great skill in the occult sciences with a dæmon whom I used to converse with, that he promised to grant me whatever I should ask of him. I desired that my soul might never pass into the body of a brute creature; but this he told me was not in his power to grant me. I then begged, that into whatever creature I should chance to transmigrate, I might still retain my memory, and be conscious that I was the same person who lived in different animals. This he told me was within his power, and accordingly promised on the word of a dæmon that he would grant me what I desired. From that time forth I lived so very unblamably, that I was made president of a college of Brachmans, an office which I discharged with great integrity till the day of my death.

I was then shuffled into another human body, and acted my part so very well in it, that I became first minister to a prince who reigned upon the banks of the Ganges. I here lived in great honor for several years, but by degrees lost all the innocence of the Brachman, being obliged to rifle and oppress the people to enrich my sovereign: till at length I became so odious, that my master, to recover his credit with his subjects, shot me through the heart with an arrow, as I was one day addressing myself to him at the head of his army.

Upon my next remove I found myself in the woods, under the shape of a jackall, and soon listed myself in the service of a lion. I used to yelp near his den about midnight, which was his time of rousing and seeking after his prey. He always followed me in the rear, and when I had run down a fat buck, a wild goat, or an hare, after he had feasted very plentifully upon it himself, would now and then throw me a bone that was but half picked for my encouragement; but upon my being unsuccessful in two or three chases, he gave me such a confounded gripe in his anger, that I died of it.

In my next transmigration I was again set upon two legs, and became an Indian tax-gatherer; but having been guilty of great extravagances, and being married to an expensive jade of a wife, I ran so cursedly in debt, that I durst not show my head. I could no sooner step out of my house, but I was arrested by somebody or other that lay in wait for me. As I ventured abroad one night in the dusk of the evening, I was taken up and hurried into a dungeon, where I died a few months after.

My soul then entered into a flying-fish, and in that state led a most melancholy life for the space of six years. Several fishes of prey pursued me when I was in the water, and if I betook myself to my wings, it was ten to one but I had a flock of birds aiming at me. As I was one day flying amidst a fleet of English ships, I observed a huge sea-gull whetting his bill and hovering just over my head: upon my dipping into the water to avoid him, I fell into the mouth of a monstrous shark, that swallowed me down in an instant.

I was some years afterwards, to my great surprise, an eminent banker in Lombard-street; and remembering how I had formerly suffered for want of money, became so very sordid and avaricious, that the whole town cried shame of me. I was a miserable little old fellow to look upon, for I had in a manner starved myself, and was nothing but skin and bone when I died.

I was afterwards very much troubled and amazed to find myself dwindled into an emmet. I was heartily concerned to make so insignificant a figure, and did not know but some time or other I might be reduced to a mite if I did not mend my manners. I therefore applied myself with greater diligence to the offices that were allotted me, and was generally looked upon as the notablest ant in the whole molehill. I was at last picked up, as I was groaning under a burden, by an unlucky cock-sparrow that lived in our neighborhood, and had before made great depredations upon our commonwealth.

I then bettered my condition a little, and lived a whole summer in the shape of a bee; but being tired with the painful and penurious life I had undergone in my two last transmigrations, I fell into the other extreme, and turned drone. As I one day headed a party to plunder a hive, we were received so warmly by the swarm which defended it, that we were most of us left dead upon the spot.

I might tell you of many other transmigrations I went through; how I was a town-rake, and afterwards did penance in a bay horse for ten years; as also how I was a tailor, a shrimp, and a tom-tit. In the last of these my shapes I was shot in the Christmas holidays by a young jack-a-napes, who would needs try his new gun upon me.

But I shall pass over these and several other stages of life, to remind you of the young beau who made love to you about six years since. You may remember, Madam, how he masked, and danced, and sung, and played a thousand tricks to gain you; and how he was at last carried off by a cold that he got under your window one night in a serenade. I was that unfortunate young fellow, whom you were then so cruel to. Not long after my shifting that unlucky body, I found myself upon a hill in Æthiopia, where I lived in my present grotesque shape, till I was caught by a servant of the English factory and sent over into Great Britain: I need not inform you how I came into your hands. You see, Madam, this is not the first time you have had me in a chain: I am, however, very happy in this my captivity, as you often bestow on me those kindnesses which I would have given the world for, when I was a man. I hope this discovery of my person will not tend to my disadvantage, but that you will still continue your accustomed favors to

Your most devoted humble servant,

PUGG.

P.S. — I would advise your little shock-dog to keep out of my way: for, as I look upon him to be the most formidable of my rivals, I may chance one time or other to give him such a snap as he won't like.

Spectator No. 452.   *Eagerness for news ridiculed.*

There is no humor in my countrymen, which I am more inclined to wonder at, than their general thirst after news. There are about half a dozen ingenious men, who live very plentifully upon this curiosity of their fellow-subjects. They all of them receive the same advices from abroad, and very often in the same words; but their way of cooking it is so different, that there is no citizen, who has an eye to the public good, that can leave the coffee-house with peace of mind, before he has given every one of them a reading. These several dishes of news are so very agreeable to the palate of my countrymen, that they are not only pleased with them when they are served up hot, but when they are again set cold before them by those penetrating politicians, who oblige the public with their reflections and observations upon every piece of intelligence that is sent us from abroad. The text is given us by one set of writers, and the comment by another.

But notwithstanding we have the same tale told us in so many different papers, and if occasion requires, in so many articles of the same paper; notwithstanding a scarcity of foreign posts we hear the same story repeated, by different advices from Paris, Brussels, the Hague, and from every great town in Europe; notwithstanding the multitude of annotations, explanations, reflections, and various readings which it passes through, our time lies heavy on our hands till the arrival of a fresh mail: we long to receive further particulars, to hear what will be the next step, or what will be the consequence of that which has been lately taken.   A westerly wind keeps the whole town in suspense, and puts a stop to conversation.

This general curiosity has been raised and inflamed by our late wars, and, if rightly directed, might be of good use to a person who has such a thirst awakened in him. Why should not a man who takes delight in reading everything that is new, apply himself to history, travels, and other writings of the same kind, where he will find perpetual fuel for his curiosity, and meet with much more pleasure and improvement, than in these papers of the week? An honest tradesman, who languishes a whole summer in expectation of a battle, and perhaps is balked at last, may here meet with half a dozen in a day. He may read the news of a whole campaign in less time than he now bestows upon the products of any single post. Fights, conquests, and revolutions, lie thick together. The reader's curiosity is raised and satisfied every moment, and his passions disappointed or gratified, without being detained in a state of uncertainty from day to day, or lying at the mercy of sea and wind. In short, the mind is not here kept in a perpetual gape after knowledge, nor punished with that eternal thirst which is the portion of all our modern newsmongers and coffee-house politicians.

All matters of fact, which a man did not know before, are news to him; and I do not see how any haberdasher in Cheapside is more concerned in the present quarrel of the Cantons, than he was in that of the League. At least, I believe every one will allow me, it is of more importance to an Englishman to know the history of his ancestors, than that of his contemporaries who live upon the banks of the Danube or the Borysthenes. As for those who are of another mind, I shall recommend to them the following letter, from a projector, who is willing to turn a penny by this remarkable curiosity of his countrymen.

Mr. Spectator,

You must have observed, that men who frequent coffee-houses, and delight in news, are pleased with everything that is matter of fact, so it be what they have not heard before. A victory, or a defeat, are equally agreeable to them. The shutting of a cardinal's mouth pleases them one post, and the opening of it another. They are glad to hear the French court is removed to Marli, and are afterwards as much delighted with its return to Versailles. They read the advertisements with the same curiosity as the articles of public news; and are as pleased to hear of a piebald horse that is strayed out of a field near Islington, as of a whole troop that has been engaged in any foreign adventure. In short, they have a relish for everything that is news, let the matter of it be what it will; or to speak more properly, they are men of a voracious appetite, but no taste. Now, sir, since the great fountain of news, I mean the war, is very near being dried up; and since these gentlemen have contracted such an inextinguishable thirst after it; I have taken their case and my own into consideration, and have thought of a project which may turn to the advantage of us both. I have thoughts of publishing a daily paper, which shall comprehend in it all the most remarkable occurrences in every little town, village, and hamlet, that lies within ten miles of London, or in other words, within the verge of the penny-post. I have pitched upon this scene of intelligence for two reasons; first, because the carriage of letters will be very cheap; and secondly, because I may receive them every day. By this means my readers will have their news fresh and fresh, and many worthy citizens, who cannot sleep with any satisfaction at present, for want of being informed how the world goes, may go to bed contentedly, it being my design to put out my paper every night at nine-a-clock precisely. I have already established correspondences in these several places, and received very good intelligence.

By my last advices from Knightsbridge I hear that a horse was clapped into the pound on the third instant, and that he was not released when the letters came away.

We are informed from Pankridge, that a dozen weddings were lately celebrated in the mother-church of that place, but are referred to their next letters for the names of the parties concerned.

Letters from Brompton advise, that the widow Blight had received several visits from John Mildew, which affords great matter of speculation in those parts.

By a fisherman which lately touched at Hammersmith, there is advice from Putney, that a certain person well known in that place, is

like to lose his election for churchwarden ; but this being boat-news,
we cannot give entire credit to it.

They advise from Fulham, that things remained there in the same
state they were. They had intelligence, just as the letters came away,
of a tub of excellent ale just set a-broach at Parson's Green ; but this
wanted confirmation.

I have here, sir, given you a specimen of the news with which I
intend to entertain the town, and which, when drawn up regularly in
the form of a newspaper, will, I doubt not, be very acceptable to many
of those public-spirited readers, who take more delight in acquainting
themselves with other people's business than their own. I hope a
paper of this kind, which lets us know what is done near home, may
be more useful to us than those which are filled with advices from Zug
and Bender, and make some amends for that dearth of intelligence,
which we justly apprehend from times of peace. If I find that you
receive this project favorably, I will shortly trouble you with one
or two more ; and in the mean time am, most worthy sir, with all
due respect,

Your most obedient and most humble servant.

Spectator No. 7. *Omens.*

Going yesterday to dine with an old acquaintance, I had
the misfortune to find his whole family very much dejected.
Upon asking him the occasion of it, he told me that his
wife had dreamt a strange dream the night before, which
they were afraid portended some misfortune to themselves or
to their children. At her coming into the room, I observed
a settled melancholy in her countenance, which I should
have been troubled for, had I not heard from whence it
proceeded. We were no sooner sat down, but, after having
looked upon me a little while, "My dear," says she, turning
to her husband, "you may now see the stranger that was in
the candle last night." Soon after this, as they began to
talk of family affairs, a little boy at the lower end of the
table told her, that he was to go into join-hand on Thursday.
"Thursday !" says she. "No, child, if it please God, you

shall not begin upon Childermas-day: tell your writing master that Friday will be soon enough." I was reflecting with myself on the oddness of her fancy, and wondering that anybody would establish it as a rule to lose a day in every week. In the midst of these my musings, she desired me to reach her a little salt upon the point of my knife, which I did in such a trepidation and hurry of obedience, that I let it drop by the way; at which she immediately startled, and said it fell towards her. Upon this I looked very blank; and observing the concern of the whole table, began to consider myself, with some confusion, as a person that had brought a disaster upon the family. The lady, however, recovering herself, after a little space, said to her husband, with a sigh, "My dear, misfortunes never come single." My friend, I found, acted but an under part at his table, and being a man of more good-nature than understanding, thinks himself obliged to fall in with all the passions and humors of his yoke-fellow. "Do not you remember, child," says she, "that the pigeon-house fell the very afternoon that our careless wench spilt the salt upon the table?" "Yes," says he, "my dear; and the next post brought us an account of the battle of Almanza." The reader may guess at the figure I made, after having done all this mischief. I despatched my dinner as soon as I could, with my usual taciturnity; when, to my utter confusion, the lady seeing me quitting my knife and fork, and laying them across one another upon my plate, desired me that I would humor her so far as to take them out of that figure, and place them side by side. What the absurdity was which I had committed I did not know, but I suppose there was some traditionary superstition in it; and therefore in obedience to the lady of the house, I disposed of my knife and fork in two parallel lines, which is the figure I shall always lay them in for the future, though I do not know any reason for it.

It is not difficult for a man to see that a person has conceived an aversion to him. For my own part, I quickly found, by the lady's looks, that she regarded me as a very odd kind of fellow, with an unfortunate aspect. For which reason I took my leave immediately after dinner, and withdrew to my own lodgings. Upon my return home, I fell into a profound contemplation of the evils that attend these superstitious follies of mankind; how they subject us to imaginary afflictions, and additional sorrows, that do not properly come within our lot. As if the natural calamities of life were not sufficient for it, we turn the most indifferent circumstances into misfortunes, and suffer as much from trifling accidents as from real evils. I have known the shooting of a star spoil a night's rest; and have seen a man in love grow pale, and lose his appetite, upon the plucking of a merry-thought. A screech-owl at midnight has alarmed a family more than a band of robbers: nay, the voice of a cricket hath struck more terror than the roaring of a lion. There is nothing so inconsiderable, which may not appear dreadful to an imagination that is filled with omens and prognostics. A rusty nail, or a crooked pin, shoot up into prodigies.

For my own part, I should be very much troubled were I endowed with this divining quality, though it should inform me truly of everything that can befall me. I would not anticipate the relish of any happiness, nor feel the weight of any misery, before it actually arrives.

I know but one way of fortifying my soul against these gloomy presages and terrors of mind, and that is, by securing to myself the friendship and protection of that Being who disposes of events, and governs futurity. He sees at one view the whole thread of my existence; not only that part of it which I have already passed through, but that which runs forward into all the depths of eternity. When I lay me down to sleep, I recommend myself to his care;

when I awake, I give myself up to his direction. Amidst all the evils that threaten me, I will look up to him for help, and question not but he will either avert them, or turn them to my advantage. Though I know neither the time nor the manner of the death I am to die, I am not at all solicitous about it; because I am sure that he knows them both, and that he will not fail to comfort and support me under them.

Spectator No. 12. *Ghost-stories.*

At my coming to London, it was some time before I could settle myself in a house to my liking. I was forced to quit my first lodgings, by reason of an officious landlady, that would be asking me every morning how I had slept. I then fell into an honest family, and lived very happily for above a week; when my landlord, who was a jolly good-natured man, took it into his head that I wanted company, and therefore would frequently come into my chamber to keep me from being alone. This I bore for two or three days; but telling me one day that he was afraid I was melancholy, I thought it was high time for me to be gone, and accordingly took new lodgings that very night. About a week after, I found my jolly landlord, who, as I said before, was an honest hearty man, had put me into an advertisement of the Daily Courant, in the following words, "Whereas a melancholy man left his lodgings on Thursday last in the afternoon, and was afterwards seen going towards Islington; if any one can give notice of him to R. B., fishmonger in the Strand, he shall be very well rewarded for his pains." As I am the best man in the world to keep my own counsel, and my landlord the fishmonger not knowing my name, this accident of my life was never discovered to this very day.

I am now settled with a widow-woman, who has a great many children, and complies with my humor in everything.

I do not remember that we have exchanged a word together these five years; my coffee comes into my chamber every morning without asking for it; if I want fire I point to my chimney, if water to my basin: upon which my landlady nods, as much as to say she takes my meaning, and immediately obeys my signals. She has likewise modelled her family so well, that when her little boy offers to pull me by the coat, or prattle in my face, his eldest sister immediately calls him off, and bids him not disturb the gentleman. At my first entering into the family, I was troubled with the civility of their rising up to me every time I came into the room; but my landlady observing, that upon these occasions I always cried pish ! and went out again, has forbidden any such ceremony to be used in the house; so that at present I walk into the kitchen or parlor, without being taken notice of, or giving any interruption to the business or discourse of the family. The maid will ask her mistress, though I am by, whether the gentleman is ready to go to dinner, as the mistress, who is indeed an excellent housewife, scolds at the servants as heartily before my face as behind my back. In short, I move up and down the house, and enter into all companies with the same liberty as a cat or any other domestic animal, and am as little suspected of telling anything that I hear or see.

I remember last winter there were several young girls of the neighborhood sitting about the fire with my landlady's daughters, and telling stories of spirits and apparitions. Upon my opening the door the young women broke off their discourse, but my landlady's daughters telling them that it was nobody but the gentleman, for that is the name which I go by in the neighborhood as well as in the family, they went on without minding me. I seated myself by the candle that stood on a table at one end of the room; and pretending to read a book that I took out of my pocket, heard several dreadful stories of ghosts as pale as ashes, that had stood at the feet of a bed, or walked over a church-yard by moon-light, and of others that had been conjured into the Red sea, for disturbing people's rest, and drawing their curtains at midnight, with many other old women's fables of the like nature. As one spirit raised another, I observed that at the end of every story the whole company closed their ranks, and crowded about the fire: I took notice, in particular, of a little boy, who was so attentive to every story, that I am mistaken if he ventures to go to bed by himself this twelvemonth. Indeed they talked so long, that the imaginations of the whole assembly were manifestly crazed, and, I am sure, will be the worse for it as long as they live. I heard one of the girls, that had looked upon me over her shoulder, asking the company how long I had been in the room, and whether I did not look paler than I used to do. This put me under some apprehensions, that I should be forced to explain myself if I did not retire; for which reason I took the candle in my hand, and went up into my chamber, not without wondering at this unaccountable weakness in reasonable creatures, that they should love to astonish and terrify one another. Were I a father, I should take a particular care to preserve my children from these little horrors of imagination, which they are apt to contract when they are young, and are not able to shake off when they are in years. I have known a soldier that has entered a breach, affrighted at his own shadow; and look pale upon a little scratching at his door, who, the day before, had marched up against a battery of cannon. There are instances of persons, who have been terrified even to distraction at the figure of a tree, or the shaking of a bull-rush. The truth of it is, I look upon a sound imagination as the greatest blessing of life, next to a clear judgment and a good conscience. In the mean time, since there are very few whose minds are not more or less subject to these dreadful thoughts and appre-

dictates of reason and religion, *to pull the old woman out of our hearts*, as Persius expresses it, and extinguish those impertinent notions which we imbibed at a time that we were not able to judge of their absurdity. Or, if we believe, as many wise and good men have done, that there are such phantoms and apparitions as those I have been speaking of, let us endeavor to establish to ourselves an interest in Him who holds the reins of the whole creation in his hand, and moderates them after such a manner, that it is impossible for one being to break loose upon another, without his knowledge and permission.

Spectator No. 23. *Against the authors of libels and lampoons.*

There is nothing that more betrays a base ungenerous spirit, than the giving of secret stabs to a man's reputation. Lampoons and satires, that are written with wit and spirit, are like poisoned darts, which not only inflict a wound, but make it incurable. For this reason I am very much troubled when I see the talents of humor and ridicule in the possession of an ill-natured man. There cannot be a greater gratification to a barbarous and inhuman wit, than to stir up sorrow in the heart of a private person, to raise uneasiness among near relations, and to expose whole families to derision, at the same time that he remains unseen and undiscovered. If, besides the accomplishments of being witty and ill-natured, a man is vicious into the bargain, he is one of the most mischievous creatures that can enter into a civil society. His satire will then chiefly fall upon those who ought to be the most exempt from it. Virtue, merit, and everything that is praiseworthy, will be made the subject of ridicule and buffoonery. It is impossible to enumerate the evils which arise from these arrows that fly in the dark, and I know no other excuse that is or can be made for them, than that the wounds they give are only imaginary, and produce nothing more than a secret shame or sorrow in the mind of the suffering person. It must indeed be confessed, that a lampoon or a satire do not carry in them robbery or murder; but at the same time, how many are there that would not rather lose a considerable sum of money, or even life itself, than be set up as a mark of infamy and derision? and in this case a man should consider that an injury is not to be measured by the notions of him that gives, but of him that receives it.

Those who can put the best countenance upon the outrages of this nature which are offered them, are not without their secret anguish. I have often observed a passage in Socrates's behavior at his death, in a light wherein none of the critics have considered it. That excellent man, entertaining his friends, a little before he drank the bowl of poison, with a discourse on the immortality of the soul, at his entering upon it, says, that he does not believe any the most comic genius can censure him for talking upon such a subject at such a time. This passage, I think, evidently glances upon Aristophanes, who writ a comedy on purpose to ridicule the discourses of that divine philosopher. It has been observed by many writers, that Socrates was so little moved at this piece of buffoonery, that he was several times present at its being acted upon the stage, and never expressed the least resentment at it. But, with submission, I think the remark I have here made shows us, that this unworthy treatment made an impression upon his mind, though he had been too wise to discover it.

When Julius Cæsar was lampooned by Catullus, he invited him to a supper, and treated him with such a generous civility, that he made the poet his friend ever after. Cardinal Mazarin gave the same kind of treatment to the learned Quillet, who had reflected upon his Eminence in a famous Latin poem. The Cardinal sent for him, and after some kind expostulations upon what he had written, assured him of his esteem, and dismissed him with a promise of the next good abbey that should fall, which he accordingly conferred upon him in a few months after. This had so good an effect upon the author, that he dedicated the second edition of his book to the Cardinal, after having expunged the passages which had given him offence.

Sextus Quintus was not of so generous and forgiving a temper. Upon his being made pope, the statue of Pasquin was one night dressed in a very dirty shirt, with an excuse written under it, that he was forced to wear foul linen, because his laundress was made a princess. This was a reflection upon the pope's sister, who, before the promotion of her brother, was in those mean circumstances that Pasquin represented her. As this pasquinade made a great noise in Rome, the pope offered a considerable sum of money to any person that should discover the author of it. The author relying upon his Holiness's generosity, as also on some private overtures which he had received from him, made the discovery himself; upon which the pope gave him the reward he had promised, but at the same time, to disable the satirist for the future, ordered his tongue to be cut out, and both his hands to be chopped off. Aretine is too trite an instance. Every one knows that all the kings in Europe were his tributaries. Nay, there is a letter of his extant, in which he makes his boasts that he had laid the Sophy of Persia under contribution.

Though, in the various examples which I have here drawn together, these several great men behaved themselves very differently towards the wits of the age who had reproached them, they all of them plainly showed that they were very sensible of their reproaches, and consequently that they received them as very great injuries. For my own part, I would never trust a man that I thought was capable of giv-ing these secret wounds; and cannot but think that he would hurt the person, whose reputation he thus assaults, in his body or in his fortune, could he do it with the same security. There is indeed something very barbarous and inhuman in the ordinary scribblers of lampoons. An innocent young lady shall be exposed, for an unhappy feature; a father of a family turned to ridicule, for some domestic calamity; a wife be made uneasy all her life, for a misinterpreted word or action; nay, a good, a temperate, and a just man, shall be put out of countenance by the representation of those qualities that should do him honor. So pernicious a thing is wit when it is not tempered with virtue and humanity.

I have indeed heard of heedless, inconsiderate writers, that without any malice have sacrificed the reputation of their friends and acquaintance, to a certain levity of temper, and a silly ambition of distinguishing themselves by a spirit of raillery and satire: as if it were not infinitely more honorable to be a good-natured man, than a wit. Where there is this little petulant humor in an author, he is often very mischievous without designing to be so. For which reason I always lay it down as a rule, that an indiscreet man is more hurtful than an ill-natured one; for as the latter will only attack his enemies, and those he wishes ill to; the other injures indifferently both friends and foes. I cannot forbear, on this occasion, transcribing a fable out of Sir Roger L'Estrange, which accidentally lies before me. 'A company of waggish boys were watching of frogs at the side of a pond, and still as any of them put up their heads, they'd be pelting them down again with stones. Children, says one of the frogs, you never consider, that though this may be play to you, it is death to us.' As this week is in a manner set apart and dedicated to serious thoughts, I shall indulge myself in such speculations as may not be altogether unsuitable to the season; and in the mean time, as the set-ling in ourselves a charitable frame of mind is a work very proper for the time, I have in this paper endeavored to expose that particular breach of charity which has been generally overlooked by divines, because they are but few who can be guilty of it.

Spectator No. 494. *A cheerful piety recommended.*

About an age ago it was the fashion in England, for every one that would be thought religious, to throw as much sanctity as possible into his face, and in particular to abstain from all appearances of mirth and pleasantry, which were looked upon as the marks of a carnal mind. The saint was of a sorrowful countenance, and generally eaten up with spleen and melancholy. A gentleman, who was lately a great ornament to the learned world, has diverted me more than once with an account of the reception which he met with from a very famous Independent minister, who was head of a college in those times. This gentleman was then a young adventurer in the republic of letters, and just fitted out for the university with a good cargo of Latin and Greek. His friends were resolved that he should try his fortune at an election which was drawing near in the college, of which the Independent minister whom I have before mentioned was governor. The youth, according to custom, waited on him in order to be examined. He was received at the door by a servant, who was one of that gloomy generation that were then in fashion. He conducted him, with great silence and seriousness, to a long gallery which was darkened at noon-day, and had only a single candle burning in it. After a short stay in this melancholy apartment, he was led into a chamber hung with black, where he entertained himself for some time by the glimmering of a taper, till at length the head of the college came out to him from an inner room, with half a dozen nightcaps upon his head, and religious horror in his countenance. The young man trembled; but his fears increased, when, instead of being asked what progress he had made in learning, he was examined how he abounded in grace. His Latin and Greek stood him in little stead; he was to give an account only of the state of his soul; whether he was of the number of the elect; what was the occasion of his conversion; upon what day of the month and hour of the day it happened; how it was carried on, and when completed. The whole examination was summed up with one short question, namely, *Whether he was prepared for death?* The boy, who had been bred up by honest parents, was frighted out of his wits at the solemnity of the proceeding, and by the last dreadful interrogatory; so that, upon making his escape out of the house of mourning, he could never be brought a second time to the examination, as not being able to go through the terrors of it.

Notwithstanding this general form and outside of religion is pretty well worn out among us, there are many persons, who, by a natural uncheerfulness of heart, mistaken notions of piety, or weakness of understanding, love to indulge this uncomfortable way of life, and give up themselves a prey to grief and melancholy. Superstitious fears and groundless scruples cut them off from the pleasures of conversation, and all those social entertainments which are not only innocent, but laudable: as if mirth was made for reprobates, and cheerfulness of heart denied those who are the only persons that have a proper title to it.

Sombrius is one of these sons of sorrow. He thinks himself obliged in duty to be sad and disconsolate. He looks on a sudden fit of laughter as a breach of his baptismal vow. An innocent jest startles him like blasphemy. Tell him of one who is advanced to a title of honor, he lifts up his hands and eyes: describe a public ceremony, he shakes his head: show him a gay equipage, he blesses himself. All the little ornaments of life are pomps and vanities. Mirth is wanton, and wit profane. He is scandalized at youth for being lively, and at childhood for being playful. He sits at a christening, or a marriage feast, as at a funeral; sighs at the conclusion of a merry story, and grows devout when the rest of the company grow pleasant. After all, Sombrius is a religious man, and would have behaved himself very properly, had he lived when Christianity was under a general persecution.

I would by no means presume to tax such characters with hypocrisy, as is done too frequently; that being a vice which I think none but he, who knows the secrets of men's hearts, should pretend to discover in another, where the proofs of it do not amount to a demonstration. On the contrary, as there are many excellent persons who are weighed down by this habitual sorrow of heart, they rather deserve our compassion than our reproaches. I think, however, they would do well to consider whether such a behavior does not deter men from a religious life, by representing it as an unsociable state, that extinguishes all joy and gladness, darkens the face of nature, and destroys the relish of being itself.

I have, in former papers, shown how great a tendency there is to cheerfulness in religion, and how such a frame of mind is not only the most lovely, but the most commendable in a virtuous person. In short, those who represent religion in so unamiable a light, are like the spies sent by Moses to make a discovery of the land of Promise, when by their reports they discouraged the people from entering upon it. Those who show us the joy, the cheerfulness, the good-humor, that naturally spring up in this happy state, are like the spies bringing along with them the clusters of grapes and delicious fruits, that might invite their companions into the pleasant country which produced them.

An eminent Pagan writer has made a discourse, to show that the atheist, who denies a God, does him less dishonor than the man who owns his being, but at the same time believes him to be cruel, hard to please, and terrible to human nature. For my own part, says he, I would rather it should be said of me, that there never was any such man as Plutarch, than that Plutarch was ill-natured, capricious, or inhuman.

If we may believe our logicians, man is distinguished from all other creatures by the faculty of laughter. He has a heart capable of mirth, and naturally disposed to it. It is not the business of virtue to extirpate the affections of the mind, but to regulate them. It may moderate and restrain, but was not designed to banish gladness from the heart of man. Religion contracts the circle of our pleasures, but leaves it wide enough for her votaries to expatiate in. The contemplation of the divine Being, and the exercise of virtue, are in their own nature so far from excluding all gladness of heart, that they are perpetual sources of it. In a word, the true spirit of religion cheers as well as composes the soul; it banishes indeed all levity of behavior, all vicious and dissolute mirth, but in exchange fills the mind with a perpetual serenity, uninterrupted cheerfulness, and an habitual inclination to please others, as well as to be pleased in itself.

Spectator No. 558. *The folly of discontent with one's own lot.*

It is a celebrated thought of Socrates, that if all the misfortunes of mankind were cast into a public stock, in order to be equally distributed among the whole species, those who now think themselves the most unhappy, would prefer the share they are already possessed of before that which would fall to them by such a division. Horace·has carried this thought a great deal farther in his first satire, which implies that the hardships and misfortunes we lie under are more easy to us than those of any other person would be, in case we could change conditions with him.

As I was ruminating on these two remarks, and seated in my elbow chair, I insensibly fell asleep; when, on a sudden, methought there was a proclamation made by Jupiter, that every mortal should bring in his griefs and calamities, and throw them together in a heap. There was a large plain appointed for this purpose. I took my stand in the centre of it, and saw with a great deal of pleasure the whole human species marching one after another, and throwing down their several loads, which immediately grew up into a prodigious mountain, that seemed to rise above the clouds.

There was a certain lady of a thin airy shape, who was very active in this solemnity. She carried a magnifying glass in one of her hands, and was clothed in a loose flowing robe, embroidered with several figures of fiends and spectres, that discovered themselves in a thousand chimerical shapes as her garment hovered in the wind. There was something wild and distracted in her looks. Her name was Fancy. She led up every mortal to the appointed place, after having officiously assisted him in making up his pack, and laying it upon his shoulders. My heart melted within me to see my fellow-creatures groaning under their respective burdens, and to consider that prodigious bulk of human calamities which lay before me.

There were, however, several persons who gave me great diversion upon this occasion. I observed one bringing in a fardel very carefully concealed under an old embroidered cloak, which, upon his throwing it into the heap, I discovered to be Poverty. Another, after a great deal of puffing, threw down his luggage, which, upon examining, I found to be his wife.

There were multitudes of lovers saddled with very whimsical burdens, composed of darts and flames; but what was very odd, though they sighed as if their hearts would break under these calamities, they could not persuade themselves to cast them into the heap when they came up to it;

but after a few faint efforts, shook their heads and marched away, as heavy loaden as they came. I saw multitudes of old women throw down their wrinkles, and several young ones who stripped themselves of a tawny skin. There were very great heaps of red noses, large lips, and rusty teeth. The truth of it is, I was surprised to see the greatest part of the mountain made up of bodily deformities. Observing one advancing toward the heap with a larger cargo than ordinary upon his back, I found upon his near approach that it was only a natural hump, which he disposed of with great joy of heart among this collection of human miseries. There were likewise distempers of all sorts; though I could not but observe that there were many more imaginary than real. One little packet I could not but take notice of, which was a complication of all the diseases incident to human nature, and was in the hand of a great many fine people; this was called the Spleen. But what most of all surprised me, was a remark I made, that there was not a single vice or folly thrown into the whole heap; at which I was very much astonished, having concluded within myself, that every one would take this opportunity of getting rid of his passions, prejudices, and frailties.

I took notice in particular of a very profligate fellow, who I did not question came loaden with his crimes; but upon searching into his bundle I found that instead of throwing his guilt from him, he had only laid down his memory. He was followed by another worthless rogue, who flung away his modesty instead of his ignorance.

When the whole race of mankind had thus cast their burdens, the phantom which had been so busy on this occasion, seeing me an idle Spectator of what had passed, approached towards me. I grew uneasy at her presence, when all of a sudden she held her magnifying glass before my eyes. I no sooner saw my face in it, but I was startled at the shortness of it, which now appeared to me in its utmost aggravation. The immoderate breadth of the features made me very much out of humor with my own countenance, upon which I threw it from me like a mask. It happened very luckily that one who stood by me had just before thrown down his visage, which it seems was too long for him. It was indeed extended to a most shameful length; I believe the very chin was, modestly speaking, as long as my whole face. We had both of us an opportunity of mending ourselves; and all the contributions being now brought in, every man was at liberty to exchange his misfortunes with those of another person. But as there arose many new incidents in the sequel of my vision, I shall reserve them for the subject of my next paper.

Spectator No. 559. *The same subject continued.*

In my last paper I gave my reader a sight of that mountain of miseries which was made up of those several calamities that afflict the minds of men. I saw with unspeakable pleasure the whole species thus delivered from its sorrows; though at the same time, as we stood round the heap, and surveyed the several materials of which it was composed, there was scarcely a mortal in this vast multitude who did not discover what he thought pleasures and blessings of life, and wondered how the owners of them ever came to look upon them as burdens and grievances.

As we were regarding very attentively this confusion of miseries, this chaos of calamity, Jupiter issued out a second proclamation, that every one was now at liberty to exchange his affliction, and to return to his habitation with any such other bundle as should be delivered to him.

Upon this Fancy began again to bestir herself, and parcelling out the whole heap with incredible activity, recommended to every one his particular packet. The hurry and

confusion at this time was not to be expressed. Some observations which I made upon the occasion I shall communicate
to the public. A venerable, gray-headed man, who had laid
down the colic, and who I found wanted an heir to his estate,
snatched up an undutiful son that had been thrown into the
heap by an angry father. The graceless youth, in less than
a quarter of an hour, pulled the old gentleman by the beard,
and had like to have knocked his brains out; so that meeting the true father, who came towards him with a fit of the
gripes, he begged him to take his son again, and give him
back his colic; but they were incapable either of them to
recede from the choice they had made. A poor galley slave,
who had thrown down his chains, took up the gout in their
stead, but made such wry faces, that one might easily perceive he was no great gainer by the bargain. It was pleasant enough to see the several exchanges that were made,
for sickness against poverty, hunger against want of 'appetite, and care against pain.

The female world were very busy among themselves in
bartering for features; one was trucking a lock of gray
hairs for a carbuncle; another was making over a short
waist for a pair of round shoulders, and a third cheapening
a bad face for a lost reputation: but on all these occasions
there was not one of them who did not think the new blemish, as soon as she had got it into her possession, much
more disagreeable than the old one. I made the same
observation on every other misfortune or calamity which
every one in the assembly brought upon himself in lieu of
what he had parted with; whether it be that all the evils
which befall us are in some measure suited and propor-
tioned to our strength, or that every evil becomes more
supportable by our being accustomed to it, I shall not determine.

I could not from my heart forbear pitying the poor hump-
backed gentleman mentioned in the former paper, who

went off a very well-shaped person with a stone in his bladder; nor the fine gentleman who had struck up this bargain with him, that limped through a whole assembly of ladies, who used to admire him, with a pair of shoulders peeping over his head.

I must not omit my own particular adventure. My friend with the long visage had no sooner taken upon him my short face but he made such a grotesque figure in it, that as I looked upon him I could not forbear laughing at myself, insomuch that I put my own face out of countenance. The poor gentleman was so sensible of the ridicule, that I found he was ashamed of what he had done; on the other hand, I found that I myself had no great reason to triumph; for as I went to touch my forehead, I missed the place, and clapped my finger upon my upper lip. Besides, as my nose was exceeding prominent, I gave it two or three unlucky knocks as I was playing my hand about my face, and aiming at some other part of it. I saw two other gentlemen by me who were in the same ridiculous circumstances. These had made a foolish swap between a couple of thick bandy legs and two long trapsticks that had no calves to them. One of these looked like a man walking upon stilts, and was so lifted up into the air, above his ordinary height, that his head turned round with it; while the other made such awkward circles as he attempted to walk, that he scarcely knew how to move forward upon his new supporters. Observing him to be a pleasant kind of fellow, I stuck my cane in the ground, and told him I would lay him a bottle of wine, that he did not march up to it on a line that I drew for him in a quarter of an hour.

The heap was at last distributed among the two sexes, who made a most piteous sight, as they wandered up and down under the pressure of their several burdens. The whole plain was filled with murmurs and complaints, groans and lamentations. Jupiter, at length, taking compassion on the poor mortals, ordered them a second time to lay down their loads, with a design to give every one his own again. They discharged themselves with a great deal of pleasure; after which, the phantom which had led them into such gross delusions, was commanded to disappear. There was sent in her stead a goddess of quite a different figure; her motions were steady and composed, her aspect serious but cheerful. She every now and then cast her eyes toward heaven, and fixed them upon Jupiter; her name was Patience. She had no sooner placed herself by the Mount of Sorrows, but, what I thought very remarkable, the whole heap sunk to such a degree, that it did not appear a third part so big as it was before. She afterwards returned every man his own proper calamity, and, teaching him how to bear it in the most commodious manner, he marched off with it contentedly, being very well pleased that he had not been left to his own choice as to the kind of evil which fell to his lot.

Besides the several pieces of morality to be drawn out of this vision, I learned from it never to repine at my own misfortunes, or to envy the happiness of another, since it is impossible for any man to form a right judgment of his neighbor's sufferings; for which reason also, I have determined never to think too lightly of another's complaints, but to regard the sorrows of my fellow-creatures with sentiments of humanity and compassion.

Tatler No. 96. *The Tatler explains whom he means by the expression "dead men."*

It has cost me very much care and thought to marshal and fix the people under their proper denominations, and to range them according to their respective characters. These my endeavors have been received with unexpected success in one kind, but neglected in another: for though I have many readers, I have but few converts. This must certainly proceed from a false opinion, that what I write is designed rather to amuse and entertain, than convince and instruct. I entered upon my Essays with a declaration that I should consider mankind in quite another manner than they had hitherto been represented to the ordinary world; and asserted, that none but an useful life should be, with me, any life at all. But, lest this doctrine should have made this small progress towards the conviction of mankind, because it may have appeared to the unlearned light and whimsical, I must take leave to unfold the wisdom and antiquity of my first proposition in these my Essays, to wit, that "every worthless man is a dead man." This notion is as old as Pythagoras, in whose school it was a point of discipline, that if among the "probationers," there were any who grew weary of studying to be useful, and returned to an idle life, they were to regard them as dead; and, upon their departing, to perform their obsequies, and raise them tombs, with inscriptions to warn others of the like mortality, and quicken them to resolutions of refining their souls above that wretched state. It is upon a like supposition, that young ladies, at this very time, in Roman Catholic countries, are received into some nunneries with their coffins, and with the pomp of a formal funeral, to signify, that henceforth they are to be of no farther use, and consequently dead. Nor was Pythagoras himself the first author of this symbol, with whom, and with the Hebrews, it was generally received. Much more might be offered in illustration of this doctrine from sacred authority, which I recommend to my reader's own reflection; who will easily recollect, from places which I do not think fit to quote here, the forcible manner of applying the words *dead* and *living*, to men as they are good or bad.

I have, therefore, composed the following scheme of exist-

ence for the benefit both of the living and the dead; though
chiefly for the latter, whom I must desire to read it with all
possible attention. In the number of the dead I comprehend
all persons, of what title or dignity soever, who bestow most
of their time in eating and drinking, to support that imaginary existence of theirs, which they call life; or in dressing
and adorning those shadows and apparitions, which are
looked upon by the vulgar as real men and women. In
short, whoever resides in the world without having any
business in it, and passes away an age without ever thinking on the errand for which he was sent hither, is to me a
dead man to all intents and purposes; and I desire that he
may be so reputed. The living are only those that are
some way or other laudably employed in the improvement
of their own minds, or for the advantage of others; and
even amongst these, I shall only reckon into their lives that
part of their time which has been spent in the manner above
mentioned. By these means, I am afraid, we shall find the
longest lives not to consist of many months, and the greatest part of the earth to be quite unpeopled. According to
this system we may observe, that some men are born at
twenty years of age, some at thirty, some at threescore, and
some not above an hour before they die: nay, we may
observe multitudes that die without ever being born, as well
as many dead persons that fill up the bulk of mankind, and
make a better figure in the eyes of the ignorant, than those
who are alive, and in their proper and full state of health.
However, since there may be many good subjects, that pay
their taxes, and live peaceably in their habitations, who are
not yet born, or have departed this life several years since,
my design is, to encourage both to join themselves as soon
as possible to the number of the living.

Tatler No. 97. *The same subject continued.*

Having swept away prodigious multitudes in my last paper, and brought a great destruction upon my own species, I must endeavor in this to raise fresh recruits, and, if possible, to supply the places of the unborn and the deceased. It is said of Xerxes, that when he stood upon a hill, and saw the whole country round him covered with his army, he burst out into tears, to think that not one of that multitude would be alive an hundred years after. For my part, when I take a survey of this populous city, I can scarce forbear weeping, to see how few of its inhabitants are now living. It was with this thought that I drew up my last bill of mortality, and endeavored to set out in it the great number of persons who have perished by a distemper, commonly known by the name of idleness, which has long raged in the world, and destroys more in every great town than the plague has done at Dantzic. To repair the mischief it has done, and stock the world with a better race of mortals, I have more hopes of bringing to life those that are young, than of reviving those that are old. For which reason, I shall here set down that noble allegory which was written by an old author called Prodicus, but recommended and embellished by Socrates. It is the description of Virtue and Pleasure, making their court to Hercules under the appearance of two beautiful women.

When Hercules, says the divine moralist, was in that part of his youth, in which it was natural for him to consider what course of life he ought to pursue, he one day retired into a desert, where the silence and solitude of the place very much favored his meditations. As he was musing on his present condition, and very much perplexed in himself on the state of life he should choose, he saw two women of a larger stature than ordinary approaching towards him. One of them had a very noble air, and graceful deportment; her beauty was natural and easy, her person clean and unspotted, her eyes cast towards the ground with an agreeable reserve, her motion and behavior full of modesty, and her raiment as white as snow. The other had a great deal of health and floridness in her countenance, which she had helped with an artificial white and red; and endeavored to appear more graceful than ordinary in her mien, by a mixture of affectation in all her gestures. She had a wonderful confidence and assurance in her looks, and all the variety of colors in her dress that she thought were most proper to show her complexion to an advantage. She cast her eyes upon herself, then turned them on those that were present, to see how they liked her, and often looked on the figure she made in her own shadow. Upon her nearer approach to Hercules, she stepped before the other lady, who came forward with a regular composed carriage, and running up to him, accosted him after the following manner:

"My dear Hercules," says she, "I find you are very much divided in your own thoughts, upon the way of life that you ought to choose. Be my friend, and follow me; I will lead you into the possession of pleasure, and out of the reach of pain, and remove you from all the noise and disquietude of business. The affairs of either war or peace shall have no power to disturb you. Your whole employment shall be, to make your life easy, and to entertain every sense with its proper gratification. Sumptuous tables, beds of roses, clouds of perfumes, concerts of music, crowds of beauties, are all in readiness to receive you. Come along with me into this region of delights, this world of pleasure, and bid farewell for ever to care, to pain, to business."

Hercules, hearing the lady talk after this manner, desired to know her name; to which she answered, "My friends, and those who are well acquainted with me, call me Happiness; but my enemies, and those who would injure my reputation, have given me the name of Pleasure."

By this time the other lady was come up, who addressed herself to the young hero in a very different manner.

"Hercules," says she, "I offer myself to you, because I know you are descended from the Gods, and give proofs of that descent by your love to virtue, and application to the studies proper for your age. This makes me hope you will gain both for yourself and me an immortal reputation. But, before I invite you into my society and friendship, I will be open and sincere with you, and must lay down this as an established truth, That *there is nothing truly valuable, which can be purchased without pains and labor.* The Gods have set a price upon every real and noble pleasure. If you would gain the favor of the Deity, you must be at the pains of worshipping him; if the friendship of good men, you must study to oblige them; if you would be honored by your country, you must take care to serve it. In short, if you would be eminent in war or peace, you must become master of all the qualifications that can make you so. These are the only terms and conditions upon which I can propose happiness." The Goddess of Pleasure here broke in upon her discourse. "You see," said she, "Hercules, by her own confession, the way to her pleasure is long and difficult, whereas that which I propose is short and easy." — "Alas!" said the other lady, whose visage glowed with a passion made up of scorn and pity, "what are the pleasures you propose? To eat before you are hungry, drink before you are a-thirst, sleep before you are a-tired, to gratify appetites before they are raised, and raise such

"As for me, I am the friend of the Gods and of good men, an agreeable companion to the artizan, an household guardian to the fathers of families, a patron and protector of servants, an associate in all true and generous friendships. The banquets of my votaries are never costly, but always delicious; for none eat or drink at them who are not invited by hunger and thirst. Their slumbers are sound, and their wakings cheerful. My young men have the pleasure of hearing themselves praised by those who are in years; and those who are in years, of being honored by those who are young. In a word, my followers are favored by the Gods, beloved by their acquaintance, esteemed by their country, and, after the close of their labors, honored by posterity."

We know by the life of this memorable hero, to which of these two ladies he gave up his heart; and I believe, every one who reads this will do him the justice to approve his choice.

I very much admire the speeches of these ladies, as containing in them the chief arguments for a life of virtue, or a life of pleasure, that could enter into the thoughts of an heathen; but am particularly pleased with the different figures he gives the two Goddesses. Our modern authors have represented Pleasure or Vice with an alluring face, but ending in snakes and monsters. Here she appears in all the charms of beauty, though they are all false and borrowed; and by that means composes a vision entirely natural and pleasing.

I have translated this allegory for the benefit of the youth of Great Britain; and particularly of those who are still in the deplorable state of non-existence, and whom I most earnestly entreat to come into the world. Let my embryos show the least inclination to any single virtue, and I shall allow it to be a struggling towards birth. I do not expect of them that, like the hero in the foregoing story, they should go about as soon as they are born, with a club in their hands, and a lion's skin on their shoulders, to root out monsters, and destroy tyrants; but, as the finest author of all antiquity has said upon this very occasion, though a man has not the abilities to distinguish himself in the most shining parts of a great character, he has certainly the capacity of being just, faithful, modest, and temperate.

Spectator No. 111.   *On immortality.*

The course of my last speculation led me insensibly into a subject upon which I always meditate with great delight, I mean the immortality of the soul.   I was yesterday walking alone in one of my friend's woods, and lost myself in it very agreeably, as I was running over in my mind the several arguments that establish this great point, which is the basis of morality, and the source of all the pleasing hopes and secret joys that can arise in the heart of a reasonable creature.   I considered those several proofs, drawn:

First, From the nature of the soul itself, and particularly its immateriality; which, though not absolutely necessary to the eternity of its duration, has, I think, been evinced to almost a demonstration.

Secondly, From its passions and sentiments, as particularly from its love of existence, its horror of annihilation, and its hopes of immortality, with that sweet satisfaction which it finds in the practice of virtue, and that uneasiness which follows in it upon the commission of vice.

Thirdly, From the nature of the Supreme Being, whose justice, goodness, wisdom, and veracity, are all concerned in this point.

But among these and other excellent arguments for the immortality of the soul, there is one drawn from the perpetual progress of the soul to its perfection, without a pos-

sibility of ever arriving at it; which is a hint that I do
not remember to have seen opened and improved by others
who have written on this subject, though it seems to me to
carry a great weight with it.   How can it enter into the
thoughts of man, that the soul, which is capable of such
immense perfections, and of receiving new improvements to
all eternity, shall fall away into nothing almost as soon as
it is created ?   Are such abilities made for no purpose ?   A
brute arrives at a point of perfection that he can never pass :
in a few years he has all the endowments he is capable of;
and were he to live ten thousand more, would be the same
thing he is at present.   Were a human soul thus at a stand
in her accomplishments, were her faculties to be full blown,
and incapable of farther enlargements, I could imagine it
might fall away insensibly, and drop at once into a state of
annihilation.   But can we believe a thinking being that is
in a perpetual progress of improvements, and travelling on
from perfection to perfection, after having just looked abroad
into the works of its Creator, and made a few discoveries
of his infinite goodness, wisdom, and power, must perish
at her first setting out, and in the very beginning of her
inquiries ?

A man, considered in his present state, seems only sent
into the world to propagate his kind.   He provides himself with a successor, and immediately quits his post to
make room for him.   He does not seem born to enjoy life,
but to deliver it down to others.   This is not surprising to
consider in animals, which are formed for our use, and can
finish their business in a short life.   The silk-worm, after
having spun her task, lays her eggs and dies.   But a man
can never have taken in his full measure of knowledge, has
not time to subdue his passions, establish his soul in virtue, and come up to the perfection of his nature, before he
is hurried off the stage.   Would an infinitely wise being
make such glorious creatures for so mean a purpose ?   Can

he delight in the production of such abortive intelligences, such short-lived reasonable beings ? Would he give us talents that are not to be exerted; capacities that are never to be gratified ? How can we find that wisdom which shines through all his works, in the formation of man, without looking on this world as only a nursery for the next, and believing that the several generations of rational creatures, which rise up and disappear in such quick successions, are only to receive their first rudiments of existence here, and afterwards to be transplanted into a more friendly climate, where they may spread and flourish to all eternity ?

There is not, in my opinion, a more pleasing and triumphant consideration in religion than this, of the perpetual progress which the soul makes towards the perfection of its nature, without ever arriving at a period in it. To look upon the soul as going on from strength to strength, to consider that she is to shine for ever with new accessions of glory, and brighten to all eternity; that she will be still adding virtue to virtue and knowledge to knowledge; carries in it something wonderfully agreeable to that ambition which is natural to the mind of man. Nay, it must be a prospect pleasing to God himself to see his creation ever beautifying in his eyes and drawing nearer to him by greater degrees of resemblance.

Methinks this single consideration of the progress of a finite spirit to perfection, will be sufficient to extinguish all envy in inferior natures, and all contempt in superior.

That cherubim, which now appears as a god to a human soul, knows very well that the period will come about in eternity, when the human soul shall be as perfect as he himself now is: nay, when she shall look down upon that degree of perfection as much as she now falls short of it. It is true, the higher nature still advances, and by that means preserves his distance and superiority in the scale of being; but he knows that, how high soever the station is of which he stands possessed at present, the inferior nature will at length mount up to it, and shine forth in the same degree of glory.

With what astonishment and veneration may we look into our own souls, where there are such hidden stores of virtue and knowledge, such inexhausted forces of perfection! We know not yet what we shall be, nor will it ever enter into the heart of man to conceive the glory that will be always in reserve for him. The soul, considered with its Creator, is like one of those mathematical lines that may draw nearer to another for all eternity without the possibility of touching it: and can there be a thought so transporting, as to consider ourselves in these perpetual approaches to him who is not only the standard of perfection but of happiness?

Spectator No. 565. *Contemplation of the divine perfections suggested by the sky at night.*

I was yesterday about sun-set walking in the open fields, till the night insensibly fell upon me. I at first amused myself with all the richness and variety of colors, which appeared in the western parts of heaven: in proportion as they faded away and went out, several stars and planets appeared one after another, till the whole firmament was in a glow. The blueness of the ether was exceedingly heightened and enlivened by the season of the year, and by the rays of all those luminaries that passed through it. The galaxy appeared in its most beautiful white. To complete the scene, the full moon rose at length in that clouded majesty which Milton takes notice of, and opened to the eye a new picture of nature, which was more finely shaded, and disposed among softer lights, than that which the sun had before discovered to us.

As I was surveying the moon walking in her brightness,

and taking her progress among the constellations, a thought rose in me which I believe very often perplexes and disturbs men of serious and contemplative natures. David himself fell into it in that reflection, "When I consider the heavens, the work of thy fingers, the moon and the stars which thou hast ordained; what is man, that thou art mindful of him, and the son of man that thou regardest him?" In the same manner, when I considered that infinite host of stars, or, to speak more philosophically, of suns, which were then shining upon me, with those innumerable sets of planets or worlds, which were moving round their respective suns; when I still enlarged the idea, and supposed another heaven of suns and worlds rising still above this which we discovered, and these still enlightened by a superior firmament of luminaries, which are planted at so great a distance that they may appear to the inhabitants of the former as the stars to us; in short, whilst I pursued this thought, I could not but reflect on that little insignificant figure which I myself bore amidst the immensity of God's works.

Were the sun, which enlightens this part of the creation, with all the host of planetary worlds that move about him, utterly extinguished and annihilated, they would not be missed, more than a grain of sand upon the sea-shore. The space they possess is so exceedingly little in comparison of the whole, that it would scarce make a blank in the creation. The chasm would be imperceptible to an eye, that could take in the whole compass of nature, and pass from one end of the creation to the other; as it is possible there may be such a sense in ourselves hereafter, or in creatures which are at present more exalted than ourselves. We see many stars by the help of glasses, which we do not discover with our naked eyes; and the finer our telescopes are, the more still are our discoveries. Huygenius carries this thought so far, that he does not think it impossible there may be stars whose light is not yet travelled down to us

since their first creation.   There is no question but the
universe has certain bounds set to it; but when we consider
that it is the work of infinite power, prompted by infinite
goodness, with an infinite space to exert itself in, how can
our imagination set any bounds to it?

To return therefore to my first thought, I could not but
look upon myself with secret horror, as a being that was not
worth the smallest regard of one who had so great a work
under his care and superintendency.   I was afraid of being
overlooked amidst the immensity of nature, and lost among
that infinite variety of creatures, which in all probability
swarm through all these immeasurable regions of matter.

In order to recover myself from this mortifying thought,
I considered that it took its rise from those narrow conceptions, which we are apt to entertain of the divine nature.
We ourselves cannot attend to many different objects at
the same time.   If we are careful to inspect some things,
we must of course neglect others.   This imperfection which
we observe in ourselves, is an imperfection that cleaves in
some degree to creatures of the highest capacities, as they
are creatures, that is, beings of finite and limited natures.
The presence of every created being is confined to a certain
measure of space, and consequently his observation is stinted
to a certain number of objects.   The sphere in which we
move and act and understand, is of a wider circumference to
one creature than another, according as we rise one above
another in the scale of existence.   But the widest of these
our spheres has its circumference.   When therefore we
reflect on the divine nature, we are so used and accustomed
to this imperfection in ourselves, that we cannot forbear in
some measure ascribing it to him in whom there is no
shadow of imperfection.   Our reason indeed assures us
that his attributes are infinite, but the poorness of our conceptions is such that it cannot forbear setting bounds to
every thing it contemplates, till our reason comes again to

our succor, and throws down all those little prejudices which rise in us unawares, and are natural to the mind of man.

If we consider Him in his omnipresence: His being passes through, actuates, and supports the whole frame of nature. His creation, and every part of it, is full of him. There is nothing he has made, that is either so distant, so little, or so inconsiderable, which he does not essentially inhabit. His substance is within the substance of every being, whether material or immaterial, and as intimately present to it, as that being is to itself. It would be an imperfection in him, were he able to remove out of one place into another, or to withdraw himself from anything he has created, or from any part of that space which is diffused and spread abroad to infinity. In short, to speak of him in the language of the old philosopher, he is a being whose centre is every where, and his circumference no where.

In the second place, he is omniscient as well as omnipresent. His omniscience indeed necessarily and naturally flows from his omnipresence. He cannot but be conscious of every motion that arises in the whole material world, which he thus essentially pervades; and of every thought that is stirring in the intellectual world, to every part of which he is thus intimately united. Several moralists have considered the creation as the temple of God, which he has built with his own hands, and which is filled with his presence. Others have considered infinite space as the receptacle or rather the habitation of the Almighty: but the noblest and most exalted way of considering this infinite space is that of Sir Isaac Newton, who calls it the *sensorium* of the Godhead. Brutes and men have their *sensoriola,* or little *sensoriums,* by which they apprehend the presence, and perceive the actions, of a few objects that lie contiguous to them. Their knowledge and observation turn within a very narrow circle. But as God Almighty cannot but perceive and know every thing in which he resides, infinite

space gives room to infinite knowledge, and is, as it were,
an organ to omniscience.

Were the soul separate from the body, and with one
glance of thought should start beyond the bounds of
the creation, should it for millions of years continue its
progress through infinite space with the same activity, it
would still find itself within the embrace of its Creator, and
encompassed round with the immensity of the Godhead.
Whilst we are in the body he is not less present with us
because he is concealed from us. "O that I knew where
I might find him!" says Job. "Behold, I go forward, but
he is not there; and backward, but I cannot perceive him:
on the left hand where he does work, but I cannot behold
him: he hideth himself on the right hand, that I cannot see
him." In short, reason as well as revelation assures us,
that he cannot be absent from us, notwithstanding he is
undiscovered by us.

In this consideration of God Almighty's omnipresence
and omniscience every uncomfortable thought vanishes.
He cannot but regard every thing that has being, especially
such of his creatures who fear they are not regarded by him.
He is privy to all their thoughts, and to that anxiety of
of heart in particular, which is apt to trouble them on this
occasion: for as it is impossible he should overlook any of
his creatures, so we may be confident that he regards with an
eye of mercy those who endeavor to recommend themselves
to his notice, and in an unfeigned humility of heart think
themselves unworthy that he should be mindful of them.

Spectator No. 441. *Trust in God.*

*　　　*　　　*　　　*　　　*　　　*

David has very beautifully represented this steady reliance
on God Almighty in his twenty-third psalm, which is a kind

of pastoral hymn, and filled with those allusions which are
usual in that kind of writing.   As the poetry is very exquisite, I shall present the reader with the following translation
of it : —

The Lord my pasture shall prepare,
And feed me with a shepherd's care:
His presence shall my wants supply,
And guard me with a watchful eye:
My noon-day walks he shall attend,
And all my midnight hours defend.

When in the sultry glebe I faint,
Or on the thirsty mountain pant,
To fertile vales, and dewy meads,
My weary wand'ring steps he leads ;
Where peaceful rivers, soft and slow
Amid the verdant landscape flow.

Though in the paths of death I tread,
With gloomy horrors overspread,
My steadfast heart shall fear no ill,
For thou, O Lord, art with me still ;
Thy friendly crook shall give me aid,
And guide me through the dreadful shade.

Though in a bare and rugged way,
Through devious lonely wilds I stray,
Thy bounty shall my pains beguile:
The barren wilderness shall smile,
With sudden greens and herbage crown'd,
And streams shall murmur all around.

Spectator No. 453.   *Providence.*

*   *   *   *   *   *

I have already communicated to the public some pieces of
divine poetry ; and, as they have met with a very favorable
reception, I shall from time to time publish any work of the

same nature, which has not yet appeared in print, and may
be acceptable to my readers.

When all thy mercies, O my God,
  My rising soul surveys,
Transported with the view, I'm lost
  In wonder, love, and praise.

O how shall words with equal warmth
  The gratitude declare
That glows within my ravish'd heart?
  But thou canst read it there.

Unnumber'd comforts to my soul
  Thy tender care bestow'd,
Before my infant heart conceived
  From whom those comforts flow'd.

When in the slippery paths of youth
  With heedless steps I ran,
Thine arm unseen convey'd me safe,
  And led me up to man.

Through hidden dangers, toils, and deaths,
  It gently clear'd my way,
And through the pleasing snares of vice,
  More to be fear'd than they.

When worn with sickness, oft hast thou
  With health renew'd my face,
And when in sins and sorrows sunk,
  Revived my soul with grace.

Thy bounteous hand with worldly bliss
  Has made my cup run o'er,
And in a kind and faithful friend
  Has doubled all my store.

Ten thousand thousand precious gifts
  My daily thanks employ;
Nor is the least a cheerful heart,
  That tastes those gifts with joy.

Through every period of my life
  Thy goodness I'll pursue ;
And after death in distant worlds
  The glorious theme renew.

When nature fails, and day and night
  Divide thy works no more,
My ever grateful heart, O Lord,
  Thy mercy shall adore.

Through all eternity to thee
  A joyful song I'll raise ;
For, oh ! eternity's too short
  To utter all thy praise.

Spectator No. 465. *The confirmation of faith.*

* * * * * *

The Supreme Being has made the best arguments for his
own existence in the formation of the heavens and earth ;
and these are arguments which a man of sense cannot forbear attending to, who is out of the noise and hurry of
human affairs. Aristotle says, that should a man live under
ground, and there converse with works of art and mechan-
ism, and should afterwards be brought up into the open
day, and see the several glories of the heaven and earth, he
would immediately pronounce them the works of such a
being as we define God to be. The psalmist has very beautiful strokes of poetry to this purpose in that exalted strain,
" The heavens declare the glory of God : and the firmament sheweth his handy-work. One day telleth another :
and one night certifieth another. There is neither speech
nor language : but their voices are heard among them. Their
sound is gone out into all the lands : and their words unto
the ends of the world." As such a bold and sublime manner of thinking furnished very noble matter for an ode, the
reader may see it wrought into the following one : —

The spacious firmament on high,
With all the blue ethereal sky,
And spangled heavens, a shining frame,
Their great original proclaim:
Th' unwearied sun, from day to day,
Does his Creator's power display,
And publishes to every land
The work of an almighty hand.

Soon as the evening shades prevail,
The moon takes up the wondrous tale,
And nightly to the listening earth
Repeats the story of her birth:
Whilst all the stars that round her burn,
And all the planets in their turn,
Confirm the tidings as they roll,
And spread the truth from pole to pole.

What though, in solemn silence, all
Move round the dark terrestrial ball?
What though nor real voice nor sound
Amid their radiant orbs be found?
In reason's ear they all rejoice,
And utter forth a glorious voice,
For ever singing, as they shine,
"The hand that made us is divine."

Spectator No. 489.   *Thanksgiving after travel.*

*   *   *   *   *

How are thy servants blest, O Lord!
    How sure is their defence!
Eternal Wisdom is their guide,
    Their help Omnipotence.

In foreign realms and lands remote,
    Supported by thy care,
Through burning climes I pass'd unhurt,
    And breathed in tainted air.

Thy mercy sweeten'd every soil,
　Made every region please :
The hoary Alpine hills it warm'd,
　And smooth'd the Tyrrhene seas.

Think, O my soul, devoutly think,
　How, with affrighted eyes,
Thou saw'st the wide extended deep
　In all its horrors rise !

Confusion dwelt in every face,
　And fear in every heart :
When waves on waves, and gulfs on gulfs,
　O'ercame the pilot's art.

Yet then from all my griefs, O Lord,
　Thy mercy set me free,
Whilst in the confidence of prayer
　My soul took hold on thee.

For though in dreadful whirls we hung
　High on the broken wave,
I knew thou wert not slow to hear,
　Nor impotent to save.

The storm was laid, the winds retired,
　Obedient to thy will ;
The sea that roar'd at thy command,
　At thy command was still.

In midst of dangers, fears, and death,
　Thy goodness I'll adore,
And praise thee for thy mercies past,
　And humbly hope for more.

My life, if thou preserv'st my life,
　Thy sacrifice shall be ;
And death, if death must be my doom,
　Shall join my soul to thee.

Spectator No. 513. *A thought in sickness.*

*   *   *   *   *

When, rising from the bed of death,
  O'erwhelm'd with guilt and fear,
I see my Maker, face to face,
  O how shall I appear !

If yet, while pardon may be found,
  And mercy may be sought,
My heart with inward horror shrinks,
  And trembles at the thought ;

When thou, O Lord, shalt stand disclosed,
  In majesty severe,
And sit in judgment on my soul,
  O how shall I appear !

But thou hast told the troubled mind,
  Who does her sins lament,
The timely tribute of her tears
  Shall endless woe prevent.

Then see the sorrows of my heart,
  Ere yet it be too late ;
And hear my Saviour's dying groans,
  To give those sorrows weight.

For never shall my soul despair
  Her pardon to procure,
Who knows thine only Son has died
  To make her pardon sure.

MACAULAY'S ESSAY

ON THE

LIFE AND WRITINGS OF ADDISON.

(July, 1843.)

The Life of Joseph Addison. By Lucy Aikin. London: 1843.

Some reviewers are of opinion that a lady who dares to publish a book renounces by that act the franchises appertaining to her sex, and can claim no exemption from the utmost rigor of critical procedure. From that opinion we dissent. We admit, indeed, that in a country which boasts of many female writers, eminently qualified by their talents and acquirements to influence the public mind, it would be of most pernicious consequence that inaccurate history or unsound philosophy should be suffered to pass uncensured, merely because the offender chanced to be a lady. But we conceive that, on such occasions, a critic would do well to imitate the courteous knight who found himself compelled by duty to keep the lists against Bradamante. He, we are told, defended successfully the cause of which he was the champion; but, before the fight began, exchanged Balisarda for a less deadly sword, of which he carefully blunted the point and edge.[1]

Nor are the immunities of sex the only immunities which Miss Aikin may rightfully plead. Several of her works,

[1] Orlando Furioso, xlv., 68.

and especially the very pleasing Memoirs of the Reign of James the First, have fully entitled her to the privileges enjoyed by good writers. One of those privileges we hold to be this, that such writers, when, either from the unlucky choice of a subject, or from the indolence too often produced by success, they happen to fail, shall not be subjected to the severe discipline which it is sometimes necessary to inflict upon dunces and impostors, but shall merely be reminded by a gentle touch, like that with which the Laputan flapper roused his dreaming lord, that it is high time to wake.

Our readers will probably infer from what we have said that Miss Aikin's book has disappointed us. The truth is, that she is not well acquainted with her subject. No person who is not familiar with the political and literary history of England during the reigns of William the Third, of Anne, and of George the First, can possibly write a good life of Addison. Now, we mean no reproach to Miss Aikin, and many will think that we pay her a compliment when we say that her studies have taken a different direction. She is better acquainted with Shakspeare and Raleigh than with Congreve and Prior; and is far more at home among the ruffs and peaked beards of Theobald's than among the Steenkirks and flowing periwigs which surrounded Queen Anne's tea-table at Hampton. She seems to have written about the Elizabethan Age because she had read much about it; she seems, on the other hand, to have read a little about the age of Addison because she had determined to write about it. The consequence is that she has had to describe men and things without having either a correct or a vivid idea of them, and that she has often fallen into errors of a very serious kind. The reputation which Miss Aikin has justly earned stands so high, and the charm of Addison's letters is so great, that a second edition of this work may probably be required. If so, we hope that every paragraph will be revised, and that every date and fact about which there can be the smallest doubt will be carefully verified.

To Addison himself we are bound by a sentiment as much like affection as any sentiment can be, which is inspired by one who has been sleeping a hundred and twenty years in Westminster Abbey. We trust, however, that this feeling will not betray us into that abject idolatry which we have often had occasion to reprehend in others, and which seldom fails to make both the idolater and the idol ridiculous. A man of genius and virtue is but a man. All his powers cannot be equally developed, nor can we expect from him perfect self-knowledge. We need not, therefore, hesitate to admit that Addison has left us some compositions which do not rise above mediocrity, some heroic poems hardly equal to Parnell's, some criticism as superficial as Dr. Blair's, and a tragedy not very much better than Dr. Johnson's. It is praise enough to say of a writer that, in a high department of literature, in which many eminent writers have distinguished themselves, he has had no equal; and this may with strict justice be said of Addison.

As a man, he may not have deserved the adoration which he received from those who, bewitched by his fascinating society, and indebted for all the comforts of life to his generous and delicate friendship, worshipped him nightly in his favorite temple at Button's. But, after full inquiry and impartial reflection, we have long been convinced that he deserved as much love and esteem as can be justly claimed by any of our infirm and erring race. Some blemishes may undoubtedly be detected in his character; but the more carefully it is examined, the more will it appear, to use the phrase of the old anatomists, sound in the noble parts, free from all taint of perfidy, of cowardice, of cruelty, of ingratitude, of envy. Men may easily be named in whom some particular good disposition has been more conspicuous than in Addison.   But the just harmony of qualities, the exact temper between the stern and the humane virtues, the habitual observance of every law, not only of moral rectitude, but of moral grace and dignity, distinguish him from all men who have been tried by equally strong temptations, and about whose conduct we possess equally full information.

His father was the Reverend Lancelot Addison, who, though eclipsed by his more celebrated son, made some figure in the world, and occupies with credit two folio pages in the Biographia Britannica.   He rose to eminence in his profession and became one of the royal chaplains, a Doctor of Divinity, Archdeacon of Salisbury, and Dean of Lichfield.   It is said that he would have been made a bishop after the Revolution if he had not given offence to the Government by strenuously opposing, in the Convocation of 1689, the liberal policy of William and Tillotson.

In 1672 his son Joseph was born.   Of Joseph's childhood we know little.   He learned his rudiments at schools in his father's neighborhood, and was then sent to the Charter House.   The anecdotes which are popularly related about his boyish tricks do not harmonize very well with what we know of his riper years.   There remains a tradition that he was the ringleader in a barring out, and another tradition that he ran away from school and hid himself in a wood, where he fed on berries and slept in a hollow tree, till after a long search he was discovered and brought home.   If these stories be true, it would be curious to know by what moral discipline so mutinous and enterprising a lad was transformed into the gentlest and most modest of men.

We have abundant proof that, whatever Joseph's pranks may have been, he pursued his studies vigorously and successfully.   At fifteen he was not only fit for the university, but carried thither a classical taste and a stock of learning

which would have done honor to a Master of Arts. He
was entered at Queen's College, Oxford; but he had not
been many months there, when some of his Latin verses
fell by accident into the hands of Dr. Lancaster, Dean of
Magdalene College, who found it easy to procure for his
young friend admittance to the advantages of a foundation
then generally esteemed the wealthiest in Europe.

At Magdalene Addison resided during ten years. He
was, at first, one of those scholars who are called Demies,
but was subsequently elected a fellow. His college is still
proud of his name; his portrait still hangs in the hall; and
strangers are still told that his favorite walk was under the
elms which fringe the meadow on the banks of the Cher-
well. It is said, and is highly probable, that he was distinguished among his fellow-students by the delicacy of his
feelings, by the shyness of his manners, and by the assiduity
with which he often prolonged his studies far into the night.
It is certain that his reputation for ability and learning
stood high. Many years later, the ancient doctors of Magdalene continued to talk in their common room of his boyish
compositions, and expressed their sorrow that no copy of
exercises so remarkable had been preserved.

It is proper, however, to remark that Miss Aikin has
committed the error, very pardonable in a lady, of overrat-
ing Addison's classical attainments. In one department of
learning, indeed, his proficiency was such as it is hardly
possible to overrate. His knowledge of the Latin poets
was singularly exact and profound. He understood them
thoroughly, entered into their spirit, and had the finest and
most discriminating perception of all their peculiarities of
style and melody; nay, he copied their manner with admirable skill, and surpassed, we think, all their British imita-
tors who had preceded him, Buchanan and Milton alone
excepted. This is high praise; and beyond this we cannot
with justice go. It is clear that Addison's serious attention

during his residence at the university was almost entirely concentrated on Latin poetry, and that, if he did not wholly neglect other provinces of ancient literature, he vouchsafed to them only a cursory glance. He does not appear to have attained more than an ordinary acquaintance with the political and moral writers of Rome; nor was his own Latin prose by any means equal to his Latin verse. His knowledge of Greek, though doubtless such as was, in his time, thought respectable at Oxford, was evidently less than that which many lads now carry away every year from Eton and Rugby. A minute examination of his works, if we had time to make such examination, would fully bear out these remarks.

It is probable that the classical acquirements of Addison were of as much service to him as if they had been more extensive. The world generally gives its admiration, not to the man who does what nobody else even attempts to do, but to the man who does best what multitudes do well. Bentley was so immeasurably superior to all the other scholars of his time that few among them could discover his superiority. But the accomplishment in which Addison excelled his contemporaries was then, as it is now, highly valued and assiduously cultivated at all English seats of learning. Everybody who had been at a public school had written Latin verses; many had written such verses with tolerable success, and were quite able to appreciate, though by no means able to rival, the skill with which Addison imitated Virgil. His lines on the Barometer and the Bowling-green were applauded by hundreds, to whom the Dissertation on the Epistles of Phalaris was as unintelligible as the hieroglyphics on an obelisk.

The Latin poems of Addison were greatly and justly admired both at Oxford and Cambridge, before his name had ever been heard by the wits who thronged the coffee-houses round Drury Lane Theatre. In his twenty-second

year, he ventured to appear before the public as a writer
of English verse. He addressed some complimentary lines
to Dryden, who, after many triumphs and many reverses,
had at length reached a secure and lonely eminence among
the literary men of that age. Dryden appears to have been
much gratified by the young scholar's praise; and an inter-
change of civilities and good offices followed. Addison was
probably introduced by Dryden to Congreve, and was certainly presented by Congreve to Charles Montague, who
was then Chancellor of the Exchequer, and leader of the
Whig party in the House of Commons.

At this time Addison seemed inclined to devote himself
to poetry. He published a translation of part of the fourth
Georgic, Lines to King William, and other performances of
equal value, that is to say, of no value at all. But in those
days the public was in the habit of receiving with applause
pieces which would now have little chance of obtaining the
Newdigate prize or the Seatonian prize. And the reason is
obvious. The heroic couplet was then the favorite measure. The art of arranging words in that measure, so that
the lines may flow smoothly, that the accents may fall cor-
rectly, that the rhymes may strike the ear strongly, and
that there may be a pause at the end of every distich, is an
art as mechanical as that of mending a kettle or shoeing a
horse, and may be learned by any human being who has
sense enough to learn anything. But, like other mechanical arts, it was gradually improved by means of many experiments and many failures. It was reserved for Pope to
discover the trick, to make himself complete master of it,
and to teach it to everybody else. From the time when his
Pastorals appeared, heroic versification became matter of
rule and compass; and, before long, all artists were on a
level. Hundreds of dunces who never blundered on one
happy thought or expression were able to write reams of
couplets which, as far as euphony was concerned, could not

be distinguished from those of Pope himself, and which very clever writers of the reign of Charles the Second, Rochester, for example, or Marvel, or Oldham, would have contemplated with admiring despair.

Ben Jonson was a great man, Hoole a very small man. But Hoole, coming after Pope, had learned how to manufacture decasyllable verses, and poured them forth by thousands and tens of thousands, all as well turned, as smooth, and as like each other as the blocks which have passed through Mr. Brunel's mill in the dockyard at Portsmouth. Ben's heroic couplets resemble blocks rudely hewn out by an unpractised hand, with a blunt hatchet. Take as a specimen his translation of a celebrated passage in the Æneid:—

> This child our parent earth, stirr'd up with spite
> Of all the gods, brought forth, and, as some write,
> She was last sister of that giant race
> That sought to scale Jove's court, right swift of pace,
> And swifter far of wing, a monster vast
> And dreadful. Look, how many plumes are placed
> On her huge corpse, so many waking eyes
> Stick underneath, and, which may stranger rise
> In the report, as many tongues she wears.

Compare with these jagged, misshapen distichs the neat fabric which Hoole's machine produces in unlimited abundance. We take the first lines on which we open in his version of Tasso. They are neither better nor worse than the rest:—

> O thou, whoe'er thou art, whose steps are led,
> By choice or fate, these lonely shores to tread,
> No greater wonders east or west can boast
> Than yon small island on the pleasing coast.
> If e'er thy sight would blissful scenes explore,
> The current pass, and seek the further shore.

Ever since the time of Pope there has been a glut of lines of this sort; and we are now as little disposed to admire a man for being able to write them as for being able to write his name. But in the days of William the Third such versification was rare; and a rhymer who had any skill in it passed for a great poet, just as in the dark ages a person who could write his name passed for a great clerk. Accordingly Duke, Stepney, Granville, Walsh, and others whose only title to fame was that they said in tolerable metre what might have been as well said in prose, or what was not worth saying at all, were honored with marks of distinction which ought to be reserved for genius. With these Addison must have ranked, if he had not earned true and lasting glory by performances which very little resembled his juvenile poems.

Dryden was now busied with Virgil, and obtained from Addison a critical preface to the Georgics. In return for this service, and for other services of the same kind, the veteran poet, in the postscript to the translation of the Æneid, complimented his young friend with great liberality, and indeed with more liberality than sincerity. He affected to be afraid that his own performance would not sustain a comparison with the version of the fourth Georgic, by "the most ingenious Mr. Addison of Oxford." "After his bees," added Dryden, "my latter swarm is scarcely worth the hiving."

The time had now arrived when it was necessary for Addison to choose a calling. Everything seemed to point his course toward the clerical profession. His habits were regular, his opinions orthodox. His college had large ecclesiastical preferment in its gift, and boasts that it has given at least one bishop to almost every see in England. Dr. Lancelot Addison held an honorable place in the Church, and had set his heart on seeing his son a clergyman. It is clear, from some expressions in the young man's rhymes, that his intention was to take orders. But Charles Montague interfered. Montague had first brought himself into notice by verses, well timed and not contemptibly written, but never, we think, rising above mediocrity. Fortunately for himself and for his country, he early quitted poetry, in which he could never have attained a rank as high as that of Dorset or Rochester, and turned his mind to official and parliamentary business. It is written that the ingenious person who undertook to instruct Rasselas, Prince of Abyssinia, in the art of flying, ascended an eminence, waved his wings, sprung into the air, and instantly dropped into the lake. But it is added that the wings, which were unable to support him through the sky, bore him up effectually as soon as he was in the water. This is no bad type of the fate of Charles Montague, and of men like him. When he attempted to soar into the regions of poetical invention, he altogether failed; but as soon as he had descended from that ethereal elevation into a lower and grosser element, his talents instantly raised him above the mass. He became a distinguished financier, debater, courtier, and party leader. He still retained his fondness for the pursuits of his early days; but he showed that fondness not by wearying the public with his own feeble performances, but by discovering and encouraging literary excellence in others. A crowd of wits and poets, who could easily have vanquished him as a competitor, revered him as a judge and a patron. In his plans for the encouragement of learning, he was cordially supported by the ablest and most virtuous of his colleagues, the Lord Chancellor Somers. Though both these great statesmen had a sincere love of letters, it was not solely from a love of letters that they were desirous to enlist youths of high intellectual qualifications in the public service. The Revolution had altered the whole system of government. Before that event, the Press had been controlled by censors, and the Parliament had sat only two months in eight years. Now the Press was free, and had begun to exercise unprecedented influence on the public mind. Parliament met annually, and sat long. The chief power in the State had passed to the House of Commons. At such a conjuncture, it was natural that literary and oratorical talents should rise in value. There was danger that a government which neglected such talents might be subverted by them. It was, therefore, a profound and enlightened policy which led Montague and Somers to attach such talents to the Whig party, by the strongest ties both of interest and of gratitude.

It was in the year 1699, when Addison had just completed his twenty-seventh year, that the course of his life was finally determined. Both the great chiefs of the ministry were kindly disposed towards him. In political opinions he already was what he continued to be through life, a firm, though a moderate, Whig. He had addressed the most polished and vigorous of his early English lines to Somers, and had dedicated to Montague a Latin poem, truly Virgilian, both in style and rhythm, on the Peace of Ryswick. The wish of the young poet's great friends was, it should seem, to employ him in the service of the crown abroad. But an intimate knowledge of the French language was a qualification indispensable to a diplomatist; and this qualification Addison had not acquired. It was, therefore, thought desirable that he should pass some time on the Continent in preparing himself for official employment. His own means were not such as would enable him to travel, but a pension of three hundred pounds a year was procured for him by the interest of the lord chancellor. It seems to have been apprehended that some difficulty might be started by the rulers of Magdalene College. But the Chancellor of the Exchequer wrote in the strongest terms to Hough. The State — such was the purport of Montague's letter — could not, at that time, spare to the Church such a man as Addison. Too many high civil posts were already occupied by adventurers, who, destitute of every liberal art and sentiment, at once pillaged and disgraced the country which they pretended to serve. It had become necessary to recruit for the public service from a very different class, from that class of which Addison was the representative. The close of the minister's letter was remarkable. "I am called," he said, "an enemy of the Church. But I will never do it any other injury than keeping Mr. Addison out of it."

This interference was successful; and, in the summer of 1699, Addison, made a rich man by his pension, and still retaining his fellowship, quitted his beloved Oxford, and set out on his travels. He crossed from Dover to Calais, proceeded to Paris, and was received there with great kindness and politeness by a kinsman of his friend Montague, Charles, Earl of Manchester, who had just been appointed ambassador to the court of France. The countess, a Whig and a toast, was probably as gracious as her lord; for Addison long retained an agreeable recollection of the impression which she at this time made on him, and, in some lively lines written on the glasses of the Kit Cat Club, described the envy which her cheeks, glowing with the genuine bloom of England, had excited among the painted beauties of Versailles.

While Addison was at Paris, an event took place which made that capital a disagreeable residence for an Englishman and a Whig. Charles, second of the name, King of Spain, died; and bequeathed his dominions to Philip, Duke of Anjou, a younger son of the Dauphin. The King of France, in direct violation of his engagements both with Great Britain and with the States General, accepted the bequest on behalf of his grandson. The house of Bourbon was at the summit of human grandeur. England had been outwitted, and found herself in a situation at once degrading and perilous. The people of France, not presaging the

calamities by which they were destined to expiate the perfidy of their sovereign, went mad with pride and delight.
Every man looked as if a great estate had just been left
him.

"The French conversation," said Addison, "begins to
grow insupportable; that which was before the vainest
nation in the world is now worse than ever." Sick of the
arrogant exultation of the Parisians, and probably foreseeing that the peace between France and England could not
be of long duration, he set off for Italy.

In December, 1700, he embarked at Marseilles. As he
glided along the Ligurian coast, he was delighted by the
sight of myrtles and olive trees, which retained their verdure under the winter solstice. Soon, however, he encountered one of the black storms of the Mediterranean. The
captain of the ship gave up all for lost, and confessed himself to a Capuchin who happened to be on board. The
English heretic, in the mean time, fortified himself against
the terrors of death with devotions of a very different kind.
How strong an impression this perilous voyage made on
him appears from the ode, " How are thy servants blest, O
Lord!" which was long after published in The Spectator.
After some days of discomfort and danger, Addison was
glad to land at Savona, and to make his way, over mountains where no road had yet been hewn out by art, to the
city of Genoa.

At Genoa, still ruled by her own Doge, and by the nobles
whose names were inscribed on her Book of Gold, Addison
made a short stay. He admired the narrow streets over-
hung by long lines of towering palaces, the walls rich with
frescoes, the gorgeous temple of the Annunciation, and the
tapestries whereon were recorded the long glories of the
house of Doria. Thence he hastened to Milan, where he
contemplated the Gothic magnificence of the cathedral with
more wonder than pleasure. He passed Lake Benacus

while a gale was blowing, and saw the waves raging as they raged when Virgil looked upon them.   At Venice, then the gayest spot in Europe, the traveller spent the Carnival, the gayest season of the year, in the midst of masques, dances, and serenades.   Here he was at once diverted and provoked by the absurd dramatic pieces which then disgraced the Italian stage.   To one of those pieces, however, he was indebted for a valuable hint.   He was present when a ridiculous play on the death of Cato was performed.   Cato, it seems, was in love with a daughter of Scipio.   The lady had given her heart to Cæsar.   The rejected lover determined to destroy himself.   He appeared seated in his library, a dagger in his hand, a Plutarch and a Tasso before him; and, in this position, he pronounced a soliloquy before he struck the blow.   We are surprised that so remarkable a circumstance as this should have escaped the notice of all Addison's biographers.   There cannot, we conceive, be the smallest doubt that this scene, in spite of its absurdities and anachronisms, struck the traveller's imagination, and suggested to him the thought of bringing Cato on the English stage.   It is well known that about this time he began his tragedy, and that he finished the first four acts before he returned to England.

On his way from Venice to Rome, he was drawn some miles out of the beaten road, by a wish to see the smallest independent state in Europe.   On a rock where the snow still lay, though the Italian spring was now far advanced, was perched the little fortress of San Marino.   The roads which led to the secluded town were so bad that few travellers had ever visited it, and none had ever published an account of it.   Addison could not suppress a good-natured smile at the simple manners and institutions of this singular community.   But he observed, with the exultation of a Whig, that the rude mountain tract which formed the territory of the republic swarmed with an honest, healthy, and contented peasantry, while the rich plain which surrounded the metropolis of civil and spiritual tyranny was scarcely less desolate than the uncleared wilds of America.

At Rome Addison remained on his first visit only long enough to catch a glimpse of St. Peter's and of the Pantheon. His haste is the more extraordinary because the Holy Week was close at hand. He has given no hint which can enable us to pronounce why he chose to fly from a spectacle which every year allures from distant regions persons of far less taste and sensibility than his. Possibly, travelling, as he did, at the charge of a government distinguished by its enmity to the Church of Rome, he may have thought that it would be imprudent in him to assist at the most magnificent rite of that Church. Many eyes would be upon him; and he might find it difficult to behave in such a manner as to give offence neither to his patrons in England, nor to those among whom he resided. Whatever his motives may have been, he turned his back on the most august and affecting ceremony which is known among men, and posted along the Appian Way to Naples.

Naples was then destitute of what are now, perhaps, its chief attractions. The lovely bay and the awful mountain were indeed there. But a farm-house stood on the theatre of Herculaneum, and rows of vines grew over the streets of Pompeii. The temples of Pæstum had not, indeed, been hidden from the eye of man by any great convulsion of nature; but, strange to say, their existence was a secret even to artists and antiquaries. Though situated within a few hours' journey of a great capital, where Salvator had not long before painted, and where Vico was then lecturing, those noble remains were as little known to Europe as the ruined cities overgrown by the forests of Yucatan. What was to be seen at Naples, Addison saw. He climbed Vesuvius, explored the tunnel of Posilipo, and wandered among the vines and almond trees of Capreæ. But neither the won-

ders of nature nor those of art could so occupy his attention
as to prevent him from noticing, though cursorily, the abuses
of the Government and the misery of the people. The
great kingdom which had just descended to Philip the Fifth
was in a state of paralytic dotage. Even Castile and Aragon
were sunk in wretchedness. Yet, compared with the Italian
dependencies of the Spanish crown, Castile and Aragon
might be called prosperous. It is clear that all the observations which Addison made in Italy tended to confirm him
in the political opinions which he had adopted at home. To
the last, he always spoke of foreign travel as the best cure
for Jacobitism. In his Freeholder, the Tory fox-hunter
asks what travelling is good for, except to teach a man to
jabber French, and to talk against passive obedience.

From Naples Addison returned to Rome by sea along the
coast which his favorite Virgil had celebrated. The felucca
passed the headland where the oar and trumpet were placed
by the Trojan adventurers on the tomb of Misenus, and
anchored at night under the shelter of the fabled promon-
tory of Circe. The voyage ended in the Tiber, still over-
hung with dark verdure, and still turbid with yellow sand,
as when it met the eyes of Æneas. From the ruined port
of Ostia the stranger hurried to Rome; and at Rome he
remained during those hot and sickly months when, even in
the Augustan Age, all who could make their escape fled
from mad dogs and from streets black with funerals, to
gather the first figs of the season in the country. It is
probable that, when he, long after, poured forth in verse
his gratitude to the Providence which had enabled him to
breathe unhurt in tainted air, he was thinking of the
August and September which he passed at Rome.

It was not till the latter end of October that he tore himself away from the masterpieces of ancient and modern art
which are collected in the city so long the mistress of the
world. He then journeyed northward, passed through

Siena, and for a moment forgot his prejudices in favor of
classic architecture as he looked on the magnificent cathedral. At Florence he spent some days with the Duke of
Shrewsbury, who, cloyed with the pleasures of ambition, and
impatient of its pains, fearing both parties, and loving
neither, had determined to hide in an Italian retreat talents
and accomplishments which, if they had been united with
fixed principles and civil courage, might have made him the
foremost man of his age. These days, we are told, passed
pleasantly; and we can easily believe it. For Addison
was a delightful companion when he was at his ease; and
the Duke, though he seldom forgot that he was a Talbot, had
the invaluable art of putting at ease all who came near him.

Addison gave some time to Florence, and especially to
the sculptures in the Museum, which he preferred even to
those of the Vatican. He then pursued his journey through
a country in which the ravages of the last war were still
discernible, and in which all men were looking forward
with dread to a still fiercer conflict. Eugene had already
descended from the Rhætian Alps to dispute with Catinat
the rich plain of Lombardy. The faithless ruler of Savoy
was still reckoned among the allies of Lewis. England had
not yet actually declared war against France; but Manchester had left Paris; and the negotiations which produced the Grand Alliance against the house of Bourbon were
in progress. Under such circumstances, it was desirable for
an English traveller to reach neutral ground without delay.
Addison resolved to cross Mont Cenis. It was December;
and the road was very different from that which now
reminds the stranger of the power and genius of Napoleon.
The winter, however, was mild; and the passage was, for
those times, easy. To this journey Addison alluded when,
in the ode which we have already quoted, he said that for
him the Divine goodness had warmed the hoary Alpine
hills.

It was in the midst of the eternal snow that he composed his Epistle to his friend Montague, now Lord Halifax. That Epistle, once widely renowned, is now known only to curious readers, and will hardly be considered by those to whom it is known as in any perceptible degree heightening Addison's fame. It is, however, decidedly superior to any English composition which he had previously published. Nay, we think it quite as good as any poem in heroic metre which appeared during the interval between the death of Dryden and the publication of the Essay on Criticism. It contains passages as good as the second-rate passages of Pope, and would have added to the reputation of Parnell or Prior.

But, whatever be the literary merits or defects of the Epistle, it undoubtedly does honor to the principles and spirit of the author. Halifax had now nothing to give. He had fallen from power, had been held up to obloquy, had been impeached by the House of Commons, and, though his peers had dismissed the impeachment, had, as it seemed, little chance of ever again filling high office. The Epistle, written at such a time, is one among many proofs that there was no mixture of cowardice or meanness in the suavity and moderation which distinguished Addison from all the other public men of those stormy times.

At Geneva the traveller learned that a partial change of ministry had taken place in England, and that the Earl of Manchester had become Secretary of State. Manchester exerted himself to serve his young friend. It was thought advisable that an English agent should be near the person of Eugene in Italy; and Addison, whose diplomatic education was now finished, was the man selected. He was preparing to enter on his honorable functions, when all his prospects were for a time darkened by the death of William the Third.

Anne had long felt a strong aversion, personal, political,

and religious, to the Whig party. That aversion appeared in the first measures of her reign. Manchester was deprived of the seals, after he had held them only a few weeks. Neither Somers nor Halifax was sworn of the privy council. Addison shared the fate of his three patrons. His hopes of employment in the public service were at an end; his pension was stopped; and it was necessary for him to support himself by his own exertions. He became tutor to a young English traveller, and appears to have rambled with his pupil over great part of Switzerland and Germany. At this time he wrote his pleasing treatise on Medals. It was not published till after his death; but several distinguished scholars saw the manuscript, and gave just praise to the grace of the style, and to the learning and ingenuity evinced by the quotations.

From Germany Addison repaired to Holland, where he learned the melancholy news of his father's death. After passing some months in the United Provinces, he returned about the close of the year 1703 to England. He was there cordially received by his friends, and introduced by them into the Kit Cat Club, a society in which were collected all the various talents and accomplishments which then gave lustre to the Whig party.

Addison was, during some months after his return from the Continent, hard pressed by pecuniary difficulties. But it was soon in the power of his noble patrons to serve him effectually. A political change, silent and gradual, but of the highest importance, was in daily progress. The accession of Anne had been hailed by the Tories with transports of joy and hope; and for a time it seemed that the Whigs had fallen never to rise again.

But the country gentlemen and country clergymen were fated to be deceived, not for the last time. The prejudices and passions which raged without control in vicarages, in cathedral closes, and in the manor-houses of fox-hunting squires, were not shared by the chiefs of the ministry. Those statesmen saw that it was both for the public interest and for their own interest to adopt a Whig policy, at least as respected the alliances of the country and the conduct of the war. But if the foreign policy of the Whigs were adopted, it was impossible to abstain from adopting also their financial policy. The natural consequences followed. The rigid Tories were alienated from the Government. The votes of the Whigs became necessary to it. The votes of the Whigs could be secured only by further concessions; and further concessions the queen was induced to make.

Such was the state of things when tidings arrived of the great battle fought at Blenheim on the 13th August, 1704. By the Whigs the news was hailed with transports of joy and pride. No fault, no cause of quarrel, could be remembered by them against the commander whose genius had, in one day, changed the face of Europe, saved the imperial throne, humbled the house of Bourbon, and secured the Act of Settlement against foreign hostility. The feeling of the Tories was very different. They could not indeed, without imprudence, openly express regret at an event so glorious to their country; but their congratulations were so cold and sullen as to give deep disgust to the victorious general and his friends.

Lord Treasurer Godolphin was not a reading man. Whatever time he could spare from business he was in the habit of spending at Newmarket or at the card-table. But he was not absolutely indifferent to poetry; and he was too intelligent an observer not to perceive that literature was a formidable engine of political warfare, and that the great Whig leaders had strengthened their party, and raised their character, by extending a liberal and judicious patronage to good writers. He was mortified, and not without reason, by the exceeding badness of the poems which appeared in honor of the battle of Blenheim. One of these poems has been rescued from

> Think of two thousand gentlemen at least,
> And each man mounted on his capering beast;
> Into the Danube they were pushed by shoals.

Where to procure better verses the treasurer did not know. He understood how to negotiate a loan, or remit a subsidy: he was also well versed in the history of running horses and fighting cocks; but his acquaintance among the poets was very small. He consulted Halifax; but Halifax affected to decline the office of adviser. He had, he said, done his best, when he had power, to encourage men whose abilities and acquirements might do honor to their country. Those times were over. Other maxims had prevailed. Merit was suffered to pine in obscurity, and the public money was squandered on the undeserving. "I do know," he added, "a gentleman who would celebrate the battle in a manner worthy of the subject; but I will not name him." Godolphin, who was expert at the soft answer which turneth away wrath, and who was under the necessity of paying court to the Whigs, gently replied that there was too much ground for Halifax's complaints, but that what was amiss should in time be rectified, and that in the mean time the services of a man such as Halifax had described should be liberally rewarded. Halifax then mentioned Addison, but, mindful of the dignity as well as of the pecuniary interest of his friend, insisted that the minister should apply in the most courteous manner to Addison himself; and this Godolphin promised to do.

Addison then occupied a garret up three pair of stairs, over a small shop in the Haymarket. In this humble lodging he was surprised, on the morning which followed the conversation between Godolphin and Halifax, by a visit from no less a person than the Right Honorable Henry Boyle, then Chancellor of the Exchequer, and afterward Lord Carleton. This high-born minister had been sent by the Lord Treasurer as ambassador to the needy poet.

Addison readily undertook the proposed task, a task which, to so good a Whig, was probably a pleasure. When the poem was little more than half finished, he showed it to Godolphin, who was delighted with it, and particularly with the famous similitude of the Angel. Addison was instantly appointed to a commissionership worth about two hundred pounds a year, and was assured that this appointment was only an earnest of greater favors.

The Campaign came forth, and was as much admired by the public as by the minister. It pleases us less, on the whole, than the Epistle to Halifax. Yet it undoubtedly ranks high among the poems which appeared during the interval between the death of Dryden and the dawn of Pope's genius. The chief merit of the Campaign, we think, is that which was noticed by Johnson, the manly and rational rejection of fiction. The first great poet whose works have come down to us sung of war long before war became a science or a trade. If, in his time, there was enmity between two little Greek towns, each poured forth its crowd of citizens, ignorant of discipline, and armed with implements of labor rudely turned into weapons. On each side appeared conspicuous a few chiefs whose wealth had enabled them to procure good armor, horses, and chariots, and whose leisure had enabled them to practise military exercises. One such chief, if he were a man of great strength, agility, and courage, would probably be more formidable than twenty common men; and the force and dexterity with which he flung his spear might have no inconsiderable share in deciding the event of the day. Such were probably the battles with which Homer was familiar. But Homer related the actions of men of a former generation, of men who sprung from the gods, and communed with the gods face to face, of men one of whom could with ease hurl rocks which two sturdy hinds of a later period would be unable even to lift. He therefore naturally represented

their martial exploits as resembling in kind, but far surpass-
ing in magnitude, those of the stoutest and most expert
combatants of his own age. Achilles, clad in celestial
armor, drawn by celestial coursers, grasping the spear
which none but himself could raise, driving all Troy and
Lycia before him, and choking Scamander with dead, was
only a magnificent exaggeration of the real hero, who,
strong, fearless, accustomed to the use of weapons, guarded
by a shield and helmet of the best Sidonian fabric, and
whirled along by horses of Thessalian breed, struck down
with his own right arm foe after foe. In all rude societies
similar notions are found. There are at this day countries
where the Lifeguardsman Shaw would be considered as a
much greater warrior than the Duke of Wellington. Bona-
parte loved to describe the astonishment with which the
Mamelukes looked at his diminutive figure. Mourad Bey, distinguished above all his fellows by his bodily strength, and by
the skill with which he managed his horse and his sabre, could
not believe that a man who was scarcely five feet high, and
rode like a butcher, could be the greatest soldier in Europe.

Homer's descriptions of war had therefore as much truth
as poetry requires. But truth was altogether wanting to
the performances of those who, writing about battles which
had scarcely anything in common with the battles of his
times, servilely imitated his manner. The folly of Silius
Italicus, in particular, is positively nauseous. He undertook to record in verse the vicissitudes of a great struggle
between generals of the first order; and his narrative is made
up of the hideous wounds which these generals inflicted
with their own hands. This detestable fashion was copied
in modern times, and continued to prevail down to the age
of Addison. Several versifiers had described William turning thousands to flight by his single prowess, and dyeing
the Boyne with Irish blood. Nay, so estimable a writer as
John Philips, the author of The Splendid Shilling, repre-

sented Marlborough as having won the battle of Blenheim
merely by strength of muscle and skill in fence. The following lines may serve as an example: —

Churchill, viewing where

The violence of Tallard most prevail'd,
Came to oppose his slaughtering arm. With speed
Precipitate he rode, urging his way
O'er hills of gasping heroes, and fallen steeds
Rolling in death. Destruction, grim with blood,
Attends his furious course. Around his head
The glowing balls play innocent, while he
With dire impetuous sway deals fatal blows
Among the flying Gauls. In Gallic blood
He dyes his reeking sword, and strews the ground
With headless ranks. What can they do? Or how
Withstand his wide-destroying sword?

Addison, with excellent sense and taste, departed from
this ridiculous fashion. He reserved his praise for the
qualities which made Marlborough truly great, energy,
sagacity, military science. But, above all, the poet extolled
the firmness of that mind which, in the midst of confusion,
uproar, and slaughter, examined and disposed everything
with the serene wisdom of a higher intelligence.

Here it was that he introduced the famous comparison of
Marlborough to an angel guiding the whirlwind. We will
not dispute the general justice of Johnson's remarks on this
passage. But we must point out one circumstance which
appears to have escaped all the critics. The extraordinary
effect which this simile produced when it first appeared,
and which to the following generation seemed inexplicable,
is doubtless to be chiefly attributed to a line which most
readers now regard as a feeble parenthesis,

Such as, of late, o'er pale Britannia pass'd.

Addison spoke, not of a storm, but of the storm. The
great tempest of November, 1703, the only tempest which

in our latitude has equalled the rage of a tropical hurricane, had left a dreadful recollection in the minds of all men. No other tempest was ever in this country the occasion of a parliamentary address or of a public fast. Whole fleets had been cast away. Large mansions had been blown down. One prelate had been buried beneath the ruins of his palace. London and Bristol had presented the appearance of cities just sacked. Hundreds of families were still in mourning. The prostrate trunks of large trees, and the ruins of houses, still attested, in all the Southern counties, the fury of the blast. The popularity which the simile of the angel enjoyed among Addison's contemporaries has always seemed to us to be a remarkable instance of the advantage which, in rhetoric and poetry, the particular has over the general.

Soon after the Campaign, was published Addison's Narrative of his Travels in Italy. The first effect produced by this Narrative was disappointment. The crowd of readers who expected politics and scandal, speculations on the projects of Victor Amadeus, and anecdotes about the jollities of convents and the amours of cardinals and nuns, were confounded by finding that the writer's mind was much more occupied by the war between the Trojans and Rutulians than by the war between France and Austria; and that he seemed to have heard no scandal of later date than the gallantries of the Empress Faustina. In time, however, the judgment of the many was overruled by that of the few; and, before the book was reprinted, it was so eagerly sought that it sold for five times the original price. It is still read with pleasure: the style is pure and flowing; the classical quotations and allusions are numerous and happy; and we are now and then charmed by that singularly humane and delicate humor in which Addison excelled all men. Yet this agreeable work, even when considered merely as the history of a literary tour, may justly be censured on account of its faults of omission. We have already said that, though rich in extracts from the Latin poets, it contains scarcely any references to the Latin orators and historians. We must add that it contains little or rather no information respecting the history and literature of modern Italy. The truth is, that Addison knew little, and cared less, about the literature of modern Italy. His favorite models were Latin. His favorite critics were French. Half the Tuscan poetry that he had read seemed to him monstrous, and the other half tawdry.

His Travels were followed by the lively opera of Rosamond. This piece was ill set to music, and therefore failed on the stage, but it completely succeeded in print, and is indeed excellent in its kind. The smoothness with which the verses glide, and the elasticity with which they bound, is, to our ears at least, very pleasing. We are inclined to think that if Addison had left heroic couplets to Pope, and blank verse to Rowe, and had employed himself in writing airy and spirited songs, his reputation as a poet would have stood far higher than it now does. Some years after his death, Rosamond was set to new music by Doctor Arne, and was performed with complete success. Several passages long retained their popularity, and were daily sung, during the latter part of George the Second's reign, at all the harpsichords in England.

While Addison thus amused himself, his prospects, and the prospects of his party, were constantly becoming brighter and brighter. In the spring of 1705, the ministers were freed from the restraint imposed by a House of Commons in which Tories of the most perverse class had the ascendancy. The elections were favorable to the Whigs. The coalition which had been tacitly and gradually formed was now openly avowed. The Great Seal was given to Cowper. Somers and Halifax were sworn of the council. Halifax was sent in the following year to carry the decorations of the Order of the Garter to the Electoral Prince of Hanover, and was accompanied on this honorable mission by Addison, who had just been made Under-secretary of State. The Secretary of State under whom Addison first served was Sir Charles Hedges, a Tory. But Hedges was soon dismissed to make room for the most vehement of Whigs, Charles, Earl of Sunderland. In every department of the State, indeed, the High Churchmen were compelled to give place to their opponents. At the close of 1707, the Tories who still remained in office strove to rally, with Harley at their head. But the attempt, though favored by the queen, who had always been a Tory at heart, and who had now quarrelled with the Duchess of Malborough, was unsuccessful. The time was not yet. The Captain General was at the height of popularity and glory. The Low Church party had a majority in Parliament. The country squires and rectors, though occasionally uttering a savage growl, were for the most part in a state of torpor, which lasted till they were roused into activity, and indeed into madness, by the prosecution of Sacheverell. Harley and his adherents were compelled to retire. The victory of the Whigs was complete. At the general election of 1708 their strength in the House of Commons became irresistible; and, before the end of that year, Somers was made Lord President of the Council, and Wharton Lord Lieutenant of Ireland.

Addison sat for Malmsbury in the House of Commons which was elected in 1708. But the House of Commons was not the field for him. The bashfulness of his nature made his wit and eloquence useless in debate. He once rose, but could not overcome his diffidence, and ever after remained silent. Nobody can think it strange that a great writer should fail as a speaker. But many, probably, will think it strange that Addison's failure as a speaker should have had no unfavorable effect on his success as a politician. In our time, a man of high rank and great fortune might, though speaking very little and very ill, hold a considera-

ble post.   But it would now be inconceivable that a mere
adventurer, a man who, when out of office, must live by his
pen, should in a few years become successively Under-secretary of State, Chief Secretary for Ireland, and Secretary of
State, without some oratorical talent.   Addison, without'
high birth, and with little property, rose to a post which
dukes, the heads of the great houses of Talbot, Russell, and
Bentinck have thought it an honor to fill.   Without opening his lips in debate, he rose to a post the highest that
Chatham or Fox ever reached.   And this he did before he
had been nine years in Parliament.   We must look for the
explanation of this seeming miracle to the peculiar circumstances in which that generation was placed.   During the
interval which elapsed between the time when the censor-
ship of the Press ceased, and the time when parliamentary
proceedings began to be freely reported, literary talents
were, to a public man, of much more importance, and
oratorical talents of much less importance, than in our
time.   At present, the best way of giving rapid and wide
publicity to a fact or an argument is to introduce that
fact or argument into a speech made in Parliament.   If a
political tract were to appear superior to the Conduct of the
Allies, or to the best numbers of The Freeholder, the circulation of such a tract would be languid indeed when compared with the circulation of every remarkable word uttered
in the deliberations of the legislature.   A speech made in
the House of Commons at four in the morning is on thirty
thousand tables before ten.   A speech made on the Monday
is read on the Wednesday by multitudes in Antrim and
Aberdeenshire.   The orator, by the help of the shorthand
writer, has to a great extent superseded the pamphleteer.
It was not so in the reign of Anne.   The best speech
could then produce no effect except on those who heard it.
It was only by means of the press that the opinion of the
public without doors could be influenced; and the opinion

of the public without doors could not but be of the highest importance in a country governed by parliaments, and indeed at that time governed by triennial parliaments. The pen was, therefore, a more formidable political engine than the tongue. When these things are duly considered, it will not be thought strange that Addison should have climbed higher in the State than any other Englishman has ever, by means merely of literary talents, been able to climb. Swift would, in all probability, have climbed as high, if he had not been encumbered by his cassock and his pudding sleeves. As far as the homage of the great went, Swift had as much of it as if he had been Lord Treasurer.

To the influence which Addison derived from his literary talents was added all the influence which arises from character. The world, always ready to think the worst of needy political adventurers, was forced to make one exception. Restlessness, violence, audacity, laxity of principle, are the vices ordinarily attributed to that class of men. But faction itself could not deny that Addison had, through all changes of fortune, been strictly faithful to his early opinions and to his early friends; that his integrity was without stain; that his whole deportment indicated a fine sense of the becoming; that, in the utmost heat of controversy, his zeal was tempered by a regard for truth, humanity, and social decorum; that no outrage could ever provoke him to retaliation unworthy of a Christian and a gentleman; and that his only faults were a too sensitive delicacy, and a modesty which amounted to bashfulness.

He was undoubtedly one of the most popular men of his time; and much of his popularity he owed, we believe, to that very timidity which his friends lamented. That timidity often prevented him from exhibiting his talents to the best advantage. But it propitiated Nemesis. It averted that envy which would otherwise have been excited by fame so splendid, and by so rapid an elevation. No man is

so great a favorite with the public as he who is at once an
object of admiration, of respect, and of pity; and such were
the feelings which Addison inspired. Those who enjoyed
the privilege of hearing his familiar conversation declared
with one voice that it was superior even to his writings.
The brilliant Mary Montague said that she had known all
the wits, and that Addison was the best company in the
world. The malignant Pope was forced to own that there
was a charm in Addison's talk which could be found no-
where else. Swift, when burning with animosity against
the Whigs, could not but confess to Stella that, after all,
he had never known any associate so agreeable as Addison.
Steele, an excellent judge of lively conversation, said that
the conversation of Addison was at once the most polite
and the most mirthful that could be imagined; that it was
Terence and Catullus in one, heightened by an exquisite
something which was neither Terence nor Catullus, but
Addison alone. Young, an excellent judge of serious conversation, said that when Addison was at his ease, he went
on in a noble strain of thought and language, so as to chain
the attention of every hearer. Nor were Addison's great
colloquial powers more admirable than the courtesy and
softness of heart which appeared in his conversation. At
the same time, it would be too much to say that he was
wholly devoid of the malice which is, perhaps, inseparable
from a keen sense of the ludicrous. He had one habit
which both Swift and Stella applauded, and which we hardly
know how to blame. If his first attempts to set a pre-
suming dunce right were ill received, he changed his tone,
"assented with civil leer," and lured the flattered coxcomb
deeper and deeper into absurdity. That such was his practice we should, we think, have guessed from his works.
The Tatler's criticisms on Mr. Softly's sonnet, and The
Spectator's dialogue with the politician who is so zealous
for the honor of Lady Q—p—t—s, are excellent specimens

Such were Addison's talents for conversation. But his rare gifts were not exhibited to crowds or to strangers. As soon as he entered a large company, as soon as he saw an unknown face, his lips were sealed, and his manners became constrained. None who met him only in great assemblies would have been able to believe that he was the same man who had often kept a few friends listening and laughing round a table, from the time when the play ended till the clock of St. Paul's in Covent Garden struck four. Yet, even at such a table, he was not seen to the best advantage. To enjoy his conversation in the highest perfection, it was necessary to be alone with him, and to hear him, in his own phrase, think aloud. "There is no such thing," he used to say, "as real conversation, but between two persons."

This timidity, a timidity surely neither ungraceful nor unamiable, led Addison into the two most serious faults which can with justice be imputed to him. He found that wine broke the spell which lay on his fine intellect, and was therefore too easily seduced into convivial excess. Such excess was in that age regarded, even by grave men, as the most venial of all peccadilloes, and was so far from being a mark of ill-breeding that it was almost essential to the character of a fine gentleman. But the smallest speck is seen on a white ground; and almost all the biographers of Addison have said something about this failing. Of any other statesman or writer of Queen Anne's reign, we should no more think of saying that he sometimes took too much wine than that he wore a long wig and a sword.

To the excessive modesty of Addison's nature we must ascribe another fault which generally arises from a very different cause. He became a little too fond of seeing himself surrounded by a small circle of admirers, to whom he was as a king, or rather as a god. All these men were far inferior to him in ability, and some of them had very serious faults. Nor did those faults escape his observation; for, if

ever there was an eye which saw through and through men,
it was the eye of Addison. But, with the keenest observation, and the finest sense of the ridiculous, he had a large
charity. The feeling with which he looked on most of his
humble companions was one of benevolence, slightly tinc-
tured with contempt. He was at perfect ease in their company; he was grateful for their devoted attachment; and
he loaded them with benefits. Their veneration for him
appears to have exceeded that with which Johnson was
regarded by Boswell, or Warburton by Hurd. It was not
in the power of adulation to turn such a head, or deprave
such a heart, as Addison's. But it must in candor be admitted that he contracted some of the faults which can
scarcely be avoided by any person who is so unfortunate as
to be the oracle of a small literary coterie.

One member of this little society was Eustace Budgell,
a young Templar of some literature, and a distant relation
of Addison. There was at this time no stain on the character of Budgell, and it is not improbable that his career
would have been prosperous and honorable, if the life of his
cousin had been prolonged. But when the master was laid
in the grave, the disciple broke loose from all restraint,
descended rapidly from one degree of vice and misery to
another, ruined his fortune by follies, attempted to repair it
by crimes, and at length closed a wicked and unhappy life
by self-murder. Yet, to the last, the wretched man, gam-
bler, lampooner, cheat, forger, as he was, retained his affection and veneration for Addison, and recorded those feelings
in the last lines which he traced before he hid himself from
infamy under London Bridge.

Another of Addison's favorite companions was Ambrose
Philips, a good Whig and a middling poet, who had the
honor of bringing into fashion a species of composition
which has been called, after his name, Namby Pamby. But
the most remarkable members of the little senate, as Pope

long afterward called it, were Richard Steele and Thomas Tickell.

Steele had known Addison from childhood. They had been together at the Charter House and at Oxford; but circumstances had then, for a time, separated them widely. Steele had left college without taking a degree, had been disinherited by a rich relation, had led a vagrant life, had served in the army, had tried to find the philosopher's stone, and had written a religious treatise and several comedies. He was one of those people whom it is impossible either to hate or to respect. His temper was sweet, his affections warm, his spirits lively, his passions strong, and his principles weak. His life was spent in sinning and repenting; in inculcating what was right, and doing what was wrong. In speculation, he was a man of piety and honor; in practice, he was much of the rake and a little of the swindler. He was, however, so good-natured that it was not easy to be seriously angry with him, and that even rigid moralists felt more inclined to pity than to blame him, when he diced himself into a spunging house or drank himself into a fever. Addison regarded Steele with kindness not unmingled with scorn, tried, with little success, to keep him out of scrapes, introduced him to the great, procured a good place for him, corrected his plays, and, though by no means rich, lent him large sums of money. One of these loans appears, from a letter dated in August, 1708, to have amounted to a thousand pounds. These pecuniary transactions probably led to frequent bickerings. It is said that, on one occasion, Steele's negligence, or dishonesty, provoked Addison to repay himself by the help of a bailiff. We cannot join with Miss Aikin in rejecting this story. Johnson heard it from Savage, who heard it from Steele. Few private transactions which took place a hundred and twenty years ago are proved by stronger evidence than this. But we can by no means agree with those who condemn Addison's severity. The

most amiable of mankind may well be moved to indignation, when what he has earned hardly, and lent with great
inconvenience to himself, for the purpose of relieving a
friend in distress, is squandered with insane profusion.
The real history, we have little doubt, was something like
this: A letter comes to Addison, imploring help in pathetic
terms, and promising reformation and speedy repayment.
Poor Dick declares that he has not an inch of candle, or a
bushel of coals, or credit with the butcher for a shoulder of
mutton.   Addison is moved.   He determines to deny himself some medals which are wanting to his series of the
Twelve Cæsars; to put off buying the new edition of
Bayle's Dictionary; and to wear his old sword and buckles
another year.   In this way he manages to send a hundred
pounds to his friend.   The next day he calls on Steele, and
finds scores of gentlemen and ladies assembled.   The fiddles
are playing.   The table is groaning under champagne, bur-
gundy, and pyramids of sweetmeats.   Is it strange that a
man whose kindness is thus abused should send sheriff's
officers to reclaim what is due to him ?

Tickell was a young man, fresh from Oxford, who had
introduced himself to public notice by writing a most ingenious and graceful little poem in praise of the opera of
Rosamond.   He deserved, and at length attained, the first
place in Addison's friendship.   For a time Steele and Tickell were on good terms.   But they loved Addison too much
to love each other, and at length became as bitter enemies
as the rival bulls in Virgil.

At the close of 1708, Wharton became Lord Lieutenant
of Ireland, and appointed Addison Chief Secretary.   Addison was consequently under the necessity of quitting London for Dublin.   Besides the chief secretaryship, which
was then worth about two thousand pounds a year, he obtained a patent appointing him keeper of the Irish Records
for life, with a salary of three or four hundred a year.

Budgell accompanied his cousin in the capacity of private secretary.

Wharton and Addison had nothing in common but Whiggism. The Lord Lieutenant was not only licentious and corrupt, but was distinguished from other libertines and jobbers by a callous impudence which presented the strongest contrast to the Secretary's gentleness and delicacy. Many parts of the Irish administration at this time appear to have deserved serious blame. But against Addison there was not a murmur. He long afterward asserted, what all the evidence which we have ever seen tends to prove, that his diligence and integrity gained the friendship of all the most considerable persons in Ireland.

The parliamentary career of Addison in Ireland has, we think, wholly escaped the notice of all his biographers. He was elected member for the borough of Cavan in the summer of 1709; and in the journals of two sessions his name frequently occurs. Some of the entries appear to indicate that he so far overcame his timidity as to make speeches. Nor is this by any means improbable; for the Irish House of Commons was a far less formidable audience than the English House; and many tongues which were tied by fear in the greater assembly became fluent in the smaller. Gerard Hamilton, for example, who, from fear of losing the fame gained by his single speech, sat mute at Westminster during forty years, spoke with great effect at Dublin when he was secretary to Lord Halifax.

While Addison was in Ireland, an event occurred to which he owes his high and permanent rank among British writers. As yet his fame rested on performances which, though highly respectable, were not built for duration, and which would, if he had produced nothing else, have now been almost forgotten, on some excellent Latin verses, on some English verses which occasionally rose above mediocrity, and on a book of travels, agreeably written, but not indicating any extraordinary powers of mind. These works showed him to be a man of taste, sense, and learning. The time had come when he was to prove himself a man of genius, and to enrich our literature with compositions which will live as long as the English language.

In the spring of 1709, Steele formed a literary project, of which he was far indeed from foreseeing the consequences. Periodical papers had during many years been published in London. Most of these were political; but in some of them questions of morality, taste, and love casuistry had been discussed. The literary merit of these works was small indeed; and even their names are now known only to the curious.

Steele had been appointed gazetteer by Sunderland, at the request, it is said, of Addison, and thus had access to foreign intelligence earlier and more authentic than was in those times within the reach of an ordinary news-writer. This circumstance seems to have suggested to him the scheme of publishing a periodical paper on a new plan. It was to appear on the days on which the post left London for the country, which were, in that generation, the Tuesdays, Thursdays, and Saturdays. It was to contain the foreign news, accounts of theatrical representations, and the literary gossip of Will's and of the Grecian. It was also to contain remarks on the fashionable topics of the day, compliments to beauties, pasquinades on noted sharpers, and criticisms on popular preachers. The aim of Steele does not appear to have been at first higher than this. He was not ill qualified to conduct the work which he had planned. His public intelligence he drew from the best sources. He knew the town, and had paid dear for his knowledge. He had read much more than the dissipated men of that time were in the habit of reading. He was a rake among scholars, and a scholar among rakes. His style was easy and not incorrect, and, though his wit and humor were of no high order, his gay animal spirits imparted to his compositions an air of vivacity which ordinary readers could hardly distinguish from comic genius. His writings have been well compared to those light wines which, though deficient in body and flavor, are yet a pleasant small drink, if not kept too long or carried too far.

Isaac Bickerstaff, Esquire, Astrologer, was an imaginary person, almost as well known in that age as Mr. Paul Pry or Mr. Samuel Pickwick in ours. Swift had assumed the name of Bickerstaff in a satirical pamphlet against Partridge, the maker of almanacs. Partridge had been fool enough to publish a furious reply. Bickerstaff had rejoined in a second pamphlet still more diverting than the first. All the wits had combined to keep up the joke, and the town was long in convulsions of laughter. Steele determined to employ the name which this controversy had made popular; and, in April 1709, it was announced that Isaac Bickerstaff, Esquire, Astrologer, was about to publish a paper called The Tatler.

Addison had not been consulted about this scheme; but as soon as he heard of it, he determined to give his assistance. The effect of that assistance cannot be better described than in Steele's own words. "I fared," he said, "like a distressed prince who calls in a powerful neighbor to his aid. I was undone by my auxiliary. When I had once called him in, I could not subsist without dependence on him." "The paper," he says elsewhere, "was advanced indeed. It was raised to a greater thing than I intended it."

It is probable that Addison, when he sent across St. George's Channel his first contributions to The Tatler, had no notion of the extent and variety of his own powers. He was the possessor of a vast mine, rich with a hundred ores. But he had been acquainted only with the least precious part of his treasures, and had hitherto contented himself with producing sometimes copper and sometimes lead, intermingled with a little silver. All at once, and by mere accident, he had lighted on an inexhaustible vein of the finest gold.

The mere choice and arrangement of his words would have sufficed to make his essays classical. For never, not even by Dryden, not even by Temple, had the English language been written with such sweetness, grace, and facility. But this was the smallest part of Addison's praise. Had he clothed his thoughts in the half French style of Horace Walpole, or in the half Latin style of Dr. Johnson, or in the half German jargon of the present day, his genius would have triumphed over all faults of manner. As a moral satirist he stands unrivalled. If ever the best Tatlers and Spectators were equalled in their own kind, we should be inclined to guess that it must have been by the lost comedies of Menander.

In wit, properly so called, Addison was not inferior to Cowley or Butler. No single ode of Cowley contains so many happy analogies as are crowded into the lines to Sir Godfrey Kneller; and we would undertake to collect from the Spectators as great a number of ingenious illustrations as can be found in Hudibras. The still higher faculty of invention Addison possessed in still larger measure. The numerous fictions, generally original, often wild and grotesque, but always singularly graceful and happy, which are found in his essays, fully entitle him to the rank of a great poet, a rank to which his metrical compositions give him no claim. As an observer of life, of manners, of all the shades of human character, he stands in the first class. And what he observed he had the art of communicating in two widely different ways. He could describe virtues, vices, habits, whims, as well as Clarendon. But he could do something better. He could call human beings into existence, and make them exhibit themselves. If we wish to find anything more vivid than Addison's best portraits, we must go either to Shakespeare or to Cervantes.

But what shall we say of Addison's humor, of his sense of the ludicrous, of his power of awakening that sense in others, and of drawing mirth from incidents which occur every day, and from little peculiarities of temper and manner, such as may be found in every man? We feel the charm; we give ourselves up to it; but we strive in vain to analyze it.

Perhaps the best way of describing Addison's peculiar pleasantry is to compare it with the pleasantry of some other great satirists. The three most eminent masters of the art of ridicule, during the eighteenth century, were, we conceive, Addison, Swift, and Voltaire. Which of the three had the greatest power of moving laughter may be questioned. But each of them, within his own domain, was supreme.

Voltaire is the prince of buffoons. His merriment is without disguise or restraint. He gambols; he grins; he shakes his sides; he points the finger; he turns up the nose; he shoots out the tongue. The manner of Swift is the very opposite to this. He moves laughter, but never joins in it. He appears in his works such as he appeared in society. All the company are convulsed with merriment, while the dean, the author of all the mirth, preserves an invincible gravity, and even sourness of aspect, and gives utterance to the most eccentric and ludicrous fancies, with the air of a man reading the commination service.

The manner of Addison is as remote from that of Swift as from that of Voltaire. He neither laughs out like the French wit, nor, like the Irish wit, throws a double portion of severity into his countenance while laughing inwardly; but preserves a look peculiarly his own, a look of demure serenity, disturbed only by an arch sparkle of the eye, an almost imperceptible elevation of the brow, an almost imperceptible curl of the lip. His tone is never that either of a Jack Pudding or of a Cynic. It is that of a gentleman, in whom the quickest sense of the ridiculous is constantly tempered by good nature and good breeding.

We own that the humor of Addison is, in our opinion, of a more delicious flavor than the humor of either Swift or Voltaire. Thus much, at least, is certain, that both Swift and Voltaire have been successfully mimicked, and that no man has yet been able to mimic Addison.

But that which chiefly distinguishes Addison from Swift, from Voltaire, from almost all the other great masters of ridicule, is the grace, the nobleness, the moral purity, which we find even in his merriment. Severity, gradually hardening and darkening into misanthropy, characterizes the works of Swift. The nature of Voltaire was, indeed, not inhuman; but he venerated nothing. Neither in the masterpieces of art nor in the purest examples of virtue, neither in the Great First Cause nor in the awful enigma of the grave, could he see anything but subjects for drollery. Nothing great, nothing amiable, no moral duty, no doctrine of natural or revealed religion, has ever been associated by Addison with any degrading idea. His humanity is without a parallel in literary history. The highest proof of virtue is to possess boundless power without abusing it. No kind of power is more formidable than the power of making men ridiculous; and that power Addison possessed in boundless measure. How grossly that power was abused by Swift and by Voltaire is well known. But of Addison it may be confidently affirmed that he has blackened no man's character, nay, that it would be difficult, if not impossible, to find in all the volumes which he has left us a single taunt which can be called ungenerous or unkind. Yet he had detractors, whose malignity might have seemed to justify as terrible a revenge as that which men, not superior to him in genius, wreaked on Bettesworth and on

Franc de Pompignan. He was a politician; he was the best writer of his party; he lived in times of fierce excitement, in times when persons of high character and station stooped to scurrility such as is now practised only by the basest of mankind. Yet no provocation and no example could induce him to return railing for railing.

Of the service which his essays rendered to morality it is difficult to speak too highly. It is true that, when The Tatler appeared, that age of outrageous profaneness and licentiousness which followed the Restoration had passed away. Jeremy Collier had shamed the theatres into something which, compared with the excesses of Etherege and Wycherley, might be called decency. Yet there still lingered in the public mind a pernicious notion that there was some connection between genius and profligacy, between the domestic virtues and the sullen formality of the Puritans. That error it is the glory of Addison to have dispelled. He taught the nation that the faith and the morality of Hale and Tillotson might be found in company with wit more sparkling than the wit of Congreve, and with humor richer than the humor of Vanbrugh. So effectually, indeed, did he retort on vice the mockery which had recently been directed against virtue, that, since his time, the open violation of decency has always been considered among us as the mark of a fool. And this revolution, the greatest and most salutary ever effected by any satirist, he accomplished, be it remembered, without writing one personal lampoon.

In the early contributions of Addison to The Tatler his peculiar powers were not fully exhibited. Yet, from the first, his superiority to all his coadjutors was evident. Some of his later Tatlers are fully equal to anything that he ever wrote. Among the portraits, we most admire Tom Folio, Ned Softly, and the Political Upholsterer. The Proceedings of the Court of Honor, the Thermometer of Zeal, the Story of the Frozen Words, the Memoirs of the Shilling, are excellent specimens of that ingenious and lively species of fiction in which Addison excelled all men.   There is one still better paper, of the same class. But though that paper, a hundred and thirty-three years ago, was probably thought as edifying as one of Smalridge's sermons, we dare not indicate it to the squeamish readers of the nineteenth century.

During the session of Parliament which commenced in November, 1709, and which the impeachment of Sacheverell has made memorable, Addison appears to have resided in London.   The Tatler was now more popular than any periodical paper had ever been; and his connection with it was generally known.   It was not known, however, that almost everything good in The Tatler was his.   The truth is, that the fifty or sixty numbers which we owe to him were not merely the best, but so decidedly the best that any five of them are more valuable than all the two hundred numbers in which he had no share.

He required, at this time, all the solace which he could derive from literary success.   The queen had always disliked the Whigs.   She had during some years disliked the Marlborough family.   But, reigning by a disputed title, she could not venture directly to oppose herself to a majority of both Houses of Parliament; and, engaged as she was in a war on the event of which her own crown was staked, she could not venture to disgrace a great and successful general. But at length, in the year 1710, the causes which had restrained her from showing her aversion to the Low Church party ceased to operate.   The trial of Sacheverell produced an outbreak of public feeling scarcely less violent than the outbreaks which we can ourselves remember in 1820 and in 1831.   The country gentlemen, the country clergymen, the rabble of the towns, were all, for once, on the same side. It was clear that, if a general election took place before the excitement abated, the Tories would have a majority.   The services of Marlborough had been so splendid that they were no longer necessary. The queen's throne was secure from all attack on the part of Lewis. Indeed, it seemed much more likely that the English and German armies would divide the spoils of Versailles and Marli than that a marshal of France would bring back the Pretender to St. James's. The queen, acting by the advice of Harley, determined to dismiss her servants. In June the change commenced. Sunderland was the first who fell. The Tories exulted over his fall. The Whigs tried, during a few weeks, to persuade themselves that her majesty had acted only from personal dislike to the secretary, and that she meditated no further alteration. But, early in August, Godolphin was surprised by a letter from Anne, which directed him to break his white staff. Even after this event, the irresolution or dissimulation of Harley kept up the hopes of the Whigs during another month; and then the ruin became rapid and violent. The Parliament was dissolved. The ministers were turned out. The Tories were called to office. The tide of popularity ran violently in favor of the High Church party. That party, feeble in the late House of Commons, was now irresistible. The power which the Tories had thus suddenly acquired, they used with blind and stupid ferocity.

None of the Whigs suffered more in the general wreck than Addison. He had just sustained some heavy pecuniary losses, of the nature of which we are imperfectly informed, when his secretaryship was taken from him. He had reason to believe that he should also be deprived of the small Irish office which he held by patent. He had just resigned his fellowship. It seems probable that he had already ventured to raise his eyes to a great lady, and that, while his political friends were in power, and while his own fortunes were rising, he had been, in the phrase of the romances which were then fashionable, permitted to hope. But Mr. Addison the ingenious writer and Mr. Addison the chief secretary were, in her ladyship's opinion, two very different persons. All these calamities united, however, could not disturb the serene cheerfulness of a mind conscious of innocence, and rich in its own wealth. He told his friends, with smiling resignation, that they ought to admire his philosophy; that he had lost at once his fortune, his place, his fellowship, and his mistress; that he must think of turning tutor again, and yet that his spirits were as good as ever.

He had one consolation. Of the unpopularity which his friends had incurred, he had no share. Such was the esteem with which he was regarded, that, while the most violent measures were taken for the purpose of forcing Tory members on Whig corporations, he was returned to Parliament without even a contest.

The only use which Addison appears to have made of the favor with which he was regarded by the Tories was to save some of his friends from the general ruin of the Whig party. He felt himself to be in a situation which made it his duty to take a decided part in politics. But the case of Steele and of Ambrose Philips was different. For Philips, Addison even condescended to solicit, with what success we have not ascertained. Steele held two places. He was gazetteer, and he was also a commissioner of stamps. The Gazette was taken from him. But he was suffered to retain his place in the Stamp Office, on an implied understanding that he should not be active against the new Government; and he was, during more than two years, induced by Addison to observe this armistice with tolerable fidelity.

Isaac Bickerstaff accordingly became silent upon politics, and the article of news, which had once formed about one-third of his paper, altogether disappeared. The Tatler had completely changed its character. It was now nothing but a series of essays on books, morals, and manners. Steele therefore resolved to bring it to a close, and to commence a new work on an improved plan. It was announced that this new work would be published daily. The undertaking was generally regarded as bold, or rather rash; but the event amply justified the confidence with which Steele relied on the fertility of Addison's genius. On the 2d of January, 1711, appeared the last Tatler. At the beginning of 'March following appeared the first of an incomparable series of papers, containing observations on life and literature by an imaginary Spectator.

The Spectator himself was conceived and drawn by Addison; and it is not easy to doubt that the portrait was meant to be in some features a likeness of the painter. The Spectator is a gentleman who, after passing a studious youth at the university, has travelled on classic ground, and has bestowed much attention on curious points of antiquity. He has, on his return, fixed his residence in London, and has observed all the forms of life which are to be found in that great city, has daily listened to the wits of Will's, has smoked with the philosophers of the Grecian, and has mingled with the parsons at Child's, and with the politicians at the St. James's. In the morning, he often listens to the hum of the Exchange; in the evening, his face is constantly to be seen in the pit of Drury Lane Theatre. But an insurmountable bashfulness prevents him from opening his mouth, except in a small circle of intimate friends.

These friends were first sketched by Steele. Four of the club, the templar, the clergyman, the soldier, and the merchant, were uninteresting figures, fit only for a background. But the other two, an old country baronet and an old town rake, though not delineated with a very delicate pencil, had some good strokes. Addison took the rude outlines into his own hands, retouched them, colored them, and is in truth the creator of the Sir Roger de Coverley and the Will Honeycomb with whom we are all familiar.

The plan of The Spectator must be allowed to be both original and eminently happy. Every valuable essay in the series may be read with pleasure separately; yet the five or six hundred essays form a whole, and a whole which has the interest of a novel. It must be remembered, too, that at that time no novel giving a lively and powerful picture of the common life and manners of England had appeared. Richardson was working as a compositor. Fielding was robbing birds' nests. Smollett was not yet born. The narrative, therefore, which connects together the Spectator's essays gave to our ancestors their first taste of an exquisite and untried pleasure. That narrative was indeed constructed with no art or labor. The events were such events as occur every day. Sir Roger comes up to town to see Eugenio, as the worthy baronet always calls Prince Eugene, goes with the Spectator on the water to Spring Gardens, walks among the tombs in the Abbey, and is frightened by the Mohawks, but conquers his apprehension so far as to go to the theatre when the Distressed Mother is acted. The Spectator pays a visit in the summer to Coverley Hall, is charmed with the old house, the old butler, and the old chaplain, eats a jack caught by Will Wimble, rides to the assizes, and hears a point of law discussed by Tom Touchy. At last a letter from the honest butler brings to the club the news that Sir Roger is dead. Will Honeycomb marries and reforms at sixty. The club breaks up; and the Spectator resigns his functions. Such events can hardly be said to form a plot; yet they are related with such truth, such grace, such wit, such humor, such pathos, such knowledge of the human heart, such knowledge of the ways of the world, that they charm us on the hundredth perusal. We have not the least doubt that if Addison had written a novel, on an extensive plan, it would have been superior to any that we possess. As it is, he is entitled to be considered not only as the greatest of the English essayists, but as the forerunner of the great English novelists.

We say this of Addison alone; for Addison is the Spectator. About three sevenths of the work are his; and it is no exaggeration to say that his worst essay is as good as the best essay of any of his coadjutors. His best essays approach near to absolute perfection; nor is their excellence more wonderful than their variety. His invention never seems to flag; nor is he ever under the necessity of repeating himself, or of wearing out a subject. There are no dregs in his wine. He regales us after the fashion of that prodigal nabob who held that there was only one good glass in a bottle. /As soon as we have tasted the first sparkling foam of a jest, it is withdrawn, and a fresh draught of nectar is at our lips. On the Monday we have an allegory as lively and ingenious as Lucian's Auction of Lives; on the Tuesday, an Eastern apologue as richly colored as the Tales of Scheherezade; on the Wednesday, a character described with the skill of La Bruyère; on the Thursday, a scene from common life equal to the best chapters in the Vicar of Wakefield; on the Friday, some sly Horatian pleasantry on fashionable follies, on hoops, patches, or puppet shows; and on the Saturday, a religious meditation, which will bear a comparison with the finest passages in Massillon.

It is dangerous to select where there is so much that deserves the highest praise. We will venture, however, to say that any person who wishes to form a just notion of the extent and variety of Addison's powers will do well to read at one sitting the following papers: the two Visits to the Abbey, the Visit to the Exchange, the Journal of the Retired Citizen, the Vision of Mirza, the Transmigrations of Pugg the Monkey, and the Death of Sir Roger de Coverley.

The least valuable of Addison's contributions to The Spectator are, in the judgment of our age, his critical papers.

Yet his critical papers are always luminous, and often ingenious. The very worst of them must be regarded as creditable to him, when the character of the school in which he has been trained is fairly considered. The best of them were much too good for his readers. In truth, he was not so far behind our generation as he was before his own. No essays in The Spectator were more censured and derided than those in which he raised his voice against the contempt with which our fine old ballads were regarded, and showed the scoffers that the same gold which, burnished and polished, gives lustre to the Æneid and the Odes of Horace, is mingled with the rude dross of Chevy Chase.

It is not strange that the success of The Spectator should have been such as no similar work has ever obtained. The number of copies daily distributed was at first three thousand. It subsequently increased, and had risen to near four thousand when the stamp tax was imposed. That tax was fatal to a crowd of journals. The Spectator, however, stood its ground, doubled its price, and, though its circulation fell off, still yielded a large revenue both to the State and to the authors. For particular papers the demand was immense; of some, it is said, twenty thousand copies were required. But this was not all. To have The Spectator served up every morning with the bohea and rolls was a luxury for the few. The majority were content to wait till essays enough had appeared to form a volume. Ten thousand copies of each volume were immediately taken off, and new editions were called for. It must be remembered that the population of England was then hardly a third of what it now is. The number of Englishmen who were in the habit of reading was probably not a sixth of what it now is. A shopkeeper or a farmer who found any pleasure in literature was a rarity. Nay, there was doubtless more than one knight of the shire whose country-seat did not contain ten books, receipt-books and books on farriery included. In these circumstances, the sale of The Spectator must be considered as indicating a popularity quite as great as that of the most successful works of Sir Walter Scott and Mr. Dickens in our own time.

At the close of 1712 The Spectator ceased to appear. It was probably felt that the short-faced gentleman and his club had been long enough before the town; and that it was time to withdraw them, and to replace them by a new set of characters. In a few weeks the first number of The Guardian was published. But The Guardian was unfortunate both in its birth and in its death. It began in dulness, and disappeared in a tempest of faction. The original plan was bad. Addison contributed nothing till sixty-six numbers had appeared; and it was then impossible to make The Guardian what The Spectator had been. Nestor Ironside and the Miss Lizards were people to whom even he could impart no interest. He could only furnish some excellent little essays, both serious and comic; and this he did.

Why Addison gave no assistance to The Guardian during the first two months of its existence is a question which has puzzled the editors and biographers, but which seems to us to admit of a very easy solution. He was then engaged in bringing his Cato on the stage.

The first four acts of this drama had been lying in his desk since his return from Italy. His modest and sensitive nature shrank from the risk of a public and shameful failure; and, though all who saw the manuscript were loud in praise, some thought it possible that an audience might become impatient even of very good rhetoric, and advised Addison to print the play without hazarding a representation. At length, after many fits of apprehension, the poet yielded to the urgency of his political friends, who hoped that the public would discover some analogy between the followers of Cæsar and the Tories, between Sempronius and the apostate Whigs, between Cato, struggling to the last for the liberties of Rome, and the band of patriots who still stood firm round Halifax and Wharton.

Addison gave the play to the managers of Drury Lane Theatre, without stipulating for any advantage to himself. They therefore thought themselves bound to spare no cost in scenery and dresses. The decorations, it is true, would not have pleased the skilful eye of Mr. Macready. Juba's waistcoat blazed with gold lace; Marcia's hoop was worthy of a duchess on the birthday; and Cato wore a wig worth fifty guineas. The prologue was written by Pope, and is undoubtedly a dignified and spirited composition. The part of the hero was excellently played by Booth. Steele undertook to pack a house. The boxes were in a blaze with the stars of the Peers in opposition. The pit was crowded with attentive and friendly listeners from the Inns of Court and the literary coffee-houses. Sir Gilbert Heathcote, Governor of the Bank of England, was at the head of a powerful body of auxiliaries from the City, warm men and true Whigs, but better known at Jonathan's and Garraway's than in the haunts of wits and critics.

These precautions were quite superfluous. The Tories, as a body, regarded Addison with no unkind feelings. Nor was it for their interest, professing, as they did, profound reverence for law and prescription, and abhorrence both of popular insurrection and of standing armies, to appropriate to themselves reflections thrown on the great military chief and demagogue, who, with the support of the legions and of the common people, subverted all the ancient institutions of his country. Accordingly, every shout that was raised by the members of the Kit Cat was echoed by the High Churchmen of the October; and the curtain at length fell amidst thunders of unanimous applause.

The delight and admiration of the town were described by The Guardian in terms which we might attribute to partiality, were it not that The Examiner, the organ of the ministry, held similar language. The Tories, indeed, found much to sneer at in the conduct of their opponents. Steele had on this, as on other occasions, shown more zeal than taste or judgment. The honest citizens who marched under the orders of Sir Gibby, as he was facetiously called, probably knew better when to buy and when to sell stock than when to clap and when to hiss at a play, and incurred some ridicule by making the hypocritical Sempronius their favorite, and by giving to his insincere rants louder plaudits than they bestowed on the temperate eloquence of Cato. Wharton, too, who had the incredible effrontery to applaud the lines about flying from prosperous vice and from the power of impious men to a private station, did not escape the sarcasms of those who justly thought that he could fly from nothing more vicious or impious than himself. The epilogue, which was written by Garth, a zealous Whig, was severely and not unreasonably censured as ignoble and out of place. But Addison was described, even by the bitterest Tory writers, as a gentleman of wit and virtue, in whose friendship many persons of both parties were happy, and whose name ought not to be mixed up with factious squabbles.

Of the jests by which the triumph of the Whig party was disturbed, the most severe and happy was Bolingbroke's. Between two acts, he sent for Booth to his box, and presented him, before the whole theatre, with a purse of fifty guineas for defending the cause of liberty so well against a perpetual dictator. This was a pungent allusion to the attempt which Marlborough had made, not long before his fall, to obtain a patent creating him Captain General for life.

It was April; and in April, a hundred and thirty years ago, the London season was thought to be far advanced. During a whole month, however, Cato was performed to overflowing houses, and brought into the treasury of the theatre twice the gains of an ordinary spring. In the summer the Drury Lane company went down to the Act at Oxford, and there, before an audience which retained an affectionate remembrance of Addison's accomplishments and virtues, his tragedy was acted during several days. The gownsmen began to besiege the theatre in the forenoon, and by one in the afternoon all the seats were filled.

About the merits of the piece which had so extraordinary an effect, the public, we suppose, has made up its mind. To compare it with the masterpieces of the Attic stage, with the great English dramas of the time of Elizabeth, or even with the productions of Schiller's manhood, would be absurd indeed. Yet it contains excellent dialogue and declamation, and, among plays fashioned on the French model, must be allowed to rank high; not, indeed, with Athalie or Saul; but, we think, not below Cinna, and certainly above any other English tragedy of the same school, above many of the plays of Corneille, above many of the plays of Voltaire and Alfieri, and 'above some plays of Racine. Be this as it may, we have little doubt that Cato did as much as the Tatlers, Spectators, and Freeholders united to raise Addison's fame among his contemporaries.

The modesty and good nature of the successful dramatist had tamed even the malignity of faction. But literary envy, it should seem, is a fiercer passion than party spirit. It was by a zealous Whig that the fiercest attack on the Whig tragedy was made. John Dennis published remarks on Cato, which were written with some acuteness, and with much coarseness and asperity. Addison neither defended himself nor retaliated. On many points he had an excellent defence; and nothing would have been easier than to retaliate; for Dennis had written bad odes, bad tragedies, bad comedies: he had, moreover, a larger share than most men of those infirmities and eccentricities which excite laughter; and Addison's power of turning either an absurd book or an absurd man into ridicule was unrivalled. Addison, however, serenely conscious of his superiority, looked with pity on his assailant, whose temper, naturally irritable and gloomy, had been soured by want, by controversy, and by literary failures.

But among the young candidates for Addison's favor there was one distinguished by talents from the rest, and distinguished, we fear, not less by malignity and insincerity. Pope was only twenty-five. But his powers had expanded to their full maturity; and his best poem, the Rape of the Lock, had recently been published. Of his genius, Addison had always expressed high admiration. But Addison had early discerned, what might indeed have been discerned by an eye less penetrating than his, that the diminutive, crooked, sickly boy was eager to revenge himself on society for the unkindness of nature. In The Spectator, the Essay on Criticism had been praised with cordial warmth; but a gentle hint had been added that the writer of so excellent a poem would have done well to avoid ill-natured personalities. Pope, though evidently more galled by the censure than gratified by the praise, returned thanks for the admonition, and promised to profit by it. The two writers continued to exchange civilities, counsel, and small good offices. Addison publicly extolled Pope's miscellaneous pieces; and Pope furnished Addison with a prologue. This did not last long. Pope hated Dennis, whom he had injured without provocation. The appearance of the Remarks on Cato gave the irritable poet an opportunity of venting his malice under the show of friendship, and such an opportunity could not be but welcome to a nature which was implacable in enmity, and which always preferred the tortuous to the straight path. He published, accordingly, the Narrative of the Frenzy of John Dennis. But Pope had mistaken his powers. He was a great master of invective and sarcasm. He could dissect a character in terse and sonorous couplets, brilliant with antithesis; but of dramatic talent he was altogether destitute. If he had written a lampoon on Dennis such as that on Atticus, or that on Sporus, the old grumbler would have been crushed. But Pope writing dialogue resembled — to borrow Horace's imagery and his own — a wolf, which instead of biting, should take to kicking, or a monkey which should try to sting. The Narrative is utterly contemptible. Of argument there is not even the show; and the jests are such as, if they were introduced into a farce, would call forth the hisses of the shilling gallery. Dennis raves about the drama; and the nurse thinks that he is calling for a dram. "There is," he cries, "no peripetia in the tragedy, no change of fortune, no change at all." "Pray, good sir, be not angry," says the old woman; "I'll fetch change." This is not exactly the pleasantry of Addison.

There can be no doubt that Addison saw through this officious zeal, and felt himself deeply aggrieved by it. So foolish and spiteful a pamphlet could do him no good, and, if he were thought to have any hand in it, must do him harm. Gifted with incomparable powers of ridicule, he had never, even in self-defence, used those powers inhumanly or uncourteously; and he was not disposed to let others make his fame and his interests a pretext under which they might commit outrages from which he had himself constantly abstained. He accordingly declared that he had no concern in the Narrative, that he disapproved of it, and that if he answered the remarks, he would answer them like a gentleman; and he took care to communicate this to Dennis. Pope was bitterly mortified; and to this transaction we are inclined to ascribe the hatred with which he ever after regarded Addison.

In September, 1713, The Guardian ceased to appear. Steele had gone mad about politics. A general election had just taken place: he had been chosen member for Stockbridge; and he fully expected to play a first part in Parliament. The immense success of the Tatler and Spectator had turned his head. He had been the editor of both those papers, and was not aware how entirely they owed their influence and popularity to the genius of his friend. His spirits, always violent, were now excited by vanity, ambition, and faction, to such a pitch that he every day committed some offence against good sense and good taste. All the discreet and moderate members of his own party regretted and condemned his folly. "I am in a thousand troubles," Addison wrote, "about poor Dick, and wish that his zeal for the public may not be ruinous to himself. But he has sent me word that he is determined to go on, and that any advice I may give him in this particular will have no weight with him."

Steele set up a political paper called The Englishman, which, as it was not supported by contributions from Addison, completely failed. By this work, by some other writings of the same kind, and by the airs which he gave himself at the first meeting of the new Parliament, he made the Tories so angry that they determined to expel him. The Whigs stood by him gallantly, but were unable to save him. The vote of expulsion was regarded by all dispassionate men as a tyrannical exercise of the power of the majority. But Steele's violence and folly, though they by no means justified the steps which his enemies took, had completely disgusted his friends; nor did he ever regain the place which he had held in the public estimation.

Addison about this time conceived the design of adding an eighth volume to The Spectator. In June, 1714, the first number of the new series appeared, and during about six months three papers were published weekly. Nothing can be more striking than the contrast between The Englishman and the eighth volume of The Spectator, between

Steele without Addison, and Addison without Steele.   The Englishman is forgotten: the eighth volume of The Spectator contains, perhaps, the finest essays, both serious and playful, in the English language.

Before this volume was completed, the death of Anne produced an entire change in the administration of public affairs.   The blow fell suddenly.   It found the Tory party distracted by internal feuds, and unprepared for any great effort.   Harley had just been disgraced.   Bolingbroke, it was supposed, would be the chief minister.   But the queen was on her death-bed before the white staff had been given, and her last public act was to deliver it with a feeble hand to the Duke of Shrewsbury.   The emergency produced a coalition between all sections of public men who were attached to the Protestant succession.   George the First was proclaimed without opposition.   A council, in which the leading Whigs had seats, took the direction of affairs till the new king should arrive.   The first act of the lords justices was to appoint Addison their secretary.

There is an idle tradition that he was directed to prepare a letter to the king, that he could not satisfy himself as to the style of this composition, and that the lords justices called in a clerk who at once did what was wanted.   It is not strange that a story so flattering to mediocrity should be popular; and we are sorry to deprive dunces of their consolation.   But the truth must be told.   It was well observed by Sir James Mackintosh, whose knowledge of these times was unequalled, that Addison never, in any official document, affected wit or eloquence, and that his despatches are, without exception, remarkable for unpretending simplicity.   Everybody who knows with what ease Addison's finest essays were produced must be convinced that, if well turned phrases had been wanted, he would have had no difficulty in finding them.   We are, however, inclined to believe that the story is not absolutely without a foundation. It may well be that Addison did not know, till he had consulted experienced clerks who remembered the times when William the Third was absent on the Continent, in what form a letter from the Council of Regency to the king ought to be drawn. We think it very likely that the ablest statesmen of our time, Lord John Russell, Sir Robert Peel, Lord Palmerston, for example, would, in similar circumstances, be found quite as ignorant. Every office has some little mysteries which the dullest man may learn with a little attention, and which the greatest man cannot possibly know by intuition. One paper must be signed by the chief of the department; another by his deputy; to a third the royal sign-manual is necessary. One communication is to be registered, and another is not. One sentence must be in black ink, and another in red ink. If the ablest Secretary for Ireland were moved to the India Board, if the ablest President of the India Board were moved to the War Office, he would require instruction on points like these; and we do not doubt that Addison required such instruction when he became, for the first time, secretary to the lords justices.

George the First took possession of his kingdom without opposition. A new ministry was formed, and a new Parliament favorable to the Whigs chosen. Sunderland was appointed lord-lieutenant of Ireland; and Addison again went to Dublin as chief secretary.

Those associates of Addison whose political opinions agreed with his shared his good fortune. He took Tickell with him to Ireland. He procured for Budgell a lucrative place in the same kingdom. Ambrose Philips was provided for in England. Steele had injured himself so much by his eccentricity and perverseness that he obtained but a very small part of what he thought his due. He was, however, knighted; he had a place in the household; and he subsequently received other marks of favor from the court.

Addison did not remain long in Ireland. In 1715 he quitted his secretaryship for a seat at the Board of Trade. In the same year his comedy of The Drummer was brought on the stage. The name of the author was not announced; the piece was coldly received; and some critics have expressed a doubt whether it were really Addison's. To us the evidence, both external and internal, seems decisive. It is not in Addison's best manner; but it contains numerous passages which no other writer known to us could have produced. It was again performed after Addison's death, and, being known to be his, was loudly applauded.

Toward the close of the year 1715, while the rebellion was still raging in Scotland, Addison published the first number of a paper called The Freeholder. Among his political works The Freeholder is entitled to the first place. Even in The Spectator there are few serious papers nobler than the character of his friend Lord Somers, and certainly no satirical papers superior to those in which the Tory fox-hunter is introduced. This character is the original of Squire Western, and is drawn with all Fielding's force, and with a delicacy of which Fielding was altogether destitute. As none of Addison's works exhibit stronger marks of his genius than The Freeholder, so none does more honor to his moral character. It is difficult to extol too highly the candor and humanity of a political writer whom even the excitement of civil war cannot hurry into unseemly violence. Oxford, it is well known, was then the stronghold of Toryism. The High Street had been repeatedly lined with bayonets in order to keep down the disaffected gownsmen;

His fox-hunter, though ignorant, stupid, and violent, is at heart a good fellow, and is at last reclaimed by the clemency of the king. Steele was dissatisfied with his friend's moderation, and, though he acknowledged that The Freeholder was excellently written, complained that the ministry played on a lute when it was necessary to blow the trumpet. He accordingly determined to execute a flourish after his own fashion, and tried to rouse the public spirit of the nation by means of a paper called The Town Talk, which is now as utterly forgotten as his Englishman, as his Crisis, as his Letter to the Bailiff of Stockbridge, as his Reader; in short, as everything he wrote without the help of Addison.

In the same year in which The Drummer was acted, and in which the first numbers of The Freeholder appeared, the estrangement of Pope and Addison became complete. Addison had from the first seen that Pope was false and malevolent. Pope had discovered that Addison was jealous. The discovery was made in a strange manner. Pope had written The Rape of the Lock, in two cantos, without supernatural machinery. These two cantos had been loudly applauded, and by none more loudly than by Addison. Then Pope thought of the Sylphs and Gnomes, Ariel, Momentilla, Crispissa, and Umbriel, and resolved to interweave the Rosicrucian mythology with the original fabric. He asked Addison's advice. Addison said that the poem as it stood was a delicious little thing, and entreated Pope not to run the risk of marring what was so excellent in trying to mend it. Pope afterward declared that this insidious counsel first opened his eyes to the baseness of him who gave it.

Now there can be no doubt that Pope's plan was most ingenious, and that he afterward executed it with great skill and success. But does it necessarily follow that Addison's advice was bad? And if Addison's advice was bad, does it necessarily follow that it was given from bad motives? If a friend were to ask us whether we would advise him to risk his all in a lottery of which the chances were ten to one against him, we should do our best to dissuade him from running such a risk. Even if he were so lucky as to get the thirty thousand pound prize, we should not admit that we had counselled him ill; and we should certainly think it the height of injustice in him to accuse us of having been actuated by malice. We think Addison's advice good advice. It rested on a sound principle, the result of long and wide experience. The general rule undoubtedly is that, when a successful work of imagination has been produced, it should not be recast. We cannot at this moment call to mind a single instance in which this rule has been transgressed with happy effect, except the instance of The Rape of the Lock. Tasso recast his Jerusalem. Akenside recast his Pleasures of the Imagination, and his Epistle to Curio. Pope himself, emboldened no doubt by the success with which he had expanded and remodelled The Rape of the Lock, made the same experiment on The Dunciad. All these attempts failed. Who was to foresee that Pope would, once in his life, be able to do what he could not himself do twice, and what nobody else had ever done?

Addison's advice was good. But had it been bad, why should we pronounce it dishonest? Scott tells us that one of his best friends predicted the failure of Waverley. Herder adjured Goethe not to take so unpromising a subject as Faust. Hume tried to dissuade Robertson from writing the History of Charles the Fifth. Nay, Pope himself was one of those who prophesied that Cato would never succeed on the stage, and advised Addison to print it without risking a representation. But Scott, Goethe, Robertson, Addison, had the good sense and generosity to give their advisers credit for the best intentions. Pope's heart was not of the same kind with theirs.

In 1715, while he was engaged in translating the Iliad,

he met Addison at a coffee house. Phillipps and Budgell were there; but their sovereign got rid of them, and asked Pope to dine with him alone. After dinner, Addison said that he lay under a difficulty which he wished to explain. "Tickell," he said, "translated, some time ago, the first book of the Iliad. I have promised to look it over and correct it. I cannot, therefore, ask to see yours, for that would be double dealing." Pope made a civil reply, and begged that his second book might have the advantage of Addison's revision. Addison readily agreed, looked over the second book, and sent it back with warm commendations.

Tickell's version of the first book appeared soon after this conversation. In the preface, all rivalry was earnestly disclaimed. Tickell declared that he should not go on with the Iliad. That enterprise he should leave to powers which he admitted to be superior to his own. His only view, he said, in publishing this specimen was to bespeak the favor of the public to a translation of the Odyssey, in which he had made some progress.

Addison, and Addison's devoted followers, pronounced both the versions good, but maintained that Tickell's had more of the original. The town gave a decided preference to Pope's. We do not think it worth while to settle such a question of precedence. Neither of the rivals can be said to have translated the Iliad, unless, indeed, the word translation be used in the sense which it bears in the Midsummer Night's Dream. When Bottom makes his appearance with an ass's head instead of his own, Peter Quince exclaims, "Bless thee! Bottom, bless thee! thou art translated." In this sense, undoubtedly, the readers of either Pope or Tickell may very properly exclaim, "Bless thee, Homer' thou art translated indeed."

Our readers will, we hope, agree with us in thinking that no man in Addison's situation could have acted more fairly

and kindly, both towards Pope and towards Tickell, than
he appears to have done.   But an <u>odious suspicion</u> had
sprung up in the mind of Pope.   He fancied, and he soon
firmly believed, that there was a deep conspiracy against his
fame and his fortunes.   The work on which he had staked
his reputation was to be depreciated.   The subscription, on
which rested his hopes of a competence, was to be defeated.
With this view Addison had made a rival translation:
Tickell had consented to father it: and the wits of Button's
had united to puff it.

Is there any external evidence to support this grave accusation?   The answer is short.   There is absolutely none.

Was there any internal evidence which proved Addison
to be the author of this version?   Was it a work which
Tickell was incapable of producing?   Surely not.   Tickell
was a fellow of a college at Oxford, and must be supposed
to have been able to construe the Iliad; and he was a better
versifier than his friend.   We are not aware that Pope pretended to have discovered any turns of expression peculiar
to Addison.   Had such turns of expression been discovered,
they would be sufficiently accounted for by supposing Addison to have corrected his friend's lines, as he owned that
he had done.

Is there anything in the character of the accused persons
which makes the accusation probable?   We answer confidently — nothing.   Tickell was long after this time described by Pope himself as a very fair and worthy man.
Addison had been, during many years, before the public.
Literary rivals, political opponents, had kept their eyes on
him.   But neither envy nor faction, in their utmost rage,
had ever imputed to him a single deviation from the laws
of honor and of social morality.   Had he been indeed a man
meanly jealous of fame, and capable of stooping to base and
wicked arts for the purpose of injuring his competitors,

writer of tragedy: had he ever injured Rowe? He was a writer of comedy: had he not done ample justice to Congreve, and given valuable help to Steele? He was a pamphleteer: have not his good-nature and generosity been acknowledged by Swift, his rival in fame and his adversary in politics?

That Tickell should have been guilty of a villany seems to us highly improbable. That Addison should have been guilty of a villany seems to us highly improbable. But that these two men should have conspired together to commit a villany seems to us improbable in a tenfold degree. All that is known to us of their intercourse tends to prove that it was not the intercourse of two accomplices in crime. These are some of the lines in which Tickell poured forth his sorrow over the coffin of Addison:

> Or dost thou warn poor mortals left behind,
> A task well suited to thy gentle mind?
> Oh, if sometimes thy spotless form descend,
> To me thine aid, thou guardian genius, lend.
> When rage misguides me, or when fear alarms,
> When pain distresses, or when pleasure charms,
> In silent whisperings purer thoughts impart,
> And turn from ill a frail and feeble heart;
> Lead through the paths thy virtue trod before,
> Till bliss shall join, nor death can part us more.

In what words, we should like to know, did this guardian genius invite his pupil to join in a plan such as the editor of The Satirist would hardly dare to propose to the editor of The Age?

We do not accuse Pope of bringing an accusation which he knew to be false. We have not the smallest doubt that he believed it to be true; and the evidence on which he believed it he found in his own bad heart. His own life was one long series of tricks, as mean and as malicious as that of which he suspected Addison and Tickell. He was all stiletto and mask. To injure, to insult, and to save himself from the consequences of injury and insult by lying and equivocating, was the habit of his life. He published a lampoon on the Duke of Chandos; he was taxed with it, and he lied and equivocated. He published a lampoon on Aaron Hill; he was taxed with it, and he lied and equivocated. He published a still fouler lampoon on Lady Mary Wortley Montague; he was taxed with it, and he lied with more than usual effrontery and vehemence. He puffed himself, and abused his enemies under feigned names. He robbed himself of his own letters, and then raised the hue and cry after them. Besides his frauds of malignity, of fear, of interest, and of vanity, there were frauds which he seems to have committed from love of fraud alone. He had a habit of stratagem, a pleasure in outwitting all who came near him. Whatever his object might be, the indirect road to it was that which he preferred. For Bolingbroke Pope undoubtedly felt as much love and veneration as it was in his nature to feel for any human being. Yet Pope was scarcely dead when it was discovered that, from no motive except the mere love of artifice, he had been guilty of an act of gross perfidy to Bolingbroke.

Nothing was more natural than that such a man as this should attribute to others that which he felt within himself. A plain, probable, coherent explanation is frankly given to him. He is certain that it is all a romance. A line of conduct scrupulously fair, and even friendly, is pursued toward him. He is convinced that it is merely a cover for a vile intrigue by which he is to be disgraced and ruined. It is vain to ask him for proofs. He has none, and wants none, except those which he carries in his own bosom.

Whether Pope's malignity at length provoked Addison to retaliate for the first and last time, cannot now be known with certainty. We have only Pope's story, which runs thus. A pamphlet appeared containing some reflections which stung Pope to the quick. What those reflections were, and whether they were reflections of which he had a right to complain, we have now no means of deciding. The Earl of Warwick, a foolish and vicious lad, who regarded Addison with the feelings with which such lads generally regard their best friends, told Pope, truly or falsely, that this pamphlet had been written by Addison's direction. When we consider what a tendency stories have to grow, in passing even from one honest man to another honest man, and when we consider that to the name of honest man neither Pope nor the Earl of Warwick had a claim, we are not disposed to attach much importance to this anecdote.

It is certain, however, that Pope was furious. He had already sketched the character of Atticus in prose. In his anger he turned this prose into the brilliant and energetic lines which everybody knows by heart, or ought to know by heart, and sent them to Addison. One charge which Pope has enforced with great skill is probably not without foundation. Addison was, we are inclined to believe, too fond of presiding over a circle of humble friends. Of the other imputations which these famous lines are intended to convey, scarcely one has ever been proved to be just, and some are certainly false. That Addison was not in the habit of "damning with faint praise" appears from innumerable passages in his writings, and from none more than from those in which he mentions Pope. And it is not merely unjust, but ridiculous, to describe a man who made the fortune of almost every one of his intimate friends, as "so obliging that he ne'er obliged."

That Addison felt the sting of Pope's satire keenly, we cannot doubt. That he was conscious of one of the weaknesses with which he was reproached, is highly probable. But his heart, we firmly believe, acquitted him of the gravest part of the accusation. He acted like himself. As a satirist, he was, at his own weapons, more than Pope's match; and he would have been at no loss for topics. A distorted and diseased body, tenanted by a yet more distorted and diseased mind; spite and envy thinly disguised by sentiments as benevolent and noble as those which Sir Peter Teazle admired in Mr. Joseph Surface; a feeble, sickly licentiousness; an odious love of filthy and noisome images; these were things which a genius less powerful than that to which we owe The Spectator could easily have held up to the mirth and hatred of mankind. Addison had, moreover, at his command other means of vengeance which a bad man would not have scrupled to use. He was powerful in the State. Pope was a Catholic; and, in those times, a minister would have found it easy to harass the most innocent Catholic by innumerable petty vexations. Pope, near twenty years later, said that "through the lenity of the Government alone he could live with comfort." "Consider," he exclaimed, "the injury that a man of high rank and credit may do to a private person, under penal laws and many other disadvantages." It is pleasing to reflect that the only revenge which Addison took was to insert in The Freeholder a warm encomium on the translation of the Iliad, and to exhort all lovers of learning to put down their names as subscribers. There could be no doubt, he said, from the specimens already published, that the masterly hand of Pope would do as much for Homer as Dryden had done for Virgil. From that time to the end of his life, he always treated Pope, by Pope's own acknowledgment, with justice. Friendship was, of course, at an end.

One reason which induced the Earl of Warwick to play the ignominious part of tale-bearer on this occasion, may have been his dislike of the marriage which was about to take place between his mother and Addison. The Countess Dowager, a daughter of the old and honorable family of the Myddletons of Chirk, a family which, in any country but ours, would be called noble, resided at Holland House. Addison had, during some years, occupied at Chelsea a small dwelling, once the abode of Nell Gwynn. Chelsea is now a district of London, and Holland House may be called a town residence. But, in the days of Anne and George the First, milkmaids and sportsmen wandered between green hedges and over fields bright with daisies, from Kensington almost to the shore of the Thames. Addison and Lady Warwick were country neighbors, and became intimate friends. The great wit and scholar tried to allure the young lord from the fashionable amusements of beating watchmen, breaking windows, and rolling women in hogsheads down Holborn Hill, to the study of letters and the practice of virtue. These well meant exertions did little good, however, either to the disciple or to the master. Lord Warwick grew up a rake; and Addison fell in love. The mature beauty of the countess has been celebrated by poets in language which, after a very large allowance has been made for flattery, would lead us to believe that she was a fine woman; and her rank doubtless heightened her attractions. The courtship was long. The hopes of the lover appear to have risen and fallen with the fortunes of his party. His attachment was at length matter of such notoriety that, when he visited Ireland for the last time, Rowe addressed. some consolatory verses to the Chloe of Holland House. It strikes us as a little strange that, in these verses, Addison should be called Lycidas, a name of singularly evil omen for a swain just about to cross St. George's Channel.

At length Chloe capitulated. Addison was indeed able to treat with her on equal terms. He had reason to expect preferment even higher than that which he had attained. He had inherited the fortune of a brother who died Governor of Madras. He had purchased an estate in Warwickshire, and had been welcomed to his domain in very toler-

able verse by one of the neighboring squires, the poetical
fox-hunter, William Somerville.   In August, 1716, the
newspapers announced that Joseph Addison, Esquire, famous for many excellent works both in verse and prose,
had espoused the Countess Dowager of Warwick.

' He now fixed his abode at Holland House, a house which
can boast of a greater number of inmates distinguished in
political and literary history than any other private dwelling in England.   His portrait still hangs there.   The
features are pleasing; the complexion is remarkably fair;
but, in the expression, we trace rather the gentleness of
his disposition than the force and keenness of his intellect.

Not long after his marriage he reached the height of
civil greatness.   The Whig Government had, during some '
time, been torn by internal dissensions.   Lord Townshend
led one section of the cabinet, Lord Sunderland the other.
At length, in the spring of 1717, Sunderland triumphed.
Townshend retired from office, and was accompanied by
Walpole and Cowper.   Sunderland proceeded to reconstruct
the ministry, and Addison was appointed Secretary of
State.   It is certain that the Seals were pressed upon him,
and were at first declined by him.   Men equally versed in
official business might easily have been found; and his
colleagues knew that they could not expect assistance from
him in debate.   He owed his elevation to his popularity, to
his stainless probity, and to his literary fame.

But scarcely had Addison entered the cabinet when his
health began to fail.   From one serious attack he recovered
in the autumn; and his recovery was celebrated in Latin
verses, worthy of his own pen, by Vincent Bourne, who
was then at Trinity College, Cambridge.   A relapse soon
took place; and, in the following spring, Addison was prevented by a severe asthma from discharging the duties of

Craggs, a young man whose natural parts, though little improved by cultivation, were quick and showy, whose graceful person and winning manners had made him generally acceptable in society, and who, if he had lived, would probably have been the most formidable of all the rivals of Walpole.

As yet there was no Joseph Hume. The ministers, therefore, were able to bestow on Addison a retiring pension of fifteen hundred pounds a year. In what form this pension was given we are not told by the biographers, and have not time to inquire. But it is certain that Addison did not vacate his seat in the House of Commons.

Rest of mind and body seemed to have re-established his health; and he thanked God, with cheerful piety, for having set him free both from his office and from his asthma. Many years seemed to be before him, and he meditated many works, a tragedy on the death of Socrates, a translation of the Psalms, a treatise on the evidences of Christianity. Of this last performance, a part, which we could well spare, has come down to us.

But the fatal complaint soon returned, and gradually prevailed against all the resources of medicine. It is melancholy to think that the last months of such a life should have been overclouded both by domestic and by political vexations. A tradition which began early, which has been generally received, and to which we have nothing to oppose, has represented his wife as an arrogant and imperious woman. It is said that, till his health failed him, he was glad to escape from the Countess Dowager and her magnificent dining-room, blazing with the gilded devices of the house of Rich, to some tavern where he could enjoy a laugh, a talk about Virgil and Boileau, and a bottle of claret, with the friends of his happier days. All those friends, however, were not left to him. Sir Richard Steele had been gradually estranged by various causes. He considered him self as one who, in evil times, had braved martyrdom for his political principles, and demanded, when the Whig party was triumphant, a large compensation for what he had suffered when it was militant. The Whig leaders took a very different view of his claims. They thought that he had, by his own petulance and folly, brought them as well as himself into trouble, and, though they did not absolutely neglect him, doled out favors to him with a sparing hand. It was natural that he should be angry with them, and especially angry with Addison. But what above all seems to have disturbed Sir Richard was the elevation of Tickell, who, at thirty, was made by Addison Under-secretary of State; while the editor of the Tatler and Spectator, the author of the Crisis, the member for Stockbridge who had been persecuted for firm adherence to the house of Hanover, was, at near fifty, forced, after many solicitations and complaints, to content himself with a share in the patent of Drury Lane Theatre. Steele himself says, in his celebrated letter to Congreve, that Addison, by his preference of Tickell, "incurred the warmest resentment of other gentlemen"; and everything seems to indicate that, of those resentful gentlemen, Steele was himself one.

While poor Sir Richard was brooding over what he considered as Addison's unkindness, a new cause of quarrel arose. The Whig party, already divided against itself, was rent by a new schism. The celebrated bill for limiting the number of peers had been brought in. The proud Duke of Somerset, first in rank of all the nobles whose religion permitted them to sit in Parliament, was the ostensible author of the measure. But it was supported, and, in truth, devised by the Prime Minister.

Steele took part with the opposition, Addison with the ministers. Steele, in a paper called the Plebeian, vehemently attacked the bill. Sunderland called for help on Addison, and Addison obeyed the call. In a paper called the Old Whig, he answered, and indeed refuted, Steele's arguments. In style, in wit, and in politeness, Addison maintained his superiority, though the Old Whig is by no means one of his happiest performances.

At first both the anonymous opponents observed the laws of propriety. But at length Steele so far forgot himself as to throw an odious imputation on the morals of the chiefs of the administration. Addison replied with severity, but, in our opinion, with less severity than was due to so grave an offence against morality and decorum; nor did he, in his just anger, forget for a moment the laws of good taste and good breeding.

The merited reproof which Steele had received, though softened by some kind and courteous expressions, galled him bitterly. He replied with little force and great acrimony; but no rejoinder appeared. Addison was fast hastening to his grave; and had, we may well suppose, little disposition to prosecute a quarrel with an old friend. His complaint had terminated in dropsy. He bore up long and manfully. But at length he abandoned all hope, dismissed his physicians, and calmly prepared himself to die.

His works he intrusted to the care of Tickell, and dedicated them a very few days before his death to Craggs, in a letter written with the sweet and graceful eloquence of a Saturday's Spectator. In this, his last composition, he alluded to his approaching end in words so manly, so cheerful, and so tender, that it is difficult to read them without tears. At the same time he earnestly recommended the interests of Tickell to the care of Craggs.

Within a few hours of the time at which this dedication was written, Addison sent to beg Gay, who was then living by his wits about town, to come to Holland House. Gay went, and was received with great kindness. To his amazement his forgiveness was implored by the dying man. Poor Gay, the most good-natured and simple of mankind, could not imagine what he had to forgive. There was, however, some wrong, the remembrance of which weighed on Addison's mind, and which he declared himself anxious to repair. He was in a state of extreme exhaustion; and the parting was doubtless a friendly one ou both sides. Gay supposed that some plan to serve him had been in agitation at court, and had been frustrated by Addison's influence. Nor is this improbable. Gay had paid assiduous court to the royal family. But in the queen's days he had been the eulogist of Bolingbroke, and was still connected with many Tories. It is not strange that Addison, while heated by conflict, should have thought himself justified in obstructing the preferment of one whom he might regard as a political enemy. Neither is it strange that, when reviewing his whole life, and earnestly scrutinizing all his motives, he should think that he had acted an unkind and ungenerous part, in using his power against a distressed man of letters, who was as harmless and as helpless as a child.

One inference may be drawn from this anecdote. It appears that Addison, on his death-bed, called himself to a strict account, and was not at ease till he had asked pardon for an injury which it was not even suspected that he had committed, for an injury which would have caused disquiet only to a very tender conscience. Is it not, then, reasonable to infer that, if he had really been guilty of forming a base conspiracy against the fame and fortunes of a rival, he would have expressed some remorse for so serious a crime? But it is unnecessary to multiply arguments and evidence for the defence, when there is neither argument nor evidence for the accusation.

The last moments of Addison were perfectly serene. His interview with his step-son is universally known. "See," he said, "how a Christian can die." The piety of Addison was, in truth, of a singularly cheerful character. The feeling which predominates in all his devotional writings is gratitude. God was to him the all-wise and all-powerful friend who had watched over his cradle with more than maternal tenderness; who had listened to his cries before they could form themselves in prayer; who had preserved his youth from the snares of vice; who had made his cup run over with worldly blessings; who had doubled the value of those blessings, by bestowing a thankful heart to enjoy them, and dear friends to partake them; who had rebuked the waves of the Ligurian Gulf, had purified the autumnal air of the Campagna, and had restrained the avalanches of Mont Cenis. Of the Psalms, his favorite was that which represents the Ruler of all things under the endearing image of a shepherd, whose crook guides the flock safe, through gloomy and desolate glens, to meadows well watered and rich with herbage. On that goodness to which he ascribed all the happiness of his life, he relied in the hour of death with the love which casteth out fear. He died on the 17th of June, 1719. He had just entered on his forty-eighth year.

His body lay in state in the Jerusalem Chamber, and was borne thence to the Abbey at dead of night. The choir sung a funeral hymn. Bishop Atterbury, one of those Tories who had loved and honored the most accomplished of the Whigs, met the corpse, and led the procession by torchlight round the shrine of Saint Edward and the graves of the Plantagenets, to the Chapel of Henry the Seventh. On the north side of that chapel, in the vault of the house of Albemarle, the coffin of Addison lies next to the coffin of Montague. Yet a few months, and the same mourners passed again along the same aisle. The same sad anthem was again chanted. The same vault was again opened, and the coffin of Craggs was placed close to the coffin of Addison.

Many tributes were paid to the memory of Addison; but one alone is now remembered. Tickell bewailed his friend in an elegy which would do honor to the greatest name in our literature, and which unites the energy and magnificence of Dryden to the tenderness and purity of Cowper. This fine poem was prefixed to a superb edition of Addison's works, which was published, in 1721, by subscription. The names of the subscribers proved how widely his fame had been spread. That his countrymen should be eager to possess his writings, even in a costly form, is not wonderful. But it is wonderful that, though English literature was then little studied on the Continent, Spanish grandees, Italian prelates, marshals of France, should be found in the list. Among the most remarkable names are those of the Queen of Sweden, of Prince Eugene, of the Grand Duke of Tuscany, of the Dukes of Parma, Modena, and Guastalla, of the Doge of Genoa, of the Regent Orleans, and of Cardinal Dubois. We ought to add that this edition, though eminently beautiful, is in some important points defective; nor, indeed, do we yet possess a complete collection of Addison's writings.

It is strange that neither his opulent and noble widow, nor any of his powerful and attached friends, should have thought of placing even a simple tablet, inscribed with his name, on the walls of the Abbey. It was not till three generations had laughed and wept over his pages that the omission was supplied by the public veneration. At length, in our own time, his image, skilfully graven, appeared in Poet's Corner. It represents him, as we can conceive him, clad in his dressing-gown, and free from his wig, stepping from his parlor at Chelsea into his trim little garden, with the account of the Everlasting Club, or the Loves of Hilpa and Shalum, just finished for the next day's Spectator, in his hand. Such a mark of national respect was due to the unsullied statesman, to the accomplished scholar, to the master of pure English eloquence, to the consummate painter of life and manners. It was due, above all, to the

great satirist, who alone knew how to use ridicule without
abusing it; who, without inflicting a wound, effected a
great social reform; and who reconciled wit and virtue,
after a long and disastrous separation, during which wit
had been led astray by profligacy, and virtue by fanaticism.

NOTES

THE SELECT ESSAYS OF ADDISON.

———•◦•———

P. 1. **I have observed**, etc.   Though the fictitious personage represented in this paper as describing himself has many striking points of resemblance to Joseph Addison, yet the reader must guard against the mistake of thinking that the Spectator *is* Addison.   The Spectator is an imaginary person, created by Addison and Steele and their coadjutors.   The writer of each paper, whoever he may be, assumes the rôle of the Spectator, and speaks in this character, using the first person singular.   Thus the modern journalistic plural *we* stands for no one individual, but for the paper, as an impersonal institution.

This imaginary Spectator is a member of an imaginary club, of which he is the spokesman.   In this paper he is made to give an account of himself, and in the next to describe his fellow-members. One of these papers is by Addison, the other by Steele, though both papers appear as coming from the Spectator.   The fiction that a plan of the work "is laid and concerted in a club" serves to add the interest of mystery to the undertaking, and to furnish occasion for descriptions of manners and humors.   Of course the plan of the work was really laid and concerted by Addison and Steele. The writers who now and then aided them were men who had caught the spirit of the fiction, and were thus able to join the enterprise as partners in the work of invention and creation.

The young reader may find cause of confusion in the fact that the name Spectator is given to the entire collection of papers written under this pseudonym, and that the several papers are also called Spectators.

a black or a fair man. It was formerly customary to couple the words *black* and *fair* as opposites. See Shakespeare, Sonn. 147; Rom. and Jul., I., 1, 237; Oth. I., 3, 291, and elsewhere. See, also, instances of this use of *black* in Murray.

P. 3. On the coffee-houses and the theatres of the time, the reader may profitably consult Social Life in the Reign of Queen Anne, by John Ashton.

P. 5. **Spectator No. 2,** the reader will note, is by Steele. Other De Coverley papers by Steele are those on pp. 20, 26, 34 of this book. No. 116, p. 41, is by Budgell. All the while, however, it is the Spectator that speaks.

Soho Square should be looked up in Hare's Walks in London.

Lord Rochester, Sir George Etherege, and **Bully Dawson** may be looked up in the notes to Morley's edition of the Spectator.

P. 8. **humorists.** The meaning of this word, as here used, may be inferred from the context. Consider if it is used in this sense at present. See the same word on p. 18.

P. 11. **the city.** The expression is here used in its special London sense. See Murray's Dictionary, City, 5, b. See, also, Baedeker's London.

P. 18. **he is pleasant upon any of them.** The meaning of "pleasant" as here used is not given in Webster, but may be easily inferred. Consider the noun, *pleasantry.*

P. 19. **This cast of mind,** etc. The young reader must learn betimes to make his account with the peculiarities of the Addisonian syntax, and must recognize that in many points usage has changed since the early years of the eighteenth century. See a similar construction on p. 16, in the sentence beginning, "The truth of it is."

P. 22. **took off the dress he was in**; *i.e.,* raised him from the condition of servant.

P. 24. **discovered.** Do not misinterpret this word. It is no longer used in just this sense.

P. 25. **my twenty-first speculation** may be found on p. 118.

P. 41. **Spectator No. 116,** though written by Budgell, is wholly in the Addisonian vein. Budgell had successfully caught the style of his master. Boswell reports Johnson as saying that " Addison wrote Budgell's papers, or at least mended them so much that he made them almost his own."

P. 46. **I believe in general**, etc. Remember, it is the Spectator, and not Addison, that is speaking. Addison chooses not to let the Spectator boldly disavow a belief in witchcraft. Addison's own disbelief in it is abundantly inferable from the *spirit* of this very paper. It becomes interesting to consider whether in 1711 belief in witchcraft was generally entertained by educated men. Recall the date of the latest outbreak of the delusion in New England. Ascertain from any history of witchcraft, or from the article on this subject in the Encyclo. Brit., when the last witch-trials were held in England. See Knight's Popular History, Vol. V., p. 430.

P. 49. **a yeoman**. It is impossible for an American to appreciate fully the connotations of this purely English word without considerable reading. Besides looking up the definitions in the dictionaries, read, also, the chapter on the Yeomen, in Boutmy's English Constitution.

within the Game Act. A little reading will explain this. See, *e.g.*, the last paragraph of Chap. IV., Vol. VIII., of Knight's History, and the passage from Blackstone there quoted.

P. 57. **I remember to have read**. Look up the facts about the ichneumon, and see if he is as disinterested an animal as Diodorus represents him.

P. 59. **Spectator No. 130**. The authority on the Gypsies is George Borrow, whose books are all peculiarly interesting. In the introduction to his Gypsies of Spain is a short, readable account of the English Gypsies.

P. 63. **discovers**. See note to p. 24.

P. 64. **Prince Eugene**. See Knight's History, opening of Chap. XXV., Vol. V.

P. 66. **smutting one another**. See The Deserted Village, line 27.

the late Act of Parliament. This was the law against Occasional Conformity, passed in 1711. See the histories, or Encyclo. Brit., Vol. VIII., pp. 353, 354.

the Pope's Procession. See Knight's History, Vol. V., p. 377.

Baker's Chronicle. See article on Sir Richard Baker, in Encyclo. Brit.

P. 69. **the lord who had cut off**, etc.; **that martyr to good housewifery**, etc. See Hare's Walks in London, II., 257.

the two coronation chairs. See Hare, II., 303.

P. 70. **one of our English kings without a head.** See Hare, II., pp. 300–302.

P. 71. **'the Committee,'** a play by Sir Robert Howard, one of the minor comic dramatists of the Restoration.

this distressed mother. The Distressed Mother was a play by Ambrose Philips, founded on Racine's tragedy of Andromaque.

the Mohocks. See Ashton's Social Life in the Reign of Queen Anne.

P. 75. **Vauxhall Gardens.** See Hare's Walks, II., 422.

P. 76. **La Hogue.** See Macaulay's History, Chap. XVIII.

The fifty new churches. Parliament had just voted to build fifty churches in the city.

P. 80. **Spectator No. 10. The Spectator commends his papers to sundry classes of men, and especially to women.** The vein of badinage, light and playful in manner, but serious in purpose, in which the Spectator discusses the affairs of women, was novel and piquant at the beginning of the eighteenth century. The reader will remember the grossness of manners that prevailed during the immediately preceding period of the Restoration. Addison perceived the importance of woman's social influence as an auxiliary in his work of reforming the manners and morals of his countrymen, and aimed to make his paper as attractive to women as to men. The Spectator was, in fact, a family paper, and was read in cultivated households with curiosity and zest. In No. 4 Steele had written, " As these (the fair sex) compose half the world, and are, by the just complaisance and gallantry of our nation, the more powerful part of our people, I shall dedicate a considerable share of these my speculations to their service, and shall lead the young through all the becoming duties of virginity, marriage, and widowhood. When it is a woman's day, in my works, I shall endeavor at a style and air suitable to their understanding. When I say this, I must be understood to mean that I shall not lower, but exalt, the subjects I treat upon. Discourse for their entertainment is not to be debased, but refined."

P. 85. **For if we interpret his words in their literal meaning, etc.** The allusions in this passage are to Nos. 14, 81 (see p. 122, this volume), 18, 22, 36, 8.

P. 86. **nodding places**, etc.   An allusion to Horace's lines, —

> Indignor quandoque bonus dormitat Homerus:
> Verum operi longo fas est obrepere somnum;

whence Homer's nodding has become a commonplace.

P. 89. **this new imprimatur.**   See Knight's History, Vol. V., p. 394.

P. 97. **Signor Nicolini**, an Italian actor and singer; **Hydaspes**, an Italian opera.   Morley's note will be found interesting.

P. 100. **the famous equestrian statue.**   What king is meant?

P. 106. **Doggett.** See Adams's Dictionary of English Literature.

P. 108. **Mr. Rymer — that great critic.**   This is Thomas Rymer, author of the *Fœdera*, a work of the first importance to English history.   He is here, however, alluded to as a critic.   Read him up in the Encyclo. Brit., and, by all means, find Macaulay's characteristic allusion to him in the Essay on Boswell's Life of Johnson, at the end of a paragraph near the close of the essay.

P. 111.   To find the passages referred to in South's Sermons and in Pliny's Natural History would be literary enterprises of the first order.

P. 112. **Aldus and Elzevir.**   Do not fail to look up these names, the former under the family name Manutius.

With his familiar "**Harry Stephens**," Tom undoubtedly refers to the celebrated French printer and author, Henri Estienne, who may be looked up in the Encyclo. Brit., under the Anglicized form of his name, Stephens.

a late paper.   Tatler, No. 154.

P. 113. **Ah! Mr. Bickerstaff.**   The reader will note that this paper and the next are Tatlers, not Spectators.   See note to p. 263, this volume.

P. 119. **Should our clergy**, etc.   This means, "the clergy are so numerous that if, as is done by lay land-holders, they could cut up their glebes and tithes into forty-shilling freeholds, each of which would entitle the holder to vote at the election of county members, they would command most of the (county) elections in England." — *Arnold.*

P. 135. **within the bills of mortality.**   See Webster's International Dictionary.

P. 136. **the Succession to the Spanish monarchy**. See Ploetz' Epitome of Universal History, pp. 390–393. A readable account of the War of the Spanish Succession may be found in Kitchin's History of France.

P. 141. **this was the long-expected hour of projection**; *i.e.*, the hour had at length come for throwing upon the elaborately prepared metal in the crucible the powder of projection (see Webster), which was to turn this metal into gold. Note that this paper is from the Guardian, and that it is Nestor Ironside, not the Spectator, who has this adventure with the alchemist. See note to p. 275, this volume. But by all means look up the word *projection*, definition No. 7, in the Century Dictionary, and note the quotations. Chaucer, in his Canon's Yeoman's Tale, describes the frauds practised in his day by the men who pretended to skill in alchemy.

P. 142. **the Act of Uniformity; the Act of Toleration; the Act of Settlement**. See Gardiner's Student's History of England, pp. 585, 650, 672.

P. 144. The date of this paper is March 3, 1711. Bearing in mind this date, see Gardiner's History, p. 643, par. 18. Addison had, in 1706, accompanied Halifax on his mission to the electoral court of Hanover (see p. 252, this volume). But it must be remembered that Addison is not the Spectator. We could hardly expect of the Spectator that, in those extensive journeys he made in Europe, he should have foreseen what personages were destined to become great in the future.

P. 146. **the old philosopher**; Diogenes the Cynic, as reported both by Lucian, in his dialogue on the Sale of Lives, and by Diogenes Laertius.

P. 149. **Freeholder No. 22**. The fifty-five numbers of the Freeholder were all written by Addison. Hence the entire series is printed in Addison's works. These papers appeared from December, 1715, to June, 1716. To understand the title and scope of the work, the reader should look up Freeholder, No. 1. Remember that here the pronoun *I* no longer means the Spectator.

P. 150. **Dyer's Letter**. See Macaulay's History, Chap. XX., and Spectator, 43 and 127.

P. 151. **burgesses**. See the dictionaries, and Fonblanque's How we are Governed.

P. 158. **When I was at Grand Cairo**. See Spectator, No.

P. 160. '**I see a bridge standing in the midst of the tide.**' Note that this "bridge" does not lead *across* the tide. The people on it move in a direction parallel to the flow of the current.

P. 163. **Homer's balance.** Iliad, XXII., 208–215. By all means look up this most impressive passage in one or more of the famous translations of Homer, in Chapman, or Pope, or Cowper, or in the prose translation of Lang, Leaf, and Myers.

a passage of Virgil. Æneid, XII., 725–727. Look this up, either in the original or in Dryden or Conington.

those noble passages of Scripture. To be found by means of Cruden's Concordance, a book indispensable to English study.

P. 164. **Milton, in that beautiful description.** This may be found by means of the Milton Concordance, or, better, by searching Paradise Lost.

amusing. Note that this word is used in a sense now obsolete. Look it up.

P. 170. **Wapping.** The sailor quarter of London. See Hare.

P. 180. **When I look**, etc. Notice the charm which this passage has both for the mind and for the ear. Its thought is noble, elevated, and serious, its language rhythmical and melodious. Consider by what peculiarities of arrangement this effect of rhythm, or measure, is produced.

Sir Paul Rycaut. See Encyclo. Brit.

P. 183. What do you think of Addison as an apiologist?

P. 186. **The shutting of a cardinal's mouth**, etc. See Encyclo. Brit., article "Cardinal."

fresh and fresh; an intensive doubling no longer in use. We still use many similar expressions, — through and through, out and out, over and over, many and many a day, etc.

P. 187. **Zug and Bender.** In 1712 the "Toggenburg War" was causing commotion among the cantons of Switzerland. Charles XII. was intriguing at Bender, in Russia, from 1709 to 1711.

P. 188. **the battle of Almanza.** See Gardiner's Student's History of England, p. 689.

P. 195. **Pasquin.** See Webster's Dictionary.

Aretine. To be looked up under his Italian name, Aretino.

P. 196. **As this week is in a manner set apart.** This paper is dated March 27, 1711. Easter, that year, fell on April 1.

P. 197. **who was head of a college in those times.** This is probably to be understood of a Dr. Thomas Goodwin, who was President of Magdalen College, Oxford, during the Commonwealth.

P. 209. **that noble allegory.** The story is told by Xenophon, who attributes it to Prodicus. It may be pleasantly and profitably looked up in the Bohn Xenophon, Memorabilia, II., i., 21–33.

P. 213. **as the finest author of all antiquity has said.** The allusion is to Cicero, who, *De Officiis*, I., xxxii., 118, adduces Prodicus' story of Hercules, as told by Xenophon, and, a little further on, uses the language here translated by Addison. We quote Cicero's words, that the reader may consider the Spectator's rendering : —

"Si igitur non poterit sive causas defensitare sive populum contionibus tenere sive bella gerere, illa tamen praestare debebit, quae erunt in ipsius potestate, justitiam, fidem, liberalitatem, modestiam, temperantiam."

In calling him "the finest author of all antiquity," Addison rates Cicero far more highly than modern opinion would sanction.

P. 216. **that clouded majesty which Milton takes notice of.** It will be easy to find this beautiful passage in Book IV. of Paradise Lost.

P. 224. **Spectator, No. 489.** Note the biographical allusions in this hymn. See pp. 239, 242, 243, this volume.

NOTES

MACAULAY'S ESSAY ON ADDISON.

P. 228. **the Laputan flapper.** Allusions like this, and like that to Rasselas, Prince of Abyssinia, on p. 236, should be understood from direct acquaintance with the books referred to. These are specimens of the reading that the young student of literature must command as the indispensable condition of intelligent progress.

The political and literary history of England during the reigns of William III., of Anne, and of George I. was the subject to which Macaulay's studies had been especially devoted, and of which he was an acknowledged master.

Theobald's. (Pronounce *Tibbals.*) If you will read Miss Strickland's lives of Queens Elizabeth, Anne of Denmark, and Henrietta Maria, or Miss Aikin's Memoirs of the Reign of James I., you will know what Theobald's was. Good maps of England show Theobald's Park in Hertfordshire. If you have not time to read so much as is indicated above, at least look up, by means of the index, the allusions to Theobald's in Miss Strickland's work.

Steenkirks. See Macaulay's account of the battle of Steenkirk in Chap. XIX. of the History.

P. 230. **the Biographia Britannica.** See Adams' Dict. of Eng. Lit., but especially Cowper's lines, "On observing some names of little note recorded in the Biographia Britannica."

the Charter House. See Hare's Walks in London, and the article "Carthusians" in Encyclo. Brit.

P. 231. **Magdalene.** (Pronounce *Maudlin.*)

P. 233. **Charles Montague, who was then Chancellor of the Exchequer.** The reader must bear in mind that it is precisely this period of English history that is treated by Macaulay in his History of England. It will be found very interesting to look up in this, by means of the index, the careers of such men as Montague and Somers. On the constitution of the British *Cabinet*, and the functions and titles of its members, consult Albany de Fonblanque's little book, How we are Governed.

the Newdigate prize, or the Seatonian prize. In Macaulay's essay on Moore's Life of Lord Byron is a short paragraph that fully explains the former of these allusions. The Seatonian prize was founded at Cambridge, by the Rev. Thomas Seaton, for the best English poem on a subject "to be most conducive to the honor of the Supreme Being and the recommendation of virtue."

P. 235. **a critical preface to the Georgics.** This is well worth looking up and reading. The Georgics may be read in numerous English versions. The enterprising reader will find pleasure in comparing Dryden's couplets, Conington's prose, and the peculiarly charming metrical translation by Harriet Waters Preston.

P. 236. **Charles Montague** and **Lord Chancellor Somers.** Do not fail to read the pages on these men in Chap. XX. of Macaulay's History.

the Press had been controlled by censors. See a very interesting paragraph near the beginning of Chap. XXI. of Macaulay's History.

P. 237. **He had addressed the most polished, etc.** These lines constitute an introduction to the Poem to His Majesty, mentioned on p. 233. Find them on p. 3 of Vol. I. of the Bohn Addison.

P. 238. **lines written on the glasses of the Kit Cat Club.** The Kit Cat Club is abundantly described on pp. 676–678 of Vol. VI. of the Bohn Addison. Do not misinterpret the expression, "written on the glasses."

P. 239. **the ode, "How are thy servants blest, O Lord!"** See p. 224 of this book.

Book of Gold. It is with Venice, rather than with Genoa, that the Golden Book, the register or directory of patrician citizens, is chiefly associated. Yet the expression is sometimes generalized, and made to apply, not only to the other Italian republics, as here by Macaulay, but also to other countries than Italy. The

Libro d'Oro of Venice was an actual book, and has its place in Venetian bibliography. The young student can look up the subject in Edmund Flagg's Venice, the City of the Sea. The overthrow of the Republic of Venice by Napoleon, in 1797, was signalized by the burning of the Golden Book in effigy at the foot of a French liberty-tree erected in the Piazza of St. Mark. This is an interesting subject for a little historical research. See Brewer's Historic Note Book, under "Golden Book."

P. 241. **The temples of Paestum.** You may read a pleasing chapter on this subject in John Addington Symonds's Sketches in Italy.

P. 242. **The great kingdom.** See Chap. XXIII. of Macaulay's History. See, also, his essay on Mahon's History of the War of the Succession in Spain. Look up the subject in Freeman's Historical Geography of Europe, Chap. XII., Sec. 3.

the Tory fox-hunter. See p. 149.

P. 243. **the Duke of Shrewsbury.** See Chap. XXII. of the History.

Eugene had already descended, etc. To understand the military and political events here referred to, see the histories of the War of the Spanish Succession. For a brief account, see Richard Lodge's History of Modern Europe, in the Students' Series, Chap. XIII., Sec. 24.

P. 245. **Manchester was deprived of the seals.** The office from which Manchester was removed was that of "principal Secretary of State."

P. 246. **Godolphin** had been appointed lord treasurer by Queen Anne in 1702.

Newmarket. See Encyclo. Brit. See, also, very interesting accounts of Newmarket and its dissipations, in Chaps. XXI. and XXIII. of Macaulay's History.

P. 248. **The Campaign.** Do not fail to look up this poem in Addison's works; it is interesting. Look up, also, in Johnson's Life of Addison, in the Lives of the English Poets, the passage referred to below.

P. 249. **the Lifeguardsman Shaw.** Shaw, who had already attained notoriety as a pugilist, became famous by his prowess in the battle of Waterloo, where he fought as corporal in the Second Lifeguards. The story of his valor is variously told by the historians of the battle. It may be read in Siborne, p. 282, and in Gleig, p. 191. From a contemporary account of the battle we extract the following: "Shaw was fighting seven or eight hours, dealing destruction to all around him. At one time he was attacked by six of the French Imperial Guard, four of whom he killed, but at last fell by the remaining two. A comrade who was at his side a great part of the day, and who is the relater of this anecdote, noticed one particular cut, which drove through his opponent's helmet, and with it cut nearly the whole of his face at the stroke."

P. 250. Johnson's remarks on this passage should by all means be looked up and read in the class; they convey an interesting lesson in criticism.

P. 251. the advantage which, in rhetoric and poetry, the particular has over the general. See this principle more fully set forth by Macaulay in his Essay on Milton, near the beginning.

Rosamond will be found well worth looking into, at least for the sake of its pleasing metrical effect.

The Great Seal was given to Cowper. (Pronounce *Cooper.*) That is, Cowper was made "Lord Keeper." See Webster's Dictionary, under "Lord keeper." In Southey's Life of Cowper, the poet, you may trace the kinship of the two men.

the Order of the Garter. See the story of the origin of this order, briefly told in Hume's History, and more fully discussed in Encyclo. Brit., article "Knighthood."

P. 253. the queen had now quarrelled, etc. For a full account of this famous quarrel, you will of course go to Miss Strickland; but all the histories give it.

The Captain General. This was Marlborough's title.

Sacheverell figures very largely at this period of English history. You will find an interesting brief account of him in Macaulay's essay on Lord Mahon's History of the War of the Succession in Spain.

P. 254. During the interval, etc. See Samuel Rawson Gardiner's Student's History of England, pp. 663 and 779.

the Conduct of the Allies. Swift published this tract in 1712, in support of the Tory opposition to the war, which was ended next year by the peace of Utrecht. It is said that 11,000 copies of the Conduct of the Allies were sold within three months after its appearance.

P. 255. governed by triennial parliaments. See Gardiner's Student's History, pp. 530, 661, 706.

P. 256. " assented with civil leer." See note to p. 291.

Mr. Softly's sonnet. See p. 114.

Lady Q-p-t-s. See Spectator, No. 568.

P. 257. Such excess was in that age, etc. On the convivial habits of the literary men of that time, see Thackeray's English Humorists in many passages, but especially in the accounts of Addison and Pope.

P. 258. Hurd. This is Bishop Hurd, whose edition of Addison's works is often mentioned in these notes.

the last lines which he traced. See a short account of Budgell, including the "lines," in Encyclo. Brit. The very pleasing Spectator, No. 116, p. 41 of this book, is by Budgell.

has been called, after his name, Namby Pamby. The coining of this epithet is ascribed, by Dr. Johnson, to Pope. The writer of the article on Ambrose Philips in the Encyclo. Brit. credits it to Henry Carey. See Hurd's Addison.

P. 259. had tried to find the philosopher's stone. See, in Hurd's Addison, Vol. VI., p. 532, a pleasant bit of verse, in which Addison rallies his friend Steele on his erratic life. Notice in these lines an allusion to Steele's "religious treatise," which was humorously dedicated to the Pope.

The **spunging house** is well known to readers of earlier English fiction and biography. You may get a glimpse into a spunging house in Thackeray's History of Samuel Titmarsh and the Great Hoggarty Diamond, Chap. XI. The definition of spunging house in the Century Dictionary is peculiarly satisfactory.

P. 260. the rival bulls in Virgil. See the third Georgic.

P. 262. Periodical papers had during many years been published in London. The history of the newspaper is very interesting and may easily be looked up. By all means, read Macaulay's paragraphs on this subject in Chap. XXI. of his History.

gazetteer. The reference just made to Macaulay abundantly explains this word.

Will's and the Grecian. On the inns and coffee-houses of the

eighteenth century, see Knight, History of England, Vol. VII,
Chap. V., and Chap. III. of Macaulay's History. See, also, p. 27.
of this book.

P. 263. **Mr. Paul Pry**. See Dictionary of Noted Names of
Fiction, in Webster's Dictionary.

To understand the Bickerstaff-Partridge affair, you must look it
up in some life of Swift, as, *e.g.*, in Sir Walter Scott's, end of
Sec. II. It will be interesting to look up the original documents
in the case in Scott's edition of Swift's works, Vol. VIII. "Swift is
said to have taken the name Bickerstaff from a smith's sign, and
added that of Isaac, as a Christian appellation of uncommon
occurrence. Yet it was said a living person was actually found
who owned both names." Later in the century a dramatic writer
of some note bore precisely this name. Thus there are three Isaac
Bickerstaffs, — Swift's pseudonym in the Partridge episode, The
Tatler's pseudonym, and a real author.

P. 264. **Dryden.** Selections from Dryden's prose have been
edited for school use by C. D. Yonge. (Macmillan & Co.)

Temple. Macaulay has an essay on this writer.

the half French style of Horace Walpole. See Macaulay's
essay on Walpole's Letters to Sir Horace Mann.

the half Latin style of Dr. Johnson. See Macaulay's two
essays on Johnson. But, better, see Rasselas, the Rambler, or The
Lives of the Poets.

the half German jargon of the present day. Macaulay wrote
this essay in 1843, when Carlyle was 48 years old, and had produced some of his most characteristic works.

the lines to Sir Godfrey Kneller. By all means, look up
these lines in Hurd's Addison, I., p. 229. Consider if these lines
are *heroic couplets*.

Hudibras is accessible in an edition excellently annotated for
students by Alfred Milnes. (Macmillan & Co.) ·

P. 266. **Bettesworth and Franc de Pompignan** were victims
of the satire, respectively, of Swift and Voltaire, and must be
looked up in the lives of these writers, as, *e.g.*, in Scott's Swift and
Parton's Voltaire.

P. 267. **Jeremy Collier had shamed the theatres, etc.** See
Macaulay's essay on the Comic Dramatists of the Restoration.

The Tatlers named on this page are, except such as are included in this volume, Nos. 155, 160; 250, 253, 256, 259, 262; 220; 249.

P. 268. **There is one still better paper, etc.**   It has been sur-
mised that Macaulay meant Tatler, No. 257.   By all means look
up this paper, and consider why he should not have dared to
name it.

reigning by a disputed title.   See Gardiner's Student's History, p. 643, par. 18.

the outbreaks in 1820 and in 1831.   See Mackenzie's The
Nineteenth Century, a History, and Gardiner's Student's History
of England.

P. 269. **acting by the advice of Harley.**   This is explained
by the article on Harley in the Encyclo. Brit.   See under "Oxford."

Sunderland was the first who fell.   See in Encyclo. Brit.
what was Sunderland's connection with Marlborough, and from
what office he was dismissed in 1710.

directed him to break his white staff; *i.e.* dismissed him
from his office as Lord High Treasurer.

had ventured to raise his eyes to a great lady.   To be
explained further on in the essay.

P. 270. **forcing Tory members on Whig corporations.**   By
corporations are meant here the constituencies that elect members
of parliament.

P. 271. **an imaginary Spectator.**   The young reader must not
allow himself to imagine that in the papers of the Spectator the
pronoun of the first person stands for Addison.   Whoever may be
the writer of any paper, it is always "the imaginary Spectator"
that speaks.   Spectator is the pseudonym of the collective authors
of the papers.

P. 273. The seven papers named near the bottom of the page
are all in this volume, except the Journal of the Retired Citizen,
which is No. 317.

P. 274. **the stamp tax was imposed.**   See Spectator, No.
445, p. 89 of this book.

P. 275. **Nestor Ironside** is to the Guardian precisely what
Isaac Bickerstaff is to the Tatler, and Mr. Spectator to the Spectator.   He *is* the Guardian.   **The Miss Lizards** are his wards:
hence the name of the paper.

P. 278. **Athalie, Saul, Cinna,** — tragedies, respectively, by Ra-

P. 279. **the diminutive, crooked, sickly boy.** See Johnson's Life of Pope.

In the Spectator. See Spectator, No. 253.

P. 280. **a lampoon such as that on Atticus or that on Sporus.** Both these lampoons occur in the Epistle to Dr. Arbuth-not, which serves as prologue to the Satires. Of the former we shall soon hear more. Both may readily be looked up, as, *e.g.*, in the Globe edition of Pope's poetical works.

to borrow Horace's imagery and his own. Horace's verse is, *Ut neque calce lupus quemquam, neque dente petit bos.* Sat. II., 1, 55.

Pope was bitterly mortified. See Pope's Letter to Addison, in Hurd's Addison, V., 410.

P. 282. **the queen was on her death-bed,** etc. Be sure to look up Miss Strickland's account of the last days of Queen Anne.

P. 284. **a seat at the Board of Trade.** See Fonblanque's How we are Governed.

The paper on Lord Somers is Freeholder, No. 39. That on the Tory Fox-hunter is No. 22, given on p. 149 of this book.

the admonition which Addison addressed to the University is to be found in Freeholder, No. 33.

P. 285. To appreciate fairly **the estrangement of Pope and Addison,** the student should read other accounts, in addition to what Macaulay says in this essay. It will be interesting to look up the subject in Thackeray's English Humorists, and to read Professor Minto's article on Pope in the Encyclo. Brit. Johnson's Life of Pope should by all means be examined. The lives of Addison and Pope in the Men of Letters Series will also be found interesting and instructive.

P. 286. See what Johnson has to say about Akenside's recastings, and Pope's remodelling of the Dunciad.

P. 289. **The Satirist** and **The Age** were slanderous newspapers published in London in Macaulay's day.

P. 290. **The lampoon on the Duke of Chandos** is to be found in the Moral Essays, Epistle IV., beginning with line 99. The **lampoon on Aaron Hill** is probably contained in the four lines of the Dunciad, II., 295–298. The **still fouler lampoon on Lady Mary Wortley Montague** appears in the second of the Imita-tions of Horace, where her husband is called "Avidien."

P. 291. **the Earl of Warwick** was the son of the Countess of Warwick, whom Addison married in 1716.

the brilliant and energetic lines on Addison (Atticus) appear in the Epistle to Dr. Arbuthnot:—

> "Peace to all such! but were there one whose fires
> True genius kindles, and fair fame inspires;
> Blest with each talent, and each art to please,
> And born to write, converse, and live with ease;
> Should such a man, too fond to rule alone,
> Bear, like the Turk, no brother near the throne;
> View him with scornful, yet with jealous eyes,
> And hate for arts that caused himself to rise;
> Damn with faint praise, assent with civil leer,
> And without sneering teach the rest to sneer;
> Willing to wound, and yet afraid to strike,
> Just hint a fault, and hesitate dislike;
> Alike reserved to blame, or to commend,
> A tim'rous foe, and a suspicious friend;
> Dreading ev'n fools, by flatterers besieged,
> And so obliging, that he ne'er obliged;
> Like *Cato*, give his little senate laws,
> And sit attentive to his own applause;
> While wits and templars every sentence raise,
> And wonder with a foolish face of praise:—
> Who but must laugh, if such a man there be?
> Who would not weep, if ATTICUS were he?"

P. 292. **a warm encomium on the translation of the Iliad.** See Freeholder, No. 40.

P. 294. You may read the history of **Holland House** in Hare's Walks in London. Read, also, the close of Macaulay's brief essay on Lord Holland.

He owed his elevation, etc. See note 3, on p. 418 of Hurd's Addison.

P. 295. **Joseph Hume.** See Encyclo. Brit.

the house of Rich. See Hare's Walks in London, "Holland House."

P. 296. **The celebrated bill for limiting the number of peers.** See the histories generally, as, *e.g.*, Knight, Vol. VI., Chap. II. See, also, Encyclo. Brit., article "Peerage."

P. 297. See Addison's **letter to Craggs**, in Hurd's Addison, Vol. VI., p. 523.

P. 298. **The last moments of Addison.**   See Hurd's Addison, Vol. VI., p. 523.

P. 299. See Addison's favorite psalm, as versified by himself, on p. 220 of this volume.

the Jerusalem Chamber.   See Hare's Walks in London, Vol. II., p. 561.

P. 300. See **Tickell's elegy** on Addison, prefixed to Vol. I. of Hurd's edition of the works.